Further Confessions of a
Slightly Neurotic Hitwoman

Also by JB Lynn

Confessions of a Slightly Neurotic Hitwoman

Further Confessions
of a Slightly
Neurotic Hitwoman

JB LYNN

AVONIMPULSE
An Imprint of HarperCollinsPublishers

Excerpt from *Confessions of a Slightly Neurotic Hitwoman* copyright © 2012 by JB Lynn.

Excerpt from *The Forbidden Lady* copyright © 2002, 2012 by Kerrelyn Sparks.

Excerpt from *Turn to Darkness* copyright © 2012 by Tina Wainscott.

EPub Edition OCTOBER 2012 ISBN: 9780062233073

Print Edition ISBN: 9780062233080

10 9 8 7 6 5 4 3 2 1

For Doug
I dream alone, but it is with your love and support my
dreams become reality

Acknowledgments

THIS BOOK WOULD not have been possible without the support of many people (and my two dogs):

The fans of *Confessions of a Slightly Neurotic Hitwoman*. Your support made writing this book a joy.

My agent, Victoria Marini, for all her sparkly goodness.

The amazing Avon team who make this series possible, especially Lucia Macro, Esi Sogah, Pamela Spengler-Jaffee, Jessie Edwards, and everyone else who toils behind the scenes (and are thus spared my myriad of emailed questions).

My critique partners, writer friends, readers, reviewers. and book bloggers, who prove over and over again how supportive a community can be.

And last, but not least, Doug . . . who puts up with my neurotic self.

Prologue

YOU JUST KNOW it's going to be a bad day when you're stuck at a red light and Doomsday is breathing down your neck.

In this particular instance Doomsday happens to be a seventy-pound Doberman pinscher. Instead of having the voice of doom, she sounds an awful lot like an air-headed, bimbo-y blonde. "Way that! Way that!"

Did I mention that Doomsday has really lousy grammar?

"Not that way," Severus Snape drawled from the front passenger seat. Okay, not really Snape, but God . . . zilla, a talking brown anole lizard with an attitude to match his namesake.

Have you followed all this so far? The superior talking lizard is in the front passenger seat, the breathy Doberman is in the back, and I, Maggie Lee, am in the driver's seat, even though it doesn't feel as though I'm in control of this wild ride we're on.

I know this whole thing sounds crazy. I know animals can't talk, but ever since I was in a terrible car accident a month ago, I can understand them. Of course I haven't mentioned this little side effect to anyone, because I'm afraid they'll lock up my crazy ass in the nuthouse (hell, with my luck, they'd probably make me room with my mom, who's a long-term resident), and I've just got too much to do to let that happen.

Which brings me to why God and Doomsday were arguing about which direction we were headed. I needed to kill someone at a wedding.

It's a toss-up which I hate more: killing people or weddings.

Unfortunately, I'm getting pretty good at both.

Chapter One

"I SEE A disco ball in your future." Armani Vasquez, the closest thing I had to a friend at Insuring the Future, delivered this pronouncement right after she sprinkled a handful of candy corn into her Caesar salad.

Disgusted by her food combination, I pushed my own peanut butter and jelly sandwich away. "Really? A disco ball?"

If you'd told me a month ago that I'd be leaning over a table in the lunchroom, paying close attention to the bizarre premonitions of my half-crippled, wannabe-psychic coworker, I would have said you were crazy.

But I'd had one hell of a month.

First there had been the car accident. My sister Theresa and her husband, Dirk, were killed; my three-year-old niece, Katie, wound up in a coma; and I ended up with the ability to talk to animals. Trust me, I know exactly how crazy that sounds, but it's true . . . I think.

On top of everything else, I inadvertently found myself hurtling down a career path I never could have imagined.

I'm now a hitwoman for hire. Yes, I kill people for money . . . but just so you know, I don't go around killing just anyone. I've got standards. The two men I killed were bad men, very bad men.

Before I could press Armani for more details about the mysterious disco ball, another man I wanted to kill sauntered into my line of vision. I hate my job at Insuring the Future. I hate taking automobile claims from idiot drivers who have no business getting behind the wheel. But most of all I hate my boss, Harry. It's not the fact that he's a stickler for enforcing company policy or even that he always smells like week-old pepperoni. No, I hate him because Harry "likes" me. A lot. He's always looking over my shoulder (and peering down my shirt) and calling me into his office for one-on-one "motivational chats" to improve my performance.

I know what you're thinking. I should report his sexual harassment to human resources, or, if I deplore the idea of workplace conflict (and what self-respecting hitwoman wouldn't?), I should quit and find another job.

I was getting ready to do just that, report his lecherous ass and then quit (because I really do despise "helping" the general public), but then the accident happened. And then the paid assassin gig.

So now I need this crappy, unfulfilling, frustrating-as-hell clerical employment because it provides a cover for my second job. It's not like I can put HITWOMAN on my next tax return. Besides, if I didn't keep this job, my meddling aunts would wonder what the hell I'm doing with my life.

Harry, thumbs stuck into his suspenders (cuz everyone knows that suspenders are the height of fashion in a place where the typical dress code is T-shirts), strolled over to the table Armani and I occupied in the back corner of the break room. "Ladies."

Neither of us answered him. I took a giant bite of PB&J while Armani speared a piece of candy corn covered with anchovy-laced salad dressing.

"Don't forget we've got a team meeting tomorrow morning."

"How could we forget?" Armani asked. "You've sent five freaking e-mails about it."

Ignoring her, Harry focused his lusty gaze on me (I guess he thinks nothing is hotter than a woman with cheeks like a chipmunk). "We're going to have breakfast."

He made it sound like it was some sort of intimate date, not a meeting with a dozen other people present.

I just kept on chewing, waiting for him to take the hint and go away.

He transferred his gaze to Armani. "We may have to let some people go."

She raised her arm and waved her stump of a hand, the tragic result of not paying attention to her own premonitions and an out-of-control Zamboni hurtling across the ice. She wore her disability like it was some sort of magical amulet allowing her to break the rules of Insuring the Future without repercussions. She knew damn well that if someone was going to be fired, it wasn't going to be her.

I, on the other hand, wouldn't be surprised if I was on the short list of possible employees to dump. Working at a call center, listening to the umpteenth caller claim to have swerved to miss a deer at three-thirty on a Saturday morning, wears on me, and I've been known to make a snide comment—or two dozen—about drunken deer. While the audits of my recorded calls show I do an accurate job, my numbers for "customer support and empathy" swirl around the bottom of the toilet.

And they've only gotten worse since I started killing people. I'd like to blame it on the insomnia that kicked in just before the second hit I pulled off, or the fact that I'm stressed out because my niece, Katie, is in a coma, but the truth is my tolerance for bullshit is at an all-time low.

"Don't be late." Harry and his stinky breath cleared our airspace.

"He makes me sick to my stomach." The fact that Armani said this while spearing a mouthful of candy and salad turned my stomach. It was all I could do to swallow my bite of sandwich.

I never did get the details of the damn disco ball because an IT guy had an allergic reaction to something he ate, which necessitated a lot of oohing and ahhing and wringing of hands from the lunchtime crew as everyone waited to see if he was going to make it, or if his obituary would read, "Random tech guy from Insuring the Future passes on after brief battle with a Reese's Peanut Butter Cup."

There wasn't time to ask Armani about her latest premonition after work because I was on a tight schedule. I had to run over to Apple Blossom Estates, the premium care facility where Katie receives treatment for the brain injury she sustained in the car accident that killed her parents and left me responsible for her care. It had to be a quick visit, because I'd promised my Aunt Susan that I'd swing by for a family dinner. After that I was scheduled to sit down with my best friend, Alice, since we were supposed to be in full-throttle wedding-prep mode.

Rushing through the all-too-familiar hospital corridors toward Katie's room, my mind was occupied with horrendous images of chiffon and lace and tulle and beading, which is how I careened into the alleged local crime boss, Tony Delveccio. (Or maybe it was his identical twin brother, Anthony . . . if the justice system can't tell them apart, I shouldn't be expected to either.)

It is not a good idea to collide with a well-connected crime boss for many reasons. The one I was most concerned with is Vinnie, Delveccio's newly acquired, ever-present muscle. I didn't even have time to hit the ground after smashing into Tony/Anthony when I felt my arm being yanked out of its socket.

"Ow!"

I glared at the thug who'd done his best to dislocate my shoulder as he'd pulled me away from his boss. He stared down his nose, which had been broken so many times it looks more like a ragged mountain range than a facial feature, unmoved by my considerable outrage.

"Let her go, Vinnie."

The brute slid his gaze in the direction of his boss before he released my arm.

Rubbing my injured limb, I offered an apologetic smile to the nice mobster. "Sorry about that, Mr. Delveccio. I didn't hurt you, did I?"

He shook his head. "Let me buy you a chocolate pudding."

I hesitated, casting a longing look in the direction of Katie's room. My time with her was limited enough as it was, but I was pretty sure turning down a request from Tony/Anthony Delveccio was a bad idea. "Okay."

Together we walked toward the hospital cafeteria, with Vinnie following a few paces behind. Anyone watching us would think we were two strangers who spent time together waiting for our respective family members to recover from the traumas that had landed them here.

We were that.

And we were so much more.

"How's your grandson doing?" I asked. Delveccio's grandson, a small boy who occupied the room next to Katie's, lay in his hospital bed courtesy of a beating from his father, Delveccio's son-in-law.

Actually I should say his former son-in-law since I'm the one who killed him last month after Delveccio hired me to do so.

"He's the same. No change." There was no mistaking the sadness in the tough guy's voice. He might be a hardened criminal, but he obviously loved his family. "And your niece? How is she? I've heard rumblings she's improving."

"She seems to be responding to audio stimulation. It's an improvement, but she still hasn't woken up yet."

Reaching the cafeteria, Delveccio sat down at a table near a door. I tried to shake off the sense of disappointment that settled over me as I realized I wouldn't be getting any chocolate pudding after all. This was obviously not going to be just a friendly chat. There was business to be discussed.

Delveccio held up two fingers in Vinnie's direction. The paid muscle moved away from us.

"What's with the bodyguard?"

Shrugging, the crime boss examined the diamond in his pinky ring, which was closer in size to a golf ball than a pea. "Can't be too careful. Lotta people wanna know who offed Gary the Gun and why."

That would be me, because he tried to collect the money I earned for killing Delveccio's son-in-law. That and because the greedy son-of-a-bitch tried to blackmail me.

Delveccio knows this. At least the part about Gary claiming credit for work I'd done. "Figured if everyone else is acting nervous, I should too. Makes me look less suspicious to my competition."

"I see." Actually I didn't. Delveccio was the one who had suggested I off Gary the Gun, not that he paid me for *that* job . . . cheap bastard.

Vinnie lumbered up to the table and put two plastic bowls of chocolate pudding down, magically restoring my sense of well-being.

Delveccio sighed heavily. "Spoons, Vinnie. We need spoons."

The thug turned away.

"Two spoons. One for each of us." Delveccio shook his head as his henchman retreated. "And napkins! Don't forget the napkins!" He pushed a bowl of chocolaty goodness in my direction. "He's my uncle's kid. Dumber than . . . dumber than my uncle was, which, believe you me, is sayin' somethin'. But he looks the part. Spends all his dough on 'roids and all his time in the gym."

"Might as well get his money's worth."

The mobster chuckled. "That's why I like you. You've got an interesting way of looking at the world."

"Thanks."

"Which brings me to my reason for this little powwow."

I held my breath. I'd known that it was only a matter of time until Delveccio was going to ask me to kill someone else. I'd just been hoping I'd get a longer reprieve. Even though I'd taken money for killing two very bad men (okay, I was only paid for the one job, but had to do the second to collect my fee, cuz in case I haven't mentioned it, Delveccio's a cheap bastard), I haven't exactly embraced my new hitwoman identity.

"Have you ever heard of Jose Garcia?"

I closed my eyes. Heard of him? We'd been family once.

For just under a week.

"Hey, doll, you listening to me?"

I nodded.

"He's a drug dealer. Gang leader. Kind of guy that fits the criteria you've laid out for our . . . relationship."

Thankfully Vinnie returned just then with the spoons and napkins. The distraction he provided gave me the chance to get a grip on myself.

It wasn't like I had a real relationship with Jose Garcia. I hadn't seen him in years. He probably wouldn't even recognize me if he saw me. The only reason I would recognize him was that, like my current tablemate, he spent an inordinate amount of time making a mockery of the justice system. As such, his face showed up in my morning paper or on the local news with sporadic regularity.

Back when I'd known him he'd been a low-level dealer. Somehow the guy with the black handlebar mustache that made him look like a cartoon villain went from being the pot supplier for my Aunt Leslie, to the husband of her twin sister, Aunt Loretta. Even for Loretta, who's been married more times than I cared to count, and is currently engaged to the man I have christened Templeton the Rat, Garcia was a strange choice of life mate.

That's probably why she'd had the union annulled six days after they got hitched.

Delveccio shooed Vinnie away like he was a pesky pigeon. Once the bodyguard was out of earshot he continued. "Anyway, rumor has it that there's a big contract coming down the pipeline to knock him off."

I made a show of stirring my pudding, but didn't actually eat any. "No way. I'm not going to help the competition get him out of the way so that someone else can take over his territory. I've got certain standards. We talked about this."

Delveccio raised his hands defensively. "I know. I

know. Take it easy. It's not his competition that's ordering the hit. In fact, word is, it's a fine, upstanding, law-abiding citizen that's gonna take out the contract."

"That makes no sense."

"It does if the said businessman's son was killed by Garcia. You can understand that, can't you? The need for a family member to avenge their loved one?"

He waited silently, allowing me to mull that over.

Not that I needed to think about it. I'd already spent too many years contemplating that very issue. Long before I'd become a hired killer last month, I had wondered/fantasized about killing the monster who had taken my sister Darlene's life. I'd come to the conclusion that, given the opportunity, I'd do whatever it took to make him pay. Last month when I'd pulled the trigger and executed Alfonso Cifelli, I knew for certain that when the day came to avenge Darlene, I wouldn't hesitate.

"So whaddya say?"

"I'll have to think about it."

Delveccio shoveled a spoonful of pudding into his mouth. "Okay. Job hasn't been contracted yet. If it does become reality I'll contact our mutual friend and you can let me know."

"Sounds good. Listen, I'm sort of on a tight schedule. Would you mind if I went to visit Katie now?"

"You take this next job and you know her bills for this place will be covered for a month or two."

"I know." That's how I'd gotten into the assassination business, as a way to keep up with Katie's astronomical medical bills.

"Go ahead then. You're a good girl watching out for the kid like that. I'll be in touch."

Getting up, I slid my pudding across the table to the nice mobster. "Always a pleasure, Mr. D." I ignored Vinnie as I hurried away, wondering what, if anything, this had to do with a disco ball.

Chapter Two

I PULLED UP to the bed-and-breakfast that my three aunts called home and felt even more nervous than I had when sitting down with Tony/Anthony Delveccio.

Not that my aunts are criminals, or even what you'd call "bad" people, they're just . . . challenging.

I hadn't even closed my car door when I heard my name being called.

"Maggie? Maggie is that you?"

"No, Aunt Loretta, it's Dolly-freakin'-Parton!"

She leaned forward, squinting at me from the wicker rocking chair on the porch. She'd recently started to "forget" to wear her eyeglasses, reminding everyone that "men don't make passes at girls who wear glasses." I blamed this current bout of full-blown vanity on the aforementioned Templeton the Rat, her fiancé.

Even a blind woman could tell that my thirty-two-year-old, brown-haired, flat-chested self was not the Backwoods Barbie. Hell, even if I wanted to dress up as her for Halloween, there was no way I'd ever successfully pull off the look.

"What are you doing here?"

"I'm selling encyclopedias door-to-door. Can I interest you in a set?" I'd always thought Aunt Leslie was the dumb twin, but lately Aunt Loretta was winning the category hands down.

"Play nice, Margaret." Aunt Susan, Loretta's older sister, also known as She Who Can Scare the Living Crap Out of Me, emerged from around the corner with a fistful of weeds in her hands and a frown on her face. No doubt she'd been cleaning the flower beds and overheard my entire exchange with my aunt.

"I brought pie." I held up the box, both as a shield from her disapproval and as a peace offering.

"What kind of pie?" Aunt Loretta, while half blind, was not deaf.

"Maple pecan."

"But Templeton can't eat that. He's allergic to nuts."

"Oh. I forgot." I'd actually practiced my expressionless delivery of that particular lie while driving over.

The corners of Aunt Susan's mouth twitched as she fought back a smile. I wasn't sure if she was more amused by my deadpan delivery or my choice of dessert. "Go put it in the kitchen and then meet me in the barn. I need your help with something."

I headed inside, stopping just long enough to swap

air kisses with Aunt Loretta on my way. The table was already set for dinner. I did a quick count of the chairs. Eight. I wondered who was joining us.

Putting the pie on the kitchen counter, I slipped out the back door and headed toward the back of the property. The structure wasn't really a barn, it was just an oversized shed, but because it was painted red, we kids had nicknamed it the barn long ago.

Aunt Susan was already there waiting for me. "Pecan pie?"

I shrugged.

Shaking her head, she chuckled. While the rest of the world might not know it, I was privy to the fact that Aunt Susan disliked her sister's latest betrothed almost as much as me. She was just a hell of a lot better at hiding it.

"What can I help you with?"

"We need a heavier chair for Lamont. Every time he sits down for dinner, I expect to hear wood splintering."

My friend Alice and Lamont, her fiancé and baby daddy, are staying in the "Lovers' Suite" for an extended period until they find their own place. I actually thought it nothing short of miraculous that the giant of a man hadn't yet broken any of the dainty furniture that populates the B&B.

"There's a good-sized oak ladderback chair in the rear corner. Would you mind . . . ?" Susan asked.

"Sure, no problem."

Of course it was a problem.

I waded in gamely, but there was about thirty years of collected crap between me and the chair Aunt Susan wanted. It took me almost five minutes just to reach the furniture, shoving cobweb-covered odds and ends out of my path, stubbing toes on both feet, and getting poked by assorted items. Finally I reached my destination, grabbed the seat of the chair, and heaved it overhead.

And I almost fell over.

The damn thing weighed a ton. An elephant could sit down for afternoon tea on the sucker.

I couldn't put it back down because the moment I lifted it, the contents of the barn shifted and filled the void. Breaking into a sweat, I stumbled back toward the door, my muscles shaking in protest.

"I'm sorry about this, Margaret. Usually I have Dirk do the heavy . . ." She trailed off, unable to finish. Her nephew-in-law, like her beloved niece, Theresa, was no longer with us.

My own sense of grief at the unfair loss of my sister hit me hard, and my eyes filled with tears.

I hadn't been able to cry after the accident. It hadn't been until Katie had responded to my singing "The Itsy Bitsy Spider," a couple of weeks ago, that I'd shed a single tear.

Since then I'd had a hell of a time keeping the waterworks turned off. The slightest thing could make me blubber.

So now I was staggering beneath the weight of the heaviest piece of furniture known to man, tripping over assorted crap, getting poked as though I was at the doctor's examination from hell, and on top of it all, my vision was blurred by unwanted tears.

I made it all the way to the doorway before my natural lack of grace got the better of me. I tripped over something, for all I know it could have been a crack in the pavement not even visible to the naked eye, and went sprawling. The chair went one way with a sickening thud, while I scraped off the top layer of skin on my knees and elbows with an undignified grunt.

It wasn't until I'd rolled over onto my back, bloodied, drenched in sweat, gasping for air after performing the Herculean task, that I realized someone was standing beside Aunt Susan.

Oh crap.

Now I knew who was joining us for dinner.

EVERYONE WAS ALREADY seated at the dinner table by the time I got myself washed up and my wounds bandaged. That left me the seat between Lamont, who was indeed sitting in the elephant's chair, and the night's dinner guest, Paul Kowalski.

Talk about awkward.

I first met Paul last month when he pulled me over for using my cell phone while driving. While he didn't write me up a ticket, he did invite me for a drink, a date that ended in my apartment with us practically tearing each other's clothes off. That is until I remembered that I had the gun I was going to use to kill Alfonso stuck under my mattress and I, in a panic, unceremoniously kicked Paul out of my place before he stumbled on my murder weapon of choice.

We didn't fare much better on our other two dates, and since he hadn't called in a couple of weeks, I'd kinda figured I wouldn't be seeing him again. That is until I looked up after my chair wrestling debacle to find him looking down at me with an expression that could only be described as a mixture of horror and amusement.

Despite my pain and embarrassment, I'd felt the familiar zing of physical attraction as he'd helped me to my feet. My body definitely wanted the well-built cop. I just wasn't so sure about the rest of me.

Now here I was faced with the prospect of sitting beside him for the next hour.

"We've waited for you, Maggie." Aunt Leslie sounded irritated.

I hurried to my seat.

The woman had been a stoner for as long as I could remember, always mellow. I wasn't sure how I felt about her newly clean, newly bitchy persona that had taken over in the past couple of weeks. It was my own fault she'd decided to stop smoking marijuana so I knew I shouldn't complain. If I hadn't requested that she surrender her key to my apartment, she'd still be happily lighting up.

Squeezing into my place at the table, I immediately felt suffocated by the bulging biceps on either side of me. Both Paul's and Lamont's developed physiques intruded into my personal space.

"Let's say grace," Leslie demanded.

"Huh?" I asked eloquently.

"Grace. Let's say grace." She acted as though it was an everyday request.

I was fairly certain I'd never said grace in my entire life and I was pretty sure it had never been uttered around this table. I slid my gaze in Aunt Susan's direction. She was glaring at the salad bowl as though expecting hellfire to come bubbling out of it.

"Everyone join hands," Leslie ordered.

Lamont snatched up my left hand and bowed his head reverently. I guess he comes from a religious family and is well trained. The rest of us just sort of looked around the table, bewildered.

"Join hands! Join hands!" Leslie grabbed the limp appendages of her two sisters, who had the misfortune of flanking her.

I fumbled for Paul's hand, not wanting to be told a third time. He squeezed my fingers tightly, which I'm sure he thought was supportive, but actually sent a bolt of pain straight from my palm to my shoulder.

Closing her eyes, Aunt Leslie cleared her throat.

I was expecting to hear something along the lines of "Bless us" or "We give thanks" or even "Good bread, good meat, good gosh, let's eat!" I was not expecting what came next.

"God grant me the serenity to accept . . ."

The Serenity Prayer? The woman was spending way too much time at her Narcotics Anonymous meetings.

" . . . the things I cannot change." Paul joined in.

Which made no sense since I knew he drank alcohol on our dates. Had he too gone to battle with an addiction in the last couple of weeks? Maybe that's why he hadn't called. Isn't abstinence one of the twelve steps?

"Courage to change the things I can." Now Templeton was chiming in, his long nose twitching as though he smelled cheese.

Three of the eight people at the table were actually participating in this "grace."

"And the wisdom to know the difference," the three intoned like some sort of cult straight out of a bad 1970s sci-fi movie.

Aunt Susan was still glaring at the salad bowl, focusing all of her resentment on the ceramic vessel. I was sort of disappointed it didn't blow up.

"Amen," Aunt Leslie crowed triumphantly.

"Amen," echoed everyone except me and Aunt Susan. The cult's power was spreading.

"I'm starving. Pass the salad, Aunt Susan?"

She practically threw it at me. I smiled sweetly in return, glad of the excuse to let go of Paul and Lamont.

"Isn't it lovely that Paul could join us, dear?" Aunt Loretta blinked her false eyelashes at the off-duty cop.

"Lovely." So saying, I passed the bowl of greens to him with a polite smile. "Does make me wonder why you asked me what I was doing here earlier though."

"You were early."

"You're never early. You're always late," Aunt Leslie added. "Usually everyone mills around waiting for you. We still sat here waiting for you tonight."

I definitely liked her better when she just sat there in her drug-induced stupor. It would sound childish to say, *It wasn't my fault*, so I resisted the urge to tell her that my tardiness was the result of an injury. Barely.

"It was my fault she was late, Leslie." Aunt Susan coming to my defense was almost enough to knock me off my chair. "She was doing me a favor. Leave the poor girl alone. She worked all day, no doubt visited Katie, and then I put her to work. Let her eat her meal in peace."

Alice, my blonde, Amazonian, pregnant best friend, tilted back in her chair so that she could whisper behind her fiancé Lamont's back, "Did Susan dip into Leslie's stash?"

Grinning, I shook my head. Alice and I have been best friends since we were kids. This was the first time either of us had ever heard Aunt Susan stick up for me.

"It was so lucky that Templeton ran into Paul and extended the dinner invitation," Aunt Loretta trilled. I wasn't sure if she hit that particular birdlike pitch because she was trying to play mediator to her two sisters, or if she was desperate to return the conversation to her matchmaking efforts.

"I said to let the poor girl eat in peace." Susan slopped a spoonful of mashed potatoes onto her plate for emphasis. "How are the wedding plans coming along, Alice?"

Anyone else might have been apprehensive about being chosen to fill the awkward silence that hung in the room like an ill-fitting coat, but not Alice. Full of sunshine and light, she's always too happy to gush about whatever is currently occupying the bulk of her time. Right now, that's wedding plans.

Have I mentioned how much I hate weddings? I hate attending them. I hate shopping for them. Most of all, I hate listening to people prattle on about them.

And that's all anyone did for the next forty-five minutes.

I didn't partake in the discussions about venues and menus, flowers or dresses. Instead I sat there trying to figure out how, if he offered me the job, I was going to tell Delveccio that I wasn't going to kill Garcia for him. I also sat there wondering if the myths about human self-combustion were true since I was pretty sure that the heat flooding through my body as Paul pressed his left thigh into my right leg didn't occur in nature very often.

Whether or not to sleep with Paul—gotta love that euphemism, dontchya?—is yet another dilemma I find myself facing. On the one hand, there's no denying our sexual compatibility is off the charts, but more than one per— *being* in my life has warned me to stay away from him. Then again he had been awfully kind to Aunt Leslie when she passed out in my doorway, but Paul's temper does raise some red flags for me. Not to mention the whole he's-a-cop-and-I'm-a-killer thing.

Chapter Three

THE MOMENT I stood up from the table, Alice grabbed me by the arm and practically dragged me upstairs to the Lovers' Suite for more wedding talk.

"You need to help me choose the menu for the reception." She pulled out a giant folder and dumped its contents on the dusty rose comforter that topped the four-poster bed. "We've got to choose the appetizers for the cocktail hour and the menu for the dinner."

"Can't Lamont do that?"

Alice frowned. "Aren't you happy for me, Maggie?"

"Of course I'm happy for you. Lamont's a great guy."

"Then why don't you want to help me? You're my best friend, my maid of honor, you're supposed to *want* to help me." She stuck out her bottom lip in a pathetic pout.

I couldn't fathom how my best friend could have conveniently forgotten how much I hate weddings, but I thought it was probably better not to point that out during this conversation. "It's just that I've got so much on my mind right now with Katie and everything."

"I know." She flashed her most benevolent smile at me. "I won't be asking much, I promise."

I cringed inwardly, feeling like the world's biggest jerk. "Okay. I'm not sure how much help I can be. I'm not exactly a foodie. My idea of gourmet is a frozen Lean Cuisine meal."

"C'mon. It'll be fun." She plopped down on the bed and patted the spot beside her.

It took us almost an hour to decide on the various courses. I have no idea why she even asked for my input because every time I suggested something she overruled me, which was of course her prerogative since it was her day. I guess enduring this particular form of torture without complaint got me back in her good graces because she was all smiles by the time I left.

I'd been hoping that after all that time Paul would have given up on me and I would catch a break about having to make a decision about him, but I had no such luck. (I never do.) He, Lamont, Templeton, and Loretta were all sitting out on the front porch, puffing on cigars.

"Please tell me you got the menu all picked out," Lamont pleaded the moment I stepped outside. The pathetic appeal coming from the big man made me feel a bit better. Apparently I wasn't the only one being driven crazy by his fiancée.

After I was done choking on the smoke cloud that enveloped the porch, I moved to the stairs. "All done."

"You're an angel."

"Did you hear that, Paul? Our Maggie's an angel," Loretta couldn't resist pointing out.

I sent Paul an apologetic shrug. He didn't look as though he was annoyed by my aunt's blatant matchmaking. "Except that I'm chronically tardy."

"Oh, you know Leslie didn't mean that," Loretta chided. "Her irritability is just a symptom of her withdrawal. She could also be depressed or experience a loss of appetite."

Aunt Loretta is obsessed with looking up, on the Internet, every symptom and disease known to man.

"Besides, you've never been late to one of our dates." Paul smiled, his dark eyes sparkling with flirtatious mischief. "Maybe it's just a matter of motivation."

The remark came across as smarmy to me, considering that the man had once told me that no other woman had ever turned him down for sex before. I was grateful. It made my decision to go home alone that much easier.

"I'm beat. I've got a big staff meeting tomorrow morning, so I'm going to head home."

"Walk her to her car, Paul," Loretta urged.

Obediently he got to his feet and followed me down the stairs.

"Good night!"

"Good night, dear!" Loretta leaned over and whispered something to Templeton and Lamont as soon as I was out of earshot, no doubt telling them what a perfect catch Paul was for me.

"Are you mad I accepted the dinner invitation?" Paul asked as I pulled my car keys out.

"Surprised."

"I ran into Loretta and Templeton at Angelo's Restaurant and they insisted I come."

I unlocked my car door.

"She's a very difficult woman to turn down."

"I know."

"I could follow you home. Make sure you get inside safely."

I shook my head. "Not tonight. It's been a long day and I really do have a big meeting tomorrow morning."

"Can I at least kiss you good night?"

Jerking my chin in the direction of the three sitting on the porch watching us, I asked. "For the enjoyment of the audience?"

He didn't bother to answer me. Instead he kissed me. Not a chaste peck on the cheek, or a subtle brushing of lips, but a full-on, tonsil-touching kiss that stole my breath and sent my heartbeat into overdrive. He was at least a gentleman in that he angled his body so that all anyone on the porch could see was his broad back. "We should try going on another date, Maggie."

I nodded, not trusting myself to speak.

"I'll call you."

I nodded again, slipped into my car, and drove away before I asked him to come back to my place.

It was a good thing I didn't. A very good thing.

MY PLANS WERE simple as I unlocked the front door of my apartment. I was going to walk the dog, take a shower, set up my coffeepot for the next morning, and hit the sack for some much needed rest.

You know what they say about plans.

I was so tired that I didn't notice right away that something was amiss when I walked into my home. Instead, I blithely tossed my purse in the corner and kicked off my shoes. It wasn't until I was barefoot, keyless, and without a makeshift weapon in hand that I heard it.

Thud. Thud. Thud.

Not far away.

Thud. Thud. Thud.

It was then that I realized that the dog hadn't greeted me at the door. In the weeks she'd lived with me, she always welcomed me home with a whining chorus of "Gotta! Gotta! Gotta!" which meant she had to pee that very second or her excuse for a brain was going to explode.

Thud. Thud. Thud.

I froze, not knowing what to do. Should I turn and flee? Realistically, how far could I get without my shoes or car keys? Or should I turn on the light and face down the intruder waiting for me in the shadows?

I held my breath, straining to hear whether God was telling me what to do. I didn't hear anything. The jerk had probably overindulged in crickets and was sleeping it off.

Deciding to make a run for it, I reached behind me, searching for the cold metal of the door handle.

"Hello, Mags. Didn't mean to scare you."

So saying, the man in my living room lit up a cigarette lighter and held the flickering flame near his chin so that he looked like a kid telling ghost stories around a campfire.

"Patrick." Weak with relief, I slumped back against the door.

Thud. Thud. Thud.

Holding the light away from his body, I saw that Patrick, my murder mentor, was sitting on the floor, a giant, dark shadow splayed across his lap. Now I knew where the dog was and what was making the thudding sound.

Doomsday the Doberman was having her belly rubbed and kicking her rear leg against the floor signaling her delight.

"I can't believe you kept her," Patrick said.

Doomsday's former owner had been Gary the Gun, the hitman I'd killed just a couple of weeks earlier.

"Not much of a watchdog, is she?" I said, knowing full well that she understood every word I said.

"She's a good girl, Mags. Don't be too hard on her. She was guarding the place when I got here."

"I've got to take her for a walk."

Thud. Thud. Thud.

"Did that when I got here. Fed her too."

"Oh, thanks." Without turning on the light, I moved to sit beside him on the floor, leaning back tiredly against my couch. I figured that whatever it was he was here to discuss was better talked out under the cover of darkness. I hadn't seen or spoken to the tall redhead in two weeks, not since I'd dissolved into a blubbering mess when he'd told me he thought my sister Marlene was alive.

I'm pretty sure that as a detective, he must be fairly

accustomed to women sobbing hysterically, but as my murder mentor, he probably wasn't all that pleased to witness my emotional breakdown. Maybe that was why he was here. Maybe he wanted to dissolve our working relationship. Maybe he'd figured out that killing people is not my forte.

If that were the case, it meant I'd have no need to kill Jose Garcia. I was completely comfortable with having that difficult decision being wrenched away from me. Though I would need to figure out a way to raise more cash to keep Katie at Apple Blossom Estates.

"Why are we sitting on the floor?" I asked.

"I wasn't sure whether the dog is allowed on the furniture."

"I haven't decided that myself."

"How've you been, Mags?"

"Okay." I was grateful for the shadows. Sometimes when Patrick Mulligan looked at me, I got the unnerving impression that he saw more than I wanted him to. I really wasn't okay. In fact, I felt as though I was teetering on the edge of losing it, of losing everything, but I didn't need him knowing that. The last thing I wanted was to see that look of pity he sometimes directed my way when he thinks I'm not looking. "How are you?"

"I've been better. Finally healing from that beating I took at Gary's."

Unsure of whether he was talking about Gary the Gun assaulting him, or the rough way Doomsday and I had dragged him from the burning house, I stayed silent.

"How's your niece?"

"The doctors are hopeful."

"What about you? Are you hopeful?"

"Of course." The only reason I'd agreed to kill anyone in the first place was that I believed that with the best care possible, my niece would wake up.

"Good. That's good. Delveccio said he saw you today."

"Uh-huh."

"Said you didn't look too happy about the contract that might be coming our way."

"Our way?" I hated the way my voice cracked with uncertainty.

I heard Patrick's sharp intake of breath and then nothing but the soft panting of the dog. Finally he said, "I know the last job didn't go as planned."

"That's an understatement." Gary the Gun had almost killed both of us.

"I let you down."

The forlorn note in the detective/hitman's voice made me wince. Patrick Mulligan was a man who didn't believe in letting anyone down, which was why he currently had two wives and supported two families.

"No, no, no. That's not it. I figured after I screwed up the Cifelli hit and then messed everything up at Gary's . . ." Having the it's-not-you-it's-me talk with a hitman was definitely one of the oddest conversations I'd ever had . . . and I'd had some really weird conversations in the past month.

"You did the job. You killed him. Not to mention you saved my life."

"And you saved mine. I just figured you were giving

up on me. I understand, I really do. Working with a rank amateur like me has got to be a liability."

"I'd never give up on you, Mags."

I did my best to ignore how special that simple statement made me feel. Besides having the ability to see through my bull, Patrick Mulligan seemed to actually like who he saw. For the life of me, I couldn't figure out why. If he didn't have two wives already, I'd say he was the perfect guy for me.

"So why the hesitation with Delveccio?"

"I'm not sure . . . I'm not sure I'm cut out for—"

"You don't have to do it, Mags. You can walk away anytime." Reaching out, he patted my shoulder reassuringly.

Flinching, I jerked away.

"Sorry," he muttered.

"Again, not you," I told him. "I was moving furniture earlier and now my shoulders are killing me."

"If you say so."

The man had plenty of reason not to believe me. More than once I'd thought he was going to kill me. Still, it pained me to know I was causing him to feel guilty. Despite that his second job involved killing people, he was, in fact, a gentle soul. "Really, Patrick." Reaching out, I tried to pat his arm. My hand ended up on his thigh instead.

He captured it with his own hand before I could move it in the wrong direction . . . whichever way that might have been.

Doomsday immediately laid her head on top of our

intertwined fingers, trapping us. I tried to tug free, but neither the man nor the dog budged.

"We need to talk about that other thing."

That other thing was my sister Marlene. The one who'd run away after her twin had been murdered. The one I'd been sure was dead, but who Patrick had said was not. "I can't. Not tonight."

"Mags . . ."

"Please, Patrick." I know it was cowardly of me to avoid the conversation, but I wasn't quite ready to tackle it.

He sighed his displeasure, but thankfully didn't ask me why I was unwilling to talk about my sister. "If the Garcia contract comes through, what do you want me to do?"

I stroked Doomsday's ears with my free hand. "I don't know."

"How 'bout I ask you again, if, or when, the time comes?"

"I'd appreciate that."

Pulling my hand out from under the dog's head, he raised it to his lips, pressing a quick kiss to the back of it before releasing me. "You sound tired. I'll let you get some sleep."

Pushing the dog off of him, he got to his feet. "I really am sorry I let you down at Gary's."

"You didn't," I assured him, struggling to stand.

I thought I saw him shake his head, but in the shadows, it was impossible to tell for certain. "I'll be in touch."

Patting Doomsday on the head, he said, "Keep an eye

out for her." With that, he walked out of my apartment.

Once he was out of sight I locked the door, switched on the light, and turned on the dog with a vengeance. "What the hell is wrong with you? You're supposed to tell me if someone's here. You're eating me out of house and home, the least you could do is pretend to be a guard dog."

Doomsday cocked her head to the side and looked at me as though I were some sort of rabid squirrel she didn't quite know what to do with. "Sorry?"

It never ceases to amaze me how she can convey in one breathy word how much of an airhead she is.

"Damn right you should be sorry. I'm coming home to an empty house and—"

"Not," she interrupted.

"Not what?"

"Here Doomsday. Here God."

It was my turn to cock my head at her. She was right. Technically I no longer came home to an empty house. Instead I lived with a dingbat dog and a smugly superior lizard. Which reminded me . . . why the hell hadn't God warned me of Patrick's presence? The Doberman had the excuse of being a few brain cells short of a full load, the lizard did not.

Stalking into my bedroom, the mutt following closely on my heels, too closely considering the mood I was in, I went to confront Godzilla. In the light flickering from the television I'd left on for him, I could see that he was draped over a branch in a corner of his glass-enclosed terrarium, eyes closed and belly bulging.

"Wake up!" I pounded on the lid of his home like I was the Big Bad Wolf getting ready to blow his house down.

Startled, he fell off the branch in an undignified mess of legs and tail. "Earthquake! Earthquake!"

"It's not an earthquake. It's me."

He drew himself up to his full height (which is only a couple of inches so it's not nearly as impressive as he'd like to think it is), crossed his arms over his chest, and leveled an unblinking stare at me. "Why," he asked in his snootiest, wannabe-a-British-aristocrat voice, "why did you do that?"

"Because you didn't warn me that Patrick was sitting in my living room."

"Was he?"

"Yes! He was! And neither of you thought to tip me off to that particular fact. I almost had a heart attack when I realized I wasn't alone here."

"Not!" Doomsday interjected.

"Not what?" God asked.

"She thinks I'm not alone because the two of you are here."

"She's right."

Thud. Thud. Thud.

A quick glance at the dog revealed that she was grinning from ear to ear (the sight of a Doberman beaming is downright scary if you ask me), obviously pleased that God had said she was right about something.

"Technically . . ." I conceded grudgingly.

"You should get used to the idea." The lizard climbed

back onto his branch and lay down. "We're not going anywhere."

Doomsday licked my hand for emphasis.

"Now go to bed. You look exhausted," God lectured.

Without showering or changing clothes I flopped onto my bed tiredly. Doomsday jumped up and curled against me.

Just then, feeling the warmth of my canine companion and listening to God snore, I've got to admit that a strange sense of peace stole over me as I drifted off to sleep.

It wouldn't last though. All hell was about to break loose.

Chapter Four

I SHOULD HAVE known something was up the moment I
walked into Insuring the Future and saw Armani sitting
at her desk. Glancing at the clock on the wall, I assured
myself that I wasn't late for work. That meant Armani was
on time . . . a few minutes early, in fact. In the entire time
I've worked at the insurance company, she has shown up
late every single day.

Maybe it was Harry's offer of a free breakfast, but I
thought it was more likely the imminent threat of heads
rolling that had scared her into acting like a model em-
ployee.

"Morning, Chiquita!" she practically chirped as I
strolled up to her desk.

"Morning. Meeting start yet?"

"Uh-uh. E-mail sent out this morning says the start's
been delayed by an hour. Think that means Harry's bailing on the breakfast deal?"

I shook my head. "I think it means he's fucking with our heads. Showing us who's in control."

Nodding, she held out a purple silk bag. "Pick."

I hesitated. I knew what was in the bag. Scrabble tiles. My partially disabled pal claims to be able to read the future in them, sort of like reading tea leaves.

She shook the bag impatiently.

Sighing, I indulged her, pulling seven tiles from the bag and placing them on her desk. Up until a few weeks ago I would have told you that I didn't buy into this psychic act at all, but things had changed. I now was open to the possibility that my work friend could catch glimpses of the future. Unfortunately I was just as convinced that her interpretation of those visions was usually way off base.

Shaking her mane of thick, dark hair so that it partially obscured her face, she quickly put them in alphabetical order: DEFIRRU. Pitching her voice deeper, a standard part of her fortune-telling act, she mused, "Eleven. Not such a great number." She's also superstitious about the numerical value, as computed by Scrabble tiles, of people's names and important words or phrases.

Big surprise there. Only an idiot would have suggested that my life was filled with sunshine and roses. Even though Armani knew nothing of my murder-for-hire venture, she was well acquainted with Katie being in the hospital and the car accident that had put her there.

She stared intently at the letters, as though willing them to reveal my future to her.

"Armani, I—"

"Shh!"

I smelled pepperoni a split second before Harry spoke from behind me, "Good morning, ladies."

"Hey, Harry." I answered for both of us since Armani was engrossed in her study of the tiles. "What's for breakfast?"

"Donuts. Could I speak to you for a moment alone, Maggie?"

"Sure." I tried to catch Armani's eye as I followed Harry into his office, but she was busy moving the Scrabble pieces around.

The second Harry shut the door to his office, I forgot all about the faux prophecy being dreamed up, because Harry draped an arm around my shoulders. A hot, sweaty, possessive arm. "We have to talk, Maggie."

I tried to gracefully pull away, but he was one wily octopus.

"It's about your future here."

"My future?" Shoving his arm off of me, I made a point of putting a chair between us before I turned to face him.

"Your reviews are consistently problematic. I've done what I can to protect you, but . . ." He let his unspoken threat hang in the air for a second before he made his move. "I think you need more one-on-one help. Some additional training outside the office."

I have many faults. Among them is my tendency to imagine the worst of any situation. It's something I'm working on, so I did my best to give him the benefit of the doubt. "You mean at headquarters?"

He chuckled. "With me. Over dinner."

"You're asking me out?"

He nodded, smiling.

"No."

His face fell. "That would be a mistake, Maggie."

"Are you threatening me?" I'd gotten away with murder. Twice. I was pretty sure I could knock off this smug son-of-a-bitch and get away with it.

"I'll give you until the end of the day to make your decision. Just remember that your job is hanging in the balance." He opened his office door and said loudly enough for half his employees to hear, "I'll see you in the meeting."

Steaming, I marched back out to Armani's desk, intent on sharing what I'd just endured, but I never got the chance.

The moment I was within earshot she blurted out, "Bad news, Chiquita."

"What now?"

She pointed to my letters which she'd laid out: RUF RIDE "You're in for a rough ride."

I didn't need a freakin' psychic to tell me that.

The meeting consisted of stale donuts, burnt coffee, and Harry doing his best to play benevolent dictator while threatening to "let go" twenty percent of the department who had "less than stellar" reviews. Basically this meant me, Armani, a couple of alcoholics who stumbled in late and hungover on a consistent basis, and the twenty-something slackers who were more suited to bagging groceries at a snail's pace.

To be honest, I was miffed to be counted among the

company of the others. I was punctual (despite what Aunt Leslie might say), accurate, and efficient. I just "lacked empathy" for the idiots sucking up valuable space on Earth who called in their accident reports day in and day out.

"I was thinking about the rough ride thing. Maybe you just need new shock absorbers in your car," Armani said as I ended my last call of the day.

I glanced from her to the clock on the far wall. In two minutes I would be free of this place. Free from the worrying glances Armani kept shooting in my direction. Free from Harry and his pepperoni breath. Free from the morons who couldn't spell the name of the street they lived on, but had still managed to somehow pass a written driver's test.

"Maggie?"

"Yeah. I'll have a mechanic check out the car."

"Ice, ice, baby." It was a none-too-subtle reminder that she'd ignored one of her own visions and been run over by an out-of-control Zamboni, resulting in a bum leg and hand that she tended to milk for all they were worth. "On the other hand, that dream about a disco ball may mean you have something to celebrate soon, so don't go around feeling sorry for yourself." Settling her hip on the edge of my desk so that she could take the weight off her bad leg, Armani picked up my newest addiction and sniffed it suspiciously.

"They're Life Savers. Candy. Mints." I'd started chomping on them whenever I felt anxious because they reminded me of Patrick, the only calm and stabilizing influence in my life. Yes, I know it's pathetic that a hitman is the best person I know, but it's the truth.

"Have you made a decision, Maggie?"

I didn't even bother to swivel my chair around to face Harry, who'd crept up behind me. Instead I rolled my eyes at Armani. To her credit, she didn't react at all.

"I have."

"And?" He sounded . . . hopeful.

"The answer is still no."

"No?"

"No."

"I'm not sure you understand the seriousness of this issue, Maggie." Now he sounded . . . put out . . . pissed off . . . offended.

I spun my chair around, looked the lecherous louse in the eye, and said loudly enough for half my coworkers to hear, "No, Harry. I won't go to dinner with you to save my job."

A dozen heads swiveled in our directions. A cacophony of gasps, chuckling, and throat clearing filled the office.

His mouth working, but no sounds coming out, Harry turned a most unflattering shade of purple.

I smiled my satisfaction. I'd killed people. He didn't intimidate me.

"Time to go." Armani slid off my desk, grabbed my arm, and hauled my ass straight out of there.

"I don't think a mechanic is going to be able to fix this," she muttered as we bulldozed a path through our gossipy coworkers.

She was right. I was in for a rough ride.

MY DAY DIDN'T get any better while I was at the hospital for my daily after-work visit with Katie. Her condition remained unchanged, which meant her small, still body was tucked into the hospital bed, just like every other visit. I smoothed my hand down her cheek. The bruises she'd sustained in the accident had faded, but her skull was still encapsulated in a cast. It was a terrible look for a three-year-old. "Aunt Maggie's here, Katie."

Pulling the visitor's chair up to her bedside, I took her limp hand in mine and began our nightly ritual. "The itsy bitsy spider went up the water spout."

Some days she responded to my silly song, her fingers twitching against mine. Some days she didn't move at all. This was one of the latter.

The doctors had told me not to read too much into her reaction or lack of reaction, but each time she failed to respond, I panicked anew that I'd lost her forever.

After an hour of singing and telling her how God was doing in his lizard world, it was time for me to go.

I got to my feet tiredly and shuffled out of the room.

Vinnie the Muscled Meathead was waiting for me. "Boss wants to talk to you."

I glanced toward the room where Tony/Anthony Delveccio's grandson lay in a bed just like Katie's.

"He said to get yourself a chocolate pudding. His treat."

"Big spender."

Vinnie grabbed my arm, squeezing tightly. "Don't you go disrespecting the boss!"

Yanking free, I glared at him. "Don't you go putting

your hands on me." I'd killed Delveccio's son-in-law. I'd murdered a professional hitman. I was considering taking out Harry. I had no problem adding this steroid-fueled animal to my to-do list, but if I was going to do that, it wouldn't be prudent to get into a public tiff with him, so I turned on my heel and marched toward the land of chocolate pudding.

I'd eaten two bowls' worth by the time Delveccio showed up. Vinnie was nowhere in sight.

"Where's the meathead?" I asked as Tony/Anthony slid into the seat opposite me.

"Guy gets on my nerves."

"Mine too."

"So about that job I was telling you about . . ."

"The one I'm not sure I'm going to take."

He fiddled with his giant diamond pinky ring. "How 'bout I tell you about it, you give it some consideration, and then you make a decision."

I nodded even though I was fairly certain I was out of the killing game for good.

"So you have a general idea of who Jose Garcia is?"

"He runs the second largest drug-dealing gang in the state."

"Who runs the biggest?"

"You don't want to know."

"Yeah, I do."

Delveccio frowned. "What's it matter?"

"I've got no desire to help the biggest dealer in the state knock off his main competitor."

"Some might consider that a public service. If two operations merge into one, there'd be less drive-by shootings. Less . . . oh what's the word for it? One of those Schwarzenegger movies . . ."

"*Collateral Damage.*"

"That's it!" Delveccio clapped my shoulder as though I'd just solved the mystery of life itself. "You know the damndest things. That's why I like you."

The only reason I knew what crappy movie he was talking about was that God had insisted on watching it two nights before. "I'm all for public good, but I'm not going to help a drug lord grow his empire."

"Cuz you've got standards."

I'd recently killed two men, my most meaningful conversations took place with a lizard, and I'd agreed to wear a cotton candy–colored tutu for a wedding, but yeah, somewhere in the warped recesses of my soul, I still had standards. "Yes, Mr. Delveccio. I'm afraid I do."

"Good girl! Good girl!" He pummeled my shoulder.

I had no idea why he seemed so pleased that I'd refused the job, but I was relieved. I had no desire to kill Jose Garcia. Especially since I'd once called him Uncle Jose . . . albeit for a very short time.

"It's not his competition footing the bill for this hit. It's the father of one of his victims."

I fought hard to keep hope alive that I could get out of this particular job. I really didn't want to kill Uncle Jose. "Victim?"

"Some rich kid who was in the wrong place at the wrong time and made the mistake of telling the cops what he'd seen. Garcia had him whacked as he was leaving the police station. A message to cops and anyone else paying attention that no one was going to get away with testifying against him. Rich boy's daddy brought all kinds of pressure on the D.A.'s office, but they couldn't make anything stick. So the man's given up on the law and is looking for a different kind of justice. Which is where you come in."

"I'll have to think about it." It was a feeble attempt to buy some time to think up an excuse to get me out of this situation without pissing off the mob boss sitting across from me. The chance to earn more cash for Katie's care was a powerful incentive to take the job, but knowing that the news of Garcia's death would make Aunt Loretta cry made the idea hard to stomach. (She cried every time the New Jersey Devils or New Jersey Nets lost a game . . . she was loyal like that . . . to losers . . .)

"He wants it done at a very specific time and place."

"Why?"

"He wants Garcia's family to suffer as much as his has. The hit's gotta take place in two weeks."

"Where?" I found myself asking.

"He wants it done publicly. Either at the rehearsal dinner for his daughter's wedding or at the wedding itself."

"I hate weddings."

THANKFULLY GOD AND Doomsday were the only ones in my place when I got home and they both greeted me cheerfully.

Well, in reality, God groused, "Turn on the TV. It's almost time for *Wheel of Fortune*." The lizard is obsessed with the game show despite the fact he royally sucks at it.

Doomsday smothered me with doggie kisses before whining, "Gotta! Gotta! Gotta!"

Switching on the set for the lizard, I slipped the leash on the Doberman and walked outside. "We've got to hurry. I've got somewhere else to be."

"Where?"

"Wedding dress shopping."

"Marry?"

"My friend Alice is getting married. We're going to pick out her dress." I didn't bother to explain to my four-legged friend that Alice was knocked up and was in a huge rush to get hitched before she started to show. This meant that wedding preparations were in overdrive.

"If you go fast I'll give you an extra biscuit." It was shameless bribery, but the mutt was taking her sweet time sniffing every inch of the curb.

Properly incentivized, the dog did her business in record time. Her response gave me a new perspective on the idiotic "motivational" contests Harry ran at Insuring the Future. Basically he was appealing to our base animal instincts. Yet another reason to dislike the man.

I was pondering that very thought as I rushed into The Big Day dress shop. I've been there too many times to count. My Aunt Loretta got married every couple of years, plus I'd been the maid of honor at my sister Theresa's wedding. I know the place well and I despise everything about it. The combination of the endless sea of white, the crinkle of crinoline, and the rose-scented pot-pourri made me want to hurl. But nothing compared to my unbridled hatred of the staff, who manage to come across as equal parts pandering ass-kissers and know-it-all snobs performing holy work.

Alice was already there, pawing through the racks like a miner searching for a nugget of gold.

"Find anything yet?" I asked.

"You're late."

Overly sensitive about time ever since Aunt Leslie had pointed out my habitual tardiness, I glanced over at the clock hanging over the wall of veils. "Am not. I'm three minutes early."

Ignoring me, Alice pulled a sequined and feathered gown from the rack and held it up against her. "What do you think?"

"It's very Lady Gaga meets Liberace."

"Gee, thanks." Pouting, she shoved the dress back in its place.

"You asked."

"I'm sorry I did."

"I see you in something more refined," one of the male ass-kissing snobs offered from behind me.

I cringed. He'd probably spotted Alice's desperation and smelled an easy sale.

Alice smiled widely. "Zeke?"

I threw up in my mouth and had to swallow my burning bile. Not Zeke. It couldn't be Zeke.

"Alli? Oh my God, is it really you?"

As my best friend and my childhood nemesis threw

themselves at each other in an embrace worthy of a cheesy 1970s love story, I decided Armani was right. I was in for RUF RIDE.

While they made googly eyes at one another, I decided that he'd changed since the last time I'd seen him, and for the better. He'd always been a good-looking kid, but now he was a handsome man, what with his bright blue eyes, cleft chin, and a head full of wavy, chestnut hair that almost reached his shoulders.

Once they'd finished hugging and exclaiming how wonderful it was to see each other, Zeke turned his attention to me. He held out his arms, flashed that megawatt smile of his, and exclaimed, "It's my lucky day to run into both of you."

I held out my hand, not so much because I wanted to shake his, but because I didn't want him to hug me. "Hi, Zeke."

Ignoring the proffered handshake, he engulfed me in a bear hug. "It's good to see you, Maggie."

I didn't share the sentiment, so I kept my mouth shut.

SOMETIMES I FEEL cursed. I've felt this way for most of my life. Can you blame me? My mom has spent half of my life locked up in a mental ward, my dad is rotting in prison, my sister Darlene was murdered when we were kids, my sister Marlene . . . well, I don't want to talk about her, and my big sister Theresa was killed a couple of months ago in the car accident that left me with the unenviable ability to be berated by a lizard and questioned by a Doberman.

Not to mention that my niece is in a coma, my aunts drive me bat-shit, and I've inadvertently managed to become a hired killer.

Can you blame me for thinking that I'm the object of the Fates' ultimate practical joke?

But I wasn't thinking about any of that when I strolled into Insuring the Future. No, I was trying to decide which I hate more: weddings or Zeke Roble. They were pretty similar in my book, all show and pretense, and saccharine sweetness that put my teeth on edge.

Alice and I had been best friends since forever. Through the years, only one person had ever come between us, not any of our respective loser boyfriends, or insane family members, just Zeke. The boy, now man, had always had the uncanny ability to make me look bad, just like he had at the wedding dress shop. That's why I hated him. I had to keep him from worming his way back into Alice's life. I didn't mind sharing her with Lamont, but there was no way I was surrendering my best friend to my nemesis without a fight.

I was so preoccupied with my thoughts that I didn't see the empty box until I got to my desk. I eyed the paper carton suspiciously.

"It's for you." Harry appeared at my side. He must have come from downwind because I hadn't smelled his pepperoni approach. "I'm sorry, Maggie, but we're going to have to let you go."

I wondered for a moment if my boss, soon-to-be-ex-boss, and Zeke were related. At that moment I hated them equally. "You're firing me?"

Harry shrugged. "Sorry, but I did warn you."

"You're firing me because I won't go out on a date with you?"

Harry shook his head. "I know you're upset, Maggie, but we've talked about this. I've pointed out your shortcomings in all of your reviews. You've signed off on all the reports."

I looked from Harry to the box on my desk and back to Harry. He smiled smugly.

Holy hell, he'd documented my "shortcomings" over all this time, while I had never said word one to human resources about his lecherous ways. Now I needed to keep this job as my cover. The little shit had outfoxed me and he knew it.

I glanced at my desk wondering what I could use to kill him. I'm a pretty resourceful murderer. After all I used a leg of lamb to off the last guy I slaughtered.

I could smash Harry over the head with the Insuring the Future mug I'd received for my perfect attendance last year. Once he was crumpled at my feet, I could break the mug and use a shard to slice open his jugular.

"I've arranged for you to receive a month's severance," Harry said. "Assuming you leave quietly."

It seemed as though Mr. Pepperoni Breath had thought of everything. He had to know how badly I need my paycheck with Katie in the hospital. Outmaneuvered again, I snatched up my framed picture of Katie and me at the pumpkin patch last year and my bag of Life Savers. There was nothing else in the desk or in that place that mattered to me.

Harry looked at me expectantly. I wondered if my begging to keep my job was part of his evil plan. I wouldn't give that particular satisfaction.

He leaned over and said, "You're not really fired."

"What?"

"I just wanted you to know what it could feel like if it did happen," he said with a smug grin. "I don't want to fire you, Maggie. I like you."

I stared at him. "So this was . . ."

"A dress rehearsal for what could happen if your attitude doesn't improve. But don't worry, your job is safe . . . for now."

My fingers twitched, wanting to grab the mug and clobber him with it. Instead I turned on my heel and stalked away, trying to regain a semblance of control over my temper.

I almost bowled over Armani on my way.

"I have to talk to you, Chiquita," she said, once she'd regained her balance. Grabbing my arm, she dragged me outside toward the picnic tables. "I've got to tell you something important about your Scrabble tiles."

I wanted to tell her that I didn't have time for her psychic act today, but since I'd just been fired, but not really fired, I decided I was entitled to a long break. "What?"

"I may have been wrong about you being in for a RUF RIDE."

"I doubt that," I said, thinking about the arrival of Zeke and the evil plan of Harry.

"But look!" Using her good hand she pulled seven Scrabble tiles from her pocket and tossed them onto the table like she was playing craps. Which was appropriate considering my life was crap. "It doesn't just spell out RUF RIDE, they also say, U R FIRED. See?"

"You're right."

"So you see it too?"

"No, I mean, you're right. Harry just threatened to fire me. This time he used props."

Armani collapsed onto a picnic bench. "Oh my God. Do you know what this means?"

"It means that in the near future I'm going to have to find a new job or apply for unemployment."

"No."

"No?"

"It means that I was right. My predictions are right. I've been doubting my gift, but now . . . but now . . . I've got to call my mother and tell her."

I stared at my work friend, marveling at how she could turn my bad news into her own good news. "Congratulations."

Missing my sarcastic nuances, Armani bobbed her head. "Thanks. Thanks. I can't believe it."

I turned away and strode toward my car. I should got to HR right now and tell them what that scumbag had just done to me, but I couldn't take the chance now.

"Maggie?"

I didn't break stride. Harry couldn't say shit about my leaving. Not if I kept quiet.

"Maggie, watch out for the disco ball I told you about!"

Ignoring her, I started cramming minty fresh Life Savers into my mouth. They didn't make me feel any better. In fact I felt worse as I realized that Patrick was going to kill me for almost getting fired.

I CONSIDERED CALLING Patrick and asking him to kill my boss, but I wasn't in the mood for a Life Lesson lecture.

Instead I drove over to the hospital, thinking I could get a visit in with Katie without risking running into Delveccio and getting pressured for an answer about the job. I'd been sitting with Katie for over an hour, reading books to her and singing songs, when I heard the familiar clickety-clack of an aging sex kitten's stilettos tattooing their way down the hall. Looking up, I wasn't surprised to see Aunt Loretta arrive in the doorway. I peered around her to see if she had her fiancé, Templeton, in tow. The rat was nowhere in sight.

"Oh my!" Loretta exclaimed breathlessly. "Is everything all right? Has there been a change in Katie's condition? Has she gotten worse?"

I sighed. Aunt Loretta could be such a drama queen. "She's fine. No change."

"Then what are you doing here? It's not even noon yet."

Realizing that it was my presence that had alarmed her, I felt guilty for labeling her a drama queen. "I'm sorry I startled you. I . . ." If I told her that I'd almost lost my job, it would just give her, Leslie, and Susan something else to worry about. They already had too much to lose sleep over. It had always been pretty easy to get away with lying to Aunt Loretta, since she was the most gullible. "I took the day off."

"Good for you! You've been looking tired lately. A day off is probably just what you need."

I stood up and motioned for her to sit in the visitor's chair.

She bent over the bed and blew air kisses at Katie before sitting down. Taking the child's limp hand in her own, she confided in a whisper, "Your Aunt Maggie has met the most delightful fellow. His name is Paul. I think he might be the one."

"I don't think so, Aunt Loretta."

"And why not?" She turned her heavily mascaraed eyes on me. "He's very interested in you. Asks a ton of questions about you. That's a good sign, you know. A man being interested in his woman's secrets."

"I'm not his woman."

"He's a good catch."

"How would you know?"

"He's got a good, stable job in law enforcement."

Unlike your ex, Jose Garcia, I thought.

"And he's not hard on the eyes."

I had to agree with her on that. Paul Kowalski is a fine looking man. "He has his faults."

"Such as?"

"He has a temper."

Loretta shrugged. "All that means is that he's passionate. You wouldn't want a man who didn't feel anything, would you?"

It was my turn to shrug. It wasn't as though I could

tell her that both Patrick and God didn't trust him.

"You should go out with him. You could use some love in your life."

It took all my self-control not to roll my eyes. Taking love life advice from a woman who'd been married as many times as my aunt sort of felt like listening to a hooker preach abstinence. Wanting to get her attention off Paul, I changed the subject to another topic I knew she loved to talk about. "Last night I went to The Big Day with Alice."

"And did she find something?"

"Mmmm."

"Is that a yes or a no, Maggie?"

"Yes." The absolute joy in my best friend's eyes when she looked at herself in the mirror had been touching. Technically it had been Zeke who had found the perfect dress for Alice. He'd reached into the racks and pulled out the wedding gown of Alice's dreams. She'd practically babbled her gratitude at him, which had been . . . unsettling. After all, I was her best friend, but there she was gushing over the moment with him. "Zeke's back in town."

"I always liked that boy."

That was the problem. Everyone liked Zeke. Everyone except me.

"I HAVE NEVER understood how Zeke's able to fool so many people. He's tricky and conniving and . . . evil, just downright evil." I poured out my troubles to Doomsday as we walked. Well, as I tried to walk and she kept stopping every three-point-five inches to sniff something.

"Fetch he does?"

"What?" Unlike God, I was still having some difficulty understanding the Doberman's grammar . . . or lack thereof.

"Fetch he?"

"I don't know if he plays fetch." I thought about her question for a moment. "I doubt it. If memory serves, it says Most Likely to Iron His Underwear under his picture in our high school yearbook. I'm thinking that means he probably wouldn't pick up anything that's covered with dog spit."

"Squirrel!"

That was the only warning I received. Suddenly Doomsday was doing her damndest to dislocate my shoulder. She bounded away. If I hadn't had her leash wrapped around my wrist she would have been gone. Instead, she dragged me with her. Fighting to stay upright, I screamed, "Stop! For the love of—"

Twisting my ankle, I lost my balance and took a knee-skinning header for the second time that week. Except this time, my journey didn't end when I hit the ground. I kept moving. "Doomsday!"

My battered body bounced along the ground.

I'm not sure if it was my desperate shriek or the fact that she was now dragging my dead weight across the ground, but she seemed to realize that we were attached. "Game!"

"No, it's not a game. You almost killed me. You can't—"

Ignoring my protestations, she enthusiastically licked my face. "Maggie love. Maggie love."

Pushing her away, I struggled to my feet. "Don't do that again. You almost broke my wrist." I held it up, pointing at the red welts where the leash had cut into my skin. "See what you did?"

Doomsday hung her head.

I glared at her. "You hurt me."

"Sorry." The apology came out as a pathetic whine.

My knees hurt, my wrist ached, and I'd almost gotten fired. I had every right to be pissed at the badly behaved mutt. Didn't I?

Doomsday pawed at my shin. "Doomsday sorry."

"Margaret?"

I closed my eyes. Like my day wasn't bad enough.

"Margaret?"

I turned around to face the car that had pulled to a stop behind me and forced myself to smile. It made my cheeks hurt as much as my knees. "Hi, Aunt Susan, what are you doing here?"

"Move slowly, Margaret. Don't startle it. Just get in the car."

There was no missing the panic in my normally calm and collected aunt's voice and face. My fake smile morphed into a genuine one. "It's okay."

"It's not okay. That's a dangerous animal. Get away from it!"

Doomsday turned around to look behind her. "Animal where?"

Throwing open the door of her car, Susan leapt out brandishing a folded-up umbrella.

"So much for moving slowly."

"I'll hit it." She raised the umbrella overhead. "You jump in the car."

"No."

"Margaret, that dog is dangerous."

"Doomsday?" the dog whined.

"Shoo!" Susan shouted.

Doomsday ran behind me, burying her head into the back of my knees, almost knocking me over.

"Calm down, Aunt Susan. She's not going to hurt anyone. She's a good dog."

"Good dog," Doomsday repeated.

"Get away from my niece, you vicious beast!" Susan took a wild swing in the canine's direction.

"Give me that!" I shouted, grabbing the umbrella and yanking it away from her. "She's my dog and you're scaring her."

Aunt Susan's eyes went wide and her jaw dropped open. The only other time I'd witnessed such an expression of horror on her face was when the police had broken her favorite vase as they tried to arrest my father in her living room. Aunt Susan is not an animal lover. In particular she complains about the smell and mess dogs make. But the truth is, she's absolutely terrified of the four-legged creatures.

Doomsday ripped the umbrella from my grip and chomped on it. It made a sickening crunch.

"Bad dog! Stop that!" Grabbing it away from her, I held it out to my aunt.

"It has . . . teeth marks."

She was right. There were distinct puncture marks ripping through the material. "Sorry about that. She didn't mean it."

"It's a dangerous animal, Maggie. I think it has rabies. It could attack at any second."

Doomsday rolled on her back, belly exposed, in the most submissive posture imaginable. She wiggled her stump of a tail.

"Oh yeah," I drawled. "She's definitely vicious. I can see why you're afraid."

"I can understand that you've been shaken up by all that's happened," Susan said slowly. "Heaven knows, we all have been."

I felt a twinge of guilt as I heard a slight waver in my aunt's voice.

She cleared her throat, regaining control of her emotions. "And I understand that you're probably feeling alone, but that . . . thing . . ." She slid a sideways glance in Doomsday's direction.

The dog grinned back at her, displaying all her sharp teeth.

Susan shuddered. "That thing is not the solution to your problems. You should move back home."

"Never!" I spit out automatically. I'd rather have monkey sex with Harry than move back home.

"Would it be so bad to be with your family who loves you?"

I resisted telling her that their love was smothering. More than that, they drove me crazy. "I like being on my own."

Turning away, she got back in her car.

"Is that why you came by? To tell me to come home?"

"It's nice having Alice hanging around. It would be nicer if you were there too. You wouldn't have to pay rent. You could eat something that isn't designed to be heated in the microwave. It bothers the twins that you're here all alone."

"I'm not alone." I pointed to Doomsday.

Susan shook her head. "You're . . ."

"I'm what?"

"You're the only one we have left, Margaret," she said softly, before closing the door and driving away.

Chapter Five

THE NEXT MORNING as I was taking my shower, before I went to work at Insuring the Future, I heard a distant, unfamiliar ringing. It started and stopped, started and stopped, started and . . .

"Answer the damn phone," God bellowed. His words echoed off the glass of his terrarium as though he'd shouted in the middle of the Grand Canyon.

Turning off the water, I stepped out of the tub. "It's not my phone!" My house phone had a decidedly muffled ring because I kept it under my bed. I never wanted to speak to anyone who had that number. My cell phone quacked like a duck. I definitely heard a trilling ring, which stopped abruptly the moment I wrapped a towel around my torso.

"The bloody phone is in your purse!" God screamed when it started to ring again.

I'd forgotten that Patrick had given me a burn phone. One that only he had the number of.

"Answer it! Answer it!" The lizard was beating on the glass wall of his enclosure as though he'd been driven mad by the sound.

"Chill, big guy." I rummaged in my purse while staring at him. If it's possible for a lizard to be bug-eyed, he was.

"Hello?"

"Morning, Mags. I didn't wake you, did I?" I could practically hear the warm smile in Patrick's voice.

"I was in the shower. You could have left a message instead of calling a dozen times." I tried to push Doomsday away from me, but she was intent on licking the shower water off my ankles.

"I wanted to talk to you before you left for work."

"About what?"

"A lesson."

I swallowed hard. The one and only "lesson" we'd had consisted of me learning to shoot a gun and then rolling around in the hay of a barn together. That close physical contact had left me considering the possibility of having sex with the cop/hitman . . . that is until I'd learned he was married . . . with two wives. Still, the memory of our bodies pressed together . . .

"Are you there, Mags?"

"Hey! That tickles! Will you get off of me for two seconds?" I shoved the dog, who'd worked her way up to my knees, intent on getting every last bit of moisture off my skin with her pink tongue.

"You should have said you weren't alone." Patrick's tone was cold and hard.

"Stop licking my legs!" I shrieked.

"Jesus," Patrick muttered. "I'm hanging up now."

"Bad dog!" I swatted Doomsday's nose.

The dog lay down and whined, "Sorry Doomsday."

"Next time I'm going to lock you up." My threat caused the dog to flatten her ears.

"You're talking to the dog?" Patrick asked.

"Who else would I be talking to?"

God made a harrumphing sound, reminding me that he was a sterling conversationalist.

"I thought . . . never mind. I want you to meet me for a lesson."

"I've got work and then I'm visiting Katie."

"Afterward."

"That's usually when I eat dinner."

"I promise you won't starve. I'll see you at the mall at seven."

I looked at the dog, who'd rolled over on her back and was surreptitiously licking my big toe. "Can't. I've got to let the dog out."

"Bring her along. I'll see both of you at the mall at seven-thirty. Have a good day." He hung up.

It was my turn to harrumph. The idea of me having a good day was about as likely as my crazy mother saying something rational.

SPEAKING OF CRAZY women, Armani Vasquez was stalking me. Every time I looked up from my desk at Insuring the Future, she was watching me, but the moment she realized I saw her, she looked away, ducking behind her sheet of thick black hair. She not only observed me from her desk, but I saw her peeking at me through the fronds of the plastic potted palm by the ladies' room, furtively glancing at me when she stood by the copier, and stealing a quick look from behind the coffeemaker.

I felt like I was under surveillance, but instead of Big Brother watching me, I had the semi-psychic, semi-paralyzed, totally loco Latina chick noting my every move.

I, of course, reacted with grace under pressure. Whenever I caught her staring I alternated flipping her the bird, sticking my tongue out, and circling my finger by my ear in the universal sign of *You're a fucking loon.*

This netted me some strange looks from my other co-workers.

Finally, when lunchtime rolled around, I called her on her bizarre behavior. She was sitting outside at our favorite picnic table, her back to me, when I walked up to her and rapped my knuckles against the table to get her attention.

Startled, she turned toward me. "Hey, Chiquita," she said, as though it was the first time she'd seen me that day. "*Que pasa?*"

"Don't you *que pasa* me. What the hell are you up to?"

"What do you mean?" She had the sense to look away.

"What's with watching my every move?"

"You should sit."

"I don't want to sit. I want an answer."

"Sit, Maggie."

Her tone was so sad and serious that a sense of fore-boding pooled in the pit of my stomach. I sank onto the bench opposite her. "Is something wrong? Are you sick? What's going on?"

"I was worried about you."

"Me? Why?"

"I started dreaming about the spider web again."

A chill swept through me.

She had dreamed about a crystal spider web before the terrible car accident that had killed my sister, landed my niece in a coma, and bestowed the ability to talk to animals on me. Unable to make sense of her vision, Armani hadn't told me about it until afterward, when she'd shown me the sketch she'd made of the web. It had matched the pattern of the car's cracked windshield perfectly.

That, along with her bizarre prediction to "meet the man," which ended up being the way I killed Gary the Gun, has made me a semi-believer in her semi-accurate prophecies.

"What do you think it means?" I asked.

She shrugged. "Interpreting isn't my strong suit. I just get the visions. I suck at figuring out what they mean, but I'm thinking the web combined with RUF RIDE means you should stay away from cars."

"Stay away from cars? How the hell am I supposed to do that?"

"I'm sure Harry would be happy to set up a cot for you in his office."

"I'd rather die."

She chuckled, but then grew somber. "Seriously, Chiquita. I'm worried about you. You need to be careful."

"Is that why you were stalking me?"

"I was trying to read your aura."

"My aura?"

She nodded excitedly. "My grandmother could read auras. Maybe I can too."

"I thought you read Scrabble tiles . . . and had those prophetic dreams. Now you can read auras too? What the hell are you doing working here? I'm sure California Psychics would give you a job in an instant."

Tears filled Armani's eyes and she turned away from me.

I felt about two inches tall. She was my friend, trying to help me, and I'd gone and made fun of her for it. "I'm sorry."

She ignored me. Not that I could blame her.

"I didn't mean it. I'm just really stressed out." Because a mob boss wants me to kill a drug dealer that I used to call Uncle.

"Youneedewetaid," she muttered.

"What?"

She turned to look at me. "You need to get laid," she shouted.

Our coworkers, intentionally inhaling carcinogens by the door, stopped puffing long enough to laugh at my expense.

My cheeks burned. "That's your solution to everything."

"It would certainly fix things with Harry."

"Not funny."

"But true."

"Not happening."

"What about the cop?"

An image of red-haired, green-eyed Patrick sprang to mind, but I knew that wasn't who she was referring to. She meant muscle-bound Paul. "I don't trust him."

"News flash, Chiquita: You don't have to trust 'em to screw 'em."

Wise words.

AFTER WORK, A day that was mercifully Harry-free, I went to visit Katie. Before I entered her room, I knew by the telltale clicking that Aunt Susan was there, pecking away at her computer keyboard like a crazed woodpecker.

"Hello, Margaret." She didn't look up from her typing.

"Hi." I bent over Katie and pressed a kiss to her forehead. "Hey there, Baby Girl. Aunt Maggie is here." I held my breath, hoping that she'd open her eyes.

She didn't.

I sighed my disappointment, which made Susan's fingers falter. The sudden silence echoed through the room.

Taking Katie's tiny hand in mine, I sank into the seat beside her bed. I sang "The Itsy Bitsy Spider." Even that didn't garner a response from her. I swallowed down the painful lump that rose in my throat. The doctors had said her recovery, if she made one, would be slow, but I kept hoping for a miracle. Every day that she failed to improve, my sense of optimism wavered.

Aunt Susan cleared her throat. "You'll never guess who Alice brought by last night."

I looked over at her and saw that she too had unshed tears in her eyes. "Who?"

"Zeke."

I rolled my eyes. "Yeah, I saw him last night."

"Where?"

"At The Big Day. We were looking for a wedding dress for her and he popped up like some deranged fairy godmother, pulling out the perfect gown."

"He's a nice boy. He was always patient with your mother."

I didn't say anything. Aunt Susan had always had a soft spot for Zeke. I couldn't expect her to understand that beneath his smooth charm lurked the heart of an evil wizard, able to cast a spell over everyone I knew.

"Alice said the dress he chose was perfect, everything she'd dreamed of finding."

"She does look beautiful in it," I admitted grudgingly.

"Lamont didn't like the fact she brought Zeke home. I was afraid he was going to sit on the poor boy."

Hope surged through me, lifting my spirits and bringing a smile to my face. Finally! Someone who saw Zeke for the conniving little weasel he is! My fondness for Alice's fiancé tripled in that moment. "He's not a boy. He's my age."

She tilted her head and considered that. "But he's not bitter, which makes him seem younger."

Frowning, I looked away.

"His family disowned him," Susan reminded me quietly, before I had a chance to launch into my litany of reasons why I was bitter. "Do you remember how you begged us to take him in?"

I nodded. The anti-drug campaign had been in full swing at our high school when Zeke had called the cops on his own drug-dealing father at the end of our junior year. When his dad was sent to prison, his mother kicked Zeke out of the house for "destroying the family."

Way back then, I'd felt a sort of kinship with Zeke since we had the most fucked-up families in the neighborhood. That and the fact I'd nursed a crush on him when we were juniors. He'd needed a place to stay until he finished high school, so I'd asked my aunts to help my friend/crush, but everything changed our senior year. That's when I'd found out that he was gay and it was when he'd tried to steal my best friend.

I sighed. "I made a mistake."

"You made me proud."

I snapped my attention back to her. Her eyes were trained on her computer screen. "Really?"

"I'm constantly surprised by what you're capable of, Margaret."

The conversation went no further than that, because Aunt Loretta teetered in, pollinating the room with air kisses and taking over the conversation. I couldn't tell if she was wearing even more blush than usual, or if she was hot and bothered about something.

I didn't have to wait long to find out.

She frowned at me. "Are you going to wear a tuxedo?"

I looked to Aunt Susan for a clue as to what the hell her sister was talking about. She shrugged at me helplessly, her fingers hovering above her keyboard. "A tuxedo?" I asked Aunt Loretta.

"To the wedding!"

"To your wedding?" I asked, totally confused.

"Heaven help us," Aunt Susan muttered, and began banging away on her computer with undue vigor.

"Not *my* wedding," Aunt Loretta huffed. "How vulgar!"

"I have no idea what you're talking about," I confessed, feeling the dull throb of a headache take root behind my eyes.

"To Alice's wedding! Are you wearing a tuxedo to Alice's wedding?"

"I'm wearing a tutu."

Aunt Susan's clickety-clacking stopped long enough for her to ask, "Really? She's having you wear a tutu?"

I shook my head. "No. It just looks like a tutu. It's pink and frilly and has this giant crinoline skirt."

"Ughhh," Loretta groaned.

Apparently, in her estimation, a tutu was even more vulgar than wearing a tuxedo to her wedding. And I hadn't even mentioned that it was cotton candy pink.

"So no tuxedos," I told her with faux cheeriness.

"He can't wear a tutu." Loretta tapped her stiletto for emphasis.

"Lamont?" I asked.

She stopped tapping and looked at me as though I

were even crazier than her sister, my mom, who is locked up in the nuthouse. "Why would Lamont wear a tutu?"

"Loretta!" Aunt Susan said sharply. "Why are you going on about tuxedos and tutus?"

Her sister blinked her false eyelashes, signaling she was hurt by Susan's tone. "I wasn't the one who brought up tutus."

Aunt Susan glared at her. "Tuxedo?"

"What's Zeke going to wear to the wedding?"

The throbbing behind my eyes increased to the intensity of war drums. I had a horrible feeling that I knew where this was going. "Why would it matter what Zeke wears?"

"Because," Aunt Loretta said, "Alice asked him to be one of her bridesmaids."

Even though I'd suspected as much, the confirmation still stung. I turned away from my aunts so they wouldn't see the tears I was fighting. Blindly I picked up a pink teddy bear that had been sent to Katie.

"You're a bull in a china shop, Loretta," Aunt Susan chided.

"What?" Aunt Loretta asked. "It's a legitimate concern."

"She didn't know," Aunt Susan said gently.

"Oh. I didn't know. I'm sorry, Margaret."

"It's okay," I said, my back still to them. "One would assume that the bride would let her maid of honor in on such decisions."

Thankfully, Aunt Leslie barged in just then, effectively ending the conversation. Hyped up from all the caffeine she was ingesting at her NA and AA meetings, she talked faster than an auctioneer about "sharing" and "steps" and "amends." It didn't take me long to zone out. I was preoccupied about the night's "lesson" with Patrick. I really wasn't up to any more surprises.

Chapter Six

I WAS STILL worrying about what the lesson would entail as I left Katie's room, leaving behind the three cackling witches.

"Miss Lee?" a man called. "Miss Lee?"

Holding my breath, I turned slowly in the direction of the unfamiliar voice. The first strange man who'd greeted me by my name here in the hospital was Delveccio. The second had been Gary the Gun. Neither of those meetings had resulted in moments that gave me the warm fuzzies. Call me superstitious, but I'm a great believer in bad things happening in threes. Unlike the mob boss and the hired gun, the man approaching me from the waiting area didn't appear to be menacing. He looked tired and sad. I didn't recognize him, but maybe he too had someone lying in one of these beds. Maybe, like me, he'd been ground down by the weight of the endless waiting.

"How can I help you?" I asked as kindly as I could.

"Would you mind if we sat down and talked?" He waved at the waiting area.

"Of course."

For once the space was visitor-free. Our only company would be the television tuned to the local station. I'd learned more about my fair state because of that damn TV than I had after a childhood spent in the public school system. We sat on a pair of chairs opposite one another. Neither of us spoke. He nervously fiddled with his wedding ring, a simple band that had seen better days.

"What can I do for you?" I finally asked.

"My name is Bruce . . . Bruce Calvin." He waited, watching my reaction as the name sank in.

A vise tightened around my chest, making it difficult to breathe.

"My wife"—he glanced down at the symbol of their love encircling his finger—"my wife was Lois Calvin. I wanted to say, I wanted to tell you, to make sure you knew, how very sorry I am . . ." he said in a rush before trailing off lamely with "for what happened."

"For what happened?" My voice, shaking with emotion, was barely more than a growl. "You mean that your wife murdered my sister and put my niece in a coma?"

He flinched. "I'm sorry."

"Sorry won't bring my sister or Katie back."

He hung his head. "This was a bad idea."

"No," I said, jumping to my feet, "your wife getting behind the wheel while higher than the Empire State Building, that was a bad idea. This was just a colossal waste of time." I stalked away from him, my legs shaking from the righteous anger flooding my entire body.

"I tried to stop her!" he called.

I spun back. "You didn't try hard enough."

He'd gotten to his feet and had followed after me. "I got my daughter, Martha, she's four . . . I got her out of the car and brought her inside. I went back out to get the keys from Lois, but she was gone."

We stood there, staring at one another, each reeling from our respective losses.

Finally, when I thought I could speak without screaming, I asked, "What is it you want from me, Mr. Calvin?"

"Forgiveness?"

I laughed. Or at least tried to, but the sound that came out sounded like a grunt of pain. "You're asking the wrong person."

"Please," he begged. "Haven't you ever made a wrong choice? Haven't you ever, in the moment, gone right when you should have gone left? Don't you have any regrets about things you could have, should have done differently?"

An image of young Marlene tugging on my arm at the carnival, while I instead focused on our mother and her outlandish behavior, flashed through my mind. All too familiar regret and self-recrimination flooded through me. Instinctively I tensed against it, balling my fists.

I looked anew at Mr. Calvin and saw again how tired and sad he looked. I understood what it was like to carry that kind of guilt around. I knew what it felt like to need to be absolved for that kind of mistake.

I closed my eyes, gathering myself. I could do this. I could offer this man, who'd inadvertently destroyed my family, the one thing he wanted most. The very thing my own family had denied me.

I opened my eyes, the words *I forgive you* on the tip of my tongue, but the countenance of the man I faced was no longer desperately pleading. He stared past me, as though I didn't even exist, with a consuming hatred.

I turned to see the target of his hate and realized he was watching the TV.

I recognized the face the camera was following. Jose Garcia.

"It's all his fault," Calvin ground out through gritted teeth.

"How?" I asked softly.

"He's the one who got her hooked. We met him at a party some stupid work friend of hers threw, and he gave her a 'free sample.' It was all downhill from there. We had a life, a family, and now . . . now I have nothing." He collapsed into the nearest chair, burying his face in his hands.

"You have Martha," I reminded him gently.

"But he killed her!"

"And my sister." My anger left as quickly as it had arrived. A cold, calculating need for revenge filled the void it left.

I never even thought about the decision. In that moment, I knew I was going to tell Delveccio that I'd kill Jose Garcia.

"I'm going to kill him," I told Patrick as Doomsday clambered into the back of his truck du jour. This one was forest green and smelled . . . delish.

Patrick waited until I'd climbed inside, before inquiring mildly, "Aren't you going to put on your seat belt?"

As soon as I'd clicked my safety belt, he handed me a brown paper bag that smelled heavenly.

"What is it?" I asked, momentarily forgetting my need for revenge as I was overcome by the aroma of fresh-cooked food that hadn't come out of a microwave.

"Dinner."

"Me feed. Me feed," Doomsday whined piteously.

"Okay, okay, big fella," Patrick said, reaching behind us and rubbing the Doberman's snout. "I didn't forget about you."

"She's a girl," I reminded him as I opened up the bag and pulled out a sandwich wrapped in aluminum foil. Shredded lettuce and chopped tomatoes fell into my lap, but I didn't care. I took a giant bite.

"This isn't a burger," I said through my mouthful of food. Aunt Susan would have been appalled by my lack of manners.

"No." Patrick chuckled, pulling another brown bag out and rummaging in it. "It's a falafel. It won't kill you to eat some vegetables. Don't you like it?"

Considering that Patrick had bought me more meals in the short time I'd known him than all the other men I knew had in the past three years, I didn't think it was right to complain. "It's . . . interesting."

"Did you bring the lizard?"

"No. Should I have?"

"No, but I thought maybe you'd bring him along for luck. I mean, you did bring it to a hit." He tossed a piece of something that looked suspiciously like steak to the dog.

She gobbled it up greedily.

"You got me vegetables and the mutt a steak?" I asked incredulously.

"It's lamb."

Doomsday grinned at me. "Good. Good."

"How come she gets lamb and I get . . . this?"

"Because she's a good dog who is stuck eating dry kibble and you're a grown woman who seems to subsist on microwavable meals, olives, and fast food. You should take better care of yourself."

"I—"

"You," he interrupted, "can do whatever you choose, but that doesn't mean that *I* need to enable your self-destructive habits." He tossed another piece of lamb to Doomsday.

Scolded, I slouched in my seat and concentrated on polishing off my sandwich.

Patrick pulled the truck out of the parking space and pulled onto the road. "See that blue Camaro up there? Keep your eyes on it."

"That's a car, right?"

"It's not just a car, it's a classic."

"So that means it's old, right?" I leaned forward, squinting. "Why didn't you just say, 'See that old car up there'? Then I would have known what you were talking about."

"So you see it?"

"Yup. What's important about it?"

"Nothing."

I turned to glare at him. "So why the hell are you having me watch it?"

"It's part of a lesson."

"What kind of lesson?"

"How to tail someone. In our business it's helpful to know how to follow someone."

"I think I can handle that," I groused. "How hard can it be?"

"Where'd it go?" he asked with deceptive mildness.

I looked back at the road. We were approaching an intersection. The old blue car was nowhere in sight. My mouthful of falafel got stuck in my throat. "I don't know."

Patrick sighed his disappointment.

"Don't do that."

"What?"

"Sigh at me."

Patrick slid a sideways glance in my direction as he pulled onto a side street. "Sighing is off limits now?"

"Sighing is the universal symbol for *Maggie's a screw-up*." The sharpness of my tone made Doomsday whine.

"Or," he replied calmly, "it's a sign that Patrick's had a bad day."

"You had a bad day too?" Here I'd been all wrapped up in my problems and the man beside me had endured an equally bad day. Maybe worse, since I'd never heard him complain before. "What happened?"

He shrugged.

I opened my mouth to ask why he'd bothered to bring it up if he didn't want to talk about it, when I spotted the old, blue car, pulling into a driveway. "There it is! The Canary!"

"Camaro, it's a Camaro, not a Canary." He drove past the classic. "Nice job spotting it."

"Nice enough that it warrants you telling me why you had a bad day?"

A faint smile tugged at the corners of his mouth. "My daughter's mother wants to move to California."

"Oh." I mean what do you say to a guy when he tells you that his wife, who isn't really his wife since he's already married to someone else, is leaving him?

"She's found someone else. She's been seeing an old friend from Iraq and apparently they're going to get married."

"Oh." Was I supposed to say I was sorry to hear that?

"I'm happy for her. She's never been happy here . . . or with me."

The sadness in his voice had Doomsday licking the back of his ear.

Reaching back, he rubbed her head affectionately. "I'm happy for her, but Daria, our daughter, is freaking out. The moment she found out her mom is moving across the country she burst into tears and threatened to drop out of school. She called me a dozen times today." He dragged his hand down his face, signaling his frustration. "There's nothing I can do to make this better for her. All these years trying to protect her and it's her mom who knocks her world off its axis. I'm at a loss."

"Understandable," I murmured. "Does her mother want her to go with her?"

He shook his head. "She understands that Daria's life is here. She wants her to visit and to go to the wedding, but she doesn't expect her to move there."

We rode in silence for a few moments. We didn't appear to be tailing anyone. I finished my sandwich.

Finally he said, "So, why did you have a bad day?"

"I met the husband of the woman who killed Theresa."

Patrick let out a low whistle.

Doomsday thumped her stump of a tail against the door.

"How'd that happen?"

"He came to the hospital looking for me."

"Why?"

"He wanted my forgiveness."

"Fat chance of that," Patrick muttered.

"What's that supposed to mean?" I asked sharply.

Patrick glanced at me, an emotion I couldn't identify flickering in the depths of his green gaze. "You do like to nurse your grudges."

"So you think I can't be empathetic toward a man who's looking for forgiveness?"

Instead of answering me, Patrick eased over to the side of the road, parking beneath a streetlight. He twisted in his seat so that he faced me.

My stomach flipped nervously. I had the sudden urge to open my door and run from the truck.

As though he heard my thoughts, he caught my left wrist in his hand, gently trapping me.

Swallowing hard, I looked down at where our bodies met, wondering if he could feel how my pulse had sped up. I tried to tug away, but his fingers tightened, not painfully, just determinedly, on my skin.

"Do you believe in forgiveness?" he asked softly.

I looked up at him in surprise. The moment he'd touched me I'd forgotten what we'd been discussing.

He watched me with that quiet intensity of his that made me feel both special and frightened. My mouth went dry.

"Do you believe in forgiveness?" he prompted.

"Do you?"

He tilted his head to the side, considering the question. "It depends on whether it's deserved."

"Agreed."

"Really?" His tone indicated he didn't believe me.

Afraid of what he might see with his searching gaze, I turned away to look out the passenger window. Quite the trick considering he still held my wrist.

The only sound in the truck was Doomsday's panting.

I heard Patrick expel a long breath. "I shouldn't have pushed you."

"You shouldn't do a lot of things," I snapped, tugging my wrist for emphasis.

He let go immediately. I tried not to think about how much I missed the contact.

"So you want to kill him?" Patrick asked, retreating to a safe topic of conversation. Murder was that between us. "The husband?"

"No." I turned so that I was facing him again. "Garcia."

"I thought you were on the fence about him. And after a little digging and seeing that he was married to your aunt, I understand why. Delveccio can find someone else for the job."

"I don't want anyone else," I insisted. "I want to do it."

The venom in my tone made Doomsday whine.

Patrick's gaze narrowed. "Why the change of heart?"

"The husband."

"I don't follow."

"Revenge."

Patrick frowned. "I'm still lost."

"The husband told me that Garcia got his wife hooked on drugs, so really it's his fault that Theresa's dead. Now he's got to pay."

I hadn't realized I was yelling until Patrick winced.

"That's a really bad idea," he said quietly.

"Why?"

"Because . . ." He turned away, staring out the windshield, choosing his words with care. "Revenge never gets you what you want, and being this emotionally involved in a job multiplies the chances of you screwing up and getting caught."

"I don't care," I assured him, emboldened by my righteous anger and my newfound hatred of Jose Garcia.

"Then who will take care of Katie?" Patrick asked.

Chapter Seven

"HE DOES HAVE a point," God drawled superiorly from his glass terrarium, which I'd put in the middle of my kitchen table. "If you get caught, what will happen to Katie? And me?"

"Doomsday?" the dog barked.

"Yes," the lizard griped. "And the slobbering beast. No one in their right mind would take her in."

I didn't like being reminded of people in the right minds when I was in the midst of a conversation with a lizard and a dog. It made me feel like I could end up sharing a room with my mother in the mental hospital at any moment. I frowned at God over the refrigerator door. "I'd been looking for some support, not for you to take Patrick's side."

"I'm not taking his side," God said. "I'm advocating for Katie and myself."

"Doomsday!" the dog yipped.

"And the beast," the lizard added grudgingly.

I turned away from them and considered the contents of my fridge. The hitman was right. I did eat too many olives. I had seven different kinds on the shelves.

"So you're not going to do it, right?" the lizard nagged.

I sighed. The burning hatred in my gut had been replaced by the cold fear that I wouldn't be able to help Katie. Maybe Patrick was right. Maybe God was right. Maybe I should just go with my initial reaction and turn down this particular job.

"Well?" God asked.

I took out a container of garlic-stuffed olives. I opened it and popped one in my mouth. "I wouldn't want the two of you to end up homeless."

Doomsday licked my hand in appreciation. That or she was after the olive brine.

"A wise choice," the little guy assured me.

I felt a little better having made the choice. I ate another olive to celebrate and closed up the refrigerator.

"Who's suing you?" the lizard asked casually.

"What?"

He pointed at the pile of unopened mail beside his enclosure. "You got something from a lawyer."

I rifled through the pile until I found the envelope he was referring to. He was right, it was from an attorney's firm. Hands trembling, I ripped it open.

"Please don't be bad news," I begged. "Please no more bad news."

I flopped down on the chair and read it. I only read

the first paragraph before I jumped back up. "Son-of-a-bitch!"

Doomsday ran out of the room and even God seemed to cower against the rear wall of his terrarium.

"Son-of-a-bitch!" I shouted again, throwing the papers on the floor and jumping up and down on them like a demented four-year-old.

"What is it?" God asked cautiously.

"They want her."

"Who wants who?"

"Katie's aunt wants Katie. She's suing me for custody."

I didn't know it was possible for an anole lizard to pale, but Godzilla did. "She can't," he whispered.

"She is." I pointed at the offending papers.

"What are we going to do?"

"I'm not letting her have Katie. She's never even met her."

God nodded. "Maybe you can get the redhead to kill her."

I considered that for a second. "Maybe."

"You need to hire a lawyer," the lizard said, his color coming back.

"With what money?" I asked.

He shrugged.

I snapped my fingers. "I'll tell Delveccio I need an advance for killing Garcia."

The lizard didn't try to talk me out of it.

As eager as I was to tell my favorite mobster that I needed an advance on my contract to kill Garcia, I still had to spend the next day at Insuring the Future. But before that, I had to take Doomsday, piteously whining, "Gotta! Gotta! Gotta!" for her morning constitutional.

God, complaining that he had a case of cabin fever, insisted on coming along too, perched precariously on my shoulder, his tail wrapped around my neck for balance.

We'd barely gotten out the door when the dog emptied her bladder on my neighbor's golf green welcome mat.

"Doomsday," I scolded. "I've told you to only go on the grass."

"Grass!" She scratched at the plastic turf.

"That's not grass, dingbat," God told her with a smirk in his voice.

"Dingbat not!" the dog snarled.

"Yes, you are," I assured her, bending down to gingerly pick up the ruined mat, taking care not to spill the puddle in the middle. "And destructive. First Aunt Susan's umbrella and now this."

"While we're using D adjectives to describe the mutt, I want to add *disgusting*," God said. "As in: It's disgusting you're picking that up."

"Like cleaning your terrarium is any better," I muttered. "My life was a lot easier before the two of you."

"Sorry Doomsday." The dog nudged my hand in apology, upsetting my delicate balancing act and splashing her pee all over me.

"Aaaah!" God screamed, clambering on top of my head as if to escape sulfuric acid.

"Aaaah!" I echoed, throwing the soiled mat at the dog and trying to knock the lizard off my head. "Idiots!"

"Imbecile!" God countered.

Doomsday took off. I hadn't even realized I'd dropped her leash until she was twenty yards away.

"Doomsday!" I called.

She didn't look back. Ears flattened, she ran faster than I'd thought her capable of.

"Come back!"

She ignored me.

"Get back here right now or so help me . . ." I trailed off, partly because she was already out of earshot, but also because I realized I sounded an awful lot like my father.

"Look what you did," God said reproachfully.

"What I did? You were the one who called her a dingbat and disgusting."

"But I," he drawled haughtily, perched on my head, "didn't assault her."

"I didn't assault her."

"You threw the mat at her."

"I didn't throw it *at* her . . . I threw it and it happened to hit her."

God harrumphed his disbelief.

"If you don't get off my head this instant I'm going to throw you off." I reached upward, ready to make good on my threat.

"I have sensitive skin," he practically shrieked, clambering back onto my shoulder. "What are you going to do now?"

I frowned in the direction Doomsday had disappeared. "I'm going to work. I assume you are going to spend all day watching cooking shows."

"But what about the beast?" A tinge of concern wove through the lizard's voice.

I shrugged.

"You should go after her."

"I wouldn't even know where to start looking. She'll find her way home."

"Like Marlene has?" God goaded.

The mere mention of my missing sister's name made my bad day even worse. Ignoring the lizard's dig, I picked up the soiled mat, tossed into the Dumpster, and stalked back to my apartment.

"I can't believe you're going to leave Doomsday to cope on her own," the lizard griped as he climbed back into his terrarium.

"She'll be fine."

"She can't even compose a proper sentence and now she's out there . . . lost and afraid."

I felt a twinge of guilt, but wasn't about to let him know that. "She took off. She's probably having the time of her life."

He flicked his tail, signaling his disagreement, and turned his back on me.

Even though I was running late, after changing into urine-free clothes, I took the long way to work, hoping to catch a glimpse of the AWOL dog. I didn't spot her.

I'd barely parked my car at Insuring the Future when Harry came barreling toward me. One look at his red face and wild eyes had me considering locking my doors and getting the hell out of there.

Then I remembered I've killed a mobster and a professional hitman and I was going to kill a drug dealer, so an irate pencil pusher with a penchant for pepperoni was no one to be afraid of. I got out of my car, but kept a tight grip on my keys, my handiest weapon.

"Who did you talk to and what did you say?" Harry spluttered, rocking to a stop a few feet away.

I backed up so as not to be in range of his enraged spittle. "What?"

"What did you tell them?" he squeaked, obviously panicked.

I considered him for a second. I hadn't said anything to anyone, but he obviously thought I had. Whatever it was freaked him out. I liked watching him squirm. I smiled.

My smile unnerved him further. He paled.

"Surely there must be a way to fix this," he said in his most conciliatory tone.

"The ball's in your court, Harry." I smiled again for good measure.

He turned and practically ran away.

That should have amused me, but watching him distance himself from me just made me think of Doomsday. I wondered if she'd ever come back, or, if like so many others in my life, she'd abandoned me for good.

My eyes burned with tears. Dashing them away with the back of my hand, I squared my shoulders. I'd survived a lot worse than a doggie desertion.

"Why the long face, Chiquita?"

Whirling, I realized that Armani had snuck up behind me, quite the accomplishment for someone who drags her bad leg behind her.

"Was Harry giving you a hard time?" she asked.

"He seems to think I told someone something about him and now he's scared to death of me."

She ignored my revelation. "There was a cute guy looking for you earlier."

"For me?"

"Blue eyes, cleft chin, needs a haircut." She headed toward the building.

I fell into step beside her. "Zeke," I muttered, wondering what the hell he wanted from me.

"Zeke?" Stopping, she flashed a pleased grin. "What's it short for?"

I rolled my eyes, knowing that Armani judged people's worth based on the Scrabble value of their name, and kept walking. "It's worth seventeen points all on its own. Why does it need to be short for anything?"

She hurried to catch up. I slowed down so she could.

"It's short for something, isn't it?" she asked.

"Ezekiel."

"What the hell kind of name is that?"

"Biblical."

"Where'd you find him?"

"He crashed into me."

"Oh my God, the spider web," Armani's breath was suddenly shallow.

"With a sled," I told her hurriedly, not in the mood to

hear any more about her psychic predictions. "We were ten."

"Oh." She sounded disappointed.

"Did he say what he wanted?"

"He asked what time you took lunch and said he'd be back then."

My bad day was getting worse.

I spent the entire morning wondering what Zeke wanted from me and then the jerk never showed up. Armani was disappointed by his no-show status. I was relieved.

The rest of the workday passed uneventfully with Harry giving me a wide berth, which meant I was less stressed than usual when I got to the hospital. I'd even almost forgotten about the MIA dog. Almost.

A quick glance at the waiting area showed no sign of Tony/Anthony Delveccio or his hired muscle, so I decided to visit with my niece before doing business.

Mercifully none of my aunts were in with Katie when I got to her room. "Hey, Baby Girl," I cooed, settling into my usual seat and picking up her limp hand. I stroked two fingers down her cheek, blinking back tears.

Once again, I felt a burning hatred for Jose Garcia because of what he'd done to my family. Realizing I was holding my breath, I slowly exhaled, trying to expel some of the anger.

Returning my focus to Katie, I began manipulating her fingers and singing "The Itsy Bitsy Spider."

My voice cracked when I could have sworn I felt her fingers twitch.

I stopped singing and stared at her hand wondering if I'd felt an *inadvertent muscle contraction* as the doctors called her movements, or if she'd actually responded to me.

I cleared my throat, which felt as though it was being squeezed closed by a vise and started singing again. "The itsy bitsy spider went up the—"

This time I definitely felt her squeeze my fingers. She was responding. My heartbeat doubled its pace.

I forced myself to keep singing around the lump of tears lodged in my throat. "Down came the rain—" I looked up at her face. Her eyelids were trembling.

"C'mon, Baby Girl. Open your eyes. Open your eyes for Aunt Maggie." I stroked her cheek. "Please, Katie. Please."

I could have buzzed for a nurse, I probably should have, but it never even occurred to me. The only thing I could think of in that moment was willing Katie to open her eyes.

"It's okay, Katie. Aunt Maggie's here."

She opened her eyes.

My heart leapt and I thought my cheeks might crack, my smile was so wide.

My moment of elation was short-lived when I realized there was no recognition in her gaze. There was nothing.

Chapter Eight

THE DOCTORS AND nurses tried to convince me that Katie squeezing my hand and opening her eyes were encouraging signs, but as much as I wanted to, I couldn't believe them. The blank stare of the little girl frightened me. It made me think that my niece was lost to me forever.

That loss weighed on me as I left the hospital and stumbled toward my car, having forgotten I'd planned on finding Delveccio. I dropped my keys as I got to my car. Instead of picking them up, I leaned my head tiredly against the window. The glass felt cool.

"Maggie?"

I turned slowly in the direction of the voice.

"What's wrong?"

Zeke stood a few paces away, worry lines creasing his forehead. Armani was wrong. He wasn't "cute." He'd done "cute" as a teenager, now he was just ridiculously handsome in a movie star kind of way. I couldn't totally stop crushing on him just a little, even knowing he was gay, was my sworn enemy, and was trying once again to steal my best friend.

"Maggie, what's wrong?" he asked again, concern deepening his tone.

I busied myself with bending to pick up my fallen keys. I couldn't tell him how monumentally unfair it was that he was gay and I didn't want to give voice to my fears about Katie. What was it Aunt Susan always said? The best defense is a strong offense? "Are you stalking me, Zeke? First you go to where I work and now you're here. I spent the whole day waiting for you to show up."

A devilish glint flashed in his eyes, a grin dancing on his lips. "Were you disappointed when I didn't?"

I grabbed my keys. "Annoyed, but not surprised. You never were the responsible kind."

His eyes narrowed and his smile vanished at my attack. "I needed to talk to you."

I stood up slowly. "About what?"

"The bridal shower. I think Alice is expecting one this weekend."

I leaned back weakly against the car. "This weekend?"

"Well, the wedding is next weekend, so this would be the only chance."

"There's no way . . ."

"And I think she's expecting a bachelorette party."

I closed my eyes.

"So," he said in a rush, "I was thinking we could do the shower this weekend and the bachelorette party on Wednesday night."

"I can't."

"We can do it Tuesday or Thursday." He moved closer as he spoke. "We can just make a quick trip to Atlantic City to one of the casinos. She won't be drinking because of her condition, so it should be a pretty short night."

I watched him with grudging amazement. He'd done this when we were kids too, cheerily bulldozed his way through a conversation, as though he could achieve the desired outcome through pure strength of will.

When he paused to take a breath, I said hurriedly, "I'm not doing a shower or a bachelorette party. She'll understand."

He stared at me, shocked. "But she's your best friend."

"Don't try to put this on me." I poked his chest with my finger. "I'm not the one who saddled everyone with this ridiculous time frame."

Zeke looked down at where I'd poked him. "It's not like she did it on purpose."

"There you go again," I muttered, shoving at his chest with the palm of my hand.

Caught off guard, he stumbled backward a step.

"You always take her side. You're always kissing up to her."

He considered me for a long moment, but didn't refute my accusation. Instead he asked, "Why won't you do the shower or party?"

"Because"—I waved an arm at the hospital—"I can't drop everything just because she got herself knocked up and still wants all the white wedding crap. She doesn't get to have everything go right for her while everything goes wrong for me." The unfairness of it all hit me in the solar plexus and I found myself gasping for air with tears running down my face. "I can't do it. I won't do it."

I sensed Zeke step toward me and held up my hands to stop him.

"You're not going to hit me, are you?" he asked. "You've already poked and shoved me."

Guiltily I covered my face with my hands and sobbed.

Somehow I found myself leaning on his shoulder. Catching a whiff of his aftershave, something bright and fresh with notes of sandalwood, made me cry harder.

"I'll take care of everything, Maggie," he soothed. "I'll plan everything and decorate and order the food. All you'll have to do is show up."

I could have hated him even more in that moment when he said he'd take on all of the bridesmaid duties, but I was just so relieved that everything wasn't falling to me that I was filled with gratitude. "Th-thank you," I said on a hiccuping sob.

"Hey!" a Neanderthal boomed. "The boss wants to see you."

I jumped away to find Vinnie, Delveccio's muscle-head nephew, frowning at me from a few paces away.

"Who the hell are you?" Zeke countered, stepping between us protectively, like he couldn't see that Vinnie could bench press him with just his pinky.

Vinnie ignored him. "Now."

"I'll be there in a couple minutes." I wiped away my tears.

"Who the hell is this guy?" Zeke asked, every muscle in his body tense, looking surprisingly alpha male.

Vinnie looked him up and down, deciding whether he could take Zeke. Considering he pumped iron and Zeke primped tulle, I didn't think it would be much of a fight.

While part of me still hated Zeke, he *had* just offered to shoulder most of the bridesmaid duties, so I didn't want anything to happen to him.

I jumped between the two men.

"The boss said—" Vinnie began.

"And I said I'll be there in a couple minutes," I interrupted. "Leave." I made a shooing motion in his direction.

He glared at me, the veins in his neck bulging.

I glared right back. "Now."

Grudgingly he turned away and trudged toward the hospital.

Zeke turned to face me. "Who the hell is that?"

"A family member of one of the patients." Technically that was true, so I wasn't lying.

Zeke eyed me suspiciously. "And who's his boss?"

"His uncle. The boy's grandfather. We've sort of bonded." Again, not a lie. "His grandson isn't much older than Katie."

"I'll go back inside with you," Zeke offered.

"Thanks, but . . ." I said slowly. I needed to talk to Delveccio about killing Garcia and I was pretty sure bringing along Zeke would be in direct violation of Patrick's Don't Get Caught rule. "Thanks, but I can do this on my own."

"Are you sure? That guy looked sketchy."

"Sketchy?" I teased. "There's something I haven't heard in a while. I seem to remember you telling Alice that Louis Lauer was sketchy."

"And I was right."

I nodded. He had tried to warn Alice about her boyfriend when we were fifteen. Alice hadn't listened. Louis, like most of her loser boyfriends, had broken her heart. He probably would have broken her arm too at the Spring Semi-Formal our junior year, if Zeke and I hadn't gotten her away from him. The Monday afterward, Zeke had shown up to school with a black eye he refused to explain. I was never sure if it was his dad or Louis who gave it to him.

"What do you think of Lamont?" I asked.

"I think he doesn't like me."

"I don't like you either." The words were out of my mouth before I could stop them.

Zeke didn't appear hurt or angry. In fact, he smiled. "I guess I'll have to work my way back into your good graces, starting with planning this shower."

I stared at him, not knowing how to respond.

"Anything you don't want at the shower?"

"Games."

"Games?"

"I hate those lame-ass games people insist on. They're like grown-up versions of Pin the Tail on the Jackass."

"Okay. No games. You sure you don't want me to go in there with you?" He jerked his thumb in the direction of the hospital.

"Dead sure."

"You're the boss." He crossed the space between us and pressed a kiss to my cheek, whispering in my ear, "You *are* going to like me."

I stared at him dumbfounded as he winked at me and then strolled across the parking lot.

Once he was out of sight, I returned to the hospital for my meeting with Delveccio. The whole way to the cafeteria, I mentally rehearsed how I was going to convince him to give me some money in advance of the Garcia job, but I completely forgot my speech when Aunt Leslie accosted me before I reached the mobster.

Well, she didn't so much accost me as she almost ran me over with a loaded wheelchair.

"Hey," I protested, having barely escaped with my toes intact. "Watch where you're going."

"What are you doing here?" she asked, but before I could reply, she patted her wheelchair passenger on the shoulder and said, "Bertram, this is my niece Maggie. She was my rock bottom. Maggie, this is Bertram."

"Hi," I said weakly to the wizened old man who had a death grip on the arms of the wheelchair, wondering how many people my newly clean aunt told I was her rock bottom.

"What are you doing here?" Leslie asked again.

"I was visiting Katie." I tried to assess whether she was chemically impaired or just all-naturally wacky.

She gave me the same look right back. "Why else would you be at the hospital?"

"But you just asked . . ."

"I meant," she said with exaggerated patience, "what are you doing in this wing?"

I couldn't very well tell her that I was there to talk to a mobster about killing her twin's ex. "I was hungry and they have great chocolate pudding. What are you doing here?"

"I'm a Candy Striper!" She did a little happy dance that looked a lot like the hokey pokey. "Of course they don't call it that anymore, but that's what I am. It was my sponsor's idea that I do something in service to others, so here I am." She leaned toward me. "And guess what? I'm good at it."

Having witnessed her wheelchair-driving skills, I wasn't so sure about that, but I didn't want to be the one to burst her "service to others" bubble. "That's great."

"Well I've got to get Bertram back to his room, but it was nice seeing you," she said as though I were an old neighbor she'd run into at the grocery store. "See you soon."

I had to jump out of the way as she and Bertram careened wildly away. I looked down to make sure all my toes were still attached.

When I looked back up, I saw Vinnie standing at the cafeteria entrance glaring at me. "The boss doesn't like to be kept waiting."

Ignoring him, I strode past and made my way to where Delveccio sat. As usual, his shirt was unbuttoned almost to his belly button.

"Sorry I made you wait." I slid into the seat opposite him.

He swept his gaze over me and I knew what he was thinking. The first time we'd met, I'd come to the hospital straight from Theresa's funeral and had been wearing a black dress and high heels. He preferred my femme fatale look to my "blending in" jeans and polo shirt. Little did he know that the little black dress only came out of the closet for funerals or really promising dates. I hadn't had a promising date in years, despite what Aunt Loretta thought about Paul.

Finally Delveccio said, "Vinnie said you gave him lip."

I shot a dirty look at the bodyguard on the opposite side of the room. "He rubs me the wrong way."

Delveccio chuckled. "Me too. You want a pudding?"

I nodded.

The mobster flashed two fingers at his muscled henchman. "Did you decide about the Garcia thing?"

"Yes."

"Yes, you've decided? Or yes, you're going to do it?"

"Both."

"Our mutual friend seems to think giving you the contract is a bad idea."

I made a mental note to tell Patrick to stay the hell out of my business. "What do you think?"

"I like you. You want it, the job's yours."

"I want an advance," I blurted out, which was so not the way I'd rehearsed asking the mobster for money.

His gaze narrowed. "What for?"

"Expenses." I held my breath as Vinnie arrived with our chocolate puddings.

He put them down and walked away.

"Spoons!" Delveccio boomed.

Vinnie flinched and scurried away.

"I swear they were scraping the bottom of the brains barrel when they created that moron," Delveccio griped.

Considering that his mother, an Atlantic City showgirl, named her identical twins Tony and Anthony, I was pretty sure the DNA pool of his family tree was a kiddie pool, not Olympic-sized. I kept that thought to myself. Instead I said, "So what do you say? Will you give me an advance?"

He waited until Vinnie had placed spoons and napkins in front of us before he answered. "You are one ballsy chick."

"Thank you."

"Since you did me a solid with Gary the Gun, I'm considering your request."

The solid referred to the fact he hadn't paid me for offing the hitman and had ended up with a two-for-one deal when I'd killed his son-in-law.

I forced myself to eat a bite of creamy, chocolaty goodness while waiting for his decision.

"How 'bout I front you a quarter of the fee?"

"What's the fee?"

"A hundred . . . minus my brokerage fee of fifty percent."

I almost choked on my pudding. He was pocketing fifty grand while I took all the risk and did the work?

He watched me steadily, waiting for me to call him on the unfairness of the deal.

I did the calculations in my head. A quarter of fifty

thousand dollars was a little over twelve . . . that had to be enough to retain a lawyer. "Okay."

He blinked, surprised. "Okay?"

I nodded.

"Tell you what," he offered. "Since you're not being a whiny pansy ass like a lot of guys I deal with, if you earn the bonus, I'll let you keep the whole thing."

"Bonus?"

"You do the job in the next twelve days *and* if you do it publicly, there's an extra hundred in it for you."

"Hundred thousand?" I practically squeaked.

"Yeah. It's good money, but only if you don't get caught."

Chapter Nine

"HE AGREED TO the deal," I shouted as I entered my apartment.

God didn't answer me and I realized I wasn't being greeted by a chorus of "Gotta! Gotta! Gotta!" from Doomsday. That's when I remembered she was gone. The pain of loss shot through me. Knees weak, I stumbled, catching myself on the wall, my hand brushing against her leash hanging there.

I missed her. I missed the eat-me-out-of-house-and-home, grammatically challenged dingbat so much it hurt.

"I'm going to look for the beast. Want to come along?"

Again God didn't answer me.

"Seriously? You're giving me the silent treatment?"

Nothing.

I stalked into the kitchen, ready to have it out with him. I stopped short when I realized his terrarium, sitting smack in the middle of my kitchen table, was empty, the lid slightly ajar. I wouldn't have thought the scrawny guy would be strong enough to move it. Bending down, pressing my nose to the glass, I double-checked whether he was hiding beneath the driftwood he liked to recline on.

No lizard.

I grabbed the kitchen table for support as a sinking feeling in the pit of my stomach made the world spin. "God?" I whispered.

Not him too. He was the only . . . friend I could confide in and count on in the midst of my crazy life.

"Godzilla?" I shouted.

When he didn't answer, I knew he wasn't in the apartment.

"Where did you go?" I wondered aloud, even though I was pretty sure I knew the answer.

Hurrying back toward the front door I grabbed Doomsday's leash off the wall. Throwing open the door, I bounced off a chest.

Not a piece of furniture, but the chest of a man. A well-muscled, buttons-stretched-to-their-limit kind of chest.

"Going somewhere, Maggie?" Paul Kowalski, wearing his police uniform, looked amused as I stumbled backward, carefully catching myself against the wall.

"What are you doing here?" I didn't know if my breathlessness was a result of my hurrying, crashing into him, or because I was startled.

"I was coming to see you." He flashed his most charming smile.

At least I would have found it charming when we'd first met. Now it seemed to have a slightly predatory gleam that had me tightening my grip on the leash. "You could have called."

"And you could have screened my call." He reached out and straightened the family portrait I'd recently rehung in the foyer.

This was the third time Paul had been in my home. The first time I'd been ready to have sex with him (until God had reminded me I'd had a gun tucked under my mattress). The second time I'd been grateful for his help as he'd helped me deal with my Aunt Leslie who'd passed out on my doorstep. But this time . . . this time I wanted him gone, because this visit just didn't feel right.

"Sorry," I said with as much fake cheer as I could muster. "If you'd called, I could have told you I was on my way out."

"Where are you going?"

"To look for my dog."

"You don't have a dog."

"I do now." At least I hoped I did. I had to find her first.

He focused on the leash I held for the first time. "What kind of dog?"

"A Doberman."

His smile wavered a little. "Why'd you get a Dober-man?"

I shrugged, figuring it was safer than telling the police officer that the dog had belonged to a hitman I'd killed with a leg of lamb.

"Anyway," he said, seemingly undeterred by my desire to get rid of him. "Your Aunt Loretta said you need a date to the wedding."

"Did she?" I made a mental note to duct tape Loretta's painted lips closed.

"So I thought you and me, some dancing, some romance."

"That's sweet," I said slowly, "but it wouldn't be fair to you. I'm going to be swamped with maid of honor duties." Behind my back, I crossed my fingers to offset the lie. Zeke was the one taking care of everything. "And Lamont's best man isn't getting in until the day before . . ."

"Oh." He looked genuinely disappointed.

"I'm sorry."

"Well if you change your mind, you can always call me. You do still have my number, don't you?"

I nodded.

"So you'll call?"

"Sure."

"Why do I feel like you're giving me the brush-off?"

Because I was. "I've got a lot going on, Paul. I just don't have the time for a relationship right now. It wouldn't be fair to you."

"Who's talking about a relationship? I'm just talking about having some fun together." He winked at me. "We *have* had some fun together, haven't we?"

I couldn't help but smile at his blatant flirtation, even as I waited for him to leave. Despite the fact I didn't trust him, and I worried about his temper, I couldn't deny that he was sexy as hell and we had shared some pretty hot kisses and groping.

Part of me wished I had the time or the disposition to take him up on his offer of "fun." The other part of me remembered that both Patrick and God didn't like him. The only person who did was Aunt Loretta, and she's not exactly the best judge when it comes to the characters of the men she meets.

As I locked the door of the apartment, I heard the engine of his car roar away. When I turned around, he was gone from sight.

I scanned the area, but didn't see my MIA lizard or dog.

"God?" I whispered. "Where are you?"

Pacing the length of the parking lot, I was relieved I didn't spot his smooshed brown corpse anywhere. I peered beneath all the parked cars, but couldn't find him.

How far could the little guy have gotten?

I tried to think like him, but then realized that he had probably tried to think like a dog. All that thinking gave me a headache.

Spotting a squirrel, I called out, "Hey! Have you seen a big, black, airheaded dog running around loose?"

The squirrel fixed his beady little eyes on me, wrinkled his nose with distaste, twitched his tail, and bounded off.

I set off in the direction Doomsday had disappeared. A block later I saw a pair of feral cats Dumpster diving behind a diner. "Excuse me?"

The stopped and eyed me with disdain.

"Have you seen a big, black dog? Her name is Doomsday."

Arching its back, one hissed at me. The other yowled.

I couldn't understand what either was saying. So much for being the clone of Doctor-freakin'-Dolittle.

Discouraged, I trudged on.

I'd lost my dog.

I'd lost my lizard.

And if I didn't kill Jose Garcia, I was going to lose my niece.

Trying to brush away tears that blurred my vision, I staggered, catching myself against a "Children at Play" sign. Resting my forehead against the pole, I closed my eyes and let out a hiccupping sob.

A car pulled to a stop beside me.

Squeezing my eyes shut, I prayed they'd just move along and not ask me why I was holding on to a street sign for dear life.

"Mags?"

I opened one eye and looked at the car, an unfamiliar blue sedan.

"Whatchya doing?" the driver asked, peering through the lowered passenger window.

I opened my other eye so that I could focus properly on the redhead behind the wheel. "Are you following me?"

Patrick tilted his head. "I prefer to call it tailing. Do you want a ride?" Without waiting for an answer, he leaned over and pushed the passenger door open for me.

"Why were you tailing me?"

"I'm pretty sure the sign can stand all by itself. Get in."

Unable to come up with a smart-ass answer, I got in the car. It smelled like stale cigar smoke.

"Seat belt," Patrick prompted.

I put the seat belt on and he drove away.

"What's going on?" he asked. "Delveccio said you took the job. I thought we'd agreed you wouldn't since it's so dangerous. Then I see Kowalski leaving your place, and now you're walking around talking to yourself."

There was no anger or judgment in his tone, only curiosity and concern. Somehow that made me feel worse.

"I lost my dog, I lost my lizard, and I'm going to lose my niece."

He slid a sidelong glance in my direction as if to ascertain whether I'd lost my mind too. "Was that an answer to what I asked, or just some random rant?"

"I had to take the job. Katie's aunt is suing me for custody."

"Marlene?" he asked, referring to my runaway sister.

"No, not Marlene. Who knows whether Marlene is even alive?"

"I do. She is, though now she's going by the name Jewel. I keep trying to talk to you about her, but you won't let me." A note of exasperation threaded through his tone.

"She's not the point." I really couldn't deal with talking about Marlene with everything else that was going on. "Dirk the Jerk's sister, Abilene Plude, is."

"Plude?" Something sharpened Patrick's tone, but I was mid-rant.

"She didn't even come for her brother's funeral, and, I might add, has never laid eyes on Katie, but now she wants her." I sank into my seat.

"So you took the Garcia job because . . . ?"

"I need to hire an attorney."

"Oh."

"Unless you want to kill her for me?" I suggested hopefully. "It would be kind of obvious if I did it myself, but you could. What do you say?"

He didn't say anything, just concentrated on driving.

"Yeah," I muttered, turning away and looking out the window. "I knew that's what you'd say. Those damn criteria about a victim deserving it . . ."

After a few minutes of riding in silence he asked, "So . . . you and Kowalski?"

"There is no me and Kowalski. My Aunt Loretta would like there to be and I'm guessing he would like there to be since he showed up at my door, but there's definitely no Kowalski and me." Saying it aloud helped me to know I'd made the right decision.

Patrick nodded, a hint of a smile tugging at his lips.

Since I was unburdening myself, I told him the rest. "Doomsday and God ran away."

"God?"

"Godzilla. The lizard. They both ran away."

"Together?"

"No. Doomsday took off this morning. God disappeared sometime after that. He was pissed that I didn't go find her right away."

Patrick gave me that suspicious, sidelong look again.

I guess it did seem kind of crazy that my pet lizard was annoyed with me.

"And why were you walking around talking to yourself?"

I couldn't very well tell him that I can talk to and understand some animals. He might have driven me straight to the loony bin and gotten me into the room adjoining my mom's. So I said, "I was looking for them. Calling their names."

I wasn't sure if he believed me. I decided to distract him.

"Where are we going?"

"My place."

My stomach fluttered. "Why?"

"There's someone you should see."

My throat closed, preventing me from speaking. I couldn't believe he was ambushing me like this. I was in no shape to see Marlene. Finally, as he pulled to a stop in front of his place, I managed to say, "You can't do this."

Turning off the car, he turned to face me. "Do what?"

"Make me see her."

Worry creased his forehead. "You don't want to see her?"

I shook my head.

"Why not?"

"I'm not prepared."

"What kind of preparation do you need?"

"I'm too . . . raw. I can't . . . please . . ."

I hadn't realized I was trembling until he reached over and pulled me to him, cradling my head against his shoulder. He was warmer and more solid than the stupid signpost. With him holding me, I didn't feel like I was going to shatter into a billion bits.

"Take it easy, Mags. Just take a breath."

I did. He smelled like soap and peppermint.

"Now listen carefully to me. You think I've got your sister in my place?"

I nodded.

He leaned back, catching my chin so that I had to look into his reproachful gaze. "You should know I wouldn't do that to you."

He was right. He might be a paid assassin, but he'd never treated me with anything with fairness and respect.

Guiltily I looked away. "Then who?"

"Come see."

He hopped out of the car. I followed slowly.

"Wake up, Sleeping Beauty," he called as he unlocked the door of the tiny apartment.

"Maggie! Maggie! Maggie!" a breathy bimbo panted as she jumped up and knocked me over.

Doomsday and I collapsed to the floor in Patrick's entryway.

"How?" I asked as she licked my face, practically drowning me.

"She was nosing around outside of the falafel place." Pulling the dog off me, he helped me to my feet. "I'm guessing the scent of the lamb was familiar after the other night."

"Meat! Meat!" Doomsday whined.

"I was there for lunch," Patrick continued, absentmindedly petting the Doberman. "I had to get back to work and it hasn't gone too well the last couple of times I went to your place unannounced, so I brought her here."

Doomsday wagged her stump of a tail. "Cheese! Cheese!"

"I take it you fed her?" I asked.

"Cheese. It was the only thing in the fridge besides beer. I went by your place tonight to tell you about her, but I saw Kowalski's car . . ."

"And you decided to tail me."

"Actually I wanted to make sure he wasn't following you. He looked pretty angry when he got back in his car."

I wasn't surprised at that nugget of information. "Thanks."

"That's what friends are for."

"Is that what we are?" I asked without thinking. "Friends?"

An uncomfortable tension stretched between us as we both considered ramifications of the question. Sure I was attracted to him, but even with only one wife in the picture now, he wasn't the guy for me. He was still a professional killer, no matter how caring and considerate he came across.

Finally he said, "Among other things. Do you want to talk about the Garcia hit?"

I nodded, grateful to be back on safer ground: killing a person for profit. "Where do you want to start?"

THE PLAN, AT least in its rudimentary form, was to kill Jose at the rehearsal dinner he was throwing for his daughter. It would be quick and public, like it was supposed to be, but Patrick thought there would be less risk of getting caught since there would be fewer people in attendance and fewer photographers who might inadvertently snap my picture.

Plus, scheduling-wise, it was a lot more convenient for me. Apparently Jose's wife was the superstitious type, and her psychic told her holding the rehearsal dinner the night before the wedding would bring bad luck. As a result, the Garcia rehearsal dinner was scheduled for the weekend before the nuptials. This meant I'd be obligation-free the weekend of Alice's wedding.

After we'd worked out the general details, Patrick drove me home, with Doomsday riding along, head hanging out the window, in the backseat. He dropped us off two blocks away from my apartment, leaving the dog and me to walk the rest of the way.

As soon as Patrick left, I bent down, wrapped my arms around Doomsday's neck, and hugged her tightly. "I'm so sorry about this morning."

"Okay." She licked my face, signaling her forgiveness.

I wished people could forgive so easily.

"I have to tell you something upsetting," I said, straightening and heading for home. "Godzilla is missing."

The dog fell into step beside me, completely oblivious of the leash hanging from her collar. "Why?"

"I'm not sure. I think he may have gone looking for you."

"Am here I."

I took that to mean, *Here I am*. We walked the rest of the way in silence.

As we approached the door of my apartment, a superior voice said, "It's about time."

I spun around. "God?"

"Who else were you expecting?"

"Missing not," Doomsday panted excitedly. She scampered over to where the lizard was perched on the railing, but stopped abruptly, taking care not to crash into him. Lowering her head, she sniffed him. "Home everyone."

A painful lump rose in my throat as I watched him reach out with his tiny front foot to pat the tip of her nose.

"It's wet!" He wiped the dog snot onto the railing. "Disgusting."

"Inside, Doomsday," I said, pushing the apartment door open.

She bounded in.

I squatted down to get a better look at God. "Where'd you go?"

"How did you find her?" he countered.

"I didn't. Patrick did."

"And yet you were cavorting with Mr. 'Roid Rage."

"You saw Paul? Where were you?"

"I notice you're not denying the cavorting."

"I wasn't cavorting with him. If you must know, he stopped by, uninvited, and suggested I take him as my date to the wedding."

"If you ask me, that would be a bad idea."

"But I didn't ask you. My knees are starting to hurt from squatting like this."

"That's from the cavorting."

"I didn't cavort with him," I snarled. I put out my hand, palm up. "Do you want a lift inside, or did you plan on staying out here the whole night insulting me?"

Gingerly he stepped onto my palm. "Don't forget, I have sensitive skin."

I carried him inside and let him climb from my hand onto the driftwood in his enclosure. "I turned him down on the wedding date thing."

"Wise move."

"I'm glad you approve."

It was difficult to tell which of us was more sarcastic. We glared at one another. It's stupid to get into a staring contest with a lizard since they don't have eyelids and can't blink.

I'd been doing a lot of stupid things, and was about to do a lot more.

Chapter Ten

"SO ABOUT THAT disco ball . . ." Armani said.

We were at one of the picnic benches outside Insuring the Future. I was having a peanut butter and jelly sandwich for lunch; she was eating what looked like tuna salad with gummi worms.

"Did you have another dream about it?"

Instead of answering me, she stared over my shoulder.

"Tell me it's not Harry," I said.

"Nope. It's your cute guy."

"He's not my cute guy."

"He could be, if you'd unleash your inner Chiquita."

I rolled my eyes. This wasn't the first time she'd suggested I let out the fun-loving gal she believed was stifled in the depths of my psyche. "Trust me, I'm not his type."

"Hey there, gorgeous," Zeke called as he approached the table.

Armani waved to him with her good hand.

I turned to face him. "What's up?"

"I needed to run a couple of things past you for the shower." He slid onto the bench beside me. "Hi, Armani. How are you?"

"My day's getting better getting the chance to look at you," she practically cooed.

Instead of being flustered by her outrageous flirtation, he smiled. "You're good for my ego."

Pitching her voice lower, she said suggestively, "I'm good for a lot of things."

"I bet you are, but"—he sighed sadly—"I'm a man on a mission. No time for distractions, no matter how enjoyable they might be."

"What do you want with the Chiquita?"

"I wanted to get her okay for the menu. He pulled a folded menu from a local catering hall out of his back pocket. "I figured Italian since it's Alice's favorite." He put the menu down in front of me.

Scanning the items he'd marked, I said, "Good choice."

"Great. Now what do you think about decorations?" He reached out and stole the half of my PB&J I hadn't eaten from yet and took a big bite, eyes twinkling like he expected me to give him a hard time about it.

I wouldn't give him the satisfaction. "I think they're the stuff landfills are made of. We should skip the decorations."

Armani gasped. "You *have* to have decorations."

"Why?" I asked. "You spend a small fortune on them, they're out for a couple of hours, and then you throw them away. They're a waste of resources and money."

"But we're going to have them," Zeke said. "Because you know as well as I do that Alice is going to want them. So help a guy out and tell me how to do them."

"How should I know?"

"You go to a lot of weddings."

"Not by choice."

"Everything's a choice," Zeke countered. "You choose to be the kind of person people can count on even when you're doing something you despise."

I frowned at him. "Have you been drinking the same Kool-Aid as Aunt Susan?"

"What's that supposed to mean?"

"Nothing." I took another bite of the half a sandwich he hadn't taken.

"What are the wedding colors?" Armani asked.

I eyed her suspiciously, worried she was one of those women who spent her weekends curled up with a pint of ice cream, watching marathons of the wedding shows that litter television. "I don't know."

"How can you not know? You're the maid of honor. What color is your bridesmaid dress?"

"Pink."

"Salmon," Zeke corrected. "The dress is salmon."

Armani wrinkled her nose. "Uh-uh-gly."

Zeke nodded his agreement.

"You should decorate the room in salmon," Armani told him helpfully. "And since the color is ugly, you should use a lot white stuff. White tablecloths, maybe white candles or flowers, and you can get a lot of white things like wedding bells."

"All this for the knocked-up virgin bride," I muttered.

"Wedding bells?" he asked, ignoring me.

"They're these paper things you unfold and hang everywhere."

"Great ideas, thank you."

I watched him and Armani discuss possible decorating ideas for the next ten minutes, feeling more than a twinge of jealousy. I had no interest in planning the shower, but I did wish I was the one Zeke was laughing with. I knew it was silly, especially since, as I'd told Armani, I knew I wasn't his type, but it would have been nice to have been the recipient of his charming attentiveness.

After he'd taken copious notes of Armani's suggestions, he focused on me. "Have you thought about a gift?"

"That I've got under control." I'd known what I was going to give Alice when she got married since we were fifteen.

"What's a good gift to give at a bridal shower?" Zeke asked Armani.

"Well," she said slyly, "I usually give lingerie."

Zeke held up his hands in surrender. "Are you trying to get me killed? Have you seen her fiancé? Nice guy, but on the jealous side. You don't want my boyish good looks to be messed with, do you?"

Armani giggled. She actually giggled. Why did every woman I know have to succumb to Zeke's charm?

"Give her something off the registry," I said.

The smiles dropped off their faces at my sharp tone.

"What's wrong?" Armani asked.

"Nothing. He's right. If he gives Alice some sort of lingerie, Lamont will get the wrong idea and beat the crap out of him. He's better off just getting something off the registry."

"And leave the lingerie to Loretta?" he teased gently.

I couldn't help but smile a bit at that. "You know her too well."

He brushed the hair off my face, skimming my cheek.

My heart rate sped up.

"I know all of you," he said, looking into my eyes with an intimate intensity.

My stomach fluttered. I forgot to breathe as I got lost in those blue eyes of his. I wondered if he knew that I'd carried a torch for him all those years earlier. I wondered if he had any idea the effect he still had on me.

"Pick," Armani ordered, breaking the strange spell Zeke had cast over me.

She held out her bag of Scrabble tiles to Zeke. He took one.

"Take six more," she told him.

"I don't have time for a game. Maybe next time?"

"It's not a game. Pick six."

He looked to me for guidance.

"She's sort of psychic," I told him.

"Not sort of," she muttered.

"She has dreams and visions and reads Scrabble tiles."

"So pick six more." She shook the bag at him, making the tiles click against one another.

Obediently he pulled six more. She held out her good hand and he dumped them into her upturned palm.

"I need to think about these for a while," she said. "I'll tell Maggie what they mean at the end of the day and she'll tell you."

"Okay. Thanks. I've never had my fortune told before."

"I'm not a fortune teller. I'm a psychic."

Zeke flashed her a smile. "Well either way, it'll be a first for me." He turned his attention back to me. "Anything else you need from me?"

I hadn't been aware I'd needed anything from him until he showed up.

He pressed a kiss to my cheek as he stood up. "Places to go. People to see."

"What do you do, Zeke? For a living," Armani asked.

"A little bit of this. A little bit of that."

Armani frowned. "What does that mean? You're unemployed?"

"Leave him alone," I interrupted. "He works at The Big Day."

"No I don't." He sounded surprised. "You think I work at the bridal shop?"

I looked up at him. "You don't?"

He shook his head.

"But . . . Why the hell were you there then? And how'd you find the perfect dress for Alice?"

"You really think it's the perfect dress for her?"

"Yeah, she looks gorgeous in it."

"She looks gorgeous in just about anything."

I winced. It wasn't easy having a best friend that everyone thought was stunning. I'd long ago resigned myself to the fact that she'd always outshine me, but that didn't mean it didn't sting.

Seeing my discomfort, Zeke hurried to say, "I didn't mean—"

"Why were you there?"

"I was there to see somebody else. It was just luck that I ran into you."

I'd known Zeke a long time and could have sworn I saw something falter in his usually easy smile, but before I could press him about it, we were interrupted.

"Ladies."

I barely suppressed a groan as I turned to see Harry standing a few paces away.

"I was just wondering whether you were planning on attending this afternoon's training session." Harry looked to Armani for an answer, seeming to take care to not make eye contact with me.

"Are there going to be cookies?" Armani asked.

Harry nodded slowly.

"Chocolate cookies?"

Harry's eyes widened and his Adam's apple bobbed, but he nodded again.

"Then we'll be there," Armani said. "Right, Chiquita?"

"Uh-huh."

"I'll let you all get back to work." Zeke said, moving quickly away from the table in the direction of the parking lot.

"Me too." Harry beat an even hastier retreat.

"Thanks for your help, Armani!" Zeke called.

She watched him go. "You'd be a fool to pass that one up, Maggie."

"I told you. I'm not his type."

She rolled her eyes. "You also thought he worked at a bridal shop. I'm thinking you don't know him as well as you think you do. You should definitely get to know that man better."

SOMEONE I DON'T want to get to know any better is my father, and yet, after work, instead of going to visit Katie, I found myself in the waiting room of East Jersey State Prison, where he currently resides. He's a permanent guest of the state for robbery and murder. The murder of a cop's wife, who happened to be working as a teller at the bank he was robbing, might very well be an unjust conviction. I had believed my dad had done it, up until last month when he'd confided he hadn't. I sort of believed him. It didn't mean he wasn't a crook, though, and a lousy husband and father.

Alice would hear none of that, though. Ever since he'd saved her from her monstrous stepfather she'd always seen him as her personal knight in rusty, dented armor, which is why I found myself waiting to see him. She'd begged me to take her for a visit before she got married.

"Are you bringing a date to the wedding?" Alice asked, nervously eyeing the guard in the corner of the visiting room. I'd warned her that she'd be patted down, but the professional groping had unnerved her.

"Nope. Going solo."

"Because Loretta said you might be bringing that cop."

"I'm not."

"You could. He's hot."

"And he's got a hot temper."

"So would you mind being Zeke's date? He's not bringing anyone either. I told him he could, told him we'd be cool with it, but he said he's not going to. Maybe you could dance with him a couple times."

"Maybe."

Alice smiled, a far-off look in her eyes. "There was a time you'd have killed for a chance to dance with him."

I winced inwardly at her choice of words. "You would have too."

Before we'd found out he was gay, we'd both had teen-age crushes on Zeke.

She laughed. "How far we've come."

Glancing around at the gray walls of the prison, I didn't think that where we'd ended up was any better than where we'd been.

My father appeared on the other side of the Plexiglas partition. He lowered himself into a chair so that he was eye level with us.

"Mr. Lee!" Alice squealed with delight.

He beamed back, looking like a benevolent department store Santa Claus rather than a convicted felon. "Such a nice surprise. You're more beautiful than ever,

Alice." He switched his gaze over to me. "It's good to see you, Maggie May."

I tilted my head in Alice's direction. "She wanted to see you."

He nodded, his joy fading, accepting that his daughter hadn't wanted to see him.

"I'm getting married, Mr. Lee." Alice displayed the sparkling engagement ring Lamont had put on her finger.

"Congratulations."

"And I'm pregnant!"

"That's wonderful news."

"We're very excited."

"You have a lot to celebrate." Leaning forward, he looked to me. "What about you, Maggie? Has Katie given you any reason to celebrate?" His affection for his granddaughter was evident.

I nodded slowly. "She's opened her eyes a couple of times." Just the once when I was there, but she'd done it a few more times when my various aunts were visiting. "The doctors are cautiously hopeful."

"Cautiously hopeful is good." He relaxed a bit in his chair. "So tell me, what else is new with you two girls?"

"Zeke is back in town," Alice gushed. "He's helping with the wedding. He's a godsend."

"I actually wanted to ask you something," I said, interrupting her waxing poetic about my frenemy.

A flicker of surprise flashed in my father's eyes. He wasn't accustomed to me asking anything of him. "Shoot."

"Did Theresa ever mention Dirk's sister, Abilene?"

"Why?"

"You can't just answer the question?"

"It's out of character for you to ask," he countered.

"Forget I asked." Folding my arms over my chest, I glared at him.

"He didn't say he wasn't going to tell you," Alice interjected, playing peacemaker. "He just asked why you were asking."

I really didn't want to tell them, but I really needed to know if Theresa had said something that might help to swing the odds in my favor in the upcoming custody battle. "She's suing me for custody of Katie."

"She can't do that," Alice said.

"She is. So, *Dad*." I emphasized the name to remind him that he owed me something. "What did Theresa say about her?"

He pulled on his white beard thoughtfully. "Dirk was afraid of her."

My stomach soured. Dirk may have been a jerk, but he'd never struck me as a man easily scared. "Why?"

"She has a lot of power, a lot of money."

Two things I definitely didn't have.

"You can't let her take Katie," my father said.

"I know."

"You have to do whatever it takes to keep her."

I nodded, wondering if that would involve killing Abilene.

"According to Theresa, the woman always hated Dirk. She destroyed his toys when he was a kid, wrecked his relationships as they got older. He moved across the country, from Vegas to here, just to get away from her. Did you know she managed to get their old man to name her as head of the family business, even though Dirk had worked his butt off for ten years?"

I shook my head, feeling a twinge of guilt for how I'd regarded Dirk when he was alive.

"This Abilene woman is dangerous, Maggie." Dad took a deep breath. "Maybe you could ask the bit . . . the witches for help."

Alice sucked in her breath. Like me, she knew that my father usually referred to my aunts as "the bitches." Like me, she knew he despised them and would never ask them for help. Like me, she now realized how big a threat Abilene must be.

"And what do you think a control freak, a nymphomaniac, and a recovering addict are going to be able to do to help?" I asked.

"Leslie's clean?" Dad's eyes grew round with astonishment.

"She was the last time I saw her a couple of days ago."

"That's amazing. Good for her."

"Good for her, bad for the rest of us."

"She's a bit . . . touchy right now," Alice chimed in helpfully.

"Bitchy is more like it," I corrected. "But the point is, there's not much they can do to help. I know they'd want to, but if this Abilene has as much money and power as you say, I can fight her, but I'm not sure I have a chance in hell of winning."

Chapter Eleven

"WHICH WAS PRETTY much what the lawyer said," I told God, filling him in on what was going on. The lizard perched on the top of his terrarium listening intently.

"When did you go to a lawyer?"

"I left work an hour early, saw the lawyer, and then took Alice to the prison."

"Quite the day."

"So the lawyer's number one suggestion was that I move back into the bed-and-breakfast."

"Food?" Doomsday panted hopefully from where she lay against the fridge.

I hadn't known she was even paying attention to the conversation. Instead of trying to explain to the mutt what a bed-and-breakfast is, I tossed her a biscuit. "She said—"

"She being the lawyer?" God asked.

"Yes. She said that if I moved back in with my aunts,

it would illustrate that I have a stable home and support system to bring Katie back to."

"Stable?" God snorted.

"I know. I know. But the lawyer seemed to think it was the strongest weapon I've got against this Abilene Plude."

Doomsday rested her heavy head in my lap. "Back move never."

I looked to God for translation. He shrugged.

"I don't understand, sweetie," I told the dog. "What do you mean?"

"Back move never lady umbrella."

"Oh for Pete's sake," God groused. "When are you going to learn how to construct a proper sentence?"

"Leave her alone," I muttered. "I know what she meant."

"Care to share?"

"I told my Aunt Susan I'd never move back."

"Never say never." He imparted it like it was the greatest line of wisdom ever imparted.

I wanted to smack him. Instead I said, "She hates dogs."

"Oh . . ." God said worriedly.

"Hate Doomsday?" the dog asked.

"She hates dogs in general. Not you in particular." I realized that wasn't terribly soothing, but I had to tell her the truth.

"Hate Doomsday?"

"You did chomp on her umbrella," I reminded her.

She immediately lay down and rolled over on her back. "Sorry! Sorry!"

"I know you are." I absentmindedly rubbed her belly.

"So it's going to come down to choosing between Katie and the beast?" God asked, eyeing the dog.

"No." I buried my head in my hands. "I don't know. We're getting ahead of ourselves. I don't even know whether I'm going to consider moving in with them or not. I mean what would be the point if I'm going to lose Katie anyway?"

The lizard started pacing the length of his enclosure. "But you have to position yourself in the best possible way to win the case."

"Don't you think I know that?"

"Happen Doomsday what?" the dog whined.

She looked at me with those big brown eyes, so sad, so scared, and a vise tightened around my chest. "We'll figure something out."

"Alone Doomsday?"

I looked to God for help, but he had turned his back on us. It looked as though his shoulders were heaving. The little guy was as fond of the big dog as I was.

"An impossible choice," I muttered, brushing away the tears that spilled down my cheeks. "It's not fair."

"Not impossible," God said, his voice strained. "Not impossible, just ridiculously difficult and unfair."

Doomsday got up from the floor and put her head in my lap. Licking my tears from my hands, she said, "Okay."

I didn't know what she was trying to tell me, but I threw my arms around her and squeezed as tightly as I could. "Everything will work out."

"Liar," God whispered.

THE NEXT MORNING, after another night of insomnia, I went to meet Patrick at his favorite cemetery.

I'm not sure why he's so fond of the cemetery, maybe because it's calm and quiet. I think it's kind of creepy. Doomsday, who I'd taken along for the trip, thought it was a wonderful spot. She ran around happily, sniffing headstones and chasing squirrels.

Seeing her so joyous increased my sense of guilt. What would happen to her if I moved in with aunts? She deserved a good home.

Patrick pulled up in a mud-splattered green Jeep.

"Patrick! Patrick!" Doomsday panted, running over to greet him.

He greeted her enthusiastically, bending down to pet her. "Hey there, beautiful." He smiled at me over her.

I did my best to smile back.

Worry flickered in his gaze, but all he said was "Hungry?"

"Yes!" Doomsday barked. "Yes! Yes!"

"She is," I told him.

He chuckled. "I think she's always hungry."

Reaching into the Jeep, he pulled out a white paper bag and proceeded to lay an impromptu picnic break-fast on the hood. On a bed of paper napkins he placed a couple of sandwiches, a Styrofoam container of bacon, and two fruit cups.

"Can you get the coffee?" he asked, tilting his head toward the interior of the Jeep.

I did, thinking I'd never had a man in my life take care of me the way he did. He'd probably make a great owner for Doomsday, giving her the kind of home she deserved.

When I emerged from the vehicle holding two cups of coffee, he was feeding the dog a strip of bacon, further cementing the idea in my head.

"You're spoiling her," I said.

"I think she had a rough life. She deserves to be spoiled a little." He threw a piece of bacon and the dog chased after it happily. "You look like you had a rough night."

Self-consciously I smoothed my hair, wondering how bad he thought I looked. "I had trouble sleeping."

"Something on your mind?" He handed me a sandwich wrapped in foil.

I nodded. "Thanks."

"The Garcia job?"

"No. I went to see my father yesterday."

He looked surprised. Every cop in town knew who Archie Lee was, but not every cop knew that when my father called from prison I screened his calls. "He upset you?"

"No. I asked him if he knew anything about Abilene, Katie's aunt. He said she had a lot of money and power and some lifelong vendetta against Dirk, Katie's dad."

He took a bite of his sandwich, circling his finger, indicating I should keep rolling with my story.

"I went to visit a lawyer yesterday who specializes in custody cases. She wasn't very encouraging. She said that if Abilene Plude could prove she could provide better for Katie's care, the court might award her custody."

"And you can't prove where you get most of your

income from," he said, meaning the money Delveccio paid me for being his go-to killer chick.

"Not to mention my dad is in prison and my mom resides in a mental ward. The only advice she really had was that I move back in with my aunts to show I have a stable family and support system to bring Katie back home to."

"And you don't want to do that?"

"In the worst way." I looked over at Doomsday, her stub of a tail quivering joyfully as she stalked a caterpillar creeping along the top of a headstone. "If I do, I'll have to get rid of the dog." I turned to face him. "Maybe you can take her?"

His eyes flicked from my face to the dog and back to me. "I can't, Mags."

"Okay," I said quickly, trying to mask my disappointment.

"It wouldn't be fair to her," Patrick tried to explain. "My hours are crazy. My life is crazy."

"I understand." I unwrapped my packet of food, revealing an egg and cheese sandwich on a roll, and took a big bite, hoping to end the conversation.

Patrick sighed. "I feel like I'm always letting you down."

I froze mid-chew. That was how I always felt when it came to everyone in my life.

"I screwed up with Gary the Gun, refused to kill Katie's aunt for you, and now I'm not agreeing to give your dog a home." He speared his hand through his hair. "I'm sorry. I really am."

Having finished chewing and swallowing I said, "Everything worked out with Gary, I get why you won't kill Abilene, and you're probably right about Doomsday."

That he didn't believe me was written all over his face.

Reaching out, I patted his arm. "Really. It's okay."

He looked down at where I was touching him. "You're a complication I hadn't anticipated, Mags." His voice had a husky note and when he looked back into my eyes, something I couldn't quite identify flickered in their depths.

I swallowed hard. "I don't mean to be."

Covering my hand where it lay against his arm with his own, he slipped his fingers around my wrist, stroking the tender skin underneath in a strangely intimate caress.

My pulse sped up beneath his touch and my breath hitched as he leaned closer.

"Bacon! Bacon!" Doomsday jumped between us, dislodging our physical contact.

I stepped back, unsure whether I was relieved or disappointed by the interruption. I knew getting any more involved with Patrick Mulligan was a bad idea, but there were times when the attraction I felt for him drowned out any semblance of common sense I had.

"Bacon!" Doomsday barked.

"I think she's hungry," I said.

The police detective/hitman nodded and tossed her another piece of meat. She swallowed it whole and licked his hand to express her gratitude.

"Thanks for breakfast." I took another bite of the egg sandwich.

"Someone's got to feed you," he muttered. "I've got

something else for you." He climbed into the Jeep and rummaged in the glove compartment.

The dog looked at me hopefully so I chucked a chunk of my sandwich in her direction. She gobbled it up with a wolfish grin.

"Here you go." Patrick reemerged with a necklace dangling from his fingers.

I didn't think we'd progressed to the stage where he'd buy me jewelry. I wasn't sure if we'd ever get there and I didn't want to give him the wrong impression and lead him on. "That's very nice, but I can't accept."

Ignoring me, he held up the necklace and said, "Turn around."

Even though my better judgment told me not to, I did what he asked.

He stepped behind me, reached over my head, and lowered the large, silver, cylindrical pendant so that it rested in the valley between my breasts. I flinched as the cool metal came in contact with my bare skin. I'd had no idea when I'd thrown on the V-neck T-shirt that morning that it would become the sexiest item of clothing I owned, but suddenly I felt like a temptress, with Patrick standing behind me, peering down my shirt.

And it wasn't anything like when Harry stares down my shirt. When Harry does it, I want to throw up. Whereas with Patrick, I wanted to throw myself at him.

But I didn't.

I just stood there, frozen, holding my breath, waiting to see what he'd do next.

"Lift your hair," Patrick said softly.

Reaching back with one hand, I held my hair away from the back of my neck. I could feel him fiddling with the clasp and then he dropped the chain against my neck.

"There you go." His breath tickled the back of neck.

I shivered uncontrollably, as my insides turned to molten mush.

Taking my raised wrist, he gently lowered the hand holding up my hair, to my side, causing me to rock back and lean on his chest. My eyes fluttered closed as he steadied my hip with his free hand.

We stood like that for a long moment, neither willing to take the next step, but neither wanting to pull away.

Being so close to him without actually doing anything was a delicious kind of torture. Every nerve in me was on high alert, waiting, but I couldn't gather the courage to act on the desires screaming through my body.

Finally he cleared his throat. "Make sure you don't take that off."

"Why not?"

"It contains the poison you're going to use to kill Jose Garcia."

Talk about a mood killer. My eyes snapped open and I stepped away from him as I reached up to finger the pendant.

"You wouldn't want anyone to accidentally get into it." He waved in the general direction of the dog.

"Poison?" I asked.

Reaching out, he plucked the cylinder from my fingers, the backs of his knuckles brushing against my sternum. A current of pleasure shot from the contact through my entire body, almost causing my knees to buckle.

Seemingly unaware of the effect he was having on me, Patrick explained. "It's colorless and tasteless. A drop or two, poured into his drink or something he's going to eat, and he'll die within a minute or two of ingestion."

"Poison?" I asked again. I'd shot a man to death and broken the neck of another with a leg of lamb; poison seemed . . . less violent than what Garcia deserved after all the heartache he'd caused.

"It's the safest way. There's no way you can risk trying to get a gun in and out of a place like this. Nobody should look twice at the necklace, but if they do, you can always tell them it's Holy Water."

"Holy Water?"

"Are you okay?"

My hormones were in overdrive and I was stressed to the max. "Sure. I just wasn't expecting the poison angle."

"Rule Number One: Don't Get Caught."

I nodded, even though I personally thought Rule Number One should be: Don't Fall for Your Murder Mentor.

Rule Number Two should be: Always Listen to Your Gut.

Chapter Twelve

I KNEW I should have listened to my gut and figured out a way to get out of the bridal shower. I was tired and stressed out beyond belief, but God had insisted if I wanted to be a good friend to Alice, I should dutifully show up. When I got to the VFW Hall where the impromptu party was being held, I got an instant headache. Zeke had taken Armani's advice and bought every single white wedding decoration sold in the state. Which wouldn't have been too bad if he hadn't draped every table in the place with the most hideous salmon-colored tablecloths.

Even that probably wouldn't have given me a headache if I hadn't heard the witches cackling in the midst of the virginal fishiness.

They hadn't seen me, and I actually backed up two steps to make my escape, but then a hand snaked around my waist from behind and lips were pressed against my ear. "Na-ah, I've been stuck here with them for an hour, you're not getting away that easily," Zeke whispered in my ear.

Pulling away from him, I spun around and glared at his smug expression. "I wasn't going anywhere. I just forgot something in my car."

"You always were a terrible liar, Maggie." He reached out and stroked a finger down my suddenly burning cheek.

I swatted his finger away.

He grinned, winked at me, and then had the audacity to boom, "There you are, Maggie!"

"Jerk," I growled under my breath as his overly loud greeting had its desired effect and my aunts descended upon me like flies to a picnic.

I heard him chuckling as he walked away.

"You're here!" Aunt Loretta trilled, smothering me with air kisses.

"You're early." Aunt Leslie made it sound like I'd never been on time to anything in my life.

I clamped my jaw shut to keep from countering with *You're not high*.

"We're making a flock of doves," Loretta said excitedly. "Come help."

I allowed them to lead me to a table in the center of the room. Aunt Susan sat there, surrounded by dozens of puffy, paper doves. She looked about as thrilled as I felt.

"Zeke has done a marvelous job," Loretta said, sitting down in a chair and opening yet another package of paper birds.

"Of course he has," I muttered, wondering where he'd managed to escape to.

"Alice is lucky to have him," Leslie said. "Especially since you're no one's idea of Maid of Honor of the Year."

I wasn't sure why she'd decided that I was one to be her personal punching bag, but I wasn't about to take any more shots without swinging back. "I liked you better when you were drugged out of your mind," I snapped.

"Margaret." Loretta gasped, appalled.

Leslie burst into tears and ran off.

"Look what you've done." Loretta tottered off after her twin, the rat-tat-tat of her stilettos echoing in the hall.

I frowned at Aunt Susan, daring her to say anything to me.

She extended a dove and a sad smile. "Your mother had paper doves at her shower. Not as many as this, but a lot of them. Of course they didn't come prepackaged then. The twins and I had to cut them all by hand."

Her melancholy reminiscing deflated my righteous anger. I sank into the chair beside her.

"The twins were so excited. They'd fallen for Archie's charms and thought that your mother was going to live some fairy-tale life."

"But you didn't." I didn't even bother to make it a question.

Susan put down the dove she was working on so that she could pat my hand, which lay limply in my lap. "Would it surprise you to know that I don't think your father is a bad man, Margaret?"

"It'd shock the shit out of me."

She winced. "Language."

"Sorry."

"I don't think Archie's a bad man. I think he has terrible judgment and that he makes horrible choices, but I don't think he's mean or malicious."

"You don't? I always thought you hated him."

She shook her head slowly. "No. I thought he was the wrong person for Mary and a not-so-great father to you girls, but he could have been worse. He genuinely loves your mother and he never hurt or harmed you kids."

"That's debatable," I muttered.

She looked over at where Zeke stood on the other side of the room setting up a ladder. "Your father never beat you, Margaret," she said pointedly.

I nodded slowly. That was true.

"And you were never the victim of the kinds of things Alice endured. What your father did to that man . . ." She paused, remembering how Dad had beaten Alice's perverted stepfather to within an inch of his life. " . . . that was a good thing. Not a smart thing. Maybe not the right thing in the eyes of the law, but a good thing. That's who your father is, someone driven by desires and passions the rest of us can't understand. He does things that are at best questionable and at worst simply wrong, but he does them for the right reasons."

I swallowed hard, realizing that the same description could be applied to me.

"But I look at all these stupid paper doves and all I can think of is how they didn't bring your mother peace and happiness. They were the beginning of her downfall."

I flinched as she ripped the head off a bird to illustrate her point. I didn't know what to say to make her feel better so we sat there, each of us lost in our own thoughts for a couple of minutes, watching as Zeke hung salmon-colored streamers.

"Is your dress really that color?" Susan finally asked.

"I dunno. I thought it was pink, but Zeke insisted it's salmon."

"Has he seen it?"

"No, but I get the impression he's hanging on every word Alice says. No doubt she told him it's salmon. Leslie's right. Alice is lucky to have him." I sighed, feeling like I was failing my friend. "I guess I should go apologize to her."

"You could," Aunt Susan said, "but personally I don't think it's necessary."

"You don't?" That was the second shocking thing she'd said.

"She's been a real bitch to you."

"Language, Aunt Susan!" I teased.

She smiled. "Sometimes you remind me so much of your mother."

"Because I'm a bitch?"

"Because of your warped sense of humor." Her smile faded. "Leslie's not going to stay clean, you know."

"We can hope she will."

She shook her head. "You shouldn't. When she falls off the wagon, she's going to blame you. That's why she's giving you such a hard time now. She's constructing this story in her head about how you've wronged her, how you've upset her, how you've pushed her over the edge."

She spoke with such conviction and authority that I believed her.

"How do you know that?"

"I've talked about it with my therapist."

Third shock!

"You see a therapist?"

"How do you think I stay relatively sane in this crazy family? It might not be a bad idea for you to do the same."

"I think I'm beyond help," I murmured, knowing that she had no idea what crazy things I'd done and what I was planning on doing.

"Everyone needs help, Margaret. The trick is recognizing those who genuinely want to help you and being grateful for it."

"A little help over here?" Zeke shouted from across the room, startling both Susan and me.

She chuckled. "And sometimes you need to know when others need help. Go. I'll finish these."

Jumping up, I hurried over to where Zeke was trying to untangle the strings of a wedding bell mobile.

"Here." He thrust it at me. "This thing is driving me crazy."

Looking at the tangled mess, I suggested, "We could put it straight into the trash."

"Or . . ." he said testily, "you could at least say thank you to the man who spent way too much time and money in a party supply store." Before I could respond, he pointed at a rented helium tank leaning in the corner. "Or you could tell me you know how to use that thing."

"I do."

"That's the bride's line," he teased, his snit fit evaporating into thin air.

"And I am grateful," I told him. "For all of this . . . even the doves."

"What's wrong with the doves?"

"Long story. Let's leave the bells for later. With any luck Aunt Leslie will come back. When I was a kid she was the one who could always get my shoelaces unknotted and my kite string untangled."

"You really know how to do the balloon thing?"

"It's not rocket science. Aunt Loretta's been married so many times, under so many balloon arches, that I could practically do this in my sleep."

"I hate balloon arches. They make me break out in hives."

"Are you allergic to latex?"

"No. I'm allergic to sudden, loud noises. I hate popping balloons."

I nodded sympathetically. "I have a friend who feels the same way. So why did you get them?"

"Alice mentioned something about loving rooms filled with balloons. I figured that was a subtle hint."

"You got them despite the fact you hate them?"

He frowned. "Why do you have such a low opinion of me? Why would you think I wouldn't do everything in my power to make my friend happy?"

"I don't." I snatched up a pack of balloons, ripped one open, and positioned it at the valve of the tank. "I just figured you could have used balloon-free decorations."

"Like what?"

I filled the balloon, taking care not to overfill it. I didn't want it to pop and spook Zeke after all he'd done. "Flowers?"

"They do flowers at these things?"

I nodded.

"Armani didn't tell me that. You didn't tell me that. Nobody told me that."

"But they do balloons too," I soothed quickly, knotting the balloon and grabbing a piece of ribbon to tie on. "Everyone probably figured you'd been to a bunch of these before. That's why we didn't think to mention it."

"To a shower? Why would you think I've been to a bridal shower?"

Releasing the balloon, I watched it float up to the ceiling and dance along the tiles. "Because you're gay."

Rocking back on his heels, Zeke stared at me, eyes bulging, mouth hanging open, looking thoroughly appalled.

"I'm sorry," I said reaching out to pat his arm. "I didn't mean to make you uncomfortable." I waved my hand to encompass the room. "You've done an amazing job."

"Because I'm gay?" Usually Zeke was all smooth talking and charm, but at the moment he sounded like he was on the verge of coming unhinged.

"Well . . . not *just* because you're gay."

Disbelief and something close to anger warred in his gaze.

"Look, I'm sorry." I raised my hands in supplication. It was bad enough I'd insulted Aunt Leslie, I really didn't want to alienate Zeke too. "I said the wrong thing. I always say the wrong thing. Ask anyone. A couple of minutes ago I reduced my aunt to tears. I'm an equal opportunity foot-in-mouth-er."

"How long?"

"My whole life?"

"How long have you known I'm gay?"

"Since senior year."

"Since senior year?" his voice cracked.

I hung my head, feeling guiltily awful.

Had he thought it was a secret all this time? Even if Aunt Loretta hadn't told me, I would have figured it out myself when he rebuffed Alice's advances. No straight guy had ever turned down my leggy, blonde, Amazonian friend.

"It's okay," I assured him. "Everyone's cool with it."

"Everyone?"

I nodded.

"Even you?" He stared at me intently.

Despite the fact we were discussing the fact that he was gay, my heartbeat sped up a little as his blue eyes searched mine. I swallowed hard, quelling the desire to tell him I thought it was monumentally unfair. "Especially me." I offered what I hoped was a reassuring smile.

"What a mess," he muttered. Pulling free of my grasp, he turned on his heel and stalked away, leaving me to finish the balloons all by myself.

Not that I needed any help.

By the time I finished the balloons, Aunt Susan had finished the doves, Zeke was done hanging all his streamers, and Aunts Leslie and Loretta returned. Zeke, Leslie, and Loretta all refused to speak to, or even make eye contact with me for the entire party. Not that I really minded, since I made a point of running myself ragged, trying to be the best maid of honor ever.

I served food. (I didn't get a chance to actually eat any myself, but I heard it was outstanding.) I mingled with guests, mostly Alice's friends from all of her do-gooder adventures over the years and I dutifully carried each and every gift for her to open while her friend Preppy Priscilla, the girl our high school class had voted Most Likely to Kiss Up, wrote down a list of who gave Alice what.

Zeke meanwhile stayed in the back of the room, standing in the doorway, his arms crossed over his chest and a permanent frown etched on his face.

It wasn't until Lamont had shown up, and all the gifts had been packed into his car and those of my aunts, that Zeke and I interacted.

With everyone else gone, I told him, "You did all the prep work. I can do the cleanup. Go home." I didn't relish the idea of spending the next few hours doing all the work, but the alternative was to spend them with him mad at me. My nerves were frayed, and I feared the continuing tension might just about kill me.

Zeke surveyed the mess, calculating how much time and effort it would take to clean up.

"Really," I said, all but shooing him out the door. "I've got this."

"You're right," he said, turning away.

I breathed a sigh of relief.

"It is all the stuff of landfills." He grabbed a garbage can, hauled it over to the nearest table, and began cleaning it off.

"You don't have to—"

He shot me a look, effectively silencing my protest.

"Thank you," I said weakly.

"Alice wants you to pick up your dress."

"I told her I'd do it tomorrow. I've got something to do tonight."

"Hot date?" he asked.

I had an appointment to kill a man. "No, just something I've got to take care of."

"She wants me to go with you to make sure you get the dress tomorrow."

"I don't need a chaperone." I considered popping a balloon to illustrate my point, but thought better of it. After all, he was helping me clean up.

Ignoring me, he said, "I told her I would."

"Awesome," I said sarcastically.

"I thought so." He flashed a mysterious smile at me.

He was up to something. I just didn't know what.

Chapter Thirteen

I HAD A couple of hours to fritter away between when I finished cleaning up after Alice's shower and before I was due to kill Jose Garcia, so I went home, in the hopes of taking a nap and getting some much needed sleep. Despite the cooperation of the animals, sleep eluded me.

"Tell me the plan again," God urged.

"Jose has some special silver goblet that he uses to make toasts. No one else is ever allowed to drink from it. The plan is to get the poison into that. He makes his toast, he croaks, game over."

"Frog like?" Doomsday asked.

God chuckled. "No, he doesn't croak like a frog. He dies."

I checked the outfit I was wearing for lint. It was the same black dress I'd been wearing when I met Delveccio after I'd attacked his son-in-law to prevent him from killing the mobster's young, comatose grandson. I wondered if, like baseball players and their lucky socks, this was somehow my "lucky" dress.

"How are you going to get close enough to the cup?" God asked.

I shrugged. Patrick had gotten me the poison and the information about the toast, but he'd been unable to come up with a plan as to how I could put the two together. "I'm winging it."

God covered his eyes and shook his head. "Bad idea. Bad, bad idea."

"Do you have a better one?"

"A better one than walking into a room full of drug dealers and their relatives and hoping you can get close enough to poison one? Sure. Don't do it. Walk away from the job."

"I can't. I need the money for the lawyer . . . not to mention the hospital bills."

"You're going to get caught."

"I'm not going to get caught," I told him with way more bravado than I was feeling. "I'll figure it out. I'll get the job done and everything will be okay."

"Delusional," God muttered.

Ignoring him, I slipped on my black high heels, wobbled for a moment, and then headed for the front door. "I'm off to meet Patrick. He's driving me to the job. Wish me luck."

"Luck!" Doomsday panted.

"Tell the redhead to check in on us if you get caught," God said. "Otherwise we'll starve to death."

I stumbled, realizing that not only my safety was at stake, but that of the lizard and dog too. "I'll tell him."

I walked out, locking the door behind me, unsure of whether or not I'd ever return.

Leaving my car at home, I walked the couple of blocks to the bowling alley where I'd arranged to meet Patrick. In hindsight, I realize this wasn't the best of plans. Walking in a dress and high heels is enough of a challenge for me, but when the various catcalls and wolf whistles were directed at me, it became even more difficult. I did my best to hold my head high and ignore the "compliments" but I really wished I had my gun with me so that I could teach some of the pigs a lesson.

I'd worked up quite a head of outraged steam by the time a white panel van pulled alongside me, slowed, and lowered its window. "Fuck off, loser," I shouted, before the driver had a chance to say anything.

The van fell behind and I felt a moment of triumph. I resisted the urge to fist pump the air, but inside I was doing a victory dance.

Then the van pulled alongside me again.

A frisson of fear danced down my spine as I remembered every movie I'd ever seen where a kidnap victim is dragged into a panel van and never seen again. I moved as far to the far end of the sidewalk as I could and pretended not to notice I was being stalked.

"Are you planning on walking all the way, Mags?"

I stopped and so did the van.

Peering inside, I saw my favorite redhead. "You!"

He threw the van into park, hopped out, and ran around to where I stood. "You didn't really mean it when you told me to fuck off, did you?"

"I thought you were another of the dozen jerks who propositioned me on the way here."

He opened the passenger door. "I'm sorry about that. I should have realized that you walking through this neighborhood in *that* wasn't the best of ideas." He motioned for me to climb into the van.

"In that?" I asked, not budging.

He ran his eyes slowly up and down the length of my body with blatant appreciation.

I swallowed hard as every cell in my body responded to the implied caress.

"C'mon. Let's get you in." Taking my elbow in his warm, firm grip, he steered me into the van, helping me to balance on the step up. Once I was situated, he let go of my arm, but he didn't move away.

My breath caught in my throat as I looked down into his stormy green gaze. My heart stopped as he reached up, his fingers skimming the tender flesh of my throat as he adjusted the chain of the necklace.

"Ready?" he asked.

I wasn't sure if he was asking if I was ready to kiss him, or if he was asking about the upcoming assassination.

"I don't know," I whispered.

He stepped back, breaking the contact. "Seat belt."

As he climbed back into the driver's seat, Patrick said, "You don't have to do this. You can still back out."

"I've got to do it. I've got too much to lose."

Nodding, he started driving toward the restaurant where the Garcia family wedding rehearsal was taking place. "I want you to promise me, though, that if it looks like you're going to get caught, you'll abort."

"If I get caught, Delveccio will have me killed, right?"

"I don't think so."

"But you said that if I didn't kill his son-in-law, Alfonso, that he'd have me killed."

"He could have been tied to Alfonso."

"And what about Gary the Gun?"

"Him too."

"But you think it'll be different with Garcia?"

"Yes."

"Why?"

"For one thing, I get the impression he really likes you. For another, I doubt anyone could win a case against him based solely on your testimony."

"Why not?"

He glanced over at me. "You're the daughter of a convicted felon. They'd paint it that you'd cut a deal to get your father out of jail."

"I wouldn't do that!"

"Why not?"

"I just wouldn't."

"Because you think he deserves to be there?"

I shrugged.

"What if you found out he didn't really kill that teller, that all he was guilty of was robbing the bank? What if you found out there'd been a miscarriage of justice? Would you leave him there then?"

I stared at Patrick. He'd voiced the questions lightly, but I sensed an urgency behind them.

What did he know about my father's case? Could it be that my father really had told the truth when he said he wasn't a murderer? I'd entertained the idea as a possibility, but I hadn't thought much beyond that. Did my father really deserve to be free?

I examined his expression, but Patrick's face was a stoic mask I couldn't read. Instead of answering his question, I asked, "So if I get caught, I'll just rot in prison?"

He pulled to a stop at a red light. "You could probably get yourself a pretty good deal."

"How?"

He turned to face me. "You could testify against me."

"Patrick!" I gasped, stung by the suggestion. "I'd never do that."

"I know," he said with a sad smile. "Which is why I need you to promise me that if you think you're going to get caught you won't go through with it. Promise me, Mags." He stared at me with an unnerving intensity, willing me to make the pledge.

"I promise."

The horn of the car behind us blared, and Patrick returned his attention to driving.

"I need a favor though," I said.

"Name it."

"If something goes wrong and I do get caught, I need you to take care of God and Doomsday. I know you can't give them a home or anything, but if you could make sure they don't starve, and if you could find them new homes . . . good homes . . . they deserve that." I was choked up with tears by the time I finished.

He reached out and patted my knee. "Of course I will."

"Thank you."

"Don't do this. Just walk away from the job now while you're safe," he pleaded.

"I can't."

"You won't."

"You worry too much."

He glanced over at me, his eyes glittering with emotion. "That doesn't mean my advice isn't good. Speaking of which, take these." Flipping down the sun visor, he caught a pack of opened cigarettes mid-fall. He held them out.

"Thanks, but I don't smoke."

"I'd noticed."

I wondered what that meant, but before I could ask, he tossed them on my lap.

"You don't have to smoke them. They're a prop."

"A prop?"

"A useful prop. You can walk right out of a lot of situations simply by saying you need a cigarette. Plus they're a great conversation starter. You can always walk up to anyone and ask if they have a light. And last, but not least, they can help you blend in with a group you have nothing in common with except for the cigarettes in your hands."

"Oh. Thanks, I guess."

"You're welcome, I guess." He pulled the van over to the side of the road and pointed at a driveway. "That's the rear entrance."

I reached for the door handle.

"You can still change your mind."

I hesitated, unsure whether to be touched or freaked out by his concern. "You'll be here when I come out?"

"I'm going to park up a hill a block or so away. I can see both the front and rear parking lots from that vantage point."

"How?"

"Binoculars."

"I guess this is it." I smoothed my dress over my thighs, trying to quell the sense of uneasiness that was making me queasy.

"Don't get caught."

"I'll try, but if I do . . ."

"The animals will be well cared for," he promised.

I climbed out of the van and tottered down the driveway. There was no turning back now.

GETTING INTO THE restaurant was easier than I'd expected. I made a show of stuffing the cigarettes into my clutch as I approached the back door where a couple of waiters and waitresses were hanging out, smoking.

"Is this the door I came out?" I asked them.

"Not this one," a waiter said.

"But you can go in through this door," a waitress offered, holding it open for me.

"Thanks." I scooted past them, skirted around the kitchen, and found myself smack in the midst of a bustling cocktail party.

People were talking and laughing, the staff was passing out appetizers, and there was a line at the bar. I got on it, thinking it was probably the least auspicious place to stand and survey the room. I didn't see Uncle Jose. I saw a lot of unsavory characters and what looked like some hired muscle, but I couldn't spot the man I was there to kill.

"Quite the turnout," the older gentleman who'd gotten on line behind me said, as he stared at my legs.

Gritting my teeth, I smiled politely. "Have you been here before?"

"Many times."

"It's beautiful."

"Not as beautiful as you, my dear. Tell me, do you have an escort this evening?"

I managed to keep from rolling my eyes. Barely. The last thing I needed was to be saddled with this old letch for the evening. "He's here somewhere. I think he went to look for Jose. Do you know where he is?"

"No doubt in the private room upstairs. It's his daughter's day, but I imagine he's planning on making a grand entrance."

"Oh," I exclaimed. "There's my better half!" I waved at a crowded corner at the opposite side of the room. "If you'll excuse me . . ." I hurried away.

Crossing the room was a bit of an obstacle course, but I managed to dodge waitstaff and maneuver around clusters of guests without tripping in my high heels. When I looked back at the bar, I saw that the old letch was no longer watching me, but was instead focusing his unwanted attentions on another single female guest.

I slipped out of the room and wandered down a deserted hallway, searching for a stairway that would lead me to the private room and my prey.

Instead I found a pair of inquisitive, dark eyes staring out from behind a potted plant.

"Who are you?" a small voice asked.

"Who are you?" I asked the little girl.

"Christina." A five-year-old, dressed in the cutest purple party dress, emerged from behind the plant.

"What are you doing, Christina? Playing hide-and-seek?" I looked up and down the hallway, but saw no adults the child might belong to.

"I'm looking for Grampa Jose. He promised me a piggyback ride."

"Where are your mommy and daddy?" I had better things to do than watch over this kid, like kill her grandfather, but I couldn't in good conscience just leave her alone.

"Daddy's in heaven."

"Oh. I'm sorry. And where's Mommy?" I asked, hoping that I wasn't about to find out that Grampa Jose was the little girl's only living relative. That knowledge would make murdering him much more difficult.

She pointed at a restroom door.

"Is she sick?"

"She's crying."

"How about we go check on her," It felt like I'd been punched in the stomach when Christina grabbed the hand I held out to her as I remembered Katie doing the same thing countless times. I barely held it together as I walked her over to the ladies' room.

"Hi, Mommy," she said, letting go of me and running inside as I pushed the door open for her.

I let the door close before her mother could see me, but I heard her exclaim happily, "There's my girl!"

I stumbled away, my vision blurred by unshed tears. What I wouldn't give for Katie to take my hand again, but because of Jose Garcia, I might never get that chance, and I knew for sure that Theresa never would.

Fueled by anger, I flew up the first set of stairs I found. Clasping the pendant, I stopped at the top of the flight, when I spotted my target.

Jose Garcia stood not twenty feet away, his back to me, busily shining the silver cup which would deliver him to his death.

Chapter Fourteen

REVENGE WAS MINE. I could practically taste it.

"Carry this out on a silver platter for me when it's time to make the toast," Garcia ordered a young, pimply-faced waiter. "No one else touches this cup, you understand?"

The waiter nodded nervously.

"No one but me drinks from it, you got that?"

"Yes, sir."

"The wine guy knows what I want. He fills it and you bring it to me."

"Yes, Mr. Garcia."

Garcia thrust the cup at the young man, who took it with trembling hands.

"You drop that and there's gonna be hell to pay," Garcia warned.

Nodding, the waiter clasped it to his chest with both hands before hurrying in my direction. I ducked down the stairs before anyone could see me. I turned my back, pretending to be searching for something in my purse, as the waiter rushed past.

My plan had been to follow him, but that was derailed the moment I turned around, since I almost plowed into little Christina and her mother.

"Hi!" Christina waved at me. "What are you doing here?"

"Christina, where are you manners?" her mother hissed. She looked up at me with a tired smile. "I'm sorry, she's a bit of a busybody."

"Not a problem," I assured her, noticing that she had the same curly hair as her father, but while his eyes had always sparkled with mischief, this woman's were dulled by sadness. "I have a niece about the same age."

"Oh really? What's her name?"

The waiter had already disappeared with the cup and I didn't think Patrick would approve of me chitchatting with the daughter of my intended victim. "If you'll excuse me," I said with a wave to Christina, "my boyfriend must be looking for me."

Hurrying away as fast as my heels would let me, I raced down the hallway hoping to catch a glimpse of the waiter, but he was nowhere in sight.

"I should have paid attention during the tailing lesson," I muttered to myself.

"Can I help you, ma'am?" a waitress of no more than twenty asked.

I frowned. When had I become a *ma'am*?

"Ma'am?" she prompted.

"Where can I find the wine guy?" I asked.

"The sommelier?"

I nodded.

"I believe he's in the wine cellar getting a special bottle for Mr. Garcia. Would you like me to find him for you?"

"No. That's okay. Thank you for your help."

"No problem, ma'am."

I considered yanking out her perky ponytail as she walked away. Instead I went in search of the wine cellar and/or the sommelier. The necklace weighed heavily on me, each step jostling the pendant, reminding me of what I had to do.

It wasn't just getting the poison into the cup that caused me anxiety. It was that I'd never killed anyone in cold blood before. Sure, I'd gone looking for both Delveccio's son-in-law and Gary the Gun with the intent to kill them, but, both times, when push had come to shove, I'd been defending my own life as each man attacked me.

Garcia wasn't going to attack me. When he died, he was going to be standing in front of friends and family, celebrating.

I physically stumbled at the thought of his loved ones watching him die. Could I really be so cold as to do that to a group of strangers who'd never done anything to me? But then I thought about how my family had suffered, the losses we'd endured, and I suddenly felt a whole lot better about wiping Jose Garcia from the face of the Earth and preventing him from destroying any other families. I clutched the pendant as though it were some sort of magical amulet that would give me the power and resolve to pull off this assassination.

A flash of silver caught my attention, but before I could get to it, the hallway suddenly filled with partygoers as the guests moved from the cocktail hour to the dining room. I was swept up in the sea of guests and transported by the current into another room.

As soon as I could get out of the way of the flow of people entering the room, I stepped to the side, scanning the space for the silver cup. I didn't see it, but I did spot the waiter ducking through a door on the far side of the room. I made a beeline straight toward it, but before I'd gone ten steps, someone grabbed my arm.

My heartbeat stuttered and fear skittered down my spine.

"Where do you think you're going?"

I turned slowly to face my captor.

It wasn't one of Garcia's badass men who'd caught me, it was the letch from the bar. I breathed a sigh of relief as I tried to shake my arm loose from his grip.

"Still haven't found that phantom date of yours?" The letch's breath was laden with scotch.

I leaned back to escape the fumes. "He's around here somewhere."

"I don't believe you. Come sit with me."

"Can't." I glanced at the door the waiter had disappeared through, keenly aware I was running out of time to put my plan into action. "Let go."

I tried to tug free of the letch's grip, but he tightened it painfully.

"You're hurting me."

He didn't ease up. "And you're breaking my heart by

not sitting with me. How about we go outside and talk it over?" He led me toward the exit, exerting so much pressure on my arm, I worried it would snap.

Tears of pain filled my eyes. I couldn't make a scene and risk attracting attention, but I was starting to panic that if I let this guy get me alone, he'd hurt me. "Please," I pleaded. "Let me go."

He looked down and smiled malevolently at my fear and pain.

"Where are you going, Uncle Mo?" a familiar voice asked. Christina's mom stepped into our path.

My captor stopped in his tracks, but squeezed my arm even tighter. "We were just going to step outside to get some air."

"My father is going to make his toast soon. He'd be disappointed if you weren't here to hear it." There was no mistaking the implied threat in her tone.

While he didn't release me, the letch's grip slackened.

Christina's mother stared pointedly at where his fingers curled around me. He released me immediately. "You can walk me to my table." She extended her arm.

The letch had no choice but to go with her, leaving me free to make my escape.

I made my way across the room on rubbery legs. Frightened both by the violent encounter and by the fact that Christina's mother had now seen my face twice.

I could hear Patrick's voice in my head, urging me to abort if I thought I was going to be caught. I was ready to do just that when the cup appeared before me, served up on a silver platter.

The waiter carried it right past my nose and I followed closely on his heels.

He went into the kitchen and so did I, knowing that if I lost sight of it again, I'd never get my chance with the cup. He put the tray down on a counter and disappeared around a corner.

My hand trembled as I snatched up the cup. This was it, my chance. I reached for the pendant, ready to unscrew it and pour a few drops of the deadly poison.

"What the hell are you doing?" an angry male voice boomed.

Startled, I almost dropped the goblet. Instead I bobbled it like some lame-ass juggling act.

"What are you doing back here?" A man in a high white hat, which I took to mean he was a chef, glared at me. "Give me that."

Two of Garcia's goons, alerted by the chef's raised voice, hurried over. They loomed menacingly. I tried not to stare at the bulges beneath their jackets, which I knew were poorly concealed guns.

I'd been caught!

"Are you on the guest list?" the bigger goon asked suspiciously.

I swallowed hard, trying to come up with a plausible story to save my butt, but came up blank. I considered fighting my way out of the situation, but the only weapon I had was the cup and I doubted I could do any serious damage with it. I thought about making a run for it, but knew I'd never outrun a toddler in my heels, let alone hired muscle.

"Let's go have a chat," the goon said. They each grabbed one of my arms.

The chef plucked the cup from my hand. "Stay out of my kitchen."

The two scary men propelled me out of the kitchen. I probably should have screamed for help at that point, but my mouth had gone dry and I couldn't seem to make my vocal cords work.

They half carried, half dragged me down the once again deserted hallway, and I knew that worse than getting caught, I was getting myself killed. I hoped Patrick would keep his promise about God and Doomsday. I prayed that Abilene would take care of Katie.

"Let me see what the boss wants me to do with her," the goon said.

"Now?" his partner in crime asked. "He'll be pissed if you interrupt his party."

The bigger goon nodded slowly. "We'll keep her until it's over."

I took a big gulp of air, grateful for the momentary reprieve.

"Put her in the coatroom," the big guy said.

"Can I have some fun with her," the smaller one asked, staring at my legs like he'd never set eyes on a pair before.

"As long as she doesn't scream."

I tried to scream then, but all that came out was a hoarse whisper. "Help! Help!"

The leg man chuckled. "You're going to be fun."

I kneed him in the groin. I didn't even think about it, I just did it.

Grunting in pain, he bent over, loosening his grip on my arm. Wrenching free, I stumbled away.

He made a grab for me, but I ducked away. I didn't think I'd get so lucky with the bigger guy, who lunged for me as I dodged around the corner. I turned to see how close behind me he was.

From behind me, an arm snaked around my waist, lifting me off my feet. I was spun around so that my back was to the wall.

Chapter Fifteen

I SAW A flash of bright blue eyes, but as I opened my mouth to warn Zeke about the impending danger, he crushed his mouth to mine, effectively silencing me. One of his hands cradled the back of my head as he increased the pressure of the kiss. To anyone else it probably looked as though our tonsils were touching, but in reality, he kept his tongue to himself and I did the same with mine. He tilted me backward slightly and I wobbled on my heels. Instinctively I looped my arms around his neck and allowed my eyes to flutter closed, just as the bad guys came around the corner.

Even as I tried to figure out how to use this latest development to my favor, I was aware that he smelled delectable. Coming up for air, he placed a finger on my lips, keeping me quiet and smiled at me. "Thought you could hide from me, didn't you?"

Confused, I blinked at him.

Suddenly he became aware of the two men standing there staring at us. Instead of getting flustered, he nodded in their direction. "Hey."

"What are you doing here?" the bigger goon asked.

"Kissing my girl," Zeke answered smoothly, wrapping a possessive arm around my shoulders, and angling himself so that his body was between me and the men. "What's it to you?"

"Are you on the guest list?"

"Busted," he muttered.

The goon's gaze narrowed dangerously.

"Fifi here said that crashing this party was a bad idea, but I insisted." He leaned toward the man and lowered his voice to a conspiratorial whisper. "We're looking to get married here and we got the official tour and tasted the official menu, but I really wanted to get a feel for how they handle a hundred guests. I mean anyone can serve a perfect dinner for two, can't they?"

He waited a beat, but the goon didn't answer him.

"Anyway, I told Fifi that if we were going to lay out the kind of dough this place wants just for a freaking deposit, that we had to be sure it was the right place for us." He made a show of squeezing my shoulders. "I don't mind paying for the best for my girl, but it's gotta be the best. You understand that, right?"

"She ain't got no ring on her finger," the smaller goon observed.

Instinctively I glanced down at my naked fingers, wondering if he'd have thought differently about assaulting me if I'd been wearing a metal band.

"My fault," Zeke replied smoothly. "I made her break-fast in bed this morning . . . well, not really made it, but I picked some up from the bakery and put it on a tray for her."

For once I admired his gift of gab as the shorter goon hung on every word of the story he was spinning.

"When I cleaned up afterward," Zeke continued, "thinking I'd spoil her and do the dishes for once, I knocked the ring down the kitchen drain. I've got a plumber at the house right now, charging me a fortune to take apart the pipes and find it." He shook a finger in front of my face. "If I've told you once, I've told you a thousand times that you shouldn't leave it lying around, haven't I?"

I nodded obediently.

"Women," Zeke said to the two men. "Pretty to look at, but not the most practical, if you know what I mean."

The bigger goon chuckled. "You can say that again."

"C'mon, honey. Let's get out of here." He slid his hand down to the base of my spine and gave me a little shove to get me moving.

He kept it there, the warmth of his palm burning through the material of my dress, as we made our way toward the exit. The two goons followed behind.

"Where's your car?" Zeke asked, quietly enough that only I could hear him.

I thought of Patrick in the white panel van. "I don't have one."

"Perfect." As we stepped outside, he slipped his hand

into mine and gave it a reassuring squeeze. "One foot in front of the other, Maggie. We're almost home free."

I held on to him for dear life as he led me across the parking lot. I imagined that Patrick was watching our progress, but I couldn't think of a way to signal that I was in no danger from Zeke.

Reaching a fancy red sports car, Zeke opened the passenger door for me. Before I could slide inside he stepped in front of me, pulling me close to him. Off-balance, I steadied myself against his chest. I looked up at him, unsure of what was going on or what his intentions were.

"We've got to sell it," he said, lowering his mouth toward mine.

I didn't know whether it was a result of the adrenaline rush of almost getting caught or because Patrick had gotten my hormones racing in overdrive earlier, but the moment Zeke's lips touched mine, I melted into him with a soft moan of pleasure.

Almost immediately he pulled away, much to my disappointment. He looked down at me with stunned amusement, and that's when I remembered he was gay, and I was making a fool of myself mooning over him just as I had when we'd been teenagers.

Tearing away from him, I hopped into the car, not caring how my skirt rode up, giving Zeke and the goons a generous peek of skin. I fumbled with my seat belt, but had it on by the time Zeke climbed into the driver's seat.

He didn't speak while he started the car and pulled out of the lot. We were a quarter mile away before he asked, "Where's your car?"

"At home." I glanced in the rearview mirror and saw a white panel van pull up behind us.

"What the hell were you doing there?" Zeke asked, with more than a tinge of annoyance in his tone.

"I could ask you the same."

"Business," he ground out between clenched teeth.

"Me too." I fingered the pendant, remembering I'd just failed at my attempt to kill Jose Garcia.

He glanced over at me. "What kind of business?"

"The kind that's none of yours."

"Seriously? I save you from being manhandled or worse by those two thugs and you're telling me to MYOB like you did when we were ten?" Disbelief and amusement warred in his tone.

I hung my head, feeling guilty for acting so churlishly ungrateful when he had in fact saved me. "I don't know how to thank you," I said slowly.

"You want to thank me?" he asked with surprising intensity. "If you really want to thank me, promise me you'll never go back there."

"Why?" I asked, curious as to why *he'd* been there.

"There are some unsavory types. Questionable business activities."

"And how do you know that."

"I told you. Business." Jerking the steering wheel, he pulled over to the side of the road in a sudden stop.

"What?" I asked, alarmed.

He twisted in his seat to look at me. I watched the panel pull slowly past behind him.

"Promise me, Maggie. Promise me you'll never go back there."

"Okay." It was an easy thing to promise. I'd missed my chance to kill Garcia there. My next attempt would have to be somewhere else.

"Why were you there?" He searched my face intently.

I knew he'd spot a lie, so I told him a half truth. "I don't make that much at the insurance company. I need a second job."

"And you figured dressing like that would get you the job?" He motioned at the length of my bare legs.

I fought the urge to tug my hem down. "Like what?"

He opened his mouth to answer and then snapped it shut. "I'll take you home." He pulled back on the road with a spray of gravel. "Where do you live?"

We didn't speak again after I gave him my address. In the silence, I alternated between watching the reflection of the panel van, which had pulled up behind us again at the first cross street we passed, and admiring Zeke's profile. He was definitely no longer "cute." Unfortunately, he was still gay.

I sighed, partially because the adrenaline that had been coursing through me was gone and partially because life was unfair. I was attracted to two guys, one of whom already had a wife or two, and the other who wasn't the slightest bit attracted to me.

I didn't speak until we were two blocks from my place. "It's the next left and then the first right."

Zeke pulled into the parking lot and stared at the slightly decrepit building. "How long have you lived here?"

"A few years."

"And you feel safe?"

"I have a dog."

"Like Fifi?"

"No. Mine's a Doberman pinscher." I punched him in the arm playfully. "I can't believe you called me by the name of Aunt Loretta's poodle."

He put the car into park. "You remind me of her, always getting into trouble." He stared at me. "Are you in trouble now, Maggie?"

I bit back a harsh laugh. I was a hitwoman who'd just failed at pulling off the most important job of her new-found career, I could talk to animals, and I was sitting in a car with my former nemesis, wishing he wasn't gay.

"I'm fine."

"I've never seen anyone hate another living creature the way Susan hated that dog."

"She hates all dogs, but Fifi did get the worst of her wrath after she destroyed her memory box."

"Memory box?"

"It was this old wooden box. One day Aunt Susan left it open and the dog had a field day with the contents."

"What was in it?"

"I don't know." I glanced in the mirror, but couldn't see the white van. "She always kept it locked."

"I can still remember her delivering her ultimatum to Loretta. 'It's me or the dog,' " he said in a falsetto reminiscent of Aunt Susan's voice.

"And we never saw Fifi again." I smiled at him. It was nice to have someone to reminisce with.

"I smeared your lipstick." He reached over and rubbed my lower lip with the pad of his thumb.

My eyes fluttered closed as I got lost in the pleasurable sensation.

"Do you need a ride to the dress shop tomorrow?" he asked, breaking the spell.

Opening my eyes, I found him watching me carefully.

"No. I can do it. You don't have to go."

"Alice was pretty adamant that I should go with you. Maybe I can be of a help somehow."

"Can you convince her to not make me wear a fishy color?"

"I doubt it. My powers only extend so far."

I resented the implication Alice thought I needed a babysitter for such a simple task. "I can handle it on my own."

He frowned. "I don't want to unleash her inner bridezilla by not following her wishes."

"Fine." I didn't want to risk that either. "But I'll meet you there."

"Noon?"

I nodded, reaching for the door handle. "Thanks, Zeke. For everything."

I slid out of the car and tugged down my skirt, scanning the lot for the van. I couldn't see it. Maybe Patrick, after seeing I'd been delivered safely home, had left. That would be a relief, since I didn't relish the idea of telling him I'd screwed up the Garcia job and had almost been caught.

I gave a quick wave to Zeke and headed toward my apartment, making a mental note to change my shoes before I tried to walk Doomsday.

"Maggie?"

I looked back. Zeke had lowered his window and was motioning me over.

I tottered over to him. "What's up?"

"I thought you should know . . ." He trailed off, as if unsure of how to complete his thought.

"Know what?"

"What I was going to say before . . . about how you looked."

My spine stiffened. I'd thought we were finally getting along and now he was going to insult me? I was a big girl. I could take whatever he had to dish out. "So say it."

He squinted at my face as though confused by my sharp tone. "I was going to say that you look hot." His voice deepened. "Really, really sexy."

I didn't know whether to laugh or cry at the compliment. Having a gay guy tell you that you're hot is kind of like having a grandparent gush about how smart their grandchild is. It's a nice sentiment, but more than a little suspect.

"Thanks," I choked out. "See you tomorrow."

I headed inside, intent on drowning my sorrows in a quart of ice cream.

Best laid plans . . .

Chapter Sixteen

"GOTTA! GOTTA!" DOOMSDAY greeted me as I opened the door.

"I have to change clothes first."

"Gotta!"

"I know, but I've gotta first."

"How'd it go?" God called from the kitchen.

"Not so well." I kicked off my heels. The dog followed me to the bedroom.

"But you weren't caught," God said. "That's a good thing."

Ripping the dress over my head, I replied, "The whole caught thing is debatable."

"What happened?"

"Gotta!" Doomsday whined.

Instead of answering the lizard, I pulled on jeans and a T-shirt, grabbed the dog's leash, and let the mutt out the door.

"Please be a good dog on this walk," I pleaded. "I'm exhausted and my feet hurt."

"Good dog," she assured me.

It was dark out and as we walked, I observed the night sky. "Orion's out."

"Onion?"

"Orion." I started to point out the constellation to the dog and then realized what I was doing. "It's a group of stars. My sister Marlene was a real astronomy nut. She'd spend hours staring at the stars." The memory of Marlene, perched on the roof, watching the sky, was bittersweet. She'd had such big dreams, about being an astronaut, about discovering new planets . . . a kid's dreams. They'd all died the day her twin had been abducted.

The familiar guilt that I'd been watching my mother too closely to keep an eye on the girls tightened like a vise around my chest. Yet another way I'd let down my family.

Hearing footsteps approaching from behind, I whirled around. A man came toward us through the shadows and I was acutely aware that the street was deserted.

"Look mean, Doomsday."

She wagged her stump of a tail.

"Growl!" I ordered. What was the point of having a big, scary dog if she couldn't at least look scary? "Protect me. Keep him away."

She lunged toward the man, practically dislocating my shoulder and dragging me with her.

"No!" I squeaked.

"Easy girl," the man said fondly, reaching down to pet her.

Patrick.

"You shouldn't sneak up on me like that." I frowned at him.

"I shouldn't do a lot of things," he muttered mysteriously. "Let's keep walking. Mint?"

He held out a roll of Life Savers.

I took a candy and slipped it onto my tongue.

"They're wintergreen. Did you ever do that spark thing when you were a kid?"

"What spark thing?"

"When you bite them, they spark. Watch." He chomped on one to illustrate his point.

"I didn't see anything."

"That's because you're not standing close enough."

He stepped closer. I stepped away.

"So what happened, Mags? You go in to kill a man and you walked out with a date."

"He wasn't a date."

"It sure looked like you two were cozy." A strange note threaded through his tone and I wondered if he was jealous.

"He's gay."

"It sure didn't look like it. He had his hands all over you."

"You're exaggerating."

"And you're totally unaware of how . . ." He trailed off, shaking his head. "The way he was looking at you, the way he was touching you . . . Never mind. What the hell happened in there?"

I told him everything that happened.

"So you got caught."

"Not really."

"You not only got caught by Garcia's men, but you were seen by someone who knows you. Sorry to break it to you, Mags, but that's caught."

"So what do I do?"

"You cut your losses and tell Delveccio you can't do the job."

"I can't."

"You have to."

"You don't get to tell me what to do."

He turned around and headed back toward my place. Even if I'd wanted to go my own way, Doomsday was having none of it. She eagerly turned and followed Patrick, carrying me along against my will.

"Ignoring me isn't going to change my mind," I told Patrick's back.

Stopping abruptly, he spun around. Doomsday kept pulling me forward, which meant I crashed into Patrick. He grabbed my waist with both hands to steady me.

Instead of thanking him, I choked, having inadvertently swallowed my mint. I coughed and spluttered and gasped for breath.

He pounded on my back. Once my choking fit subsided he said, "I wasn't ignoring you. I was trying to keep from shaking some sense into you."

"I can do this," I assured him. "I can kill Garcia."

"And what if you get caught? What happens then?"

"Then you never have to deal with me again," I joked

lightly. "C'mon admit it, that wouldn't be such a bad thing, would it?"

He didn't answer and I felt vaguely disappointed. I'd hoped he'd say he'd at least miss me.

Finally he said, "I have to leave town."

"When?"

"Wednesday."

"But the Garcia wedding is Saturday night."

"I know."

"Wait, you're going to be out of town while I try to do the job?"

"That's why I'm telling you." It was too dark to see his expression and his tone gave nothing away.

"So that's how it is." Entering the parking lot of my building, I picked up my pace, intent on getting into the apartment as quickly as possible.

He kept step with me. "How what is?"

"You're going out of town to establish your alibi since you're convinced I'm going to get caught." It felt like a betrayal and my hand shook from a mixture of anger and grief as I tried to unlock the door. "I thought you were different."

He plucked the key from my fingers. "Different than who?"

"Everybody."

Unlocking the door, he pushed it open. "Everybody who?"

I let go of her leash and Doomsday bounded inside. "Just everybody." I was going to get my key back and leave

Patrick standing on my doorstep, but, like Zeke had earlier, he put his hand against the base of my spine, and propelled me forward.

"I'm not everybody."

The overhead light was on and it took my eyes a moment to adjust. Meanwhile, he stepped further inside, closing the door behind him and throwing the dead bolt. When he turned back, I could see the tension in his jaw and an emotion I couldn't identify flashing in his eyes.

"I'm not everybody," he said again, advancing on me.

Suddenly afraid, I retreated a step and then two, until I found myself backed against the wall. He followed, looming over me. I looked to Doomsday for help, but she was lying on the floor, watching us intently, as if we were some sort of Wimbledon match.

"I'm not your best friend who goes gallivanting all over the world."

"Alice doesn't gallivant. She does good work."

"I'm not your father, always looking to make an easy buck at the expense of your family. I'm not your mother, hiding out in some fantasy."

"That's not her fault," I defended weakly.

"And I'm not Jewel, running away from all of life's problems."

"Who's Jewel?"

"That's the name Marlene does business under. Jewel."

He leaned in closer and I felt as though all the air was sucked out of the room.

"I don't let you down and I'm not everybody," he whispered. He straightened, allowing me some breathing space, but he didn't back away. "I'm sorry that my crisis is happening at the same time as yours, but I have obligations too. You're not the only one."

"I'm not an obligation."

"No, you're a distraction. Right now my daughter needs me. You can understand that, can't you? A family member needing you?"

I nodded. "Is she okay?"

"Laila just up and left, leaving Daria to move all her belongings across the country. I can't let her do that alone. Can you imagine an eighteen-year-old all alone driving a moving van across the country? The things that could happen to her?" Concern for his daughter made his voice crack.

I knew what he was imagining. I'd imagined the same things when Darlene had been abducted. In her case, they'd been her reality.

"Of course you have to go with her." Reaching out, I patted his arm.

"So you understand?"

I nodded.

"You're interrupting my beauty sleep," God complained from the kitchen.

"You do know that the secret to a good road trip is to stock up on snacks and tunes, right?" I asked.

"Olives?"

"No. Salty, crunchy, and sweet. Chips, cookies . . . does she have a favorite candy?"

"Red licorice," he answered without hesitation.

"You're a good dad."

"Because I know what kind of candy she likes?"

"Because you're making this trip with her, even though it was her mom who created the problem. And because of the candy . . . my father would have never known what my fave was. So you've got the snacks down . . . what about the tunes?"

"How come you know so much about road trips?"

"I took one with Alice once."

"And you had fun?"

I shrugged. I'd needed to get away after Darlene's body had been discovered. I glanced at the family portrait hanging behind him. He turned to see what I was looking at.

"It's the last picture I have of us all together. My parents, my sisters . . . all alive."

"You've lost a lot."

I shrugged. "How long do you expect the trip to take you?"

Ignoring my attempt to change the topic of conversation, he said, "There's still time for you and Marlene."

"I doubt that."

"But—"

I placed a finger against his lips to silence him.

He froze.

"For the love of all that is holy, don't touch him," God yelled from the other room.

"I appreciate your efforts," I said. "I really do, but if Marlene wanted to see or talk to me, I've been easy to find. So instead of arguing about her, why don't I wish you safe travels and you wish me good luck, and we leave it at that? Because to hear you tell it, chances are I'm going to get caught and we'll never see one another again."

I took my finger away, allowing Patrick to speak.

"Don't even say that." He cupped my cheek in his palm.

"Don't kiss him!" God shouted. "Don't let him kiss you. Your life doesn't need one more complication. *I* don't need to listen to you complain about one more thing."

"Kiss?" Doomsday asked hopefully.

"I'm a realist, Patrick. I know your advice is good and your prediction is probably accurate, but I've gotta take the chance anyway."

Hanging his head, he let out a shaky sigh and rubbed the back of his neck.

"Kiss! Kiss!" Doomsday panted.

"I can't," I muttered.

"Can't what?" Patrick asked.

"Oh, this should be good," God mocked.

I looked up at him, into those familiar green eyes that saw the real me and liked me anyway. The lie I'd been about to tell was forgotten. I told him the truth. "I can't kiss you."

"We shouldn't," he agreed. "It would complicate things."

"See?" God crowed. "I told you so."

"Kiss," Doomsday urged.

"We're complicated enough already." I wasn't sure if I was trying to convince Patrick or myself.

He nodded slowly, stroking my cheek with his thumb.

I leaned into his touch.

"Then again," he said in a voice laden with seductive promise, "if this is the last time we're going to see each other . . ."

"Don't do it!" God screamed.

"Quiet!" Doomsday barked, stunning us all.

Patrick chuckled. "Maybe we should listen to the dog."

"Kiss," she panted.

"Maybe just one kiss?" I suggested.

"It's a gateway drug," God grumbled.

Doomsday growled.

"Maybe just one," Patrick agreed, bending closer as he slid his hand around the back of my neck and massaged the base of my skull, making my knees go weak.

It flashed through my head that I wasn't sure I'd be able to stop after one kiss. I knew I wouldn't want to.

He lowered his mouth toward mine.

I heard bells ringing.

Except they weren't bells . . . it was an alarm.

Chapter Seventeen

THE ALARM ENDED up being no big deal, just the result of one of my neighbors roasting marshmallows . . . indoors, but it spooked Patrick.

"I can't be seen!" he shouted, before running out of my apartment.

I didn't see him again.

Instead I spent an hour milling around the apartment complex parking lot with my fellow displaced neighbors until the fire department gave us the all-clear to return to our homes.

"Home Sweet Home." I leaned tiredly against the front door once we were back inside, slipping Dooms-day's leash off.

Keeping the seventy-pound mutt relatively still when all she'd wanted to do was chase the fire trucks had worn me out, as had listening to God's incessant snotty commentary. There was no way I could have managed the dog and his terrarium, so he had perched on my shoulder the whole time, alternating between lecturing about getting romantically involved with the redheaded hitman and telling me how stupid the actions of all my neighbors were.

I didn't even bother to get undressed as I tumbled onto my bed. It had been a hell of a day between the bridal shower, the attempted hit, and my late-night rendezvous with Patrick.

The next morning, when someone knocked on my door, waking me from a sound sleep, I was fully dressed. I jumped up to answer the door, ran about three steps, tripped over the dog, and sprawled headfirst down the hallway.

I lay there for a long moment, gasping like a beached whale, having had the air knocked out of me.

"Okay Maggie?" Doomsday sniffed my face.

I swatted her away and was rewarded with a searing pain in my wrist. I didn't think I'd broken anything, but I wasn't sure I wanted to prove my hypothesis since my knees felt as though they were on fire.

The pounding on the door intensified.

"I'm coming for chrissakes!" I shouted.

"Could you *please* keep it down?" God requested. "I have a headache."

As I unsteadily got to my feet, the poison pendant swung on its chain, smacking me in the mouth. I entertained using the contents in his water, and Doomsday's, and on the person doing their best to bang my door.

"What?" I asked, yanking open the door.

"Coffee?"

A Styrofoam cup of brewed nectar of the gods was waved beneath my nose. Transported by the delicious aroma, it took me a second to focus on the offerer.

I took the cup. "What do you need?"

Alice had the grace to look offended. "Why would you think I need something?" She moved to step past me into my apartment without answering my question, but was greeted with a chorus of "Gotta! Gotta! Gotta!" from Doomsday.

Alice stepped back with a gasp. "There's a dog in there."

"Alice, meet Doomsday. Doomsday, say hello to Alice." I reached for her leash.

Doomsday hurried forward to greet Alice, licking her shoe and then sitting and offering her paw.

I couldn't believe what I was seeing.

God couldn't either. "Her grammar is atrocious, but her manners are impeccable. Who knew?"

"Oh what a darling." Alice shook the offered paw. "What his name?"

"Her. She's wearing a pink collar because she's a her." I latched the leash onto the said collar and let the dog pull me outside.

"Fine. What's *her* name?"

"Doomsday."

Alice wrinkled her nose. "That's not very feminine."

"I didn't name her." Doomsday dragged me in the direction of the garbage Dumpsters.

"Who did?" Alice had to hurry to keep up with us.

I took a sip of coffee to keep from telling her, *The hitman who owned her before me.* "Her previous owner."

"You should give her a new name."

"Yes!" Doomsday agreed with an excited yip.

"Something not so scary. Something girly."

"You're the girly one, not me," I reminded my oldest friend.

"Girly?" Doomsday wagged her stump of a tail hopefully.

"What was the name of that dog Loretta had?"

"Fifi. I am not calling Doomsday the same thing as the prissy purebred poodle."

"DeeDee?" Doomsday asked. "DeeDee?"

"But," I said slowly. "I could call her DeeDee."

DeeDee licked my hand in gratitude.

"She likes it." Alice patted the top of the dog's head.

I nodded. "Okay, now that we've got that settled . . . what do you need?"

She looked away. "I'm worried about Susan."

As a general rule, I worried about Leslie and Loretta. I didn't normally have reason to be concerned about Susan. Alice's worry frightened me. "Why?"

"Well, you know how perfectly pressed and primped she usually is . . ."

I nodded.

"I saw her drive away wearing her pajamas this morning."

Relieved, I chuckled. "Those aren't PJs. That's her kung fu uniform. She started taking classes a few months ago."

"Susan?"

"Gotta give her credit for trying new things," I said. "Now, why don't you tell me why you're here and what you need?"

"You don't know that I need something."

"Sure I do. You brought me one of my vices." I raised the coffee as though it were evidence in a legal proceeding. "Most of the time you bring things that you think will make me better. I've got subscriptions to running magazines, a rice cooker I've never used, and a collection of chakra cleansing crystals to prove it. But today, you show up with a fully caffeinated beverage for me . . . that means you need something."

"There's nothing wrong with wanting the best for you."

"Just as there's nothing wrong with bribing me to get what you want."

"I wasn't bribing you."

I raised an eyebrow, calling her bluff.

"I was buttering you up."

"What's up?"

"First I wanted to thank you for the shower. It was terrific."

It would have been easy to just tell her she was welcome, but I felt compelled to tell her the truth. "That was more Zeke than me."

She smiled. "I know, but I also know how much you hate those things. I appreciate that you were there and you were such a good sport about it."

"You're welcome." We walked back toward my apartment in companionable silence.

"You're a good friend, Maggie."

"Ditto."

"You're picking up your dress today?"

"Yeah. I really am capable of doing that by myself. I don't need Zeke to babysit me." Unlocking my front door, I ushered her inside.

"He really wanted to go with you."

A niggling suspicion tickled the back of my brain, but before I could think about it, she dropped her bombshell.

"I need you to go see my mom."

I stared at her in disbelief. "Why?"

"I want you to ask her to come to the wedding."

I sank onto the couch, dumbfounded. Alice hadn't spoken to her mother since the day my dad had beat the crap out of her stepfather. Like Zeke, Alice had been kicked out of her home, for what her mom had called "vicious lies." Unlike Zeke, she'd had family who were only too happy to take her in. She'd lived with her paternal grandparents, right here in town, while she finished school and attended college.

"I want you to invite her to my wedding," she said again, nervously pacing the length of the living room.

"Why?"

"I dunno. I saw you and your dad together . . ."

I squinted suspiciously at my coffee, wondering if she'd laced it with something because nothing she was saying made any sense. "I don't understand."

"I saw how you two were together. You don't hate him anymore."

"Yes I do," I said quickly, without considering it.

"No. You don't. Maybe you're still nursing a grudge, but you don't hate him. I want that with my mom."

"Why?"

"Because I'm getting married. Because she's going to be a grandmother." She patted her nonexistent baby bump.

"So you're just going to forgive her for everything?"

Alice nodded.

"For what she did? For siding with him?" We'd made a pact, years earlier, to never mention her stepfather's name. Despite the fact I was upset, I honored my commitment.

"She isn't with him anymore."

"He probably hooked up with someone else with a younger daughter."

Seeing the horror in her eyes, I slapped my hand over my mouth, but it was too late. The words were already out.

"I'm sorry," I said hurriedly. "That was a stupid thing to say."

"It was mean."

I nodded, biting my tongue to keep from telling her that while it may have been mean, it was probably true.

"I want her at my wedding, Maggie."

"So why not go yourself?"

"What if she says she hates me? What if she says she never wants to see me again?" Her lower lip trembled and her eyes filled with tears. "I couldn't bear to have her say those things to my face."

I wrapped her in a big bear hug and squeezed. "Okay, okay, I'll do it."

"And you'll be nice to her?"

"If you wanted nice, you should have asked Zeke to do it."

"Zeke's not my best friend. You are."

I hugged her even more tightly. Her saying that was the first thing that had gone right in quite a while. It felt good.

Of course those good feelings evaporated the moment I put on the salmon-colored tutu.

"You SAID YOU'D take care of it," I accused Zeke as I stepped into the dress. I was in a cramped fitting room of the dress shop. He leaned against the wall, just outside the louvered door, waiting for me to come out and model the monstrous creation.

"I said I'd take care of it when I thought it would be dinner and a couple hands of blackjack, but that's not what she wants. Alice wants to go to a strip club, and *that*, I'm not doing."

I tugged the skirt over my hips. "So all this time you're Mr. Helpful, taking care of everything, lending a hand to anyone who needs it, and now, suddenly, you're bailing?"

"I'm not bailing."

I caught my reflection in the narrow mirror, contorted like a Chinese acrobat, trying to zip the dress. "I can't get the stupid thing zipped."

"I could give you a hand."

Unlatching the door, I stepped out of the dressing room, holding the front of the dress in place. "I look fishy."

"Turn around."

I did, but that was even worse, because I could now see my reflection in a large, three-sided mirror. The horror was multiplied.

Zeke stepped behind me and a shiver slipped down my spine as he grasped the zipper, his hand brushing against my bare skin.

"I look like an idiot."

"A beautiful idiot," he soothed.

Something in his voice had me searching for his face in the reflection of the mirror we stood opposite. He smiled at me, something devilish shimmering in his gaze, as he slowly inched the zipper upward.

"You're bailing," I accused again, trying to ignore the way my hormones were once again racing into overdrive for a guy who'd never be interested in me.

"It's not like the two of you need my help sticking bills in a stripper's G-string."

"They're exotic dancers," I corrected. "And I won't be doing any sticking. That's why I need you there."

"It's not my kind of thing. You're all set. You're too tense. " He started giving me a neck massage. Which was almost enough to throw me off track, but not quite.

"It's not mine either, but it's what Alice wants, so it's what we're going to do, dammit."

He chuckled, seemingly unimpressed by my attempt to be authoritative. "It's what *you* are going to do."

"Why? You watch scantily clad guys grinding and gyrating and you watch women make fools of themselves. It's no big deal. They're totally used to gay guys being there."

His eyes locked on mine in the mirror's reflection. Leaning closer, he whispered, "But I'm not gay."

He watched my reaction in the mirror as the revelation sank in.

"I thought . . ."

"You thought wrong." His breath against my ear sent delicious shivers of sensation cascading through my body.

"But . . . ." It was difficult to make my thoughts make sense when a million fireworks were exploding in my body.

His eyes gleamed devilishly as he wrapped his arms around my waist. "I could prove it to you."

I practically collapsed when he pressed his lips to the side of my neck, his hands drifting upward to brush the swell of my breasts.

"I believe you," I gasped, legs trembling.

As though he sensed my knees might fold, he grasped my hips, steadying me.

I might as well have been wearing nothing considering the way his touch burned.

"It might be fun to prove it to you, Maggie. It might take a while. I could kiss you. Touch you. Taste you."

"Stop," I pleaded. "Someone might hear you."

He glanced around. Even though there was no one in sight, he said, "You're right." Spinning me around, he gently propelled me into the fitting room.

I watched our reflections in the small mirror as he stepped in behind me, and closed the door. I moved further forward so that he was no longer touching me, hoping that the lack of physical contact would help me think.

"Turn around, Maggie."

I shook my head.

"Why not?"

"You shouldn't be in here." The accusation sounded childish, but it was the best I could come up with. The space had felt small when I'd been in there by myself, but now it felt downright cramped. "You're not who I thought you were."

"And that's a bad thing?" Even though he kept his tone light, I could hear a note of hurt in his voice.

"When I was seventeen I would have thought it was a great thing," I admitted shakily.

"Really?"

"You didn't know?" All these years I'd thought I'd made a fool of myself mooning over him with my school-girl crush.

"I knew Alice did," he said slowly. "Your Aunt Susan threatened that if I 'accepted her advances' she'd kick me out of the B&B."

"Sounds like something Susan would say and do."

"But I never got that feeling from you."

"I'm not surprised. Alice always has been the bright shining star who eclipses me." Realizing how bitter that made me sound, I hurried to add. "I'm 'remarkably, un-remarkable,' as my grandmother used to say." I offered him a weak smile in the mirror to assure him that it was okay.

He frowned back at me. "You don't believe that."

"Of course not," I said with false cheeriness. "It's just what she used to say."

"You don't really think that Alice eclipses you, do you?"

"She's beautiful, charming, and the center of attention whenever she walks into a room. Plus, she's a really good person. Look at all the causes she's supported." I shrugged, hoping to convey that it didn't bother me. "And . . . she's tall."

"Wow." He leaned back against the wall and crossed his arms over his chest. "That's really how you see her?"

"Of course." I turned around slowly to face him, intrigued by the conversation. "How do you see her?"

"She's like a little girl lost. Fragile. Needy."

"Hey," I protested. "Don't—"

He held up a single finger to silence me. "I'm not saying she's not a good person. I'm just saying she's not this glorified image you have of her. And she's definitely not you."

"And what am I?"

"Strong, dependable, tough."

"You make me sound like a garbage bag."

Uncrossing his arms, he put his hands on his hips and considered me. "What do you want me to say, Maggie? That you're smart and funny?"

I shook my head. His tone dripped with sexy promises and I could have sworn the temperature in the room had shot up at least ten degrees.

He straightened so that he was no longer leaning on the wall. "That you're bewitching?"

"It's the dress," I joked weakly.

"And desirable?"

"I'm tough and strong," I reminded him. "I don't need you to stroke my ego. I know what I am."

"You have no idea what you are." His voice was low and gruff and felt like stubble scraping over me. "Kiss me, Maggie."

I shook my head.

"Why not?"

"Because my life is too complicated right now."

"Too complicated for a single kiss?" he said seductively.

"You have to keep your hands behind your back," I blurted out. I could handle a kiss as long as he kept his hands to himself.

He put his hands behind his back. "Okay, have it your way." Sin and heat shimmered in his blue eyes.

"Just one kiss," I reminded him.

Leaning forward, he brushed his mouth against mine. I froze.

"You have to kiss me back, Maggie. That's the deal."

He teased my lips again, and against my better judgment, I kissed him back. There was no tentative sampling in his kiss, no getting-to-know-you period; he tangled his tongue with mine like we'd been going at it forever. Heat pooled between my legs and I had to grab his shoulders to keep from falling over.

As his mouth worked its magic against mine, my hands slid up his neck, and I buried my fingers in the silky curls of his hair. Lost in the sensation of the sweet ache, I moaned aloud when he pressed his thigh between my legs. I bucked against him, wanting more.

A knock at the door startled us both. We jumped apart. I would have fallen over if Zeke hadn't grabbed my arm and caught me.

"Anyone in there?" a female voice asked.

"Occupied!" I gasped, breathless from the kiss.

"Sorry," the woman said.

I looked up at Zeke and saw that he was breathing heavily too. Usually he appeared unflappable, but at the moment he looked like he'd just gotten the shock of his life.

"Turn around." His voice was hoarse.

I did what he said, watching in the mirror as he grabbed the zipper and tugged it downward. A trail of goose bumps marked where his hand glided down my back.

He glanced at the reflection of my face in the mirror. There was something almost haunted in his gaze. The warm, fuzzy bubble of euphoria I'd been enveloped in popped when I smiled at him and he didn't smile back.

He walked out of the dressing room without a word, leaving me all alone with the ugly dress. I really did look like an idiot.

Chapter Eighteen

I WASN'T SURPRISED that Zeke's red sports car wasn't in the parking lot of the dress shop when I emerged, the not-so-proud owner of a salmon dress. Disappointed, but not surprised.

Tossing the fishy monstrosity in the back of my car, I headed over to the B&B, figuring that if I ran into Alice I could show her how truly awful the dress was. At the very least, I could store the ugly thing in the attic so it wouldn't be covered in dog hair before I had to wear it the next weekend.

There were only two cars parked in the lot and I didn't recognize either.

I carried the dress inside, heading straight for the attic. I paused at the base of the attic stairs when I heard a scuffling noise coming from above. The last time there'd been that kind of racket up there was because a family of raccoons had taken up residence. They'd made a terrible mess and had been a pain to evict.

I considered turning around and leaving, but then I remembered that taking care of this sort of thing had fallen to Dirk the Jerk and he was no longer around to do it. I couldn't in good conscience leave this for my aunts to find and deal with.

Putting down my dress, I slowly climbed the stairs, hoping that I'd be able to talk to the raccoons. If I could, maybe I could reason with them, or at least negotiate, and the exterminator could be kept away. Carefully I peered into the attic.

There were no raccoons.

There was just a rat.

A big, giant rat.

Templeton.

Aunt Loretta's latest fiancé was burrowing through a hope chest, tossing old blankets and table linens every which way.

"What the hell are you doing?"

I spoke in a normal tone, but he jumped as though I'd shouted. He banged into the chest, and the lid slammed shut on his fingers.

"Dammit!" he bellowed, freeing his hand and blowing on his smashed fingers as though it would magically get rid of the pain.

I did my best not to smirk. I didn't like or trust him, but it would have been impolite to laugh at his discomfort. Aunt Susan would have been impressed with my restraint.

Recovering his composure, he said, "You scared me, Margaret."

"What were you doing?"

He looked to the chest and the pile of discarded textiles. "If you must know, I was looking for some bourbon."

"Buried in a hope chest in the attic?" I wasn't polite enough to keep my disbelief to myself.

"Susan got rid of all of the alcohol so that Leslie wouldn't be tempted, but Loretta told me she'd kept her personal supply in the house."

"Among the musty linens?"

"She didn't tell me where."

"Maybe because she doesn't trust you."

He frowned. "I never asked her. But I had a bad day and I was thinking a nip might take the edge off."

"It isn't even noon yet," I told him.

He hung his head. "Clearly this isn't my finest hour. Perhaps we could keep this just between the two of us?"

I considered it for a moment. When I'd told Aunt Loretta that I'd seen her last husband coming out of the strip club on a Wednesday afternoon she'd accused me of not wanting her to be happy. I had no doubt she'd react the same if I told her about Templeton's treasure hunt.

"Okay," I agreed. "I won't tell anyone."

He looked momentarily surprised and then flashed me a grateful grin. "So what brings you here today?"

"I wanted to—"

"Why is there a dress laid out in the hallway?" Aunt Susan demanded to know from the hallway below.

I shrugged at Templeton. "That's why I'm here." I clambered down the stairs. "I thought I'd hang it in the attic since we're getting dressed here for the wedding."

Aunt Susan, in her kung fu uniform, stared at the dress, clearly appalled. "That's what you're wearing?"

I nodded.

"It's not pink."

"Zeke says that Alice says that it's salmon."

"It's disgusting." Bending down, she examined it with morbid curiosity.

"You should see it when it's on. My hips look wider than the Grand Canyon."

"And you're actually going to wear it?"

"You're not helping matters." I snatched it up. "I already don't want to wear the thing, but you carrying on like it's the ugliest piece of clothing you've ever seen is making me want to 'accidentally' spill a bottle of ink on it." I was doing my best not to grouse about the dress since I hadn't been particularly enthusiastic about anything else wedding-related and was tired of feeling like I was being a bad sport about the whole thing.

"It's not that bad," Templeton said from behind me.

Something in Aunt Susan's gaze flickered and I got the distinct impression she wanted to use some of her kung fu moves on him.

I thrust the offensive garment at him. "If you like it so much, you can find a safe place for it in the attic."

He took with a smile. "My pleasure." He disappeared up the stairs.

"Care to come have a cup of tea with me, Margaret?" She couched it as an invitation, but I knew it was really a command.

"I'd love to."

"I visited Katie this morning."

"I haven't been there yet today. I had to pick up the dress."

She shook her head slightly, leading the way to her personal living space. "You shouldn't feel the need to account for your time. I know how much you've done for that child."

She didn't know I'd killed two men in order to have the money to provide the best possible medical care for Katie, but I didn't think I should tell her that. So I said, "Any change?"

"She opened her eyes a few times while I was there." Aunt Susan led the way through her bedroom. As always, her bed was made and nothing was out of place.

"Did she seem to see you?"

With a wave of her hand she ushered me out into the enclosed porch filled with chintz, white wicker, and sunlight. "No. She didn't seem to focus on anything."

I sank into the familiar settee, watching as she turned on the electric teakettle she always kept at the ready.

She carried her ornate wooden tea chest over to me. Opening it, she waited for me to select a bag.

I chose black currant. I always choose black currant because it's my favorite. She knows that, otherwise she wouldn't keep it stocked. Long ago, just after her body had been discovered, Darlene's orange pekoe had disappeared from the selection. I noticed that Theresa's chamomile was now gone too. Marlene's mint was still tucked into a corner.

"What was in your memory box Fifi destroyed?" I asked as Susan returned the tea chest to its place.

She glanced over at me. "That's a strange question."

"Alice and I were talking about Fifi this morning."

"Ah." She chose two china mugs from the rack near the teakettle. "She mentioned she'd met your . . . pet."

"Anyway," I said quickly, not wanting to get into an argument about my choice of companions, "I realized I never knew what was in the box that Fifi destroyed."

Susan frowned at the teakettle as if hoping she could intimidate it into whistling. "Memories." She looked out at the barn in the backyard. "Plans. Did you know that we had plans drawn up to make the barn into a living space?"

I shook my head.

"We wanted to turn it into a couple of apartments."

"For you?"

The kettle whistled. She busied herself with pouring the water into the mugs.

"We debated that. I wanted them to be for family. The twins wanted to make them long-term residences for some of the guests. They liked the idea of the family all living under one roof."

She handed me my cup of tea. "Junior Mints?"

"But I haven't had my lunch yet," I teased. "Aren't you worried I'll ruin my appetite?"

"Special dispensation for having to wear that dress." She smiled as she pulled a box of my favorite childhood candy out from behind a stack of books. "They might be a little stale."

I got choked up as I took them, realizing that while my dad might have never known what my favorite snack was, my aunt always had. She kept them on hand, even though it had been years since we'd sat here, visiting like this.

Aunt Susan was crusty and tough, but she'd always been there for me. I hadn't always liked her methods, but she'd never let me down.

I looked out at the barn, knowing what I had to do.

"There's something I need to talk to you about," I said slowly.

"The something that made you snap at Leslie?" She settled into the seat opposite me and picked up her current knitting project, which just looked like a mess of hot pink, black, and white yarn to me, but which I knew she'd transform into something beautiful.

"It's been on my mind."

"I knew there was something. I've never seen you lash out at your favorite aunt before." Her knitting needles fell into their familiar clickety-clack rhythm.

"She's not my favorite," I denied quickly.

A sad smile played at her lips. "Loretta is obsessed with herself, I'm a hard-ass, and Leslie's a squish. She was always the favorite of all you girls."

Instead of telling her that I knew she was a lot more than just a hard-ass, I blurted out, "Katie's Aunt Abilene is suing me for custody."

The needles fell silent and she closed her eyes as though the news had been a physical blow.

"I've already consulted an attorney who specializes in custody cases," I told her quickly.

Folding her hands in her lap, she opened her eyes, fixing me with a steady stare. "What did he say?"

I blew the steam off my cup, trying to figure out the best way to couch what I had to tell her, what I was going to ask of her.

"Margaret?"

"According to my father, she has a lot of power and money."

"And how would Archie know? Was he paroled and no one told me?"

"Apparently Dirk told him that he was afraid of her."

Her gaze narrowed suspiciously. "And how do *you* know this?"

I sipped my tea. "Alice wanted to tell him in person that she was getting married. She asked me to take her."

"Theresa said you always refused to go visit with her."

I shrugged.

"Margaret?"

Feeling like I was ten and had been caught doing something wrong and was going to have dessert taken away for a week, I fidgeted in my chair. The wicker creaked in protest. "I'd gone to tell him that Theresa was dead," I confessed on a breath.

"When?"

"Not long after the accident." I looked away, unable to make eye contact. I'd failed to visit my mother, her sister, at the mental health facility where she resided when I'd been asked to, but I'd gone to see my incarcerated father. What did that make me?

Picking up her needles, she picked up the rhythm that had been interrupted by the news about Abilene. "Good."

"Good?" I looked up at her, surprised.

She was staring out at the barn. "It was the right thing to do. He shouldn't have found out from a stranger that his daughter had died. What did the attorney say?"

"Well," I said slowly, "she suggested that if I could prove that I could provide a stable home environment, with a support system, that I'd have a fighting chance at maintaining custody of Katie." The last part was a wee embellishment, but I'd decided to put a positive spin on the whole thing.

Susan switched her focus from the barn to me. "And how are you supposed to do that?"

"I could move back here?" I suggested weakly. "I mean I know it would be a huge imposition and that you'd have to talk it over with Loretta and Leslie, but if I don't . . . Katie could end up in Vegas."

I waited for her to remind me that only a few days ago I'd pledged to never move back or that I'd had no problem leaving when I hadn't needed anything from them. I steeled myself for her attack, vowing to not retaliate. I'd do whatever it took to keep Katie. Taking a deep breath, I squared my shoulders, prepared for the worst.

"It's not an imposition," Aunt Susan said mildly. "This is your home, Margaret. It always has been. It always will be." She put down her needles, leaned forward, and patted my knee. "You should know that."

I sank back into my chair, deflated. "But—"

"When do you want to move back in?"

"I—"

"I had new plans drawn up for the barn last year when it looked like Theresa and Dirk might be breaking up.

I even got estimates from contractors. Even hired one. When Templeton came on the scene I got the permits, thinking I couldn't live under the same roof as that insufferable man."

"You?" My head was spinning with all she was telling me. I twisted in my seat to look at the barn. Was that going to be my new home?

"I haven't told anyone, but the construction begins the day after Alice's wedding."

"You haven't told anyone that a major construction project is going to be taking place?"

"And listen to Tweedledee and Tweedledum weigh in on it incessantly?"

I wasn't sure if she was referring to Leslie and Loretta, or Loretta and Templeton, but since she said it with such venom, I thought it wise not to ask.

"No, I had a feeling that we'd need the space. Always follow your gut, Margaret. Always."

It was good advice.

Chapter Nineteen

HAVING TACKLED ONE heavy-duty request, I went home to gather reinforcements before attempting another near-impossible feat.

"Your boyfriend was here," God called from the kitchen table the instant I walked into the apartment.

"I don't have a boyfriend." I tossed Doomsday a treat and checked God's water to make sure he had enough.

The lizard rolled his eyes . . . which was just plain gross.

"Fine. The redhead was here. Just waltzed right in and left something in the bedroom."

"What do you mean he waltzed right in?" I could have sworn I'd locked the door before leaving.

"You don't think she"—he pointed at Doomsday, who was lying on her back, waiting for a belly rub—"stopped him, do you?"

"Meat!" the dog panted.

"He fed her. Didn't even look at me, but actually brought food for the beast." God sounded put out.

Curious, I went into the bedroom. A large cardboard box sat smack in the middle of my unmade bed. Flipping it open, I reached inside and felt something cool and hard. I pulled it out.

It was a giant jar of gourmet olives.

Touched by Patrick's thoughtfulness, I smiled. Putting it aside, I reached into the box again and pulled out a folder. I scanned its contents quickly. It was a complete dossier on Jose Garcia. It contained surveillance photos of Garcia, outside his house and in his car, his home address, the location of his daughter's wedding, and even the wedding itinerary.

I reached into the box again and encountered something else cold and hard. I pulled it out slowly. It was a handgun.

Instinctively I checked to make sure the safety was on before I laid it beside the olives.

Looking into the box, I saw a pile of black fabric. I pulled it out and realized it was a waitress's uniform. The name tag said "Katie."

Short of drawing a bull's-eye on Garcia's forehead, Patrick had given me everything I needed.

"What is it?" God called from the other room.

Tossing the uniform on the bed, I snatched up the olives and dossier and went back to the kitchen. "It's what I need to kill Garcia."

"No flowers? No candy? No cheesy mix tapes?"

"I told you, he's not my boyfriend." I opened the olives. "Aren't you too young to even remember mix tapes?"

"The other one was here too."

"What other one?"

"The other boyfriend."

I considered whipping the lid of the olive jar at him like some kind of deadly ninja weapon. "I don't have a boyfriend."

"Mr. 'Roid Rage was here, but Doomsday scared him off."

"DeeDee," Doomsday whined.

The lizard shook his head at her. "Apparently she's learning the alphabet, but the only letter she knows is D."

"DeeDee," the dog barked.

"She wants to change her name from Doomsday to DeeDee," I explained.

"Why?"

I shrugged. "Apparently she doesn't think Doomsday is girly enough."

"Save me," God muttered.

"Paul was here?" I asked, trying to get the conversation back on course.

"But Doomsday scared—" the lizard began.

"DeeDee," the dog corrected.

"But *DeeDee*"—God stressed the two syllables like they were the most despicable things that had ever left his tongue—"scared him off."

"Good girl, DeeDee," I praised, tossing her an olive as a reward for her guard dog duties.

"She only growled because *I* told her to," God groused.

"What did he want?"

God stared at me like I was even stupider than the dog. "I don't know. It wasn't like he was announcing his intentions as he tried to break in."

I tilted my head to the side, acknowledging that it had been a pretty stupid thing to ask.

"I thought you were going to pick up your dress," God said. "Did you forget?"

"No, I didn't forget. I just took it to my aunts' place so no one would S-H-E-D on it."

DeeDee didn't seem to notice that I was spelling so that she wouldn't understand.

"Smart idea," God said.

"I do have them occasionally."

"*Very* occasionally."

I yawned. Not the most scintillating response, but I was tired. "I need your help."

"With what?" He flicked his tail suspiciously.

"Alice wants me to invite her mom to the wedding."

"And that's a challenge?"

"It would probably be a good thing if I did it in a nice or at least polite way."

"And you think that's too much for you to handle?"

I shrugged. "Might be."

"You know," the lizard said in his most bored tone, "there's no law that says you have to take care of everyone all the time."

"And if I don't, who will?"

"I'm just saying that time will march on and the world will keep revolving."

I thought of Marlene, of how I hadn't taken care of her and Darlene when they needed me most. "If I don't do it, someone will fall through the cracks."

"Someone already has."

I frowned. I was doing my best to care for Katie, my aunts, and my friends, but he was telling me my best wasn't good enough. Panicked, I asked, "Who?"

"You."

"I'm fine."

"Really? Because the way I see it, you're standing there, ready to fall asleep, but you're getting ready to run out and take care of someone else's problem."

"So is this your way of telling me you're not going to help me?" I frowned, surprised at how disappointed I was that the lizard was going to let me down.

He flicked his tail, signaling his frustration. "It means I'll help you, but only if you take a nap first."

"Nap DeeDee." The dog wagged her stump of a tail.

"Yes," God said. "Follow the beast's lead and get some sleep. Then I'll help you with anything you need."

I swayed uncertainly, not liking that he was black-mailing me into doing his bidding, but seeing the wisdom behind his suggestion.

"Fine. For one hour."

Knowing the box and uniform were still on my bed, I flopped onto the living room couch. DeeDee lay down on the floor beside me. I'm not sure which of us snored first.

Two hours later I awoke to the sound of whistling. For

a confused moment I thought I was back in Aunt Susan's porch and she was making me another cup of tea. Then I realized it wasn't the teakettle making a racket, it was the lizard.

"I'm awake," I muttered groggily.

"Time to get going," he chirped cheerily.

"You're the one who told me to take a nap."

"I didn't tell you to sleep the entire day away."

"Gotta! Gotta!" DeeDee panted.

"Yeah, yeah." I walked the dog, ate a handful of olives, and headed out, with God perched on my shoulder.

I filled him in on why I needed him to keep me in line as we drove over to the address Alice had given me for her mom. My apartment was in a questionable part of town. There was no question about where Alice's mom lived . . . you'd have to be half crazy to live there.

I walked up to door sixteen of the dilapidated motel I'd been sent to.

"Maybe, if I'm lucky, she won't be here," I said. "Then I could honestly tell Alice I tried, but couldn't get in touch with her."

God, who had his tail wrapped around my neck for balance, said, "Don't knock on the door. You don't know who or what has touched it."

It was good advice, so instead of knocking, I kicked it three times.

"Don't answer. Don't answer. Don't an—"

The door swung open and I was face-to-face with Alice's mother. Like her daughter, the woman was ridiculously tall, but unlike Alice, she was stooped, weighed down by a lifetime of bad choices.

"Hello, Ellen." Shocked by her appearance, I barely choked out the greeting. She'd always been vain and had insisted on always being called by her first name, instead of Mrs. Whichever-Bum-She-Was-Married-To.

The years had not been kind to her. Deep furrows lined her face, her hair was limp and lifeless, and her eyes were flat.

She stared at me blearily. "Do I know you?"

"It's Maggie. Maggie Lee. Alice's friend."

She squinted at me. "The last time I saw you, you were a pimply-faced teenager. How've you been?"

"Fine. I wanted—"

"How's your mother?"

Every muscle in my body tightened. Ellen had been the first person who'd ever publicly called my mother a lunatic.

"Easy, girl," God soothed, stroking my ear like I was a wild stallion ready to buck. "Breathe."

"She's the same." The words were tight and clipped.

Ellen pushed her door open wider, ushering inside.

I leaned forward and then hesitated.

"Don't!" God shrieked. "It's like stepping into a black hole. We might never get out."

Ellen narrowed her gaze at the squeaking sound. "What's that?"

"A lizard." She probably thought I was as nuts as my mom, what with walking around with a lizard clinging to my shoulder for no apparent reason. I wasn't sure she was wrong.

"Cute little guy."

"Cute?" God shrieked, mortally offended.

Ellen reached up to pet him.

"Sensitive skin! Sensitive skin!" God scampered half-way down my back, latching on to my bra clasp.

"He's not very friendly," I told Ellen. "But he is cute."

"Bitch!" he screamed.

Just for that I stepped into the apartment.

It was dingy and smelled of mildew, but it was neat enough that Aunt Susan would have approved.

"I see your aunt sometimes," Ellen said, settling into a rocking chair and motioning for me to sit in the only other seat in the place.

I perched on the edge, waiting for God to retake his place on my shoulder before I sat back. "Aunt Susan?" I asked, assuming she'd seen her at one of her charity activities.

"Leslie." We go to some of the same Narcotics Anonymous meetings."

"So much for them being anonymous."

"She said you're the only girl left."

"Marlene's around somewhere," I said, remembering Patrick's claims.

"What are you doing here, Maggie?"

"Be nice," God coached.

"Alice is getting married."

"So I heard."

"Leslie?"

She nodded.

I wondered if Aunt Leslie did anything besides talk

about other peoples' business while at her meetings.

"She wants to make sure I'm not going to show up and make a scene, right?" Ellen twisted her hands, her voice barely more than a whisper.

"Be kind," God prompted. "The woman's obviously a wreck. Lashing out her won't serve a purpose."

He was wrong, I wasn't about to strike out. I felt a stab of pity for her. I'd never understand why she hadn't taken her daughter's side, but now, after the events of the past month or so, I could understand how it's possible to delude oneself into thinking what's wrong is right.

"She wants you to be there," I said as gently as I could.

Something in her flat gaze shimmered for a moment as though a switch had been thrown within her.

"Really." I took out an invitation and laid it on the card table between us. "She asked me to come and invite you."

Ellen reached for the piece of cardboard with trembling hands. "She . . . she forgives me?"

"That's not my place to say, but she does want you there. I'd imagine that's a start."

Two big, fat tears slid down her cheeks, disappearing into the wrinkles time and suffering had carved.

"Say something comforting," God urged.

Nothing came to me. I just sat there, watching the older woman clasp the piece of stationery like it was a lifeline.

"I have to be going," I said after a long, uncomfortable silence, and got to my feet.

"I pray for her every day," Ellen croaked.

"You should tell Alice that when you see her."

She stood up and grabbed my hand. "I meant your niece. I pray for Alice too, but I've been praying extra hard for your little niece ever since I heard."

"Thank you," I said, touched by the sentiment. "If you need a ride to the wedding I could arrange for one."

"You're the maid of honor?"

I nodded.

"She's lucky to have you. She's always been lucky to have a friend like you, Maggie."

The moment I was out the door, God patted me on the shoulder. "Good job."

I didn't answer him.

"Is something wrong?"

"Things are going too well."

"Too well."

"Patrick gave me everything I need, Aunt Susan took the news about the custody battle extremely well, Zeke's not gay, and now this . . . Do you know what it means?"

"Apparently you've developed psychic powers and think you do?"

"I'll confer with my psychic, but I'm pretty sure the rough ride is about to begin."

Chapter Twenty

"ANY MORE PROPHETIC dreams?" I asked Armani the moment she limped into work.

"Why? Did something happen?"

I couldn't tell her that I'd almost gotten caught trying to kill my former uncle so I said, "I've got an uneasy feeling."

"I'm not surprised. I keep dreaming about the disco ball."

"That's it? That's all you've got for me?"

"Well, that and a cactus."

"A cactus?"

She nodded. "A big one.

"Where am I going to encounter a big cactus?"

"I don't know. Maybe it's symbolic. Your sex life is pretty parched."

Considering that I'd made out with Zeke and almost kissed Patrick over the course of the weekend, I didn't think the tumbleweeds would be blowing through any-time soon.

"Unless you decided to take my advice about the cop . . ."

I wrinkled my nose in disgust at the thought of Paul. "Not even a remote possibility."

Harry drifted up to us, but was careful to keep a re-spectful distance. "If you ladies wouldn't mind returning to your desks, please? We've got some managers from the main office taking a tour."

I stared at him. He was polite, bordering on pandering.

"Please?" He practically squeaked, failing to make eye contact.

"Sure." I moved away and couldn't hear whatever it was Armani said to him, but I did hear her raucous laughter as it bounced through the room.

I didn't get a chance to speak to her again until lunch.

"You should invite me," she said as she slid into the bench opposite me at our regular picnic table.

"To what?"

"To the bachelorette party."

"How do you know about that?"

"Zeke told me about it."

"When?"

"When he called me yesterday."

He'd kissed me and then called her. That rankled. I did my best to keep a straight face.

She threw back her head and laughed. "So you figured out that the cute guy is straight and interested in you, huh?"

I shrugged.

"He said I should convince you to take me along to this bachelorette deal. That he'd met all of this Alice chick's friends and they reminded him of the Stepford Wives."

"They are kinda similar."

"He said I should go along and show you how to loosen up and have a good time."

"No offense," I said. "But you're not really the one I want to show me a good time."

"Oooh, you've got it bad for him."

"I always have." I sighed, flooded with regrets.

"*Carpe mano!*"

"What?"

"*Carpe mano.* Seize the man. That's what I always say."

"I've never heard you say it."

"So what do you say, Chiquita. Can I come along and seize some men?"

"Sure," I said, against my better judgment. I hoped it wasn't a decision I'd come to regret.

After work I headed straight to the hospital. I was relieved that Vinnie, Delveccio's muscle, was nowhere in sight. I really didn't want to explain to the mobster about how I'd failed to kill Jose Garcia. All I wanted to do was visit with my niece.

Nothing is ever that simple.

She already had another visitor. Aunt Leslie sat at Katie's bedside singing, "If I Had a Hammer" to her.

I hadn't seen Leslie since I'd insulted her as we prepared for the wedding shower, so I didn't know whether or not she was speaking to me. I waited until her song was over before stepping into the room and letting my presence be known.

She turned and smiled at me. "Hi, Maggie."

I let out a breath I hadn't even realized I'd been holding. "Hi, Aunt Leslie."

"Our girl keeps opening her eyes."

"That's great." I pressed a kiss to Katie's head before settling into the seat opposite Leslie. "I saw Alice's mom yesterday."

"I see her at my NA meetings sometimes. She's a nice woman, but broken."

"She looks pretty bad."

"Life has been hard on her."

"She's coming to the wedding."

Leslie nodded. "Good. Does that mean Alice has forgiven her?"

I shrugged.

"She should."

A familiar sense of outrage began to burn in my gut. "Why? What her mother did was horrible."

Leslie shook her head with a sad smile. "You don't understand, Maggie. Forgiveness isn't for the person who did wrong, it's about the person who's been wronged to find peace."

I wondered if she'd picked up that particular nugget of wisdom at one of her meetings, but I bit the inside of my cheek and managed not to ask.

"Susan told us about the custody battle," she said,

changing the topic of conversation as though she sensed how tense it made me. She stroked Katie's cheek. "If you need money for the lawyer, I have a little set aside."

"No. I have it covered." I'd used the advance Delveccio had given me for just that.

"We're all excited you're moving home."

"Are you?" I picked up Katie's limp hand and began manipulating her fingers.

"Can I give you some advice?"

I glanced over at my aunt. Susan and Loretta were usually the sisters who doled out advice. Leslie usually just sat and listened. "Sure."

"I've been thinking about it since Susan told us yesterday. I know you left the first time because we were all driving you crazy."

"I—" I felt like I should protest, but I didn't want to lie.

"So I think it would be good idea to have a family meeting before you move back in."

I thought she had meetings on the brain. "We've never had a family meeting."

"That doesn't mean we shouldn't start."

I wondered if that meant she wanted us to all sit around and chant the Serenity Prayer or something. I thought Aunt Susan's head might explode if we did. "I don't know . . ." I said slowly.

"You could lay down some ground rules. Boundaries."

I stared at her like she was a three-headed alien. Our family didn't really do the respecting-boundaries thing. "You've got to be kidding."

"People can change, Maggie. You're a grown woman. There should be limits on how much we meddle in your life."

"You guys exist solely to meddle," I said.

She frowned. "Maybe that's why Susan is a control freak, Loretta's a nymphomaniac, and I'm a drug addict."

I blinked and I'm pretty sure my mouth dropped open. It was by far the harshest thing I'd ever heard Leslie say. True, but harsh.

"It might be too late for you," Leslie continued. "But she"—she jerked her chin in the direction of Katie's face—"she deserves better."

"You're right."

"So you'll do it?"

I nodded.

"Good." She stood up to leave. "Katie's lucky to have an aunt like you, Maggie."

Standing up, I walked around the bed and wrapped my arms around Leslie. Squeezing tightly I whispered, "And I'm lucky to have an aunt like you."

She hugged me back and then left, unshed tears shimmering in her eyes.

I collapsed into the seat she'd occupied. "Hear that, Katie? We're going to establish boundaries."

Her eyes fluttered open as though she knew I was talking to her.

I did my best to smile, even though I didn't think she saw me. "That's it, Baby Girl."

Her gaze seemed to sharpen and focus.

I leaned closer. "Can you hear me, Katie? Can you see me? It's Aunt Maggie."

She blinked. When her eyes reopened she was looking right at me.

My heart skipped a beat.

"I'm here, Katie. Aunt Maggie is right here." I grabbed her hand and squeezed it. "Can you squeeze my hand, sweetheart?"

I felt no answering pressure.

A lump rose in my throat. Was I seeing things? Deluding myself?

"Please, Baby Girl? Please squeeze my hand?"

And she did.

I could have wept, but I didn't because I didn't want to frighten her. Instead I blinked away my tears and said, "Good job. Good job, kiddo."

Someone else came into the room and Katie's gaze left mine to see who it was.

One of Katie's doctors, a young guy with an earnest demeanor, circled Katie's bed. "Hello there, Katie. I'm Dr. McCain." He pulled out one of those light things that doctors are so fond of blinding their patients with. "Can you follow this light for me, Katie?"

Holding it in front of her, he moved it slowly from side to side.

She tracked it.

Then her eyes fluttered closed again, but not before she gave my hand one more weak squeeze.

I covered my mouth to choke back a sob.

Dr. McCain looked at me and smiled. A real smile,

not one of those pitying grimaces all the doctors and nurses had been giving me. "This is a really good sign, Miss Lee. A really good sign."

I walked out of Katie's hospital room wondering if Armani's cactus was somehow a good sign about Katie's recovery. Maybe it was symbolic of survival. Those things thrive out in the desert where most things shrivel up and die. I liked that idea.

I smiled, my heart lighter than it had been in ages. Things were finally starting to turn around.

The next moment, my bubble of euphoria burst.

"Miss Lee?" An older nurse who I'd seen many times hurried over to me. "There seems to be a problem."

"A problem?" I immediately thought that something was wrong with the hospital billing. I'd done the work. I'd paid Katie's bill.

"There's a woman here claiming to be your niece's aunt."

My heart leapt and then stumbled. "Marlene?"

"No, ma'am. I believe her name starts with an A. She's giving us a very hard time, insisting on seeing Katie, but she's not on the list of approved visitors."

Abilene.

I clenched my fists, ready to do battle. "I'll take care of it. Where is she?"

"At the nurses' station."

I marched off in that direction.

The nurse hurried to keep up with me. "I think you should know . . . I mean, you're a nice person, all the staff says so . . . you should know that this woman is scary."

I smiled. "Thank you, but I think I can handle it." I had, after all, killed two men. What could one woman do to me in a hospital corridor?

In hindsight, I realized I shouldn't have been so cocky.

I spotted Abilene the moment I rounded the corner. If Aunt Loretta dressed like an aging sex kitten, Abilene was the hot mama cat. Clad in black leather from head to toe and dripping in gold, she should have looked ridiculous; instead the dominatrix-crossed-with-cartoon-villain look worked for her.

I could understand why the nurses were spooked. She looked like the type who'd eat her young.

"I've met worse," I muttered beneath my breath.

The nurse who'd come to get me quirked an eyebrow, signaling she didn't believe me.

She didn't know I was a badass, professional assassin.

By default.

Deciding that my best bet was to show no fear, I marched right up to the Lady of Darkness and extended my hand. "Hello. I'm Maggie Lee. Katie's aunt."

She stared at my offered hand, but didn't move to shake it.

Determined to keep things as civil as possible, I fell back on the empathy coaching I'd received at Insuring the Future. "My deepest condolences on the loss of your brother." I felt a twinge of pride that I'd managed to sound like a freaking Hallmark card.

She shrugged. "No loss. The world's a better place without him."

I hadn't liked Dirk, heck, there were times I'd despised

him, but I didn't believe in speaking ill of the dead. "He had his redeeming qualities."

"Like what?"

I had to think about that for a second. "He could grill a steak to medium-rare perfection without a thermometer."

"Is that why your sister married him? Because he was good with meat? She must not have been the sharpest tool in the shed."

"Hey," I warned, "that's my sister you're talking about."

She gave me a long, calculating look. I did my best to stare back stoically, knowing that the nurses were watching our exchange like it was a tennis match.

She inclined her head slightly. I didn't know if it was meant as an apology or if she was acknowledging I was a worthy opponent. Either way, it felt like I'd won that match.

"I'd like to see my niece," she said.

I resisted pointing out she'd never bothered to meet Katie before. Instead I said, "Of course," hoping I could reason with her. "This way."

She followed me to Katie's room and then stood at the bed, staring at the sleeping girl.

"She was able to open her eyes and focus today," I said softly. "The doctor said that was a good sign. Maybe if you stop by earlier in the day tomorrow, she'll be awake."

"I won't be here tomorrow. I just happened to have some business to attend to nearby so I figured I'd swing by and see her."

"I was thinking," I said carefully, hoping to reason with her, "that I'd be happy to work out a visitation schedule with you. After all, she should know both sides of her family."

She turned her hard gaze on me. "Visitation? I want full custody. I'm going to get full custody."

I tried to hang on to my composure. "But you've never even met her. Surely—"

"Surely," she interrupted, "you don't think you're going to have her. Your mother is insane, your father is a criminal, you have a go-nowhere job, a crappy apartment, and you can't keep a man." She smiled maliciously as I winced at her attack. "I know who you are, Maggie Lee. I know your weaknesses and my lawyer will exploit them."

Balling my hands into fists, I asked in an even voice, "Why are you doing this?"

"Didn't Dirk tell you?"

"I'd never even heard of you before he died."

"I want everything that's his. I took his place in the family business, took his place in our father's heart, and now, now that the old man is dying, I'm going to take Dirk's brat and use it to get Dirk's inheritance."

"She's not a brat. She's certainly not an it. And you're never going to take her."

She laughed at me. She just threw back her head and laughed as though I was the biggest joke in the universe.

"I won't let you—" I glanced at Katie, so small and peaceful in the big bed, and got too choked up to continue.

I spun around and left the room, not wanting to fight in front of Katie.

Abilene followed. "That's it. Run away like the loser you are. Admit defeat. Give up."

Turning around, I swung back and marched up to her. "I am not afraid of you! I'll kill you if you try to take her!" I screamed at the top of my lungs.

She shoved me away and I stumbled back a few steps. I would have fallen, but someone grabbed my elbow and held me up. I glanced over my shoulder and was shocked to see my savior was Vinnie. I shook free of his grasp and turned back just in time for Abilene to slap me across the face.

"Catfight!" Vinnie cried with delight.

I lunged for her, but before I could wipe the sneer off her face, someone jumped between us.

"Maggie!"

It took a moment for me to recognize the woman who'd thrown herself in front of me. At that moment, enraged, I wanted to take her head off too.

"Move," I growled.

"Maggie, don't do this," Stacy Kiernan, the social worker who'd first handled Katie's case, pleaded as she held up her hands in a defensive position.

"What do you care? You don't even work here anymore."

"You're right," Stacy said. "But I care what happens to you. I'm your friend. I need you not to do this."

"Yes, Maggie," Abilene taunted. "Listen to your friend. Give up."

Stacy Kiernan, kind and caring social worker, the woman who'd burst into tears about the state of her career and love life when she'd been trying to tell me that the hospital was going to give Katie the boot, the woman who was as sweet and cuddly as a Labrador retriever puppy, turned on Abilene. "Has anyone ever told you that you look like Tim Burton's version of the Wicked Witch? Get lost, freak."

Abilene's mouth dropped open.

Vinnie chuckled.

The nurses, who'd been mean to Stacy when she'd been employed by the hospital, actually clapped and cheered.

And I backed up a little, realizing that indulging in this scene had been a mistake. If the fight escalated, the cops would be called, and that was the last thing I needed.

So I backed off and let security escort Abilene away.

"What are you doing here, Stacy?" I asked, once the witch was gone.

"I was having coffee with a former coworker. I came up here hoping I might run into you."

"I'm glad you did." I hung my head, ashamed of my outburst. "Thank you for preventing me from doing something even stupider. Speaking of which, do you have plans for tomorrow night?"

Chapter Twenty-One

AFTER I LEFT the hospital, I stopped for a take-out burger and headed home. I brought DeeDee a burger too. There was no reason Patrick should be the only one to spoil her.

After we'd both eaten, and God had whipped my butt as we played along with *Jeopardy*, I took her for a long walk.

When we returned home, we were greeted with, "Yooohooo, is that you, Maggie?"

The voice came from my kitchen, but it wasn't God's.

DeeDee growled. She was turning into quite the watchdog.

"Who else would it be, Aunt Loretta? You're sitting at my table."

The dog and I went into the kitchen. Loretta sat there, leafing through my mail.

"She just walked right in." God flicked his tail in annoyance.

"What are you doing here?" I asked my aunt.

"You who?" DeeDee asked, walking up and sniffing her.

"She stinks," God warned broodingly.

Instead of answering me, Loretta made a fuss over the mutt. "What a beautiful girl you are." As much as Aunt Susan hates dogs, Loretta loves them. Which might explain her penchant for picking bad men.

"She had a key." God glared at me accusingly.

I nodded. I'd given all my aunts, Theresa, and Alice the keys to my place when I'd moved in. Considering how often some of them dropped in, I'd often wished I hadn't. I'd asked Aunt Leslie for hers back after she passed out on my doorstep, which had been the event that had heralded her starting with Narcotics Anonymous.

"Why are you here?" I asked Aunt Loretta again.

"What's your lovely doggie's name?" she asked, petting DeeDee's head.

The dog was lapping up the attention.

"DeeDee. Is everything okay?"

Loretta nodded. "Everything's fine." She smiled and batted her false eyelashes at me.

"So what are you doing here?"

"Do I need a reason to visit with my niece?"

I eyed her suspiciously. "You know, don't you?"

"Know what, dear?" Her innocent act wasn't convincing.

"That the bachelorette party is tomorrow night. That's why you're here, isn't it? You're trying to wrangle an invitation."

"I—" she began.

"I know you did a lot for the shower, but this isn't my call. I can ask Alice if you can come, but I can't guarantee it."

"I don't want to go."

I sank into a chair. "You don't?" I'd never heard of her passing up the opportunity to ogle nearly naked men.

"No. I'm happy with my man."

"You are?" I'd never heard her say she was happy with a man before. She said she was *in love*, but never *happy*. Maybe Templeton really was The One for her? "So why are you here?"

"Susan told me about the custody case."

I closed my eyes at the thought of the upcoming battle with leather-clad Abilene.

Loretta sucked in an audible breath. "Did something happen? Is Katie okay?"

Opening my eyes, I smiled weakly. "She opened her eyes, squeezed my hand, and was able to focus today."

Loretta clapped her delight.

"Woohoo!" God shouted.

His high-pitched squeak startled Loretta. "Is that Katie's pet?"

"Yes."

"He's cute."

I smiled widely. "He certainly is."

"I'm not cute!" God boomed.

"Quiet!" DeeDee barked.

Loretta chuckled. "Quite the noisy household we're going to have."

I stared at DeeDee sadly, not wanting to voice my doubt that she'd be joining us. I said, "I know it'll be an adjustment, an inconvenience—"

"Hush, child," Loretta admonished. She slid a small, ornate wooden box toward me. "I thought this might help."

"It's beautiful."

"Open it."

I did and found myself staring at a diamond ring.

"It's my engagement ring from Kevin," Loretta said.

"You kept his ring when you were married to the man for less than a year?"

"I kept them all, but your father pawned the rest before he was sent to prison. That's the only one I have left, besides this one." She fluttered her fingers under my nose.

I couldn't remember if she'd shown me her ring from Templeton before. "Very nice."

"I want you to use it to pay for the lawyer you're using."

"I can't." Flipping the box closed, I pushed it back toward her.

"I insist."

"I like this woman," God piped up.

"Squeaky thing, isn't he?" Loretta asked.

"He never shuts up," I told her.

Loretta patted the box. "Pawn it. Sell it. Just do whatever you need to in order to keep our Katie where she belongs."

"I am." I fingered the poison-filled pendant hanging from my neck.

Standing, she pressed a kiss to my cheek, not one of

her customary air kisses, but one that would leave lipstick on my skin. "And try to have some fun at that bachelorette party."

She teetered out on her stilettos. DeeDee walked her to the door.

I sat at the table, staring at the box.

"That's wonderful news about Katie," God said.

"It is."

"But?"

I told him about what had happened with Abilene.

"You could poison her," the lizard suggested mildly when I was done telling my tale.

"I thought of that."

"But you've got motive to kill her, which means you'd probably get caught."

I nodded. "It might be worth it though, to save Katie from whatever kind of life that woman has planned for her."

"Don't do anything rash, Maggie."

"It's not like I have a lot to lose."

"Give it some time."

"I don't have time. If I'm caught doing the Garcia job, I won't be able to stop her."

He raised his right hand and pledged, "If you are unable, I will stop her."

I snorted. "You?"

"Too me," DeeDee panted.

"With the help of the beast, yes, I pledge to never allow Katie to fall into Abilene's evil clutches."

I believed him.

There are times when the bed beside my mom's in the loony bin doesn't sound like such a bad idea.

THE NEXT NIGHT I was late getting to the bachelorette party. For once, it wasn't my fault. I was ready to leave on time, but when I went out, I discovered that I had a flat tire.

I'm as modern as the next woman, but I also know when to admit my limitations. Operating a jack and changing a tire are on my personal list of Do Not Attempt Unless You Wish to Court Injury or Death items.

So I called the auto club, waited twice as long as they said it would take, and rolled into the strip club parking lot almost an hour late.

Despite the crowd, the overzealous smoke machine, and music that could make a deaf man go mad, I had no trouble finding my group. Armani was busy spanking a dancer, clad in little more than his cowboy hat and boots, with her good hand, and the rest of the table was egging her on raucously.

I considered going back to my car, but before I could, I felt a tug on my sleeve.

I looked up to see Alice glaring daggers at me. "Hi!" I said with as much faux enthusiasm as I could muster.

Grabbing my arm, she dragged me into the bathroom. My eardrums were grateful for the break.

"Where were you?" she screamed, like one of those freaky bridezilla chicks God is fond of watching on TV.

"I—"

"You're the worst maid of honor ever," she ranted.

The other two restroom occupants, who had been touching up their makeup in the mirror, stopped what they were doing to watch the show.

"I—" I tried to defend myself.

"You weren't there for the cake tasting. Or the photographer. Or the florist." She ticked the items off on her fingers for emphasis.

"I didn't even know about them."

"You didn't *want* to know about them."

"You really do suck," one of the women commented.

Alice, thrilled to have the support of the Greek chorus, turned toward them. "I know, right?"

"I had a flat tire!" I blurted out.

"Every time?" the other woman scoffed.

"Tonight. I had a flat tire tonight, which was why I'm late. I called you. I texted."

"What about the other times?" the first woman asked. "The cake, the pictures, the flowers? What kind of maid of honor lets the bride down for those things."

"The kind that's got a lot of shit going on," I screamed, so loudly it hurt my throat.

Alice's supporters backed off.

"The kind that's wearing the world's ugliest fish-colored dress that's ever been seen without a word of complaint. The kind that goes to invite *your* mother to *your* wedding. That's the kind of maid of honor I am and if you don't like it, just bestow the title on Zeke, or Priscilla the Preppy Princess. I saw her out there, whooping it up."

"You're getting married, Alice?" a soft, familiar voice answered.

"You've got to be kidding me." I turned around and saw that someone else had entered the restroom. Even though I hadn't seen her in a couple of years, I recognized Dana Velicky immediately, not because of her pudgy nose and square jaw, but because she looked so much like her brother, Frank. Frank, who'd broken down the door of my apartment and tried to drag Alice out by her hair. I'd broken my only vase over his head.

Dana tossed a frown at me, but couldn't maintain eye contact. She blamed me for sending her brother to prison, but was too afraid of me to say so. Instead she focused on Alice. "You're getting married?"

"Yes!" Alice walked over and waved her engagement ring under Dana's nose.

"I don't think—" I started.

"Oh just shut up, Maggie," Alice said.

"When's the big day?" Dana asked.

"Next Sunday."

"I really don't—"

Alice silenced me with a glare.

I'd been going to tell her that I didn't think that it was wise to share the details of her upcoming nuptials with the sister of the guy who'd beaten her within an inch of her life, but she obviously didn't want to hear what I thought. After all, I was the worst maid of honor ever.

Pushing past them, I left the restroom and headed for the exit of the club.

"Where are you going, Chiquita?" Armani wrapped her good arm around my neck.

"Home."

She squinted at me, obviously inebriated. "But you just got here."

"And I'm just leaving." I tried to shrug her off, but she held on tight.

"But you haven't seized any men."

"And yet, I'm pretty sure I'll survive the night."

"Maggie!" another voice called.

I turned and saw Stacy Kiernan stumbling toward me. I groaned, having forgotten I'd invited her to this fiasco.

"I thought maybe you got into another fistfight and weren't going to make it," Stacy said.

Armani perked up. "Fight? Is it true, chica? You got in a fight?"

"No!"

"Yup," Stacy said simultaneously. "She's in the middle of the hospital screaming about how she's going to kill this woman. The whole place heard her."

I closed my eyes. It hadn't been my finest moment.

"And then there's this shoving match," Stacy continued.

"I didn't shove her," I protested weakly.

"Luckily," Stacy said, puffed up with self-importance, "one of her friends was there to help her out."

"Maggie has good friends," Armani slurred.

"The best," Stacy agreed.

The two of them dragged me to the table occupied by Alice's bachelorette party. I greeted the other women politely, even Preppy Priscilla, who was wearing thigh-high argyle socks that almost reached her barely there skirt. Eventually Alice rejoined the group, but we didn't talk . . . or make eye contact.

Instead, I fixated on the stage, watching as the women took turns going up and interacting with the dancers in the most lewd ways imaginable. At the end of the evening, determining that they were too drunk to drive, I piled Armani and Stacy into my car. I took Stacy home first, which proved tricky since I'd never been there before and her intoxicated directions didn't always make sense.

I'd driven Armani to work a few times when she'd had car trouble, so taking her home was easier.

"Your aura's all screwy," she told me from the backseat when we were a block from her place. "It should be all soft and cloudlike, but yours is all jagged and broken."

"Uh-huh." I resisted the urge to ask if she saw disco balls and cacti floating in my energy field.

"And it's dark, like there's a shadow over your heart."

"Sounds about right." I was pretty broken, my nerves were frayed, and my heart was heavy. I swung my car into the driveway of the tiny house she owned.

"You shouldn't do it alone."

"Do what?" I panicked. What if she was able to pick up some sort of signal revealing my plans for Garcia?

"It."

"It?"

"Yes. You definitely shouldn't do it alone."

I helped her to her front door, got the door unlocked, and gently shoved her inside. "Get some sleep, Armani.

I'll give you a call in the morning to make sure you don't miss work."

I pondered her reading of my aura, disco balls, and cacti as I drove home, until lights from a police cruiser shone in my rearview mirror.

Pulling over, I glanced at my speedometer thinking that perhaps I'd been speeding. Rolling down my window, I forced myself to take deep, calming breaths as I waited for the police officer to approach my car. Whatever this was, I could handle it.

"Out of the car, ma'am," he said.

I leaned forward. "Paul?"

"Out of the car."

A shiver skittered down my spine, but I pushed the momentary fear away. Paul might have a terrible temper, but I'd given him no reason to be upset with me. I got out.

The beam of a flashlight blinded me. I raised a hand to ward off the light.

"What are you doing out here?" Paul asked.

I couldn't see his face and something in his voice scared me.

"Was I speeding?" I asked.

"Have you been drinking?" he countered.

"Because I know I wasn't talking on the phone." That's how we'd met the first time, when he'd pulled me over for talking on my cell while driving.

"Have you been drinking?" he asked again, his tone harsh, commanding.

I shook my head. "No. I was a designated driver. I was just driving a couple of friends home."

"After leaving where?"

"Foxy's." I winced as I made the revelation.

"And you weren't drinking?"

"No. Why did you pull me over?" I asked again, annoyed that he was avoiding answering me.

"I wanted to see you."

I frowned. "Were you following me?"

"Maybe. I wanted to make sure you got home safe."

"And yet you stopped me. You do know that's creepy and not romantic, right?"

"I wanted to see if you'd changed your mind about taking me as a date to the wedding, because if you did, I've got to find someone to cover my shift."

Acutely aware of how dark and deserted the road was, I said carefully, "I'm afraid not. Like I said, I'm going to be swamped with maid of honor duties. That's what I was doing at Foxy's tonight, hosting the bachelorette party." Getting the distinct impression he wasn't happy with getting no for an answer, I decided the wisest thing to do was to extricate myself from the situation, so I threw him a bone. "Maybe after the wedding we could get together?"

"Next week?" he asked hopefully.

"Sure." I didn't ask him for permission, I just got back into my car and closed the door. "Call me."

"Drive safe," he called as I pulled away.

I watched him disappear in my rearview mirror with the distinct impression I'd just narrowly escaped something unpleasant.

"Rough ride," I muttered, heading for home.

Chapter Twenty-Two

THE REST OF the week passed in a blur of work and visiting Katie. At least one of my aunts always seemed to be there, reading to her, talking to her. She watched us carefully every visit, but hadn't attempted to interact.

Still, we were all hopeful.

I wasn't so hopeful about Alice's wedding. I didn't hear from her after the bachelorette party even though I called her three times and left messages apologizing for being late.

I hadn't heard from Zeke either. He'd kissed me and then just disappeared from the planet.

I seemed to have that effect on men, since I hadn't heard from Patrick either. Not that I had expected to since he was doing the dad thing, but I'd thought, maybe even hoped, he might call to offer a pep talk.

I could have used a pep talk. The more I studied the itinerary of Garcia's daughter's wedding, the less sure I became I'd be able to pull off the job. Thankfully I didn't run into Delveccio, although I did see his daughter a number of times during my visits to the hospital. I was relieved I didn't have him asking me how my assassination plan was coming along because, frankly, it wasn't.

I told God all of these concerns while I got ready to go over to the B&B on Friday night. His response was to yawn.

I eyed the dog. "What about you?"

"Go ready," she panted.

"Okay, but remember what we talked about, your best behavior."

"Dog good. Dog good."

I took my time driving over, glancing occasionally at the gifts on the front seat. One was for Alice, the other for Aunt Susan. I hoped they'd be accepted in the spirit they were offered and not thrown back in my face.

While anxiety twisted in my gut, DeeDee practically vibrated with excitement. Hanging her head out the window, she barked, "Dog good! Dog good!" at every dog or pedestrian we passed.

Loretta and Leslie sat on the front porch with Alice, and Aunt Susan was weeding a flowerbed when I pulled up to the B&B.

"Remember," I pleaded with DeeDee. "Gentle and polite."

"Dog good."

I handed her Susan's gift, which she took gently between her jaws. Taking her leash, I led her toward the women.

"Maggie!" Loretta trilled. "It's just us girls tonight. Lamont went to pick up his parents from the airport, but he broke down."

"In Newark?" I winced at the thought of the visitors' first impression of the beautiful Garden State being one of our rougher cities.

"Apparently they're near the arena and are oohing and ahhing over it," Susan muttered.

"Templeton's gone to get them," Leslie said.

"Hi there, DeeDee." Alice pointedly greeted the dog, but not me.

That hurt.

Aunt Susan turned in our direction, freezing when she spotted the dog. I saw her reach for something in the grass and realized her hedge clippers lay only inches away.

"Gently," I prompted under my breath.

DeeDee stepped up so that less than a foot separated her and Susan.

"It's for you," I told my aunt, who seemed rooted to the spot. "Since we ruined your last one. Take it."

Slowly and carefully Susan reached out and took the wrapped gift.

DeeDee released it gently, then rolled on her back and panted, "Sorry. Sorry. Dog good. Dog good."

Aunt Susan stared at the mutt, holding the package in a death grip.

"Isn't she just the most adorable thing," Alice gushed, coming off the porch and kneeling to rub the dog's belly. "So sweet."

"Open your present," Leslie prompted.

Susan slowly got to her feet and moved away from the dog before she ripped open the wrapping paper.

"What is it?" Loretta asked.

"An umbrella," Susan said.

"To replace the one we damaged," I explained quickly.

"Was it *your* teeth that left the puncture marks?" Susan asked, seeming convinced DeeDee wasn't about to attack her.

I let the jab go.

"I wanted to talk to the three of you for a minute if that's okay. A family meeting of sorts." I looked up at Aunt Leslie. She nodded her approval.

"C'mon, DeeDee," Alice said, getting to her feet. "Let's go in the back and play fetch. I bet Maggie's too busy to play fetch with you." Tugging the leash from my limp fingers, she led the dog to the rear of the property.

"Thank you for this." Aunt Susan waved the umbrella.

"You're welcome. I'm sorry . . . about what happened to the last one."

"Things can be replaced, people can't." She looked pointedly in the direction Alice had disappeared.

Sighing heavily, I followed her up onto the porch.

"I wanted to give Alice a wedding gift," I began nervously. "But before I do, I wanted to make sure it was okay with all of you."

My aunts leaned forward, listening intently.

"But if you think it's a bad idea, I won't."

"Just tell us," Leslie prompted kindly.

"I want to give her Mom's blue necklace," I blurted out on a single breath.

There was a long moment of silence. Leslie sat back in her chair, Loretta fiddled with the pearl bracelet she wore, and Susan studied her umbrella.

"She always loved it and Mom wanted her to have it. She told me so once, in one of her lucid moments, at least I'm pretty sure she was lucid."

"It's something old and something blue," Aunt Loretta gushed. "It's a perfect gift."

"I seem to remember Mary saying just that," Leslie said slowly.

We all looked to Aunt Susan to see if she'd give me her blessing too. She was examining the folds of the umbrella.

"Let the girl do it," Loretta prompted.

"I think it would mean a lot to Alice," I said.

Susan looked up, unshed tears making her eyes shine.

A terrible crash came from the backyard.

"That dog!" Venom dripped from Aunt Susan's accusation.

I ran into the backyard, hoping that whatever klutzy thing DeeDee had done could be fixed. I wasn't prepared for the scene I encountered. I stopped short.

The barbecue grill lay on its side, that's what had made the terrible noise, but it wasn't the problem.

"Help me!" Alice screamed in terror.

Frank Velicky, her six-foot, two-hundred-pound, violent ex, who I'd thought was still in prison, advanced on her with a baseball bat raised overhead. DeeDee stood between them growling and baring her teeth.

Aunt Susan had followed me to the backyard to see

what all the commotion was about. She barreled past me before I could stop her.

"You beast," she shouted, brandishing her hedge clippers. She was so intent on using them on DeeDee she didn't notice Frank until it was too late.

"Look out!" My shouted warning came too late.

Her momentum carried her directly into Frank's path. He easily ripped the garden tool from her grasp.

"What is it with the bitches in this family who can't mind their own business?" he roared.

Like Alice, Susan backed away from him, her eyes round with fear.

"Leave them alone," I shouted, trying to draw his attention away from them.

He swung the bat at Susan. Stumbling away, she tripped and fell to the ground.

Alice screamed.

I charged at Frank as he raised the bat to take another swing at her.

DeeDee got to him first. She hit him square in the chest, mid-leap, with enough force to knock him onto his back. He dropped the bat and clippers.

She yelped in pain when he punched her in the rib cage.

He and I both dove for the clippers. I held on to them for dear life as he tried to wrench them away from me.

"Get inside!" I shouted to Alice and Susan.

"Bitch!" Frank grunted, getting to his feet and dragging me along the ground.

"Go let!" DeeDee growled, trying to get between us.

She was trying to help, but inadvertently forced me to release the hedge clippers.

"Look out," I warned breathlessly as he swung them at her.

She dodged them . . . barely . . . and then jumped between Frank and me.

"Hurt Maggie no!" she barked.

"Stay away from him, Doomsday," I pleaded as I crawled backward, trying to put some space between myself and the violent felon. "Do as I say and get away from him."

A quick glance around revealed that Alice was nowhere in sight, but Aunt Susan was still on the ground, looking dazed.

I had to keep Frank focused on me.

"What are you doing here, Frank?"

"I wanted to talk to Alice."

"Talk? Is that how the grill got knocked over, because you were talking?"

"My sister told me she was getting married and I had to stop her."

I decided that, if I lived through this ordeal, I was going to insist that Alice listen to my warnings from now on, even when she was mad at me.

"She's mine!" Frank roared.

"Away get," DeeDee growled.

"Easy, Doomsday," I soothed. "Easy girl."

She looked at me. "DeeDee. Doomsday DeeDee."

Frank took the dog's moment of distraction to make

his move. He kicked her, hard. The dull thud broke something in my heart. She crumpled to the ground.

"Doomsday!" I screamed, scrambling to throw my body on top of hers before he could hurt her again.

"You're even dumber than Alice." Frank raised the clippers, preparing to spear me with the sharp blades.

It was ironic that after I'd killed two murderers, and was trying to kill a drug dealer, that I was going to die in the backyard of the only place I'd ever really called home.

As the blades whistled through the air toward me, I was too paralyzed by fear to even move out of the way.

The crack of the report was loud enough to make my ears ring.

It took me a moment to realize that I wasn't dead, that I hadn't been stabbed.

Frank look surprised too as he stumbled backward.

The clippers were no longer in the hands he raised to protect himself as the baseball bat arced through the air at him.

There was a sickening crunch as the wood broke bones in his hands.

He fell to the ground and before he could even plead for mercy, the bat cracked one of his kneecaps.

He howled in pain.

Realizing I was no longer in danger of dying, I was able to look up at my savior. Zeke stood over the other man, brandishing the bat, daring him to make a move.

"Are you okay?" I whispered to DeeDee, leveraging myself off her.

"Ow," she whined.

I stroked her head. "You're a good dog."

I looked over at Aunt Susan. She was sitting up, and despite the blood trickling from her temple, she seemed clearheaded.

Before I could get over to check on her, the yard filled with people. Police shouting at Zeke to lower the weapon. Aunt Loretta yelling at the police to arrest Frank.

Aunt Leslie holding a sobbing Alice.

It took a while to get everything sorted out, but eventually the police took all of our statements, Frank was hauled off, the emergency medical technicians gave Aunt Susan the all-clear, and DeeDee started whining, "Gotta! Gotta!"

"I'm going to walk the dog and then I'll be back," I told Susan and Zeke, who were sitting on patio chairs.

I didn't even bother grabbing her leash, just led her away. "You were a very brave dog," I told her as we walked.

She flashed one of her all-teeth grins at me that undoubtedly looked scary to passersby.

When we returned, Aunt Susan was alone on the patio. She held out a large bowl of water to me.

I stared at it, uncomprehending.

"I thought the dog might be thirsty," she explained.

I looked from the mutt to the bowl. "It's crystal."

"She saved our lives."

"It's lead crystal."

"She saved my life. It's my bowl and I can do whatever I want with it."

"Then you give it to her." I sank onto a patio chair and watched as Susan gingerly approached DeeDee.

She put the bowl down, pointed at it, and said, "There you go."

DeeDee, on her best behavior, looked to me for permission.

I nodded.

She lapped up the water enthusiastically.

I held my breath as Aunt Susan tentatively reached toward her and patted her back.

"Good dog," she whispered.

DeeDee lay down and rolled over. To my amazement, my aunt got down on the grass and continued to pet her.

"You okay?" Zeke asked.

I jumped, startled by his return. I turned to face the man who'd saved my life.

He looked older than I'd ever seen him. Haggard almost, as though he hadn't been sleeping.

"Thank you," I said quietly.

He pulled me into a tight embrace, pressing his cheek to mine. I could feel his heartbeat pounding.

"You scared me to death, Maggie."

"You saved my life."

"If I'd been a second later . . ."

I pressed my lips to his, effectively silencing him.

I leaned back and smiled into his haunted gaze. "But you weren't," I soothed. "That's a hell of a swing you've got."

He smiled ruefully. "I guess all the time I've spent at batting cages finally paid off."

"Is she hungry?" Aunt Susan called.

Zeke and I jumped apart.

I strode over to where my aunt was stroking my pet. Crouching down, I asked, "Are you hungry, DeeDee?"

"Meat?" she panted.

"Do you have any meat?" I asked Aunt Susan.

"I've got roasted chicken."

"She'd love some of that."

I supported Susan as she got to her feet unsteadily. "Are you okay?"

Pressing a hand to the bandage the EMT had plastered on her head, she smiled. "I'm a tough old bird, but I don't think my kung fu master is going to approve of the way I handled myself tonight."

"I think you handled yourself just fine."

She patted my arm and whispered, "See? I told you Zeke is a good boy."

I nodded.

"Come with me, Dee," she commanded, walking into the house.

DeeDee cocked her head to the side and looked at me inquiringly.

"Go ahead, but remember your manners and try not to break anything."

She pranced after my aunt.

I turned to Zeke. "How's Alice doing?"

"She's shaken up, but okay. I guess she never outgrew her tendency for choosing the wrong guys?"

I shook my head. "Until Lamont."

"You hope."

I looked at him sharply. "Do you know something I don't?"

He raised his hands defensively. "I just meant that she doesn't have the best track record when it comes to men."

"Neither do I," I muttered. "I mean what kind of woman would kiss a guy who'd walk out on her and not call for days."

He looked away.

I stepped in front of him, forcing him to meet my gaze. "What was that the other day, Zeke? Some sort of game? You drop the bombshell you're not gay, kiss me, and then just disappear."

A muscle in his jaw jumped. "It wasn't a game," he said tightly.

"You made a fool of me."

"That wasn't my intention."

"What was your intention?"

He rubbed his lower lip with his thumb, signaling his agitation. "I was pissed that you thought I was gay and I wanted to make you squirm."

"You did that," I said dryly.

"Things got out of hand. I didn't expect . . ."

"Expect what?"

He leaned forward to whisper in my ear. "I didn't expect this." He nipped my earlobe, trailed his open mouth across my chin, and covered my lips with his.

Fireworklike sensations rocketed through my body and I swayed toward him, as his tongue captured mine.

Just as abruptly he pulled away, leaving me wanting more.

"I didn't expect that," he said raggedly. "I didn't expect to practically explode the moment I touched you."

Jamming his hands into the pockets of his jeans, he turned away from me. "I'm not staying. I'll be here through the wedding and I'll finish the job I came to town to do, and then I'm gone."

"Where?"

He shrugged. "To wherever the next challenge takes me."

"So go."

"I could have slept with you and then walked out of your life." He spun around to face me again. "You deserve better than a one-night stand." A note of desperation threaded through his tone. I didn't know whether he was trying to prove to me or himself that he wasn't a bad guy.

"I appreciate that." My voice was clogged with tears.

"I hurt you."

I shook my head.

"I'm not cut out for relationships. It's not you, Maggie. You're great."

"Save me the whole it's-not-you-it's-me thing. I'm a big girl."

"And I'm a big jerk."

His voice was so heavy with regret that I took pity on him. "But you're a heroic big jerk," I joked weakly. "How did you happen to be here just when we needed you?"

"Seating arrangements."

I looked up at him, trying to decide if he was speaking in code.

"Alice has been going nuts over the seating arrangements. More of Lamont's friends and family are attending than she'd originally thought and it's thrown her into a tizzy. And me."

I grinned. "A tizzy?"

He nodded.

"You do know that there are reasons why people think you're gay, right? Using the word *tizzy* in conversation is one of them."

Chapter Twenty-Three

I WAS IN a tizzy the next morning, overwhelmed by everything I had to do. It wasn't helping matters that the animals insisted on accompanying me on my morning errands.

"The itinerary clearly states that Jose Garcia is expected to visit the venue for his daughter's wedding this morning," God harped.

"So you've said three times," I answered, scooping up his terrarium and heading for the front door.

"If you don't hurry, you're going to miss his scheduled departure."

"And if you don't shut up, you're going to miss a scheduled feeding. Come, DeeDee." The dog trailed after us as I hustled toward my car, the terrarium bouncing against my hip with every step I took.

"Shotgun!" God shouted.

I ducked down, scanning the area for the gunman. DeeDee crouched beside us.

"What in the world are you doing?" God asked in his most superior drawl. "Besides making a fool of yourself."

"You said there was a gun."

"I called shotgun," he corrected. "Meaning I get to sit in the front seat. Don't you know anything?"

I barely defeated the urge to "accidentally" drop his enclosure. I stowed it in the front seat and buckled the seat belt around it before letting DeeDee into the back.

"Air?" she panted.

I opened the rear windows for her. "Get ready for a rough ride," I warned them both, peeling out of the parking lot and speeding toward Garcia's home. We got there just in time to see his car pulling out of the driveway.

"I *told* you we were going to be late," God said.

"And yet here we are following him," I countered.

"You should shoot out his tires and force his car off a cliff and make it explode in a giant fireball that can be seen for miles."

I glanced over at him. He'd climbed out of the terrarium and planted himself on top of the headrest of the passenger seat. "You are seriously watching too much TV."

"Squirrel!" DeeDee shrieked from the backseat.

"It's a good plan," God said defensively.

"Well, it might be, *if* I was a qualified stunt driver and a crack shot, but I'm neither. Plus there are no cliffs around here."

"You get too bogged down in details."

"One of the details I'm bogged down by is the fact I need to do the job in public," I reminded him.

"Squirrel!" DeeDee squealed.

I turned to glare at her. "Will you stop?"

"Light! Light!" God squeaked.

Returning my attention to the road, I saw an amber traffic light turn red. I slammed on the brakes.

"Aaaah!" God screamed.

"Ow!" DeeDee grunted as she slammed into the back of my seat, jarring my teeth.

"Everybody okay?" I asked.

"No thanks to you," God groused.

"Okay DeeDee." Her dog breath was hot on my neck. I realized I hadn't seen which way Garcia turned. "Where'd he go?"

"Way that! Way that!" DeeDee pointed her nose to the right.

"Not that way," God drawled snootily. "Go to the left."

When the light turned green, I went straight.

We never did catch up with him.

AN HOUR BEFORE Alice's wedding rehearsal was scheduled to begin, I was slipping on my uncomfortable high-heeled shoes, getting ready to head out the door.

"I don't see the point of a rehearsal," God said for the third time. "It's like cattle being led to slaughter. Walk down a chute, stop at the end, the guy calling the shots does his thing, and boom, done. Is that really so complicated it needs to be rehearsed?"

My cell phone rang.

"Are you going to answer that?" God asked.

"No. No doubt it's someone checking up on me, because, as you so eloquently pointed out, it's a real challenge to be a cow in a chute."

It continued to ring until it went to my voicemail.

And then it started ringing again.

I groaned. "Yes, I'm on my way. No, I won't be late."

This time I snatched it up and answered without bothering to look at the caller ID. "What?"

"Miss Lee?" a startled woman asked.

"Yes."

"This is Apple Blossom Estates—"

"Something happened to Katie?" I gasped, my body going cold.

"What happened?" God demanded.

I waved him off.

"Nothing too serious," the woman said.

I sagged against the wall in relief.

"But we wanted to inform you that she pulled out her IV and so—"

"I'm on my way." I disconnected the call without letting her finish. "Katie pulled out her IV," I told God.

"Is she okay?"

"I don't know. I have to get to the hospital."

I grabbed my keys and headed for the door.

"Take me," God demanded.

"I can't. I—"

"Please, Mags," God asked, suddenly humble. "Please?"

I was torn, knowing that he cared deeply for the little girl, but unable to figure out the logistics of sneaking him into the hospital. "How?"

"Your purse looks soft."

I looked at the small black satin clutch. "What about your sensitive skin?"

"I'll survive."

"Okay." I dumped the contents of the purse onto the kitchen table, opened his terrarium, and extended a hand, and he scurried up my arm.

"Any chance you could stuff it with tissues?" he asked.

Running into the bathroom I grabbed a handful of tissues, and as I ran back out, I almost tripped over the big, black dog who'd planted herself in my path.

"Go DeeDee."

"You can't, honey," I said, tottering toward the front door on my heels. "I don't know how long this will take."

She ran in front of me and blocked the exit. "Go DeeDee."

"Let her come," God said from his perch by my right ear.

"But she'll have to stay in the car."

"Nap," DeeDee said.

"See," God chided, "the beast has a plan, do you?"

So the three of us rushed to the hospital. God climbed into the purse as I put the car into park.

"Make sure you leave the windows open for her," he said from the recesses of my handbag.

Cracking them open, I patted DeeDee on the head. "Be good. Take your nap."

Considering I could barely stay upright in the stupid shoes, I crossed the parking lot and traversed the hospital in record time. I was, however, moving too fast to stop when a man stepped in front of me in the hallway leading to Katie's room.

"Uggh," I cried as we collided. I almost dropped the purse containing God as I waved my arms, trying to regain my balance.

Fortunately the man grabbed both my arms and steadied me. "Nice dress."

I looked into Delveccio's face. He wasn't smiling.

"My niece," I panted. "They called . . ."

Something shifted in his gaze and he patted my cheek tenderly. "Go."

Hurrying past him, I rushed into Katie's room.

She wasn't there.

The bed where she'd spent all this time lay empty. There were bloodstains on the white sheets.

"No!" I gasped.

"What's going on?" God asked.

"She's gone."

"Gone?" I could have sworn I heard a hiccuping sob from the bag.

"Miss Lee?" It was the voice from the phone.

I spun around. One of the night nurses, who I'd seen a million times but never learned her name, smiled at me.

I swayed unsteadily on my feet.

"Why don't you sit?" she suggested, taking my arm and leading me out of the room to the waiting area. "An orderly is going to change the sheets."

"Where is she?" I asked, sitting rigidly in the same

chair I'd sat in when Mr. Calvin had told me his wife had killed my sister.

"They took her for an X-ray."

"An X-ray? I don't understand."

"She fell when she tried to get out of bed. Her wrist was swollen and the attending wanted to make sure it hadn't fractured."

"She tried to get out of bed? I was here this afternoon and I couldn't get her to even reach for Dino the dinosaur."

She patted my arm reassuringly and lowered her voice to a whisper. "The doctors would have my head for telling you this, but it's a good sign. A very good sign."

I looked around for disco balls or cacti, but saw none.

"Wait here," the nurse said. "I'll come get you when they bring her back."

She left and I sank back in the seat.

"Open the bag before I suffocate!" God demanded.

Hands shaking, it took me two tries to get it open. He poked his head out.

"Did you hear that?" I asked.

"Every word."

I looked up to see Delveccio lumbering toward me.

"What's all the excitement?" he asked. "What the hell is that?" He stared at my purse.

God hadn't bothered to hide.

"He's Katie's pet. I thought maybe if I brought her something from home . . ."

Delveccio nodded, staring at the lizard. "He looks . . ."

Don't say cute. Please don't say cute . . . I silently prayed.

"He looks smart," Delveccio said.

God beamed. "Finally. Someone who doesn't objectify me, but appreciates me for my true worth."

"Why's he making that noise?" Delveccio asked.

"He vocalizes a lot." I glanced around. "No Vinnie?"

"He gets Saturday nights off. He likes to go to clubs. Flex his muscles. Pick up chickies."

I bit back a smile at "chickies."

"I hear your niece is doing better."

"That's what they're telling me."

"Dominic is too."

"Really?" I asked.

"Who's Dominic?" God asked.

"They think he's dreaming now." Delveccio sat in the seat beside me. "That brainwave-thing machine is doing a tango."

"Who's Dominic?" God asked again.

"I'm happy for you, Mr. Delveccio. I'm so happy your grandson is doing better." I said to appease the lizard. I patted Delveccio's arm to make my point.

From the way he stiffened, I guessed that mobsters aren't accustomed to being touched. Before I could jerk my hand away, he covered it with his own.

"You are one strange gal, Maggie Lee."

He released me and surveyed me from head to toe. "So you're in your femme fatale outfit today."

Once again, I didn't bother explaining to him that this black dress was the only one I owned.

"Big plans for tonight?"

I remembered the rehearsal I was supposed to be at.

Alice was going to kill me. "I did have plans until the hospital called."

"You know you're running out of time, right? If you don't finish the Garcia thing today or tomorrow . . ."

I nodded. "I have a plan."

"Good. I heard about that little skirmish you got into with that woman . . . your niece's other aunt."

I sighed. "I'm sure the whole hospital heard about it."

"She's the reason you needed the advance?"

I nodded.

"You should have said."

I glanced over at him, suddenly worried. "It won't affect my work."

"No. I mean, you shoulda told me. I might have been able to get one of my boys to take care of the problem for you, but now, now no one can touch her, because the cops'll come straight to you."

"Miss Lee?" the nurse called, motioning me toward Katie's room.

I stood and looked down at the mobster. "I'm glad Dominic's doing better. I hope he continues to improve."

"Thanks. Good luck tomorrow."

"Thanks." I hurried toward Katie's room, throwing the nurse a grateful smile as I passed her.

She was alone in the room. The sides of her bed had been raised and I had to get close to the bed to see over them.

"Hey, Baby Girl," I cooed.

She smiled weakly at me, raising her arm.

I grabbed her hand and squeezed.

"She's going to sleep." An older doctor walked in. He grinned down at her. "She had quite the adventure and it's tired her out."

As if on cue, Katie's eyes drifted shut.

The doctor tilted his head, indicating we should leave the room. Grudgingly, I released her hand.

"Don't you dare leave before I get a chance to see her," God piped up from the bag.

I made an after-you motion to the doctor. Once his back was to me, I unclasped the bag and laid it on the bed before following him out to the hall.

"She made amazing progress today," he said. "She'll sleep through the night now."

"But what if she falls out of bed?"

"She didn't fall out of bed, Miss Lee. She yanked out her tubes and *attempted* to get out of bed. That's when she fell." He smiled kindly at me. "Any patient who tries to get out of bed is a good thing in my book. It means that they want to move, to live. It means she's ready to recover."

"Really?" I was so choked up with tears, I could barely speak. After all this time, all this hoping against hope, and now . . .

"Really," the doctor said. "Go home. Get some rest, Miss Lee. I get the feeling your niece is going to keep us all on our toes." He turned and walked away.

Not only was she not going to die, but she was going to recover. It was too much for me. I didn't try to stop the tears from streaming down my face.

I stumbled back into her room. God was curled up on her pillow, whispering in her ear.

He looked up at me.

Unable to speak, I held out the purse. He climbed back in.

"You did it, Maggie," he said softly. "Everything you did was worth it. Our girl is back."

Chapter Twenty-Four

THE SHOCK OF Katie's condition had worn off and a sense of giddy excitement had taken its place by the time I arrived at the restaurant where the rehearsal dinner for Alice and Lamont was being held.

I practically skipped into the room, my purse, containing a lizard, in one hand, and a wrapped box, containing my mother's necklace, in the other. The guests were all seated, eating their main course.

I scanned the room looking for the bride- and groom-to-be, intent on congratulating the happy couple. I didn't see them, but I did spot Zeke, who was hurrying toward me, consternation furrowing his usually perfect brow. I smiled at him, eager to share the fantastic news about Katie.

"Don't!" he shouted, breaking into a run.

I stopped in my tracks, trying to figure out what he didn't want me to do. Out of the corner of my eye, I saw a flash of white, and then I felt the blow.

My head snapped back, my cheek burned, and I stumbled backward. I didn't even realize that I'd been slapped, until Alice tried to do it again.

My best friend, her face contorted with rage, was screaming at me, but I couldn't make out what she was saying. My ears were ringing because she'd hit me. She hit me! And she was going to do it again.

I stared to raise my hands defensively, but God screamed, "Help!"

I dropped my hands to my side, allowing Alice to slap me across the face again.

Then Lamont was inserting his mountainous self between us.

She was still screaming. "I'm not going to let you ruin my wedding! I'm not! I won't allow you to wreck my day!"

I stumbled away from the assault and would have fallen, but Zeke caught me around the waist.

"You're not invited, Maggie," Alice shouted.

"You don't mean that, honey," Lamont soothed. "She's your best friend."

"No! She was, but not anymore!"

Straightening, I pulled free of Zeke's grasp. "I'm sorry."

"Don't," Zeke warned on a whisper.

I didn't listen to him. "I'm sorry, Alice."

"You're sorry? You missed the rehearsal, Maggie. My rehearsal."

"Cattle. Chute," God groused from inside the bag.

"I can explain." I stepped toward Alice, intent on earning her forgiveness.

She lunged at me like a wild animal.

Lamont tightened his grip on his soon-to-be-wife. "Maybe this isn't the time," he suggested gently.

I hesitated, unsure, suddenly aware that a roomful of people were staring at me, staring at the woman who was ruining Alice's wedding. My aunts look horrified, Alice's friends were smirking, and Lamont's friends and family looked befuddled.

"Get out." Alice fixed me with a look so cold that I physically shivered. "And don't you dare show up tomorrow."

"Hurrah!" God cheered from the bag. "Now you don't have to wear the ugly dress."

"C'mon," Zeke urged from behind me. "Give her some time to cool down."

"But—" I protested weakly. I begged Alice with my eyes to hear me out, to understand, to forgive me.

The room fell silent, waiting to see if I'd leave with my tail between my legs. I'd never felt more lonely in my life than I did in that room full of people.

Someone cleared their throat. The sound reverberated through the room. Footsteps crossed the room toward us. My eyes didn't leave Alice's face to see who it was.

"I, um . . . I . . ." Templeton said softly.

I whipped my gaze over to him.

"I'd actually like to hear Maggie's explanation," he said loudly enough for the room to hear.

Murmuring reached my ears as I stared at him, wondering what he was up to.

"Because," he continued, "Loretta was just telling me

a little while ago how worried she was. She said it was unlike Maggie to show up late. She said Maggie had always been there for every step of her weddings, even when Maggie hadn't approved of the unions. So, I was thinking that she probably has a really good explanation for whatever prevented her from being here."

I could have hugged the rat. I don't know why he made that little speech. Maybe it was because he was trying to look like a good guy, or maybe he felt we shared a kinship because of the whole attic thing, but whatever his reason, he threw me a lifeline when I was drowning.

He offered me an encouraging smile. "Tell them, Maggie."

"The hospital called," I started.

"Louder," Zeke prompted from behind me.

"Are you looking that bridezilla in the eye?" Godzilla asked. "Look her in the eye and let it rip!"

I took their advice.

I looked Alice in the eye, stood up straight, and spoke loudly. "The hospital called. Katie had ripped out her IV."

The room filled with murmurs.

Alice looked away.

"And she'd fallen out of bed." I shook my head. "Technically, she tried to get out of bed and she fell."

"Oh no!" I heard Loretta exclaim.

I turned in her direction. "She's okay. They thought she might have fractured her wrist, but she's okay."

I turned my attention back to Alice. Sobbing softly, she'd buried her head in her hands.

Hating that I'd made her cry, I said in a rush, "I'm

sorry that I missed the rehearsal. I'm sorry that I've been the worst maid of honor ever. But most of all I'm sorry you don't think I'm your friend." Turning, I almost crashed into Zeke.

He grabbed my elbows to keep me from toppling over. "Take it easy, Maggie," he urged on a whisper.

I gritted my teeth, trying hard not to burst into tears, while he and everyone watched.

"Maggie, wait," Alice said.

I froze, staring into Zeke's concerned blue gaze.

"Just leave," God urged.

"I'm sorry," Alice said. "I should have known . . . You saved my life last night."

Zeke leaned forward and whispered in my ear. "Don't hold on to a grudge that's just going to cause you heartache."

I stiffened. Hadn't Patrick accused me of nursing grudges? And hadn't Alice said that I was holding one against my father? Was I about to do it again? Poison a relationship?

"I'm in a tizzy," I whispered so that only Zeke could hear.

"I know." I could hear the smile in his voice. "But now's the time to show them what the amazing Maggie Lee is made of." He kissed my cheek, released my arms, and stepped back, leaving me alone to make my decision.

I turned slowly to face Alice. She looked as distraught as I felt.

She took a step toward me, but then faltered as I raised my arm, holding the box out to her.

"Take it." I stepped closer to her, the box extended.

Her hands shook as she took it.

"Open it."

She looked at me, unsure.

I nodded. "Open it."

Fingers trembling, she ripped off the silver wrapping paper, letting it fall to the ground in a pile. She hesitated before lifting the lid. Two big, fat tears dripped on the box.

"Open your friend's gift, honey," Lamont urged, reaching around her to support the bottom of the box.

Slowly she did.

Her eyes grew wide when she saw the necklace. "I can't."

"Sure you can. It's something old and something blue."

"But it's your mom's."

I closed the distance between us and lifted the blue pendant out of the box. "She wanted you to have it." Lifting it over her head, I attached the clasp. "And I want my best friend to have it."

I stepped back to admire how it looked.

She threw herself into my arms, sobbing. "I'm sorry! I'm sorry! I'm so sorry, Maggie."

"I'll forgive you this time," I joked, blinking back tears. "But you'd better never get married again"—I winked at Lamont—"because I can't stand this bridezilla shit."

"Language, Margaret!" Aunt Susan called from across the room.

The whole place erupted in laughter.

Loretta hurried over to us. Slipping her arm through Templeton's, she suggested, "Why don't you two go freshen up?"

"Good idea," Lamont said.

"I'll tell them to hold off on serving dessert," Templeton offered.

Alice turned to her soon-to-be-husband. "Your family and friends are going to think I'm crazy."

Stroking her cheek tenderly he said, "All that's important is for them to know that I'm crazy about you."

He kissed her and the room started to cheer.

"The ladies' room is down the hall and to your left," Zeke told me. He gave me a slight shove. "Go."

I hurried out, eager to get away from the curious eyes hanging on my every move, with Alice close on my heels.

"I really am sorry, Maggie."

I wasn't looking for another apology. I was trying to figure out what was going on.

When we got to the restroom, I put my purse down on the counter.

"What is that stench?" God asked as I stepped into the maroon and gold room.

I sniffed the air. "Air freshener."

I squatted down to make sure none of the stalls with ornate wooden doors were occupied. Satisfied we were alone, I turned to face Alice. "Who are you and what have you done with my best friend?"

Shaking her head, she turned to look at her reflection in the mirror as though she was looking for the same answer.

"You hit me. You physically hit me. The Alice I know would never do that. Not in a million years."

She hung her head, ashamed, leaning on the marble countertop for support.

"You carry ants outside, yet you just slapped your best friend." I grabbed her by the shoulders and shook her slightly. "What's going on?"

"Hormones?" she asked weakly.

"Hormones have caused you to completely and totally lose your mind?"

"I dunno. It's just that everything's happening so fast."

"*You* wanted it to happen fast."

"I know, but . . ." She trailed off.

The only sound was a faucet dripping.

"You could call it off. There's still time."

She bit her lower lip.

"Do you want to call it off? Is that what this is all about?"

"I love him."

"I don't get it."

"He's sweet and kind and smart and—"

"I don't get why you're intent on publicly humiliating me. You did it at Foxy's and now tonight. If you're having doubts, just come out and say so, but don't try to blame everything on me."

"I'm not."

"You have. From choosing the menu, to picking out your dress, you've been on my case at every step. I'm sorry if I can't give your wedding my full attention, but I do have other things going on in my life."

"I know."

Feeling like the conversation was going nowhere, I said, "You should get back to your guests."

"You think I'm making a mistake," she accused.

"Are you?"

She sagged against the wall. "I don't know." She started to cry again.

I opened my purse. God was lying in there like it was a hammock. He made a show of yawning before handing me a tissue. I passed it to Alice.

"You think I'm stupid," she sniffled.

"For getting knocked up?"

"She is! She is!" God shouted.

"What's that noise?" Alice asked, saving me from having to answer the question.

"What noise?" I crossed my fingers behind my back, hoping the lizard would keep quiet.

"She means me, you idiot!" God screamed.

"That squeaking noise. It sounds as though it's coming from your purse." She eyed it suspiciously.

"Oh that," I said slowly. "I brought Katie's pet to the hospital. I thought she might like to see him."

"In your purse?" Alice asked.

I shrugged. "I was on the way out the door to the rehearsal when the hospital called. It was a lot easier than carrying the terrarium around."

"So you really were going to come to the rehearsal?"

I blinked, more than a little offended. "You thought I wasn't?"

She shrugged.

"I took on Frank for you, but you thought I wouldn't show for the run-through of your wedding?" A terrible thought occurred to me. "Maybe you don't want me there. Maybe that's why you keep creating these scenes, because you don't want me to show up. If that's it, just say it. Trust me, I have other things to do tomorrow."

"She does!" God piped up. "She's got to kill a man."

"Maybe you should let the poor thing out," Alice suggested.

"He's fine."

"But maybe he's not getting enough air," Alice worried.

"Now that sounds more like the way my friend usually behaves," I said.

"Maybe there's hope for me yet?"

"Maybe." I gave her a quick hug. "Come on, let's get you back to your party."

"Promise me you'll be there tomorrow, Maggie?"

"Don't do it!" God urged.

"Of course I'll be there . . . no matter what you choose to do."

She looked again at her reflection as though expecting the mirror to hold the answers she was looking for. She touched the blue pendant. "I can't believe you remembered how much I always loved this thing. Are you sure you want me to have it?"

"It's lapis lazuli, not a fancy diamond. Besides, my mom wanted you to have it. She used to say you were the only one who appreciated it." The memory brought a warm feeling to my chest. It had been so long since I'd been able to recall anything good about my mother.

I blinked away tears that caught me by surprise.

"Do you miss her?"

Living with someone suffering from a mental illness is like waking up in a strange bed every day. You have no idea where you are or what the day holds. I didn't miss the chaos that often surrounded her, but I missed the good moments. I missed my mom. I nodded, brushing away the tears.

"I miss mine too."

We hugged.

Loretta bustled into the restroom, smiled widely when she saw we weren't pulling one another's hair out, and said, "You girls can't spend the rest of the night in here. Get out there."

Obediently Alice left. I snatched up my purse and went to follow.

Catching my arm, Loretta chided gently. "Put on some lipstick, dear. You look like Death."

I glanced at my reflection. She wasn't wrong. My pale face could have used a splash of color. "I didn't bring any."

She immediately whipped out a tube of lipstick and brandished it in front of my face. "Take it," she challenged.

I did, cringing at how bright the red shone.

Loretta beamed at me in the mirror. "That's my favorite. It's called Poison Kiss. Isn't it great?"

My gaze dropped to the vial of poison hanging around my neck. For a few minutes, I'd forgotten what I had to do the next day.

But first I had to survive the night.

Chapter Twenty-Five

I MADE IT through the rest of the rehearsal dinner unscathed. I met Lamont's family and friends, posed for pictures with Alice, and ate two pieces of cake. (I'd missed dinner and was starving.)

I was just inhaling the crumbs of the second piece when Aunt Susan walked up to me. I thought I'd found a pretty secluded corner to hide in, but I should have known that I couldn't hide from her.

"Margaret?"

I swallowed my crumbs. "I know what you're going to say." I really didn't want a lecture. I just wanted to eat my cake in peace, support Alice, and go home.

"I doubt that."

An unfamiliar man in his sixties, built as solid as an oak door, stepped up behind Susan.

Realizing that if I could engage him in conversation, Aunt Susan wouldn't get the chance to lecture me, I practically knocked her over to get him. "Hi. I'm Maggie. The maid of honor . . . well, as you probably heard, the world's worst maid of honor, but I've been forgiven that."

Smiling, he took my outstretched hand. "It's nice to meet you, Maggie. I've heard a lot about you."

There was something in his tone that made me think he wasn't just being polite with that statement. "You shouldn't believe everything you hear."

"It's almost all been good," he confided in a mock-whisper.

Confused, I asked, "I'm sorry. How do you know Alice and Lamont?"

He turned toward Susan and raised his eyebrows.

She placed a possessive hand on his elbow. "Margaret, I'd like you to meet Bob."

"Bob?" I asked, still confused.

"Bob Waites," he said.

"My date," Susan supplied.

I looked from her, to the man standing beside her, and back to her. "Your date?" I squeaked.

"Did you think she was a cloistered nun?" God asked from my handbag.

I ignored him. "Your date?" I asked again like an imbecile.

Susan nodded.

"We've been seeing each other for almost a year," Bob said, wrapping his beefy arm around my slim aunt's shoulders and squeezing.

For a moment, I was too shocked to speak. Aunt Loretta was the serial dater/marry-er in the family. I'd never known Aunt Susan to even go out for coffee with someone and now I was finding out she'd been seeing this guy for almost a year. "He's your boyfriend?" I squeaked.

She sniffed her disdain. "No adult over the age of twenty-five should ever refer to their romantic relationships as 'boyfriends' or 'girlfriends.' It sounds ridiculous."

"But," I spluttered. "How? How could you?"

"I told her it wasn't fair of her to just spring me on everyone like this," Bob said kindly. "She should have at least told you of my existence before dragging me to these shindigs."

I looked up at him. "I apologize. I've been rude. It's just . . ."

"It's just that no one in this family keeps secrets from one another," Susan said.

"Ha!" God shouted. "If you only knew!"

I gave the bag a shake to keep him quiet.

"Sensitive skin," he grumbled quietly.

"Susan's told me all you've done for your niece. Quite impressive," Bob said.

I nodded dumbly, still trying to wrap my head around the idea my uptight, straitlaced aunt had been secretly dating someone.

"My sister owns a real estate company. She's always looking to hire people with drive and initiative." He held out a business card. "You should give her a call if you're ever looking for a job."

I took the card. "Thanks."

"Bob's in construction," Susan said. "He's one of the

contractors I'd contacted about converting the barn. He's going to start working on it on Monday."

"But I don't know—" I began.

"You'll be able to tell your lawyer about it." Susan reached out and patted my arm. "It'll help you win custody."

"But I'm tapped out," I said. "I can't afford . . ."

"Don't worry about it," Susan said. "Bob's doing the job for us for cost."

"That's very kind of you, Mr. Waites, but—"

"Call me Bob," he interrupted.

"That's very kind of you, Bob, but—"

"It's been taken care of, Margaret." Aunt Susan's tone warned that I should stop arguing.

I opened my mouth, saw the determined glint in her eye, and said weakly, "Okay."

"Mind if I steal Maggie for a moment?" Zeke swept into the conversation, grabbed me around my waist, and propelled me away.

I went willingly.

"Are you okay?" he asked, leaning close, so that his breath tickled my ear.

"That's her date!"

"Yeah. I met him earlier. Nice enough guy. Solid."

"Where are we going?" I asked as he steered me across the room.

"The guests are almost all gone."

Glancing around the room, I realized he was right. The place was practically deserted.

"Say your good-byes to the happy couple," he said, "and then I'm taking you home."

I stumbled a bit, the heat in his last couple of words arrowing straight to my belly. I peeked up at him and saw the same warmth shimmering in his blue gaze. He smiled, a slow, lazy grin filled with sensual promise.

"Are you two leaving?" Alice asked, interrupting the moment.

"Unless you need us for something," Zeke responded smoothly, as though he hadn't been flirting with me the moment before.

"No. Of course not. You've done so much." Alice moved to hug him, which meant he had to let go of me.

I swayed a bit, acutely aware of the loss.

"Both of you." Alice turned to hug me. "I love the necklace, Maggie. It's perfect."

"I'm glad you like it." I hugged her tightly.

"See you tomorrow?"

"Promise."

I turned to walk away. Zeke was nowhere to be seen.

He'd done it again. Just taken off without so much as a good-bye. I hated how much that stung. Determined not to cry, I stalked out of the restaurant and marched, well, more like teetered, across the parking lot. I hated those shoes.

"Maggie! Maggie, wait up!"

I glanced over my shoulder and saw Zeke hurrying after me.

I tried to speed up, but the heels wouldn't let me.

Zeke fell into step beside me. "I had them pack up

your dinner." He held a paper bag up in front of me.

I snatched it from him. "Thanks."

"I'll drive you home," he offered.

"I can manage on my own."

"Are you mad at me?" he asked.

"You disappeared again."

"You missed dinner. I figured you'd be hungry."

Getting to the car, we were greeted by DeeDee barking, "Gotta! Gotta!"

"Hi, DeeDee." Zeke's greeting was warmly affectionate.

I wasn't happy that it took some of the edge off the mad-on I was nursing.

"Gotta! Gotta!"

"Let her out before she makes a mess," God urged from my purse.

Zeke eyed the bag curiously.

I was in no mood to explain the high-pitched squeaks coming from the clutch.

"I did tell you it would be a long wait," I muttered, yanking open the door. I barely managed to grab her leash before she went bounding for the nearest patch of grass. Her momentum plus my heels had me pirouetting like a deranged ballerina.

Fortunately, Zeke was there to catch me. Wordlessly he righted me, took the leash, and went off with the dog.

I sank into the driver's seat, glad to get off my feet.

"Let me out of this thing," God demanded.

"You're the one who insisted on coming along." I put the purse on the front passenger seat and popped it open.

Clambering out, he climbed up and settled himself on the dashboard. "What's in the bag? It smells vile."

Actually it smelled mouthwateringly good. I opened the foil container and spotted mashed potatoes, baby vegetables, and prime rib. I popped a carrot into my mouth. Even cold it tasted good.

I watched Zeke and DeeDee in the rearview mirror. He was playing with the dog, who was eating it up.

"So your best friend is a violent bitch, your—" God began.

"She is not. She's freaked out about the wedding is all."

"She *slapped* you."

"It's no big deal. We worked it out."

"It's no big deal?"

Tearing my gaze away from man and dog, I glared at the lizard. "I'm done talking about this."

He shrank back against the windshield. "What would you rather talk about? How your aunt is *getting more* than you?"

I opened my mouth to protest the crude comment, but I realized he was probably right.

"Or maybe you'd like to talk about how you're perfectly willing to stick your tongue down Mr. 'Roid Rage's throat."

"I'm not! I made a mistake with Paul. It was just a momentary lapse in judgment."

"Which would have been a worse mistake if I hadn't stopped you."

I hung my head. "Yes. You were right."

"And I was right that you shouldn't kiss the redhead," he said, pushing his advantage.

"Maybe."

"Maybe? He's married. He's a hired killer. He's a cop. Which of those reasons isn't good enough to keep you from getting involved with him?"

I shrugged, beaten.

"Which is why you should do the deed with this Zeke fellow."

I stared at him. "What?"

"From what you and Doomsday said, he saved your lives last night. He's been supportive tonight, and there's no denying that you're attracted to him."

I closed my eyes. Was I really taking love life advice from a lizard?

"Meat! Meat!" DeeDee bounded up to the car. I'd left my door open and she stared hopefully at the bag.

I pulled out the prime rib with two fingers and threw the entire thing to her. She gobbled it up greedily.

"That was supposed to be your dinner," Zeke chastised gently.

"She was starving."

"So am I." He bent and captured my lips with his.

Allowing my head to loll back against the headrest, I let him work his magic with his mouth.

"Chemistry," God observed.

Startled by the squeak, Zeke jerked away, banging his head on the car's ceiling. "What the hell was that?"

I pointed to the lizard on the dash. "Say hello to God."

Zeke eyed me strangely. "You call your lizard God?"

"His real name is Godzilla, God for short. He's actually Katie's pet, not mine."

"Oh. I understand."

I doubted he did. "I'm taking the animals home."

"I'll follow you." He let DeeDee into the backseat and closed her door.

"I—"

"Don't blow this!" God ordered.

"I'd like that," I said, surprising everyone.

Zeke smiled and closed my door.

I smiled the whole way home. Something was finally going right.

Until we got to the parking lot of my apartment complex.

"You can't let him inside!" God suddenly blurted out.

"Well I'm not going to 'do the deed' in a car like some horny teenager."

"But the Garcia plans, the waitress outfit, everything is in the apartment," God warned.

He had a point.

"Well, what am I supposed to tell him?" I glanced in my rearview mirror. Sure enough, Zeke was still following me.

"You changed your mind?"

"You do know that if I get caught tomorrow, this could be my last chance to have sex with a man for a very long time, don't you?"

"There are always prison guards . . ." God suggested.

"I bet none of them look like Zeke."

"Speaking of the Garcia thing, did you ever find out why Zeke was there? At the rehearsal dinner for Garcia's daughter?"

The warm sense of euphoria that had enveloped me since our last kiss started to fade away. "No," I admitted grudgingly.

"And you don't find it odd that he was there of all places? At the same time as you?"

"I find it odd that you told me to *do the deed* with him and now you're trying to convince me not to."

"Oxygen deprivation."

I rolled my eyes, put the car into park, and prepared to turn down what could have been the best night of my life.

"Zeke," I said, as he walked toward me.

"Delivered you home, safe and sound," he said with a smile.

It really wasn't fair how handsome he was. It made me want to throw caution to the wind. "I—"

"I'll see you tomorrow." He pecked me on the cheek, spun around, walked away, and got back into his car.

Shocked, I watched him go.

As he pulled away I muttered, "At least he said goodbye this time."

I put out my hand and God scampered up my arm to perch on my shoulder.

"Sorry about that," he said.

I shrugged. "It's probably for the best."

Grabbing DeeDee's leash, I let her lead the way to the apartment.

She stopped a couple of yards away, almost tripping me.

"Bad! Bad!" she growled.

"What's bad?" I asked, trying to nudge her forward.

"Bad."

I shoved her with my knee, moving forward enough to see what it was she thought was bad.

She wasn't wrong. It was very bad.

Chapter Twenty-Six

GASPING, I STUMBLED backward, suddenly glad that all I'd eaten all night was a baby carrot.

"What is it?" God asked, scrambling around to my other shoulder, hoping to get a glimpse of what had frightened us.

"Back to the car." Turning, I hurried away.

I didn't have to tug on the leash, DeeDee sprinted past me.

"What is it?" God asked, fear threading through his tone.

"Rats!" I exclaimed.

"Now what's wrong?" he asked as I opened the rear door of my car.

DeeDee leapt in. I closed it behind her.

"No," I told the lizard. "It's rats. Dead rats."

"Uggghhh." For a creature who considered himself to be a sterling conversationalist, you'd have thought he'd come up with something better than a groan of disgust.

"Don't you dare hurl on my shoulder." Unlocking the trunk of my car, I started rummaging through it.

"What are you doing?"

"I'm finding this." I turned on a flashlight. "I've got trash bags and I can use the bags I use for Doomsday's poop as gloves . . ."

"DeeDee," he corrected distractedly. "Use them for what?"

"I've got to get rid of the rats. Someone covered the front door with them."

"You're going to . . . touch them?"

I felt his tiny body quiver. An answering shiver ran through me. My stomach roiled traitorously. "What else am I supposed to do? Leave them there?"

"I don't know. Call someone?"

"Who? The police? All I need is for them to start wondering what the hell is going on with me."

"Your door is covered with rats," he said with horrified awe. "Who would do that?"

"I dunno. Neighborhood kids?"

"Kids egg doors. They don't hang dead rats."

I closed the trunk. "Maybe Abilene?"

"Maybe Mr. 'Roid Rage?"

I shrugged. "Maybe."

"Someone with a grudge. Someone who hates you. Someone who's trying to warn you off."

"Thanks," I said dryly. "You're making me feel much better."

"This is scary. How can you not be afraid?"

I swallowed hard. I was doing my best not to freak out. "I am scared," I said slowly. "But if my run-ins with Cifelli and Gary the Gun taught me anything, it's that nothing is ever solved by giving in to fear."

"You could hide. Hiding's good."

"Do you want to wait in the car while I clean up the mess?"

When he didn't answer, I opened the front passenger door to let him inside.

"I didn't say yes," he protested.

"I know, but—"

"I'm not going to send you to deal with those things alone."

"They're dead. They can't hurt me."

"Bad," DeeDee opined from the backseat.

"We'll all go," God decided.

DeeDee whined softly. "Bad."

"You can stay here," I assured her.

"Go DeeDee."

"You don't have to."

"Go DeeDee."

The three of us went to remove the four dead rats. They'd been hung by their tails with duct tape, in a diamond pattern. DeeDee held the flashlight in her mouth, God sat between her ears telling her how to direct the beam, and I yanked each stiff, smelly body from the door. Bile rose in my throat with each rip I made. By the time I was done, I was barely together enough to carry the bag to the Dumpster and heave it in.

My hand shook terribly as I unlocked my door. I was

terrified by what horrible scene might await me inside, but nothing looked disturbed. The dog and lizard searched the place for intruders as I waited in the doorway.

"Clear!" God shouted as they searched each room. "Clear! Clear!"

"You've been watching too many police procedurals," I muttered, but I was grateful that they were checking the place out.

Satisfied that it was just the three of us, I hurried to the gun Patrick had left for me, and loaded it with shaking hands. Ushering the animals into my bedroom, I shoved my dresser in front of the window, wedged my night table against the door, dragged my pillows and comforter off the bed, and settled into a corner of the floor.

"Are you okay?" God's concern was evident.

"You said hiding is good. I'm hiding."

"Good hiding." DeeDee lay down beside me, resting her head on my lap.

I stroked the spot between her ears and finally relaxed. We all drifted off to sleep.

Until the phone rang.

I jumped so high that I bounced her head off my lap. Her chin hit the floor with a solid thunk.

"Sorry." I scrambled for my phone and stared at the unfamiliar number.

"Maybe whoever left the rats wants to know if you're home," God whispered worriedly. "Who else would call after midnight?"

I pushed the answer button, but didn't say anything. I held my breath and listened to someone breathing.

"Mags?"

"What the hell is wrong with you? Why are you calling at this hour? You scared the hell out of me!" I shouted at Patrick.

I got silence as a reply.

"Patrick? Patrick, are you there?" I whispered, afraid he'd hung up.

"What's happened?" His concern acted as a balm for my frazzled nerves.

I told him about Paul's creepy traffic stop, Katie's improvement and scare, my altercation with Abilene, all the crap with Alice, and the rats. I left out the part about Zeke.

At the end, realizing I'd babbled for a good fifteen minutes straight, I said, "But that's probably not why you called."

"I called to see how you were doing and to wish you good luck tomorrow." He sounded tired.

"How's the road trip going? Snacks and tunes working out?"

"You were right on both counts. It's been quite the experience. Really good bonding time."

"I'm glad. When will you head home?"

"She insisted on making more sightseeing stops than we'd planned, so not until Tuesday or Wednesday. I'd hoped to be back in time to help you, but . . ." He trailed off, his tone heavy with regret.

I swallowed hard, realizing the true reason for his call. "You wanted to say good-bye?"

"You could call off the job," he pleaded. "Just tell

Delveccio you couldn't do it. He'll believe you. It won't be held against you."

"I can't."

"What if I take care of Abilene?" he offered desperately.

"After the fight I had with her at the hospital I'd be the prime suspect. It wouldn't work."

"But—"

"You promised you'd find homes for God and DeeDee," I reminded him, my vocal cords stretched to their limit as I tried not to cry.

He didn't reply.

"Patrick?"

"I promised." His voice was husky with emotion. "But if you're careful tomorrow, really careful, I won't have to. Promise me, Mags. Promise me you won't get caught."

"I'll try." The promise was weak and we both knew I didn't believe in it.

"I wish . . ." he began.

"Good-bye, Patrick." I disconnected the call, grabbed DeeDee, and sobbed into her neck, thinking about all the wishes I had that were probably never going to come true.

DESPITE THE FACT I had two weddings to attend that day, the next morning I got up and went to visit Katie.

Walking through the familiar hallways of the hospital, I fervently hoped that it wasn't going to be the last time I'd see my niece. When my cell phone rang I almost didn't answer it, but, worried that it might be Alice with a last-minute bridezilla request, I looked at the display and recognized the number of the prison.

For a split second I considered ignoring the call from my father, but I realized he was probably calling to convey good wishes to Alice on her big day. I didn't want to be responsible for not passing on his words of wit and wisdom.

"I'm at the hospital," I said as a way of greeting.

"Miss Lee?" a strange male voice asked.

I stopped walking. "Who is this?"

"I'm calling from the prison."

"Why?"

"Your father's been in a fight. He's in the infirmary."

A strange, unpleasant feeling niggled at the pit of my stomach. A memory scratched at the edge of my consciousness. "How badly is he hurt?"

"He'll live. This time." The last two words were delivered as an ominous warning.

I leaned against the wall for support, the tile cool against my palm. "I'm sorry, what did you say your name was again?"

"When you come to visit, tell the rat bastard to give up the jewels." The caller's voice had a sinister silkiness to it now. It made the hairs on the back of my neck dance. "For his own good and that of his family. Otherwise, who knows what might happen."

The call ended, but I still held the phone to my ear, trying to make sense of the threat.

Before I could regain my emotional equilibrium, I saw her.

A woman dressed a lot like me, in jeans and a T-shirt,

walked toward me. Something about her gait or carriage was so familiar that I looked twice at her despite the fact I was reeling from the phone call.

I searched her face, trying to figure out where I knew her from. My heart stopped when I locked onto her brown-eyed gaze. Recognition dawned on her familiar, yet different features. Time had changed her, life had hardened her. But I knew her.

"Marlene?" The two syllables were more barely more than a whisper.

Instead of answering me, my sister spun around and took off at a dead run away from me.

For a moment, I stood, stunned. This wasn't how I'd imagined our reunion. I'd dreamed of us falling into each other's arms. I'd had nightmares about her screaming at me that Darlene's death was all my fault, but I'd never imagined her running away from me. Again.

"Marlene! Wait!" I chased after her. "Come back!"

She might have gotten the jump on me, but I wasn't about to lose her again. I ran faster, my heart exploding, my lungs wheezing. I closed the distance between us. Reaching out, I could almost touch her. A few inches more.

Hearing my approach, she looked back over her shoulder at me, her expression fear and something I couldn't identify.

"Marlene, please!" I gasped.

She passed a patient's room and as she did, a bed was pushed into the hallway, straight into my path.

"Move!" I screamed, but the bed didn't budge.

Marlene kept running, putting more and more distance between us.

"Marlene!" I wailed, but she didn't stop.

I lost her. Again.

THE B&B WAS eerily quiet when I got there a few hours later.

"Hello?" I called as I walked in the front door, wondering what fresh hell the silence preceded. "Where is everyone?"

"Loretta and Alice are getting their hair done." Zeke rounded the corner carrying an embroidered pillow.

Startled, I grabbed my chest.

"Sorry," he said, eyeing me thoughtfully. "Didn't mean to scare you. Bob picked up Susan. Leslie left separately. I don't know where they were going."

"When should they be back?"

"Alice and Loretta left fifteen minutes ago. You could probably run over to the shop and get yours done too."

Self-consciously I smoothed my hair. It had been a rough night and a rougher morning. "I look that bad?"

A strange smile played at his lips. "You really don't know."

"Know what?"

"Why do you think Alice picked that ugly dress for you?"

"Hormones?" I suggested weakly.

"And why do you think she didn't tell you about the hair and makeup appointment?"

"Because I'm the worst maid of honor ever?" I pointed at the pillow he held. "Proof. Aunt Loretta entrusted you with her ring bearer pillow."

"Actually . . ." He stepped closer, holding it out. "She asked me to give it to you for safekeeping."

Taking it, I stared down at the familiar hearts stitched into it.

Reaching out, Zeke smoothed my hair off my face, in a movement so intimate, my breath caught.

"You have no idea, Maggie," he murmured seductively. "No idea how remarkable you are. Alice does. She doesn't want the competition on her big day."

I threw back my head and laughed. "You are crazier than my mom."

He reared back as though I'd slapped him. "You don't believe me?"

"Is that really so shocking, Zeke? That I wouldn't fall for that line of bull?"

He frowned. "It's the truth."

"Sure."

"I told you the truth and you didn't believe me."

The look of shock on his face made me start laughing all over again.

"What's wrong with you?" he asked suspiciously.

I almost blurted out that I'd seen Marlene. I almost revealed that someone had called and threatened me. I almost told him about the rats. But I didn't. "I'm excited about the day."

"Unlike me," he scoffed, "*you* are a lousy liar, Maggie Lee."

I hoped he was wrong. The success of the day depended on it.

I DID PRETTY well with the whole lying thing through helping Alice get dressed, posing for pictures, and getting to the place on time. Sure my smile might have wavered slightly and my knees might have gone a little weak when I first saw Zeke looking devastatingly handsome in his tuxedo, but I'd done my best to act like he was just another member of the bridal party, not a guy I wanted to do the deed with.

Things were going smoothly until I answered the knock at the door of the bridal suite and found myself facing Alice's mom.

"Can I see her?" Ellen asked. She'd gotten dressed up for the occasion in a light blue dress and looked ten times better than she had when I'd extended the invitation to attend. She was definitely trying.

"I . . ." I hesitated, having already gotten instructions from the bride that I was not to allow her mother to see her before the ceremony. "Let me go check."

I felt a twinge of guilt at Ellen's crestfallen expression as I closed the door in her face.

I went over to Alice. "It's your mom. She wants to see you."

"I told you—"

"You wouldn't have invited her if you hadn't wanted to see her," I said hurriedly, calling her bluff.

"What would you do?" she asked Zeke. "If your mom wanted to see you, what would you do?"

He frowned, considering the question.

In that moment, I finally got the connection they shared. I'd never fully understood what had drawn them together when we were in high school, but now I did. They'd both been rejected by their mothers. I suddenly felt ashamed for having been jealous of their bond, knowing it had been forged in pain.

"Maggie's right," he said slowly. "Why would you invite her if you didn't want to see her?"

"But what if . . . ?" Alice's lower lip quivered.

"You're going to ruin your makeup if you start to cry," I teased gently.

"What if she still doesn't . . . ?"

"No one forced her to come here today," Zeke said. "She obviously wants to see you too."

Alice looked to me for confirmation.

I nodded. "She got all dressed up in a pretty dress. She's sober. She asked nicely."

"Let her in," Alice said to me, grabbing Zeke's hand.

I opened the door. Ellen, eyes downcast, didn't even look up at me. "Come in, Ellen."

Slowly she raised her head and I saw that tears had already furrowed their way down her cheeks. I reached out and touched her elbow and offered her a reassuring smile. "Come on in."

She followed me in with faltering steps. I moved to the side so that mother and daughter could see one another for the first time in years.

"You look beautiful," Ellen said, her voice shaking.

"Mommy!" Letting go of Zeke, Alice threw herself

into her mother's arms. They both sobbed loudly as they held one another.

Feeling my own eyes growing moist, I looked over at Zeke. Hands balled into fists, he'd turned away from the reunion. My heart squeezed painfully at the sight of his distress.

As though he sensed me watching him, he pivoted to look at me, something sharp and accusing in his gaze.

I took a step back, prepared for him to launch some sort of attack, but then his expression morphed to such extreme regret that I found myself moving toward him. I didn't know what to say to make him feel better, but I desperately wanted to do something to show him that while his mother might have rejected him, his friends never would.

Throwing my arms around him, I squeezed as tightly as I could.

"Ow!" he exclaimed.

I jumped away.

"My boutonniere stabbed me," he said, pulling me back to him, and crushing me in an embrace.

"Are you okay?" I whispered after a long moment, ignoring the giggles and exclamations of Alice and Ellen.

"Coming back here was so much more challenging than I expected," he admitted with a heavy sigh.

"I'm sorry."

"You should be. You're one of the biggest complications," he muttered.

"Me?"

"You've got to stop that, Maggie. You're killing me."

"Stop what?"

"Looking like you care so much."

I straightened his bow tie. "But I do care."

"And that's a complication."

Before I could ask him why, Alice said, "Could you find the photographer? I'd like her to take a picture of me and my mom."

"Sure," Zeke said a tad too quickly, and bounded out of the room as though he were glad of the excuse to escape.

After the pictures were taken, Ellen went to join the other guests and the wedding party was lined up for the processional.

"Are you sure you know what to do?" Alice asked nervously.

I adjusted her veil. "Yes, and besides, no one will be watching anyone except you."

"Does this dress make me look pregnant?" She smoothed her hand over her still-flat belly.

"You look beautiful."

She touched my mother's necklace where it lay against her collarbone. "You were right about my mom."

"I'm glad things have worked out for you."

"I hope they work out for you too."

The processional began to play.

"Showtime!" I gave her a quick hug and then was a total pro lockstepping down the aisle behind Zeke.

The ceremony was lovely; quick, sweet, and the perfect showcase for two people deeply in love. Watching

Lamont's adoration of his bride made me wonder why she'd ever had second thoughts.

I glanced at Zeke a couple of times during the ceremony. Slight frown lines wrinkled his brow and his jaw was clenched tightly, even though he had a polite smile plastered on throughout. Something was definitely bugging him. I wasn't sure if it was me or his mother, but I vowed to get to the bottom of it during the reception.

The groom kissed the bride, everyone applauded, and we all walked into the cocktail hour.

"There's no salmon," I said as we entered the room.

"What?" the groomsman, a friend of Lamont's from college, whose arm I was hanging on, asked.

"There's no salmon." The room was done in lovely shades of lavender and gray.

Behind me, Zeke chuckled. "Now do you believe me?"

Turning, I glared at him. "So what am I supposed to be? The comic relief in the butt-ugly dress?"

The groomsman sidled away.

"You're a cliché," Zeke said, taking my arm and leading me deeper into the room. "Brides have been dressing their competition in ugly dresses since the beginning of time. Consider it a compliment. Champagne?"

I could have really used a drink at that point, but had to stay sharp if I was going to kill a man that night. I shook my head.

"Wine?"

"Seltzer," I said.

Zeke frowned.

"What? You're opposed to carbonated drinks?"

"You're not . . . ?" he asked.

"Not what?"

"Armani said you didn't drink at Foxy's either."

"I was the designated driver."

"And that's all?"

It took me a while, but I finally caught on to what he was really asking.

Grabbing his arm, I stood on my toes to hiss in his ear, "Tell me you don't think I'm knocked up like Alice."

"Glad to hear it," he said smoothly, planting a quick kiss on my cheek, disentangling himself from my grip, and moving away. "I really think you're going to need that drink."

"I don't need a drink," I muttered.

Then I turned around and realized I was wrong.

Chapter Twenty-Seven

EVERYONE'S ALWAYS SAID she's an ethereal beauty. Maybe it's her pale, delicate features, or maybe it's because she seems to glow with an inner light. Or maybe it's because when you look into her eyes, eyes that seem to shift from blue, to green, to gray, with every thought that passes through her mind, you can see how tenuous the grip the world has on her. And vice versa.

For a second I thought maybe I'd lost *my* grip on reality. It was bad enough I'd been talking to animals and going around killing people, but now I was seeing someone who shouldn't be there. Who couldn't be there.

I closed my eyes, willing the world, the real world, to come back into focus. I held my breath as I reopened them.

She was still there.

Closer now.

Close enough that I could reach out and touch her.

"Hello," she said in that familiar lilting tone.

I couldn't speak.

I couldn't turn away.

I couldn't run away.

And that's what I wanted to do. I wanted to run away.

"Surprise!" Alice cheered from behind me.

I turned my head slowly.

Alice beamed at me. "You invited my mom, so I invited your mom. Isn't it great that they're both here?"

I swiveled my gaze back toward my mother. I'd invited her mom because she'd asked me to. I hadn't asked her to invite my mom.

"Hello," Mom said again. "You let your hair grow, Midge. It looks nice."

Alice pushed past me, dragging Lamont behind her. "I'm so glad you were able to make it, Mrs. Lee. This is my fiancé, Lamont."

"Husband," my mother corrected gently with a tinkling laugh. "You're going to have to get used to calling him that, Alice."

They all laughed.

The sound seemed to dislodge me from my motionless stupor. I turned to run away and almost plowed into Armani.

"That is one *ugly* dress, Chiquita," she said.

I could have said the same about her silver-sequined jumpsuit, but instead I demanded, "What the hell are you doing here?"

"I was invited." She motioned toward Alice with the

glass of champagne she held in her good hand. "She invited me at the bachelorette party." Noticing the glass, she held it out to me. "Zeke said you need this."

Snatching it from her, I guzzled it in three gulps.

Armani raised her eyebrows, but didn't say anything about my drinking. "That's your mama? Introduce me."

"I can't." I hadn't seen or talked to my mother in years. I wasn't prepared to talk to her.

"Is it because of the stump?" Armani waved her disfigured hand in my face.

"Of course not!"

"Well then, why?"

Mom was looking past Alice and Lamont to me. If I didn't get away soon . . .

"I don't know her," I told Armani.

"How can you not know her? She's your mom."

"But she's lived in a nut— in an institution. I haven't seen her for years."

Armani looked at me like I was the one who belonged in a nuthouse. "But she's your *mom*."

My mom looked at me hopefully.

I'm not a bad person. I may be a contract killer, but I take a certain amount of pride in the effort I make to be a good person. I try to be polite to strangers, I don't overindulge in office gossip, and I'm loyal to my friends and family. If I turned away from her, it would be as bad as Marlene running away from me. I couldn't do it.

"C'mon." I grabbed Armani's shoulder and pushed her in front of me like she was a human shield.

"Mom, I'd like you to meet my friend Armani Vasquez. We work together. Armani, this is my mother, Mary Lee."

"Nice to meet you." Armani extended her good hand. "You have a beautiful aura. It sort of glitters."

My mother looked a bit surprised by the aura comment, but she shook Armani's hand. "It's nice to meet you. It's a lovely wedding, isn't it?"

"I guess," Armani said with a shrug. "If you're into the whole public-display-of-affection thing."

Mom's laughter sounded like tinkling wind chimes. "I can see why you and Midge are friends. She hates weddings too."

"Midge?" Armani asked.

"Middle Maggie," Mom explained. "Theresa was the oldest. The twins were the youngest, so Middle Maggie became Midge." Her smile faded away. "Now she's the only one left."

I held my breath, waiting for it, waiting for the disconnect that occurred when she got upset.

She blinked. "So you're a friend of Alice's too?"

"No. We just met at her bachelorette party. I'm really a friend of Maggie's, that's why I'm here, in case my girl needed some moral support or something."

I was caught off guard by her revelation and more than a little touched.

"You have good friends, Midge."

I nodded.

Armani snatched the empty champagne flute from

my hand. "Good friends don't let friends stay sober. Let me get you a refill."

Mom and I watched her limp away.

"I'm not much of a drinker," I said, not wanting my mother to think I was an alcoholic or something.

"Of course not. You were always the most serious of the girls. Do you mind if we sit down, these shoes are killing me." She pointed to the sky-high stilettos on her feet.

"Loretta's?" I asked as we sat down at a tiny round table.

"She was scandalized that I wanted to wear flats."

I smiled at the irony that my aunt was more worried about footwear than the fact that her previously institutionalized sister was wandering around the cocktail hour without a visible chaperone.

"You looked sad standing up there, Midge."

I looked away. "I've got a lot on my mind."

"So I've heard. You've seen your father?"

Nodding, I looked back at her. A person would have to be deaf to miss the note of love and yearning in her voice when she talked about him. I'd never understood their crazy obsession with one another and I never would.

"He's well?"

I doubted it, considering the phone call I'd gotten while at the hospital, but I didn't want to tell her that. "He looked good when Alice and I went to see him to share the news of her engagement."

Mom smiled forlornly. "I wish I could see him."

"Have you seen Marlene, Mom?"

She blinked, surprised the question. "No one has."

I nodded. If no one had seen her, what had she been doing at the hospital? Had she been visiting Katie or had it just been some bizarre twist of fate that had brought us face-to-face?

"I'm doing much better," Mom blurted out.

"I can see that."

"So if you wanted to come visit sometime I wouldn't be . . . you know . . ." She twirled her finger by her ear, making the "crazy" sign.

I nodded, not wanting to make any promises I couldn't keep. For all I knew I might have to use a temporary insanity defense if I got caught killing Garcia.

"I mean I know you're busy with Katie, and your job, and your friends, but . . ." She trailed off sadly.

"I'm a pretty terrible daughter."

"I was a pretty terrible mother."

"No," I protested. "You were sick."

"It's my fault that Darlene's dead." Her voice shook as she nervously wrung her hands. "If you'd been watching over them instead of me . . ." Tears glistened in her eyes.

I felt my own grow damp. "It wasn't your fault."

"It wasn't *your* fault, Midge."

"It wasn't either of your faults."

Mom and I both jumped as Aunt Susan inserted herself in the conversation. She put a hand on each of our shoulders. "It wasn't anybody's fault except the sick bastard that took her."

"Language, Aunt Susan," I teased weakly.

She smiled. "It's high time both of you forgave yourselves and moved on. Your energy is better spent working toward the future than dwelling in the past."

Out of the corner of my eye I spotted Zeke strolling over.

"Sorry to interrupt," he said. "But Alice is asking for Maggie. It's nice to see you, Mrs. Lee."

I stood up to go with him and then turned back. Bending down, I hugged Mom. "I'm glad you came." Straightening, I followed Zeke out of the room.

"You okay?" he asked as we climbed the stairs toward the bridal suite.

"I will be."

And at least in that moment, I believed it.

The rest of the reception flowed smoothly. The bride and groom danced their first dance as man and wife; cutting the cake, they refrained from smashing it into one another's faces; they tossed the bouquet and garter belt to a minimum of bloodshed.

Armani, of course, successfully fought off all the other single ladies for the bedraggled bouquet. The look on the face of the poor guy who caught the garter when she offered him her deformed leg to slide it up was priceless.

No one got too drunk, no disagreements broke out, and, except for the fact that not one, but two members of Lamont's oversized-family broke chairs just by sitting on them, there was no drama at the party.

Everyone was having too good a time. I was getting nervous, as it got later and later. I had to get home to change into my waitress uniform and then get over to the Garcia wedding. I was all for celebrating and didn't want to be the first to leave the nuptials of my best friend, but I had to go kill the guy who was responsible for my sister's death.

In a strange twist of fate, it was my mother who came to the rescue.

She and Aunt Leslie were the first to go up to the happy couple and say their good-byes. Others soon followed suit. I joined the line.

Zeke stepped up behind me. "I thought we'd be stuck here all night."

I ignored him. After all, he'd pretended I was invisible for the entire reception, dancing with every other single woman, and quite a few married ones, but not me. Apparently my silent treatment didn't bother him. He didn't say anything else to me as the line inched forward.

"Oh no!" Alice cried when she spotted us. "Are you guys going too?"

"It's been a long weekend," Zeke said smoothly, stepping past me to kiss her cheek. "I can't speak for Maggie, but I'm beat."

Hanging on Zeke's arm, Alice asked me, "You're not mad I invited your mom, are you?"

"I was. That was a hell of a thing to spring on me."

Zeke gave me a warning look.

"But I'm not now," I added hurriedly. The last thing I needed was another Alice-meltdown. I'd never get out of there. I had somewhere to be.

"She looks great and she recognized the necklace." She touched the pendant.

"She does," I agreed. "You've got other people who want to talk to you, so I'm going to go."

"*We're* going to go." Zeke threw an arm around my shoulders, content to drift off of my momentum outta there.

"I'm so glad you two are getting along so well," Alice gushed, kissing us both good-bye before turning her attention to her other guests.

I shook off his arm the second we were outside. He didn't seem to care as he made a beeline to his car, without so much as a wave in my direction. I would have been hurt if I hadn't been battling such pre-kill anxiety.

Rushing home, I told God and DeeDee about the events of the day as I changed into my disguise.

"I'm coming with you," God declared.

"You can't."

"You've been threatened, you saw your sister, you talked to your mother. Quite frankly, your head is not in the game."

The lizard was right.

"You need my help."

He was right about that too.

"I'm not carrying a purse. There's no way to carry you, and if I walk into a wedding with a lizard perched on my shoulder, I'm going to attract attention, and that's the last thing I need."

He stroked his chin thoughtfully. "You haven't lost all of your faculties."

"You couldn't just say I'm right?"

"I'll walk in when you do. No one will notice me. I can run ahead and do reconnaissance."

"You could get trampled to death."

"And you could get caught. Those are the risks we're going to have to take if we're going to keep Katie."

"What if I lose you in the crowd?"

"We'll rendezvous at the car."

"You've been watching spy movies, haven't you?"

"And military action flicks . . . I want to be all I can be."

I resisted telling him he was all of a few inches long. "It sounds like a plan."

Like plans ever work . . .

Chapter Twenty-Eight

I PARKED THREE blocks away from the location of Garcia's daughter's wedding. God, riding along on my shoulder, was uncharacteristically silent as I hurried along uneven sidewalks, fiddling nervously with the poison-filled pendant.

Reaching the parking lot, I bent down as though I was fixing my shoe and he scampered to the ground.

"For Katie," he intoned solemnly like we were swearing a blood oath or something.

"For Katie."

Climbing the steps leading to the entrance of the kitchen, I followed God, who skittered inside, unnoticed. I almost jumped out of my skin when someone grabbed my elbow.

"Hey."

I turned to look at a young woman, who couldn't have been more than twenty, holding me back.

"You forgot your mask," she said.

"Mask?" Patrick hadn't mentioned a mask. There hadn't been one in the box. My heart started to pound. If I couldn't get inside, I couldn't kill Garcia. I couldn't avenge Theresa.

She rolled her eyes. "The whole reception is a Mardi Gras theme. Have you ever heard of anything tackier?"

I shrugged. I'd spent the day in a dress the color of fish flesh.

"They've got spares," the young woman said. "Take mine. Just don't let anyone see you without it." She shook a sequin-trimmed jester mask at me.

"Thanks." The bell-tipped three points of the jester hat jingled as I slid the plastic half-face mask on, but I didn't mind. I couldn't have asked for a better disguise.

Grabbing a tray of stuffed mushrooms, I took a deep breath, and stepped into the party room. The music was already pounding, a smoke machine was churning out enough fog to put a cheesy horror movie to shame, and ravenous guests fell on my loaded tray like a pack of wild hyenas. They emptied it before I could even spot Garcia, which meant I had to return to the kitchen for a refill. It wasn't the most efficient of plans . . .

When I returned, the crowd had taken to the dance floor. I skirted the perimeter of the parquet, but couldn't find my target. Disheartened, I looked for God, hoping he'd had better luck.

It was dark, smoky, crowded, and loud, but somehow he must have known I needed him, because suddenly I could hear him calling me.

"Over here, you moronic biped!" he shouted.

Unable to see him, I hurried toward his voice.

"To the left!"

I turned.

"My left, you idiot!"

I turned in the opposite direction. That's when I spotted him, jumping up and down on a giant heart-shaped ice sculpture. I hustled over.

"Death by hypothermia," he complained, leaping off the ice and onto the back of my neck. He climbed under my hair like it was a blanket, his cold skin sending shivers down my spine. I'd never cuddled with an ice cube before.

"I can't find him," I said.

"That's because he's not here."

"What do you mean he's not here? The plan hinges on him being here. If he's not here how the hell am I supposed to—"

"Shhh." He bit my earlobe for emphasis.

I'd forgotten he had teeth. Instinctively I raised my hand to swat him away.

"Don't you dare," he said in his most superior tone.

I lowered my hand.

"Garcia isn't here because the family is in another room taking pictures."

"Why didn't you just say that?"

"Because you didn't shut up. This is your big chance. Go in there and give him a glass of spiked champagne. You'll have fewer witnesses to identify you, but you'll still do it in front of his family, which the contractor wants."

"Contractor?"

"He who laid out the terms of the deal."

"Hey, you!" a familiar voice called.

I turned slowly and saw the smaller guy who'd wanted to have "fun" with me in the coatroom when I'd gotten caught at the rehearsal dinner. I froze. "He recognizes me," I whispered.

"He can't see your face," God hissed.

"Do you got any more of dem pigs in blankets?" the guy asked.

I stared blankly at him.

"Ya know. The little hot dog things?"

God yanked on my hair and then shoved my head upward, in effect causing me to nod at the thug. "Now walk away toward the kitchen," God ordered. "He'll think you're going to get him his food."

My legs were weak, but I managed to stumble away into the kitchen. Spotting a tray with a bottle of champagne and two flutes, I picked it up and dove back into the party.

"This is it, Maggie," God said in my ear. "It's your last chance to do this. It's now or never. I'll meet you back at the car."

He leapt from my neck to a potted plant.

"Leapin' lizards," I muttered, lifting the pendant from around my neck and heading off to get my revenge against Jose Garcia.

A little girl's giggles caught my attention before I could spike a glass of champagne with the deadly poison and serve it to my target. I searched for the source of the laughter and spotted Christina, the little girl I'd met in the hallway at the rehearsal dinner. Then I saw who was making her laugh. He was pudgier and had less hair than the last time I'd spoken to him, but Jose Garcia's smile as he played with his granddaughter was familiar.

An invisible vise tightened around my chest making it difficult to breathe. A flush of white-hot anger heated my skin. Katie would never again be picked up by Theresa and spun around. I didn't know if my niece would ever even smile or laugh again.

Standing in a darkened corner, watching him twirl the laughing little girl around, I was swamped with an unexpected memory.

Theresa, Darlene, Marlene, and I were in the front yard of the B&B waiting for the ice cream truck to drive by. Aunt Susan never let us get any because she said it would ruin our dinners, but we still raced outside every time we heard the tinkling chimes.

Aunt Susan wasn't home that day. She'd had to run out to do something with our mother and had left Uncle Jose in charge of our care. Afterward, we girls all agreed it was one of the best afternoons of our lives.

Uncle Jose flagged down the ice cream truck and bought us all our favorite sweet treats. Then once we were done eating them, and running around like maniacs from our temporary sugar high, he'd picked each of us up in turn, twirling us around. So fast that we thought we could touch the sky. So fast that we got deliciously dizzy and collapsed on the grass in giggles.

Just like he was doing with Christina.

I shivered as my anger left me. I looked at the little giggling girl and knew I couldn't make her last memory of her grandfather be watching him die. Slowly, I put the necklace back on.

There was no way I could kill Jose Garcia.

And yet I couldn't lose Katie.

Then I remembered the gun Patrick had left me, I'd stowed in underneath the seat of my car. I might not be able to kill Garcia here at the party, but I might be able to do it afterward. If I shot him, I reasoned, I should be able to collect at least part of the money for the contract.

Dimly aware of the DJ asking everyone to come out to the dance floor, I turned to go to the car, hoping God would meet me there, but I got swept up in the sea of people rushing toward the center of the room.

And that's when I saw it.

The biggest, glitziest, tackiest mirrored disco ball I'd ever seen. The humongous thing had to have a diameter of at least five feet.

Just like Armani had predicted. But what did it mean?

I was so focused on the disco ball that I careened into the blue-suited back of a wedding guest with the tray.

"Sorry," I muttered, turning around to make my escape.

Fingers snaked around my biceps, not tight enough to cause pain, but enough to cause alarm to turn my legs to jelly.

"Maggie?"

I knew that voice. Holding me in place, he stepped around me.

Zeke! Concern dampened the usual sparkle in his eyes.

"What the hell are you doing here?" we said simultaneously.

Tightening his grip on my arm, Zeke practically dragged me to the outskirts of the room. My mind raced. What was he doing here? What had he been doing at the rehearsal when he'd saved me from the goons in the coatroom? He'd never said why he was back in town, except to say it was for business. Was his business with Garcia? Was he no better than the man responsible for Theresa's death and Katie's condition?

My stomach soured at the thought. Yanking my arm free of his grasp, I glared up at his blue eyes, which were narrowed at me suspiciously.

"What's with the mask?"

"All the staff are wearing them."

"Right, except you're not staff."

I showed him the tray I carried as though it was the only proof I needed.

"I keep telling you that you're a lousy liar."

There was no way I'd let him get away with acting like I was the only one with a hidden agenda. "Apparently you're not. I believed you when you told Alice you were tired, but here you are, partying the night away."

His lips, those lips that could work such magic against mine, flattened into a straight line. "I'm working."

"Working? Like you were 'working' at The Big Day when you *just happened* to run into us shopping for Alice's dress?"

"Stop it, Maggie."

"And were you *working* when you were at the rehearsal restaurant the other night?"

"I can't explain. I wish I could, but I just can't."

My heart fell. He *was* in business with Garcia. I didn't need an explanation. I'd figured it out. It had taken me a while, but I'd finally worked it out. Zeke was no better than my drug-dealing target.

"You've got to get out of here." Zeke turned his attention back to the dance floor.

Garcia was preparing to toast the bride and groom. He held out a hand, demanding champagne. It would have been the perfect opportunity to poison him.

"He killed Theresa," I blurted out.

Zeke turned back to me. "What?"

"His drugs killed my sister. The driver who hit us was an addict. He got her hooked on drugs, so he's responsible."

Something that looked like a lot like pity shimmered in Zeke's gaze.

"You're no better than him," I spat. "You're just like your dad, a drug-dealing monster."

Rearing back, he blinked, as though I'd slapped him.

A deafening snap, like a loud boom of thunder, ripped through the room. Instinctively I looked in the direction of the sound, just in time to see the disco ball fall from the ceiling. There was a crash and screams and bedlam.

Before I could figure out what had happened, Zeke grabbed my hand and started dragging me away.

"We have to get out of here!" he shouted above the din.

Dropping the champagne-laden tray, I allowed him to lead me from the chaos. We raced out of the building to the parking lot.

"Where's your car?" he asked.

"Not here," I panted.

"What the hell were you doing here, Maggie?"

"What were you?"

Instead of answering me, he pulled his keys from his pocket and remotely unlocked his car, which was parked at the far end of the lot. "Run!"

Worried that Garcia's goons would chase us, I did as he said.

We tumbled into the car and he peeled out of the lot.

Chapter Twenty-Nine

ZEKE POUNDED ON the steering wheel as he sped away. "Dammit! Dammit! Dammit!"

"Where are you taking me?" My voice wobbled, suddenly afraid of him.

Glancing over at me, he noticed I was cowering against my door. He slowed down, took a deep breath, and ran a hand through his hair. "I am *nothing* like my father or Jose Garcia."

"Where are you taking me?"

"Home. So you don't have to open that door and throw yourself out of the moving car."

I relaxed a little. We rode in silence for a few minutes.

"So what was your plan?" he asked quietly. "To get up in front of everyone and tell all his family and friends what a degenerate scumbag Garcia is?"

"Something like that." I fingered the necklace.

"It would have been useless. They already know, and he's not the kind of guy you can afford to piss off."

Something wasn't tracking. He spoke of Garcia with such disdain.

"Why were you there?" I asked.

A muscle in his jaw jumped and his fingers flexed on the steering wheel. He didn't answer me. Instead, he pulled into the parking lot of my apartment complex and escorted me to my front door.

I unlocked my front door and looked up at him.

He scowled. "Promise me you'll give up on this idea of getting your revenge on Garcia."

"Okay."

"You are the *worst* liar."

Before I could protest, he kissed me, so tenderly, I forgot how to think. Shoving my door open, he maneuvered us inside my apartment.

"God?" DeeDee panted curiously.

"God!" I groaned, tearing my lips from Zeke's. I'd forgotten the little guy and left him behind! "He's okay," I assured the dog.

"Hear that, DeeDee?" Zeke petted the dog's head. "She thinks I'm okay."

I couldn't correct him without sounding crazy, so I shut my mouth and the door, trying to gather my thoughts. I couldn't remember ever being more confused.

"Can I trust you, Maggie?"

I shrugged, keeping my back to him.

"Look at me, Maggie."

I turned slowly toward him.

"I'm not real."

"You look real."

"I'm all flash, no substance. I talk fast and think faster. You deserve better."

The pain behind his words stabbed at my heart. It wasn't Zeke the man saying these things, but the boy who'd been rejected by his own family.

Wanting to alleviate his suffering, I reached up and pulled his head down to mine. Our lips touched. "You feel real," I murmured against his mouth.

He jerked his mouth from mine, but pulled my body tight against his, squeezing me tightly as though I were an anchor he had to hold on to. Wrapping my arms around his waist, I silently signaled I was there for him.

"Loyal, loving, Maggie," he muttered into my hair. "I never deserved your friendship and I don't deserve you now."

"Zeke—"

"I'm a con man, Maggie," he confessed on a rushed breath. "That's what I am. I'm a scam artist."

I stepped away so that I could look at his face. It was twisted in a mask of shame and regret.

"I came back to town to run a con designed to take down Garcia's operation. I was at the dress shop because I'd heard his daughter was going there to pick up her gown."

He stared at me, daring me to believe him.

And I did, maybe because it was no crazier than me being a hitwoman.

"So I'm part of your con?"

He shook his head vehemently. "You weren't part of the plan, but then I saw you and Alice and something came over me, something stupid, and I wanted to re-connect. I wanted to be with people who knew my real name, knew where I came from, knew the real me." He turned away. "But I don't even know who the real me is anymore."

I knew that feeling too.

"But the way you look at me . . . it's been a major distraction. I never expected to be this attracted . . ." Agitated, he speared his fingers through his hair.

"Should I apologize?"

He whirled back around to face me, blue eyes flashing wildly. "How are you not freaking out?"

I shrugged. As much as I appreciated his confession, I wasn't about to reveal that while he conned people, I killed them. "No one's perfect. We all do things we're not proud of."

Reaching out, he cupped my cheek. "You have no idea how much I'd like to stay in town and find out where we could take this, but my employer won't let me."

"You have an employer?"

"It's complicated."

"You say that a lot."

"Life is complicated."

"God where?" DeeDee asked worriedly.

"So you're going to leave?" I asked Zeke.

"I have to."

"And I'll never see you again?"

He shook his head. "I don't know."

"So why tell me all this?"

"Because I wanted you to know . . . I needed you to

know that this is about me and not you. You have no idea what an amazing woman you are. I didn't want you to think my leaving had anything to do with you."

"But you won't stay for me," I said slowly, not even sure I'd want him to, if he did.

"I can't. I have work to do. Debts to repay . . ." He trailed off. Kissing me hard on the mouth, he turned around and left, leaving me standing there like a stunned statue.

"Now God?" DeeDee asked insistently.

It took me a second to focus on her. "Let me change into sneakers and then we can go get him."

It would be a long walk all the way across town to get back to our rendezvous point, but I couldn't let him spend the night out there alone.

Three sharp knocks on the door startled us both.

I peered through the peephole and then yanked open the door.

"Back already?"

Zeke smiled sheepishly. "There was something I forgot to tell you."

I crossed my arms over my chest and did my best to pretend I was unhappy with him.

"You should learn to accept people's help, Maggie. It'll make it easier on you and them. Trying to be your friend, helping you, is hard. You've got all those walls up."

"Is this your professional con man's opinion?" I asked sarcastically.

"Armani's trying to save your job, your aunts are trying to save your niece, and you don't cut any of them any slack," he said quickly, as though he thought I might slam the door in his face. "I'm pretty sure you may have saved me, Maggie. Thank you for reminding me who I can be."

He lifted his hand in a slight wave, ran to his car, and drove out of my life.

"Now?" DeeDee asked impatiently.

"Maybe I should ask for some help," I murmured.

Chapter Thirty

THINKING ABOUT ASKING for help and actually doing it are two very different things, when you're a hitwoman. Patrick's rule Don't Get Caught was foremost in my mind as I ran through the possibilities of who I could ask to help me get my car. I couldn't think of anyone in my life who wouldn't find it strange that I'd left it across town, which was why DeeDee and I hoofed it there, in the dark of night, with a flashlight as our only companion.

"God? God?" she started barking as soon as the car was in sight.

"Shhh! You'll wake the whole neighborhood and some-one will call the cops and tell them a suspicious character is lurking in their neighborhood and I'll get caught."

"God?" DeeDee whined pitifully.

He didn't answer. I started to panic. What if some-thing had happened to him? What if he'd become the dinner of a cat or an opossum?

Kneeling down to peer under the car, I swept the beam along its length.

"Are you there, God? It's me, Maggie."

"It's about time," he groused from above.

Scrambling to my feet, I tried to find him. "Where are you?"

"Over here on windshield." He'd wedged himself between the glass and a wiper blade. "Give me a lift."

He climbed up my extended hand slowly and stiffly.

"Okay?" DeeDee asked, jumping up to put her front feet on the hood of the car so that she could see her little friend.

"I'm fine. I just want to go home."

Getting both of them situated in the car, I said, "I'm so sorry I left."

Settling himself into the inverted baseball cap I'd placed on the front seat for him, he said, "Don't be. You were right to get out of there. The place was crawling with cops."

"Cops?" I started the car.

"Air!" DeeDee panted as though I'd deprived her of oxygen for hours.

"You didn't hear?" God asked slyly.

"Hear what?" I asked, opening the window for the mutt and putting the car into drive.

"Garcia is dead."

I stomped on the brake so hard, the car shook.

"You're a terrible driver." His voice dripped with superiority.

"Again!" DeeDee barked excitedly.

I put the car in park and turned to look at the lizard. "Tell me that bit about Garcia again."

"He's dead."

"But I never . . ."

"The disco ball."

"Fetch!" DeeDee interjected.

"Shut up!" God and I yelled at her simultaneously.

"Sorry." She stuck her head out the window.

"The disco ball?" I looked to God for clarification.

He yawned. "It fell on him. Well, technically it was going to fall on his cute little granddaughter, but he jumped in to push her out of the way."

"So Armani was right," I mused. "It all came down to a disco ball."

"So it would seem," God agreed. "The poor kid was traumatized."

Which was why I hadn't been able to poison her grandfather. "At least, when she gets older, she'll know he died protecting her."

"The scum dies a hero." The bitterness in the lizard's tone was unmistakable.

"Not exactly the justice Katie and Theresa deserve," I said aloud, but secretly, I was relieved it was over.

God was out cold by the time we got home. His snoring sounded an awful lot like a whistling teakettle. Carrying the baseball cap inside, taking care not to jostle him, I gently laid it on the kitchen table beside his terrarium. He didn't even stir.

"Couch?" DeeDee yawned.

"Sure." The two of us curled up on the couch.

Exhausted, we all slept until almost noon. I visited Katie and then spent the rest of the day vegging in front of the TV, waiting for Patrick to call and see how everything had gone. I ate all the olives I had.

He never called.

I went to bed early and slept until my alarm went off the next morning.

"Turn it off," God groaned.

I rolled off the couch, shuffled into my bedroom, slapped the clock to make it silent, and staggered into the shower.

I was glad it was a Monday morning. Otherwise I wouldn't have known what to do with myself since Alice's wedding and Garcia's death weren't on the near-horizon.

After I walked DeeDee, I checked in on God. He looked pale. "Do you need anything?" I whispered, unsure if he was still asleep since he was lying so still at the bottom of his terrarium.

"I need you to go to hell," he grumbled, turning his back on me.

Lost in thought, worrying that Alice's rehearsal dinner and the Garcia wedding had been too much for the little guy, I didn't even notice Harry's pepperoni breath when he snuck up behind me as I took a claim from someone who'd driven into her own garage door.

"Much better empathy," he said.

Startled, I jumped in my seat, almost choking to death on the mint Life Saver I'd been sucking on. I coughed so loudly, half the place turned around to see what was wrong with me.

Once I could breathe again, I gasped, "Did you want something, Harry?"

Eyes narrowed, he shook his head. "Just wanted to give you some positive feedback on the excellent job you're doing."

"Thanks, I guess?" Nice Harry was even creepier than regular Harry.

"We're good, right? You and me?" He actually pointed to indicate who was "you" and who was "me."

I shrugged. "I guess."

"Good. Good. Carry on." He hurried away.

A moment later Armani limped over to my desk. "What was that about?"

Remembering what Zeke had said about her, I said, "You tell me." I fixed a steady gaze on her, waiting to see how she'd react.

She raised her eyebrows. "When did you figure it out?"

"What exactly did you do?" I countered, offering her a candy.

Taking one, she rested the hip of her bad leg on the corner of my desk. "*Someone*," she said, unwrapping the candy, "may have let slip that *somebody* may have been building a sexual harassment suit against poor Harry. And somebody might have mentioned that you'd hired a lawyer. You *did* hire a lawyer, didn't you?"

"To fight for custody of Katie," I said slowly.

"Somebody *may* have forgotten to mention that part of the equation." She winked at me.

"I don't know how to thank you."

"You don't have to."

"But—"

"That's what friends are for."

She got up and headed back toward her own desk.

"Armani?"

She looked back at me.

"Anything else you can tell me about the cactus?"

"Maybe they're a symbol of the desert wasteland that is your love life, Chiquita." Chuckling, she turned and walked away.

Considering that she'd been right about the disco ball and that Zeke had left town, I couldn't discount her theory.

I THOUGHT ABOUT not visiting the hospital after work, but now that Katie was awake and aware, I wanted to see her even more than I didn't want to run into Delveccio.

I really needed the lizard's help figuring out how to best spin the story of what had happened with Garcia, but I didn't have time to run home. Hustling across the parking lot, I decided that my safest course of action would be to let the mobster do most of the talking. It wasn't like he was going to unleash his idiot nephew/bodyguard on me in the cafeteria.

There was a flurry of activity going on in the room of Delveccio's grandson, so I scooted past, unnoticed. I closed the door to Katie's room so that we could have some privacy, before I even greeted her.

"Hey, Baby Girl."

Turning her head, she watched my progress as I crossed the room to kiss her on her cheek.

Noticing that she was covered by a new afghan, I asked, "Was Aunt Susan here to visit you?"

She didn't respond.

Picking up a corner of the blanket, I fingered the yarn. "Wow, this is soft." Sitting on the edge of the bed, I picked up her hand. "You know, when I was in kindergarten, we had nap time. We each had little blankets that we kept in our cubbyholes in the classroom and when it was time to nap, we'd take them out, put them on the floor, and lie down." I smiled at the memory, something I hadn't thought about in years. "Most of the kids had beach towels to lie on, and a couple had store-bought blankets, but I was the only one, in the whole class, who had a blanket someone had made just for them. Guess who made me my blanket."

She didn't respond, but she hadn't taken her eyes off my face while I'd told the story.

"Aunt Susan. And do you know what she told me about that blanket?"

I waited for a second as though I expected her to answer.

"She told me it was made with love, and that no matter where I went or what I did, her love would always be wrapped around me." Tears welled in my eyes and my throat constricted painfully. "And now you have a blanket made with love too. So no matter where you go, or what you do, you'll always have love wrapped around you."

I dashed away wayward tears with the back of my hand.

"And not just Susan's love, but mine too. I love you more than all the blankets in the world! You know that, don't you?"

I stared at her, willing her to respond, but I got nothing.

I closed my eyes, telling myself that her open eyes were enough. But they weren't. I wanted more. I needed to know that the little girl I loved was still there, inside her shell of a body.

Thankfully a nurse came in at that moment, so I had the excuse to get up and walk away.

"It looks like the little boy next door is waking up too," the nurse told Katie. "Isn't that wonderful news?"

It was. It meant there was a chance Delveccio wouldn't kill me for not taking care of Garcia.

A chance.

NOT LONG AFTERWARD I was kicked out by the same nurse, who said that Katie needed her rest.

"I'll see you tomorrow, Baby Girl," I promised, waving good-bye.

She didn't wave back.

Remembering that I'd promised my aunts that I'd stop by for dinner, I hurried over to the B&B. No one was on the front porch waiting for me, but I heard voices coming from the back of the house, so I walked to the rear, dimly aware I was retracing the same steps I'd taken when Frank had attacked.

The scene in the backyard was no less shocking when I rounded the corner this time.

The top of the barn was gone. Building equipment and supplies covered the manicured lawn.

Aunt Leslie, talking to a woman in her late fifties who wore a yellow business suit, noticed me first. "Maggie! We were just talking about you." She waved me over.

I approached cautiously; leery she'd been telling the stranger that her niece was perpetually tardy. Maybe the woman was her NA sponsor and would tell her to cultivate a nonjudgmental attitude.

"Maggie, this is Elaine," Leslie introduced. "Elaine, this is my niece Maggie."

Automatically I extended my hand. "Nice to meet you, Elaine."

"Please call me Lani." The woman smiled warmly at me. Something about her was familiar, but I couldn't put my finger on what it was.

I nodded politely. "What's going on here?" I waved at the demolition that had been done to the barn.

"The construction. Susan told you it was being done, didn't she?"

My chest tightened. Thinking about moving home was one thing. Knowing it was going to happen was another. I'd lose my privacy. I'd lose my dog.

"There's our girl!" Templeton crowed from behind me.

I turned to see him and Aunt Loretta, who teetered precariously, her stilettos sinking deeper into the grass with every step, coming toward us. Part of me wanted to tell him that I'd never be his "girl," but then I remembered that he'd been the one to throw me a lifeline at Alice's rehearsal dinner when she'd been intent on making me look like the world's biggest jerk.

I air kissed with Loretta and nodded at Templeton. He beamed back.

"I don't think Alice told her," Leslie whispered dramatically to her twin.

Loretta's Poison Kissed lips formed a surprised O.

"Told me what?" I asked suspiciously. It's never a good sign when people talk about you like you're not standing right in front of him.

"She's inside," Loretta said quickly. "She should really be the one to tell you."

"Tell me what?" This time I raised my voice, panicked by what kind of crazy scheme my hormonally imbalanced best friend had come up with.

"There she is," Leslie said soothingly. "She can tell you herself."

Alice, Lamont, Aunt Susan, and her date from the wedding, Bob, walked toward us.

"I'm afraid I let the cat out of the bag," Leslie said apologetically to Alice. "I'd assumed she already knew."

"Knew what?" I asked through clenched teeth, prepared to shoot down whatever idiotic plan Alice had set into motion.

"I wanted to help," Alice began.

"*We* wanted to help," Lamont corrected.

"God help me," I muttered.

But he wasn't there.

Chapter Thirty-One

"Relax, Margaret," Aunt Susan said mildly. "You're letting your imagination get the best of you."

I observed her expression carefully. If the sanest of the bunch wasn't looking like the sky was about to fall, maybe I was overreacting a tad.

Taking a steadying breath, I switched my attention back to Alice. "What's going on?"

She glanced up at her husband. "It was Lamont's idea. He should be the one to tell you."

I looked up at the mountain of a man, doing my best not to tap my foot impatiently.

Lamont cleared his throat. "So from the moment Alice and I met, she's been telling me all of the wonderful things your family has done for her over the years. Then we showed up, out of the blue, and you gave us a place to stay and put up with our rushed wedding. I got to see firsthand how kind you all are. Crazy," he said with a smile, "but kind."

Alice stared up at her husband adoringly, nodding her head in confirmation of everything he said.

"So, when the girls . . ." He waved his arm to encompass my aunts.

Loretta giggled, Leslie beamed, Susan rolled her eyes.

"When the girls started talking about the construction and how important it was to keep your family together, I came up with the idea."

"We asked the wedding guests to contribute to the construction fund instead of giving us gifts!" Alice blurted out.

I rocked back on my heels, stunned by their generosity. "I don't know what to say."

"Say thank you," Susan prompted.

" 'Thank you' seems so inadequate."

Alice hugged me tightly. "We were happy to do it."

"And Bob's doing the job for you for cost," Lamont added charitably.

Overwhelmed by everyone's kindness, I looked from one to the next, speechless.

"We're not going to lose Katie too," Aunt Susan said determinedly.

"Group hug!" Leslie called.

Everyone, even Bob and Lani, joined in. I'd never felt more wrapped in love.

"Tell her about the dog run," Bob boomed from the outskirts of the group hug.

The group broke apart as Susan ushered me to the edge of the construction site. "Bob says we can put a dog run for DeeDee right here."

I looked sideways at my normally uptight aunt. "You hate dogs."

"How can I hate her? She saved my life. If you're moving back, she's got to come too. She's family."

The vise around my chest loosened knowing I wouldn't have to give up DeeDee. "Thank you. That's very nice of you."

"Your aunt's a pretty nice lady." Bob came up from behind her and squeezed her shoulders. She leaned into him.

"Thank you." I gestured toward the demolition. "For all of this."

"My pleasure, young lady. My pleasure. Have you met my sister yet?"

"Your sister?"

"Lani! Get you scrawny butt over here!" Bob bellowed.

"Oh, we've met," I said, realizing why her smile had seemed familiar. There was no missing the resemblance between the siblings. "Leslie didn't tell me she was your sister."

Lani joined us. "Leslie says dinner is almost ready."

"You should hire this woman to be a real estate agent," Bob said, thunking me between the shoulder blades. "I bet she'd be a natural."

"We're going to help Leslie get dinner on the table." Susan led Bob away.

I smiled, liking the way he offered her his arm so that she wouldn't stumble on the uneven footing. I wasn't surprised she refused the support.

"Do you have any experience?" Lani asked.

"What?"

"Any experience in real estate."

"None. I wasn't—"

"Neither did I when I started."

"I wasn't looking for a job. I mean, it was very nice of your brother, but . . ."

"What do you do now, Maggie?"

"I take automobile insurance claims."

"Do you like it?"

I laughed.

She smiled and handed me a business card. "Give me a call and we'll talk about the possibility of you coming to work for me. Maybe a mixture of office work and sales until you get some experience and clients under your belt."

"But I don't have any experience." And I really wasn't sure I was cut out to sell houses any more than I was to answer a phone all day.

"As I said, neither did I when I got into this business. I was a single mom with a special needs child. The flexibility the job offered was my salvation. You're in the same boat. I've heard all about how you're stepping up for your niece. That makes you the kind of quality person I want to hire. Think about it and call me."

I WAS EXCITED to tell God about the job offer when I got home, but he was still sleeping.

"Did he do that all day?" I asked DeeDee as I took her on a nice long walk.

"Day all."

"Did he complain that he was in pain or anything?"

"No."

"Did he say what was wrong?"

"Tired God."

"Maybe I should take him to a vet. Do vets even treat lizards?"

DeeDee didn't reply, she just sniffed and sniffed. And sniffed. And sniffed a nondescript clump of grass.

On the way back we stopped to get the mail.

In addition to my monthly running magazine (a gift from Alice, who thought I should take it up to reduce my stress), the mailbox contained an overnighted envelope.

"Probably more bad news," I muttered, carrying it inside.

"DeeDee eat? Go away make," the dog offered, licking the envelope tentatively.

I rubbed her head affectionately. "Thanks, sweetie, but I don't think that will help."

Not wanting to disturb the sleeping lizard, we went into the bedroom. I considered not opening the envelope, but ignoring bad news never made it go away.

I changed for bed, crawled under the covers, and let DeeDee get comfortable beside me, before I opened it.

A single postcard fell out.

There was a photograph of a large cactus in the desert and the words "Vegas: Wish You Were Here." Flipping it over, I saw that the back was blank.

"Patrick sent me a cactus," I told DeeDee.

She yawned sleepily.

Armani's predictions about a disco ball and a cactus had come about, but I still didn't understand what the cactus meant.

The next morning before I went to work, I asked God if he had any theories about it, but all he grumbled was "Let me sleep."

"You're officially scaring the shit out of me," I told him.

He ignored me.

I laid my cheek on the kitchen table so that I could be eye level with him where he lay in his terrarium. "You can't die on me." Getting choked up and teary-eyed, I begged, "Please don't die."

"No die," DeeDee whined worriedly.

"I can't take it," I told the little guy. "If I lose you too . . ." I gave up trying not to cry and allowed myself a good sob fest.

"Relax," God soothed, rousing himself to press his tiny foot against the glass. "You're not going to get rid of me that easily."

I touched the glass by his foot, as I'd seen many people do with their imprisoned loved ones when I visited my father. I found it oddly comforting.

"I just need to rest," the lizard assured me. "I'll be fine."

With that promise, I went to do my time at Insuring the Future. During lunch, after she'd made me pull seven more Scrabble tiles, I told Armani about the job offer.

She considered the tiles before commenting on the employment revelation. "It might not be a bad idea."

I stared at her, shocked. "I thought for sure you'd try to talk me out of it."

She shrugged and looked away.

"What?" I asked suspiciously. "Did the tiles tell you something?"

"Chooooo."

"Bless you," I said reflexively, despite the fact she hadn't sneezed.

"Does 'choo' mean anything to you?"

"To grind food with one's teeth?"

She laid out the tiles for me to see. CHOOOOO

"How do you know it doesn't mean OOOOOCH?" I asked. "Or see who?"

"Hello, ladies," Harry interrupted, staying a respectful distance away from our table. "I just wanted to remind you that we've got a meeting this afternoon. I look forward to seeing you both there."

Armani rolled her eyes as he strode away. "There's another reason to consider the job offer."

"So you really think I should do it?"

She nodded.

"Because of Harry and CHOOOOO?"

My cell phone rang before she could answer. "It's the lawyer's office," I said, glancing at the caller ID displayed.

Armani, despite her Scrabble tiles and crazy predictions, was a good friend. She grabbed my hand and squeezed supportively. "Whatever she says, you'll get through it."

She watched me carefully while I spoke with the lawyer, concern shadowing her gaze as my voice cracked and I trembled. She tightened her grip on my hand, imbuing me with her strength.

"What is it?" she asked, the moment I disconnected the call. "Bad news?"

"She gave up."

"Seriously?" Armani gasped, outraged. "How could she?"

I shrugged.

"But you *paid* her, right?"

"No. The lawyer didn't give up. Abilene did. She dropped her petition for custody."

"Why?"

"I don't know and I don't care."

I ALSO DIDN'T care if Delveccio saw me when I walked into the hospital that evening. I just strolled in, waving at the nurses, joking with an orderly.

"Boss says to tell you he wants to buy ya a pudding," muscle-bound Vinnie said, just as I was about to walk into Katie's room.

"Tell him I'll meet him in the cafeteria in thirty minutes." I fixed Vinnie with a hard look, daring him to challenge me about keeping the mob boss happy.

He looked like he wanted to argue, but all he said was "I'll let him know."

I walked into Katie's room with a big smile on my face. "Hey there, Baby Girl."

Katie had been watching television, but she switched her attention to me. I could have sworn she gave me the slightest smile in return, but then thought it was wishful thinking on my part.

I sat in the visitor's chair and picked up her limp hand to hold in mine as she returned her gaze to the screen. "Whatchya watchin'?"

She didn't answer. Not that she needed to. A glance at the TV told me she was watching a cartoon about a dog in a haunted house.

"I got a dog," I told her. "Her name is DeeDee. She and Godzilla are friends. I think you'd like her."

That got no response either.

The cartoon dog was chased first by a ghost and then by a giant spider.

"The itsy bitsy spider went up . . ." I started to sing.

Katie looked back at me, something like recognition flickering in the depths of her blue eyes.

" . . . the water spout," I continued, not even daring to hope. "Down came the rain and washed . . ."

She moved her hand.

I looked down at her tiny little fingers.

" . . . washed the spider out." I'd stopped breathing and barely had enough air to get the words out.

Slowly, stiffly, her pudgy fingers started to perform the pantomime that went along with the song.

I joined her in making the motions. "Up came the sun and dried up all the rain."

She smiled at me, actually smiled at me, as she matched my movements.

"And the itsy bitsy spider went up the spout again," I sang weakly.

I waited to see what she'd do next. My heart almost burst when she tapped my hand twice, our "secret" signal to do it again.

"The itsy bitsy spider went up the water spout, down came the rain," I sang through my tears. "And washed the spider out."

"Oh my God!" Aunt Susan exclaimed from behind me.

I twisted around, to see her standing a few feet away, wringing her hands.

"She's doing it," she whispered in awe.

Katie waved at her.

LEAVING KATIE WITH a gushing Aunt Susan, I went in search of my favorite mob boss. He waved me over the moment I entered the cafeteria. Vinnie was nowhere in sight.

"I heard that your grandson is doing better," I said as a way of greeting, determined to start the conversation off on a positive note.

Delveccio beamed, his smile brighter than his pinky ring for once. "It's a miracle!"

I nodded, knowing the feeling.

Vinnie appeared with two puddings, two spoons and two napkins. "Anything else, boss?"

Delveccio shook his head and Vinnie hurried away. "The boy's learning."

"Does that mean he's growing on you?"

Throwing back his head, he laughed, the sound echoing off the cafeteria's walls. "Not by a long shot, but it looks like I'm going to be stuck with him for a while longer. Can't go firing my bodyguard now that *somebody* killed Gary the Gun and Jose Garcia died under mysterious circumstances."

"About that," I said slowly, choosing my words carefully.

"It was genius! Pure genius!" He gobbled a spoonful of pudding. "I'd worried you wouldn't be able to pull off the job, but wow, you did it and you did it with style."

I stared at him. He thought I'd killed Garcia?

"My guy in the forensics lab said that you stripped the hardware with amazing precision. How'd you do it?"

I opened my mouth to tell him I hadn't, but he just kept on talking.

"The guy who ordered the hit," Delveccio continued, interrupting my train of thought, "was very happy with the job you did. Very happy. And so am I."

He snapped his fingers and Vinnie hustled over. "Get the book."

The bodyguard hurried away. The mobster eyed my untouched pudding. "Are you going to eat that?"

I pushed it across the table to him, trying to figure out how to tell him I wasn't responsible for Garcia's death.

"Your payment is in the book."

"What?"

"The cash is in the book. With a bonus."

"A bonus?" I squeaked.

"You earned it." Delveccio took a book, the size of a dictionary, from Vinnie and handed it to me.

"I think you'll enjoy it," he said with a wink.

"Thank you." Clutching the book tightly, I practically ran out of the hospital, anxious to talk to God about what had really happened at the Garcia wedding.

Chapter Thirty-Two

"DID YOU KILL him?" I blurted out the moment I walked into the apartment.

"Gotta! Gotta! Gotta!" DeeDee panted.

"You forgot to leave the idiot tube on," God drawled lazily. "All I had to amuse me all day was the beast."

"Did you kill Garcia?"

"Did you bring me dinner?" He greedily eyed the bag of live crickets I'd stopped off to buy for him.

"Gotta!" DeeDee whined.

The lizard cocked his head. "Dinner theater could be munching on them while watching you clean up her mess."

I put the chirping/jumping plastic bag down on the kitchen table beside the terrarium. Grabbing the dog's leash, I rushed her outside.

"That's cruel and unusual punishment," God called after us.

"Better God feel," the dog told me as soon as she'd relieved herself.

"That's good. I know you were worried about him." I rubbed the spot between her eyes.

She smiled at me.

Which always looked scary.

"Better Maggie too is?"

I thought about the news about Abilene and my book full of bucks. "Yes. I am better."

We went back inside.

"The phone you keep hidden under the bed has been ringing all day," God groused.

"Did they leave a message?

"Do I look like the type that would stoop to listening to someone else's answering machine?"

I noticed that his color had returned with his snark. I was relieved by both.

"So are you going to feed me or let me starve to death?"

I picked up the bag o' bugs. "Did you kill Jose Garcia?"

"In a strange twist of fate, the drug-dealing scum died saving the life of his innocent granddaughter."

"And you had nothing to do with that twisting? Or should I say *untwisting* of a screw or a bolt or whatever it was?"

He shrugged eloquently.

"Thank you."

"If you want to thank me, feed me."

Lifting the lid of his terrarium, I dumped the bugs in, shivering uncontrollably as I imagined the creepy-crawlies on me.

"Katie smiled at me today," I told him as he caught a hapless bug and started chowing down. "She played with me too."

"Dat's wunnerful."

"Don't talk with your mouth full," I admonished.

"Meat!" DeeDee barked excitedly. "Meat! Meat!"

I hung my head guiltily, having forgotten to get her something special to eat. "All we have is dog food."

Someone knocked twice on my front door. I jumped, startled.

DeeDee ran to the door. "Meat! Meat! Meat!"

"Grab a carving knife," God urged. "It could be whoever left the rats."

"I don't *own* a carving knife." I grabbed a paring knife instead.

"Meat!" DeeDee whined.

"Who is it?" I called.

"It's me, Mags."

I yanked open the door to find Patrick standing on my doorstep. "You're back."

"So it would appear," God drawled.

"You knocked," I said in amazement.

The corners of Patrick's mouth twitched. "Are you going to invite me in?"

"Meat!" DeeDee whined.

"That depends. Did you bring dinner for just the dog, or for me too?"

He bent and picked up a paper grocery bag from the ground. "Plenty for everyone."

"Then come in."

He walked into the kitchen, the dog at his heels. Taking a rotisserie chicken from the bag, he tore off a piece and tossed it to the dog.

"Meat!" she panted happily.

"You spoil her," I said.

"Somebody has to." He handed me a plastic container of olives stuffed with feta cheese. "Straight from the barrel."

I opened it, popped one in my mouth, and offered them to him. "How was the trip?"

"Plates? Better than I hoped. Daria stayed behind. Laila is getting married next week."

"Wow, that was quick." I handed him two plates.

"It's not like we were ever legally married, so she doesn't need to wait to get a divorce. Besides, it was no quicker than your friend Alice. How'd that go?"

"Better than I'd hoped." I put two forks on the table.

"Check out the domestic bliss," God remarked, chewing on a cricket leg.

I shot him a dirty look. He stuck his tongue out at me.

"And I heard you managed to pull off the Garcia job." Patrick spooned mashed potatoes onto the plates.

"That seems to be the consensus," I said carefully. "Do I strike you as the handy type who could rig a disco ball to kill a man?"

Patrick shrugged, giving us each a generous portion of peas and carrots. "You're full of surprises. You're not going to tell Delveccio you weren't responsible, are you?"

"Can't. I already handed over the advance he fronted

me to the lawyer handling the custody case. Don't worry, though, I've got your percentage for you."

"Light or dark?"

"Excuse me?"

"Light meat or dark?"

"Meat!" DeeDee declared. He rewarded her with a toss of browned skin.

"White, please." I put two bottles of water on the table for us.

"I'm more of a leg man myself." Despite the fact he had his back to me, a flirtatious note threaded through his tone.

I gulped. "Katie's making progress. Today she smiled at me and we even played a little game."

"That's great, Mags. I'm happy for you."

"She wouldn't be. If it wasn't for you," I said stiltedly. "If you hadn't helped me earn the money to keep her there, none of this would be happening."

Turning around, he put the two plates down on the table. "You did the hard work. I didn't do much at all."

He indicated we should sit, so I did.

We ate in companionable silence, taking turns feeding DeeDee scraps of food.

When we were done, he looked over at my fridge. "I see you got my postcard."

I nodded, looking at the cactus.

"And?" he prompted.

"And what?"

"Did you get what came with it?"

"It was the only thing in the envelope. Was there supposed to be something else?"

"You didn't get any . . . gifts?" He studied my face as I worked it out.

He smiled as the realization dawned.

"Abilene?" My heart pounded. "You made Abilene drop her case?"

"You did ask me to stop in Vegas."

"To kill her."

"My way was cleaner."

Leaping out of my seat, I hugged his neck and pressed a kiss to the top of his red head. "Thank you! Thank you!"

With a quick twist, he pulled me into his lap. I rested one hand on his shoulder, the other on his chest to steady myself. I could feel his heartbeat, strong and steady beneath my fingers.

"I missed you, Mags." He stared at me intensely.

I felt my own heartbeat speed up.

"DeeDee miss?" The dog interrupted the intimate moment by nudging her head between us.

I slid off his lap, remembering I had something else I needed to talk to him about.

He looked disappointed I'd jumped up.

"Did you tell Marlene about Katie being in the hospital?"

"No."

"But she was there. Did you tell her about Theresa's accident?"

"Jewel was at the hospital?"

"Her name isn't Jewel. It's Marlene."

"Sorry. Marlene was at the hospital?"

I nodded.

"Did you talk to her?"

I shook my head and looked away.

"What happened?" he asked gently, getting to his feet.

"She ran away from me. Again."

He flinched at the bitterness in my tone. "I'm sorry."

"I'm not. My life is complicated enough as it is. I don't need her in it. I don't *want* her in it."

"You don't mean that," Patrick chided softly. "You're understandably hurt, but you don't mean that."

I didn't want to talk about Marlene anymore. "I'm moving back in with my aunts," I blurted out. "I thought it was the only way to win the custody case and I'm going to need help caring for Katie. And I might quit my job and become a real estate agent because who knows what kinds of special needs Katie is going to have. And DeeDee's getting a dog run."

"Run!" DeeDee barked.

"That's good, Mags. It's all good." He put the dishes in the sink.

"Leave them."

"I'm tired from the trip and you look exhausted, so I'm going to go now."

"Okay."

"Dinner tomorrow?" he asked.

"I can't. I have a date."

His expression darkened. "With Kowalski?"

"With my mom."

A smile creased his face and lit up his eyes. "That sounds great. Later in the week then?"

"I'd like that."

He patted DeeDee on the head and walked out the door.

"I like him," God opined.

"Too DeeDee!" the mutt panted.

"Me too," I muttered. "Too bad it would never work."

The phone in the bedroom rang.

"Answer it!" God shrieked. "It's been ringing all day."

"I'm going. I'm going." Hurrying into the other room, I snatched up the phone on its fourth ring. "Hello?"

"We want the jewels," a deep voice said.

I clutched the phone tightly, trying to remember where I'd hidden my gun.

"Tell the rat we want the jewels and if we don't get 'em, his family is gonna pay." A click told me the call was over.

But another nightmare was beginning.

Want to know how
Maggie Lee got her start?
Keep reading for an excerpt from

JB Lynn's

*Confessions of a Slightly
Neurotic Hitwoman*

Available now

Prologue

YOU JUST KNOW it's going to be a bad day when you're stuck at a red light and Death pulls up behind you in a station wagon.

I'd been using the rearview mirror to touch up my lip gloss when I spotted him. Okay, maybe he wasn't really Death, but dressed in a black raincoat with the hood pulled up covering his face, he sure looked like he could pluck a scythe out of thin air.

It was one of those days when I kept catching the specter of Death everywhere. I'd catch a glimpse of him in the condensation on the bathroom mirror as I stepped out of the shower, or burnt into my morning toast, or in the pile of dog shit I narrowly missed stepping in . . . or didn't.

Death was idling behind me, and I was kinda freaked out. Which was why, completely forgetting about the damn April showers that had been falling for three days straight, I floored my crappy, beat-up, not-gently-used Honda the second that light turned green.

Hydroplaning, the car spun out into the intersection, with me pumping the brakes while wondering if I should have been steering into the skid or out of it, and berating myself for not having paid more attention during my high school Driver's Ed course.

I knew I was gonna die. I could already hear the angels singing.

Three months before, I'd had the same feeling as another car slid out of control. I hadn't been driving then; my sister's idiot husband had been behind the wheel. I'd been in the backseat, singing "Itsy Bitsy Spider" to my three-year-old niece Katie, trying to distract her from the argument her parents were having in the front seat. Suddenly the car swerved and squealed, and as we rolled over onto the driver's side, I distinctly remember thinking, *Dear God, please don't let us die.*

I didn't think that three months later. In this moment I was resigned to my fate.

But then, miraculously, my little Honda gained traction, and I achieved a semblance of control over the vehicle. I wasn't in the clear, though. Squinting at the rearview mirror, I could see that Death had followed me through the rain-soaked intersection.

And I could still hear the singing of the angels, but it wasn't a heavenly sound.

It was loud. It was annoying.

From the floor of the passenger seat, I snatched up the bag of crickets that I'd bought for Godzilla. They were making an unholy racket. I shook it hard. That shut the little fuckers up.

When I first became responsible for Godzilla's care, I tried giving him freeze-dried crickets. But that damn lizard, he's got a discerning palate and insists on the live version, which is a pain in the ass because I hate bugs. Really hate 'em. Just looking at them gives me that awful creepy-crawly feeling, but I'd pledged to Katie that I'd take good care of the only pet she'd ever been allowed.

There was no way of knowing whether she even knew I'd made her that promise. She'd been in a coma, a "persistent vegetative state," as the doctors liked to call it, ever since the car accident. Her parents had died on impact, according to police. I'd walked away unharmed . . . except for the fact that I can now talk to a lizard.

"Call me God," he'd insisted the first time I'd thought to feed him.

He'd never spoken to me before. I mean animals, or reptiles or amphibians, or whatever the hell he is, don't talk. I know that. I haven't gone totally around the bend.

But the thing is, ever since the car accident, we can converse. And we do. A lot.

Maybe I've got brain damage, or maybe it's the emotional trauma of having my sister die and almost losing Katie, but I swear that I've turned into Doctor-freakin-Dolittle.

Of course, I haven't told anyone about my newfound ability. They'd lock me up in a funny farm like my mom.

Or run a bunch of tests. Or run a bunch of tests and then lock me up. And if they did that, I wouldn't be able to visit Katie. And she'd be left all alone there, lying in a hospital bed, with only the witches to look after her.

My three aunts aren't really witches. I'm not so delusional as to think they've got magical powers. They're just extraordinarily evil in their own "helpfully" meddlesome way.

So I keep the secret conversations with God to myself. To the rest of the world, it probably appears that I'm coping pretty well. I wash my clothes, bring the newspaper in, and have even gone back to work in hell (also known as an insurance company call center).

My piddly paycheck isn't going to make much of a dent in the pile of hospital bills that are piling up faster than a Colorado snowfall, but it's a decent cover. It's not like I can go around putting HITWOMAN on my tax return.

Death, or at least the driver in the station wagon, coasted past as I turned my blinker on to signal my turn into Apple Blossom Estates. There's no such thing as apple blossoms. Three months before, God, licking his lizard lips after chowing down on a cricket, had pointed out that even he knew that. But it sounds fancy right? Or at least like the over-promising prose of a condo developer's advertising. It's not. It's just a fancy name for a brain injury rehab, or as they like to call it, a "premium care facility."

Parking in the visitors' lot, I left the bag o' bugs to

their chirping (which sounded suspiciously like Madonna's "Like a Prayer") and headed inside. It was time to tell my boss that I was ready to kill a man.

But you're probably wondering how a nice girl like me got a job like this . . .

Chapter One

SOMETIMES I THINK my first memory is the sound of the three witches cackling. Sometimes I think it's tumbling—no, wait, tumbling might insinuate that I had some sort of grace or plan. I wouldn't want to give you the wrong impression of me. I am—have been for my whole life and always will be—without an iota of grace. And planning has never been my strong suit. Okay, so sometimes I think my first memory is falling/crashing/plummeting down an entire flight of stairs and breaking my left arm when I was two.

Both those memories rushed back at me. I'm guessing it was because my entire body hurt, and I could hear the three witches. I am, if you choose to believe the traitorous date imprinted on my driver's license, thirty-two. Lying there with my body aching and my head throbbing, all I wanted was to have a good cry and take a nap. But the witches wouldn't shut up.

I cracked open one eye and squinted at the three women in their fifties gathered at the foot of the bed, huddled around what looked like some sort of clipboard. I didn't recognize the bed, or the room, or the clipboard, but I did know the three women. I groaned.

"She's awake!" Aunt Leslie, the most emotional of my three aunts, hit a note that sliced through my skull with the precision of a Ginsu knife dicing butter. Racing around the bed, she stuck her face in my face like an inquisitive cocker spaniel. "Can you hear me, Margaret?"

Recoiling, I tried to get away from the noxious fumes of her sickeningly sweet perfume. At least I told myself it was perfume. It could have been the residual odor of her daily joint (medical marijuana, she claimed, though she didn't have a prescription and hadn't seen a doctor in over a decade). Unfortunately I couldn't figure out a way to answer her without inhaling. "I hear you."

For some reason those three words made Aunt Leslie burst into tears.

"It's a miracle!" Aunt Loretta cried, as though she was praising Jesus. "It's a miracle! I have got to go find that doctor and share this happy news!"

But first she had to give herself a quick once-over in her compact mirror to make sure that her lipstick wasn't smudged and her nose wasn't shiny. Reassured that she looked her best, she shimmied out of the room in her too-tight dress and too-high heels. Even closing in on sixty Aunt Loretta was convinced that she was giving Sophia Loren and Raquel Welch a run for their money as she rocked a sex-kitten wardrobe.

"What's wrong? What happened?" I asked her twin sister, Aunt Leslie, who had worked herself into full-blown sobs in record time.

Wiping her eyes with the corner of the bed sheet, she just cried harder.

A vise of panic tightened around my solar plexus, choking off my air supply, as I tried to figure out what was going on. Everything was so fuzzy.

"Margaret," Aunt Susan, the third and oldest sister, got my attention from where she waited at the foot of the bed. If Aunt Leslie is the family pothead, and Aunt Loretta is the resident nympho, Aunt Susan is the straight arrow. She might be a pain in the ass, but I know from experience that she can be counted on to make sense in the midst of chaos. "There was a car accident."

And it all came back. The car. The rain. The fighting in the front seat. The "Itsy Bitsy Spider." The skid. The roll. The screeching and squealing of metal. The impact. The pain. Screaming.

Katie.

"Katie!" I sat straight up, and the room spun. I was weak and dizzy and nauseated. I broke into a cold sweat. The sensation reminded me of the last time I'd gone with Darlene on the tilt-a-whirl. I didn't want to think about that. I couldn't.

"Katie's alive," Susan said.

The assurance acted like a super-concentrated dose of Dramamine. The room stopped spinning. The desire to puke my guts up abated. Collapsing back down onto the pillow, I closed my eyes.

"Theresa didn't make it," Aunt Susan said softly.

That made Aunt Leslie cry harder.

I kept my eyes squeezed tightly shut as I tried to convince myself this was all a dream. After my baby sister Darlene died fifteen years ago, I'd been plagued with terrible nightmares. In them, all my family members died, one by one. Maybe this was just another bad dream. Maybe my big sister Theresa was still here.

Aunt Susan couldn't leave me well-enough-alone with my happy delusion. "Dirk died too."

Aunt Leslie didn't shed a tear for him. That's how I knew it was all real.

I thought about the submarine movie. It was a foreign film, without subtitles. I don't even recall the title. All I remember was the scene when the ship is in danger of sinking. The captain makes the decision to seal off a room, or compartment, or whatever it's called on a submarine, forfeiting the lives of the sailors trapped inside in order to keep the ship afloat.

Even though I couldn't understand a single word of dialogue, it was a horrifying, heart-wrenching scene. The idea of sacrificing part in order for the whole to be saved didn't make any sense to me.

Until my sister Darlene died. Then I understood it perfectly. In order to keep functioning, to keep my head above water, I had to shut off my emotions.

Unwilling to deal with the loss of Theresa, I slammed the door shut on the tidal wave of pain and emotion that threatened to drown me. It was the only way to survive.

I opened my eyes as Aunt Loretta came click-clacking

back into the room on the heels of a white-coated doctor.
I could see why she'd been so eager to find him. He sorta
reminded me of Tom Selleck in his *Magnum, P.I.* heyday.

"How are you feeling?" he asked as he pulled out one
of those annoying lights doctors like to shine in your eyes.

"Like shit."

"Language, Margaret!" Aunt Susan admonished.

Did I mention that straight arrow of hers is stuck up
her ass?

"Well that's understandable, considering . . ." He
leaned in close to make his examination. His touch was
cool and gentle as he tilted my chin.

"She's in shock," Aunt Leslie supplied helpfully, even
though no one had asked for an opinion. "Often with a
concussion a patient—"

Dr. Magnum P.I. rolled his eyes. No doubt Aunt Leslie
had quoted every fact she'd ever read about a head injury
to the poor man. I pitied him. Aunt Loretta rested a hand
on his arm, pretending to get a better look at me, while
groping his bicep muscle.

"Let the man do his job," I muttered.

The doctor smiled, apparently relieved that at least
someone in the family wasn't going to hassle him. "I'm
going to have to ask you ladies to step out while I examine
my patient."

"I saw online—" Aunt Leslie said.

"But we're family," Aunt Susan protested

"Is there something wrong with her?" Aunt Loretta
asked, almost hopefully. I half-expected her to press the
back of her hand to her forehead and pass out.

A nurse bustled in and hustled the witches out.

The doctor poked and prodded me. "You're one fortunate woman. Most adults don't wear their seatbelts when riding in the back of a car. Yours saved your life."

"I normally don't wear it."

"Lucky you did."

"I was just trying to set a good example for my niece." I swallowed hard. A ball of misery had lodged itself in my throat. "Can I see her? Can I see my niece?"

"As soon as we're finished here."

Once he'd finished a physical examination and I'd answered a couple dozen questions for him, he told me that with the exception of some bruised ribs, and the bump on my head, I had miraculously escaped unharmed. True to his word, he instructed the nurse who had joined us to take me to see Katie. She helped me into a wheelchair and rolled me through a series of hallways, explaining that Katie was in the pediatric intensive care unit. She also told me how lucky we were that Katie had been brought to this hospital and not to another. I found it supremely irritating that everyone kept telling me how lucky I was.

She wheeled me to Katie's bedside and left.

My eyes burned, but no tears fell, as I looked at her small, frail body, lost in the big bed. The top of her head was encapsulated in some kind of cast. Bruises and scratches marred her face. She was attached to a myriad of blinking and beeping medical monitors. She looked more like a horrible science experiment than my beautiful niece.

Always pale, her skin took on an almost translucent

quality beneath the harsh hospital lights. I traced the blue vein that snaked down her cheek, imagining I could infuse my life force into her with a mere touch. It was a foolish fantasy, but one I couldn't give up.

"I'm here, Katie," I whispered. "Aunt Maggie's here."

Before the accident, it scared me how much I loved this little girl. Her smile made me happy, her laughter, giddy. My heart squeezed every time she slipped her hand into mine, and contentment flooded through me when she climbed into my lap.

I stuck my index finger into her palm, hoping that she'd reflexively grab onto me like she used to when she was a baby, but her fingers remained limp.

"You're going to be okay, Baby Girl. Aunt Maggie will take care of you. I promise."

I'm not big on promises. I don't like making them. Maybe it's because I'm commitment-phobic, or maybe I'm just lazy.

Worse than making promises, though, is believing in them.

I know this from experience. I'd made the mistake of telling my sister Marlene that her twin, Darlene, was going to be okay a long time ago. I'd paid the price, or, more accurately, she'd paid the price, ever since.

That's because a broken promise, no matter how well-intentioned it may be, is like a pebble in a shoe. At first it's uncomfortable. Then it's irritating. Finally it becomes downright painful. And if you don't figure out a way to purge it from your shoe, or, in this case, your psyche, you can end up with a giant, raw blister than can easily infect your soul.

At least that was the theory I came up with after I broke my promise to Marlene. I had nothing else to do all those sleepless nights when she'd drifted away. Nothing else to do but blame myself for what had happened. All because of my broken promise.

I didn't get to dwell on my failures as a sister for long before Aunt Susan came into the room.

"We were looking all over for you, Margaret." There was more rebuke than concern in her voice. There always was.

I ignored her admonishment, too tired to come up with an excuse, too far past caring to offer an apology. "I don't understand. I've barely got a scratch on me, and Katie . . . she. . . . Why didn't the car seat protect her?"

"There are some papers you need to sign."

It was my turn to roll my eyes. That was Aunt Susan, all business, all the time. "Papers?"

"Authorizing me to make decisions regarding Katherine's care. With Theresa . . . with both parents out of the picture, the hospital needs a guardian to sign releases, that kind of thing."

"I can sign them." Theresa had made me sign off on a million legal papers to make sure that I'd have the right to do just that. At the time, I'd thought it was a giant headache over nothing, but now I saw the wisdom of her choice.

I heard Susan's sharp intake of breath even over the

noise of Katie's monitors. She was displeased. I didn't give a damn.

"We should talk about this in the hallway, Margaret."

Grudgingly, I attempted to wheel away from Katie's bed. But no matter how hard I pushed, the damn wheelchair wouldn't budge, a none-too-pleasant reminder that I hadn't been using my gym membership.

"There's a brake," Susan muttered.

Fumbling around, I finally disengaged it, and the wheels started to turn. I tried to make a graceful exit, but instead I ended up slamming into the pole holding Katie's IV and then some other beeping machine. I made enough noise to wake the dead, but Katie didn't stir.

"Oh for goodness' sake," Susan muttered, grabbing the wheelchair from behind and steering me out of the room.

"I've never driven one of these things before. There's a learning curve."

We barreled down the hallway, causing nurses and orderlies to leap out of our path for fear of losing their toes. "Your whole life has been a learning curve, Margaret, and you're failing at it."

I winced. I couldn't come up with a clever rebuttal, because I knew she was right. I also knew I wasn't going to give her the satisfaction of knowing her barb had hit home. "I'm Katie's legal guardian. Theresa wanted me to make the decisions regarding her care."

"You can't make a decision about what socks to wear!" Aunt Susan slammed the chair to a stop, almost dumping me onto the floor.

"Hey! There are no seatbelts with these things!"

Rounding my chariot, Aunt Susan took a deep breath, preparing to hex me, or curse at me, or, worst of all, tell me how "lucky" I was to have her around to pick up the pieces.

Lucky my ass.

I wasn't going to take it sitting down. I struggled unsteadily to my feet. My blood pressure surged, and I swayed woozily, but like a boxer facing a knock-out punch, I stayed on my feet.

And the damndest thing happened. Something, some expression I had never before witnessed on my eldest aunt's face, something that looked a lot like respect, gleamed in her eyes. Pursing her lips, she considered me carefully.

I braced myself for the harangue, the lecture, the litany of my shortcomings, but she stayed silent. We stood there, locked in silent battle for the longest time. I refused to back down. I didn't look away. I knew enough to not open my mouth and stay something stupid.

Finally she cleared her throat. I lifted my chin defiantly.

"The doctor wants to keep you overnight, but one of us, probably Loretta, since she's enamored with all the wealthy, handsome doctors, will be back in the morning to drive you home."

I shook my head. "No need. My apartment is only a couple of blocks from here."

I thought for a moment I'd pushed my rebellion a bit too far, as her hands planted themselves on her hips.

"When I said we'd bring you home, I meant to the house." The three aunts still lived in the house they'd grown up in, although now it had been turned into a prosperous bed-and-breakfast catering mostly to pharmaceutical executives tired of staying in stark hotel rooms.

The B&B is located two blocks from the middle of town and is only a fifteen or twenty minute drive to three pharmaceutical complexes, but it's tucked into a quiet residential neighborhood. My aunts' neighbors are normal Jersey folks, not the kind who show up on ridiculous reality shows, but the type who, during the summer, have sprinklers that are synchronized better than any Olympic swimming team, and during the winter indulge in a penchant for oversized inflatable holiday directions that stay up from October through March.

My apartment complex, on the other hand, is on the "seedy" side of town. It's not the best of neighborhoods, but it's not as bad as my family makes it out to be. Although there is the occasional drug bust or domestic disturbance to keep things interesting, it's mostly harmless blue-collar folks who think going "down the shore" is a dream vacation. It's the best I can afford and worth every nickel to be out from beneath my aunts' stifling roof. "No, I want to go back to my apartment," I told my aunt firmly.

Aunt Susan wrinkled her nose as though she'd smelled a skunk, but all she said was, "As you wish."

Like wishes ever come true.

About the Author

Besides being a writer, JB LYNN is a compulsive reader, a runner (of sorts), an enthusiastic cook (who doesn't get the appeal of the Food Network), and someone who has an irresistible urge to eavesdrop at all times.

JB has a great love of her husband, dogs, coffee, purple ink, spiral notebooks, running gear, hot showers, and eighties music. Given enough time, all of these things will eventually show up in her books.

In addition, she's a Twitter junkie and enjoys interacting with her readers. JB would love for you to "like" and "follow" her on the Net!

To learn more about JB and her books, please visit www.jblynn.com.

Give in to your impulses . . .
Read on for a sneak peek at two brand-new
e-book original tales of romance
from Avon Books.
Available now wherever e-books are sold.

THE FORBIDDEN LADY
By Kerrelyn Sparks

TURN TO DARKNESS
By Jaime Rush

An Excerpt from

THE FORBIDDEN LADY

by Kerrelyn Sparks

(Originally published under
the title *For Love or Country*)

Before *New York Times* bestselling author Kerrelyn Sparks
created a world of vampires, there was another world of spies
and romance . . .

Keep reading for a look at her very first novel.

CHAPTER ONE

Tuesday, August 29, 1769

"I say, dear gel, how much do *you* cost?"

Virginia's mouth dropped open. "I—I beg your pardon?"

The bewigged, bejeweled, and bedeviling man who faced her spoke again. "You're a fetching sight and quite sweet-smelling for a wench who has traveled for weeks, imprisoned on this godforsaken ship. I say, what *is* your price?"

She opened her mouth, but nothing came out. The rolling motion of the ship caught her off guard, and she stumbled, widening her stance to keep her balance. This man thought she was for sale? Even though they were on board *The North Star*, a brigantine newly arrived in Boston Harbor with a fresh supply of indentured servants, could he actually mistake her for one of the poor wretched criminals huddled near the front of the ship?

Her first reaction of shock was quickly replaced with anger. It swelled in her chest, heated to a quick boil, and soared past her ruffled neckline to her face, scorching her cheeks 'til she fully expected steam, instead of words, to escape her mouth.

"How . . . how *dare* you!" With gloved hands, she twisted the silken cords of her drawstring purse. "Pray, be gone with you, sir."

"Ah, a saucy one." The gentleman plucked a silver snuff-box from his lavender silk coat. He kept his tall frame erect to avoid flipping his wig, which was powdered with a lavender tint to match his coat. "Tsk, tsk, dear gel, such impertinence is sure to lower your price."

Her mouth fell open again.

Seizing the opportunity, he raised his quizzing glass and examined the conveniently opened orifice. "Hmm, but you do have excellent teeth."

She huffed. "And a sharp tongue to match."

"*Mon Dieu*, a very saucy mouth, indeed." He smiled, displaying straight, white teeth.

A perfectly bright smile, Virginia thought. What a pity his mental faculties were so dim in comparison. But she refrained from responding with an insulting remark. No good could come from stooping to his level of ill manners. She stepped back, intending to leave, but hesitated when he spoke again.

"I do so like your nose. Very becoming and—" He opened his silver box, removed a pinch of snuff with his gloved fingers and sniffed.

She waited for him to finish the sentence. He was a buffoon, to be sure, but she couldn't help but wonder—did he actually like her nose? Over the years, she had endured a great deal of teasing because of the way it turned up on the end.

He snapped his snuffbox shut with a click. "Ah, yes, where was I, becoming and . . . disdainfully haughty. Yes, that's it."

Heat pulsed to her face once more. "I daresay it is not surprising for *you* to admire something *disdainfully haughty*, but regardless of your opinion, it is improper for you to address me so rudely. For that matter, it is highly improper for you to speak to me at all, for need I remind you, sir, we have not been introduced."

He dropped his snuffbox back into his pocket. "Definitely disdainful. And haughty." His mouth curled up, revealing two dimples beneath the rouge on his cheeks.

She glared at the offensive fop. Somehow, she would give him the cut he deserved.

A short man in a brown buckram coat and breeches scurried toward them. "Mr. Stanton! The criminals for sale are over there, sir, near the forecastle. You see the ones in chains?"

Raising his quizzing glass, the lavender dandy pivoted on his high heels and perused the line of shackled prisoners. He shrugged his silk-clad shoulders and glanced back at Virginia with a look of feigned horror. "Oh, dear, what a delightful little *faux pas*. I suppose you're not for sale after all?"

"No, of course not."

"I do beg your pardon." He flipped a lacy, monogrammed handkerchief out of his chest pocket and made a poor attempt to conceal the wide grin on his face.

A heavy, flowery scent emanated from his handkerchief, nearly bowling her over. He was probably one of those people who never bathed, just poured on more perfume. She covered her mouth with a gloved hand and gently coughed.

"Well, no harm done." He waved his handkerchief in the

air. "*C'est la vie* and all that. Would you care for some snuff? 'Tis my own special blend from London, don't you know. We call it *Grey Mouton*."

"Gray sheep?"

"Why, yes. Sink me! You *parlez français*? How utterly charming for one of your class."

Narrowing her eyes, she considered strangling him with the drawstrings of her purse.

He removed the silver engraved box from his pocket and flicked it open. "A pinch, in the interest of peace?" His mouth twitched with amusement.

"No, thank you."

He lifted a pinch to his nose and sniffed. "What did I tell you, Johnson?" he asked the short man in brown buckram at his side. "These Colonials are a stubborn lot, far too eager to take offense"—he sneezed delicately into his lacy handkerchief—"and far too unappreciative of the efforts the mother country makes on their behalf." He slid his closed snuffbox back into his pocket.

Virginia planted her hands on her hips. "You speak, perhaps, of Britain's kindness in providing us with a steady stream of slaves?"

"Slaves?"

She gestured toward the raised platform of the forecastle, where Britain's latest human offering stood in front, chained at the ankles and waiting to be sold.

"Oh." He waved his scented handkerchief in dismissal. "You mean the indentured servants. They're not slaves, my dear, only criminals paying their dues to society. 'Tis the mother country's fervent hope they will be reformed by their experience in America."

"I see. Perhaps we should send the mother country a boat-load of American wolves to see if they can be reformed by their experience in Britain?"

His chuckle was surprisingly deep. "*Touché.*"

The deep timbre of his voice reverberated through her skin, striking a chord that hummed from her chest down to her belly. She caught her breath and looked at him more closely. When his eyes met hers, his smile faded away. Time seemed to hold still for a moment as he held her gaze, quietly studying her.

The man in brown cleared his throat.

Virginia blinked and looked away. She breathed deeply to calm her racing heart. Once more, she became aware of the murmur of voices and the screech of sea gulls overhead. What had happened? It must have been the thrill of putting the man in his place that had affected her. Strange, though, that he had happily acknowledged her small victory.

Mr. Stanton gave the man in brown a mildly irritated look, then smiled at her once more. "American wolves, you say? Really, my dear, these people's crimes are too petty to compare them to murderous beasts. Why, Johnson, here, was an indentured servant before becoming my secretary. Were you not, Johnson?"

"Aye, Mr. Stanton," the older man answered. "But I came voluntarily. Not all these people are prisoners. The group to the right doesn't wear chains. They're selling themselves out of desperation."

"There, you see." The dandy spread his gloved hands, palms up, in a gesture of conciliation. "No hard feelings. In fact, I quite trust Johnson here with all my affairs in spite of his criminal background. You know the Colonials are quite wrong in thinking we British are a cold, callous lot."

Virginia gave Mr. Johnson a small, sympathetic smile, letting him know she understood his indenture had not been due to a criminal past. Her own father, faced with starvation and British cruelty, had left his beloved Scottish Highlands as an indentured servant. Her sympathy seemed unnecessary, however, for Mr. Johnson appeared unperturbed by his employer's rudeness. No doubt the poor man had grown accustomed to it.

She gave Mr. Stanton her stoniest of looks. "Thank you for enlightening me."

"My pleasure, dear gel. Now I must take my leave." Without further ado, he ambled toward the group of gaunt, shackled humans, his high-heeled shoes clunking on the ship's wooden deck and his short secretary tagging along behind.

Virginia scowled at his back. The British needed to go home, and the sooner, the better.

"I say, old man." She heard his voice filter back as he addressed his servant. "I do wish the pretty wench were for sale. A bit too saucy, perhaps, but I do so like a challenge. *Quel dommage*, a real pity, don't you know."

A vision of herself tackling the dandy and stuffing his lavender-tinted wig down his throat brought a smile to her lips. She could do it. Sometimes she pinned down her brother when he tormented her. Of course, such behavior might be frowned upon in Boston. This was not the hilly region of North Carolina that the Munro family called home.

And the dandy might prove difficult to knock down. Watching him from the back, she realized how large he was. She grimaced at the lavender bows on his high-heeled pumps. Why would a man that tall need to wear heels? Another pair of lavender bows served as garters, tied over the tabs of his silk knee breeches. His silken hose were too sheer to hide padding, so those calves were truly that muscular. *How odd.*

He didn't mince his steps like one would expect from a fopdoodle, but covered the deck with long, powerful strides, the walk of a man confident in his strength and masculinity.

She found herself examining every inch of him, calculating the amount of hard muscle hidden beneath the silken exterior. What color was his hair under that hideous tinted wig? Probably black, like his eyebrows. His eyes had gleamed like polished pewter, pale against his tanned face.

Her breath caught in her throat. A tanned face? A fop would not spend the necessary hours toiling in the sun that resulted in a bronzed complexion.

This Mr. Stanton was a puzzle.

She shook her head, determined to forget the perplexing man. Yet, if he dressed more like the men back home—tight buckskin breeches, boots, no wig, no lace . . .

The sun bore down with increasing heat, and she pulled her hand-painted fan from her purse and flicked it open. She breathed deeply as she fanned herself. Her face tingled with a mist of salty air and the lingering scent of Mr. Stanton's handkerchief.

She watched with growing suspicion as the man in question postured in front of the women prisoners with his quizzing glass, assessing them with a practiced eye. Oh, dear, what were the horrible man's intentions? She slipped her fan back into her purse and hastened to her father's side.

Jamie Munro was speaking quietly to a fettered youth who appeared a good five years younger than her one and twenty years. "All I ask, young man, is honesty and a good day's work. In exchange, ye'll have food, clean clothes, and a clean pallet."

The spindly boy's eyes lit up, and he licked his dry, chapped lips. "Food?"

Virginia's father nodded. "Aye. Mind you, ye willna be working for me, lad, but for my widowed sister, here, in Boston. Do ye have any experience as a servant?"

The boy lowered his head and shook it. He shuffled his feet, the scrape of his chains on the deck grating at Virginia's heart.

"Papa," she whispered.

Jamie held up a hand. "Doona fash yerself, lass. I'll be taking the boy."

As the boy looked up, his wide grin cracked the dried dirt on his cheeks. "Thank you, my lord."

Jamie winced. "Mr. Munro, it is. We'll have none of that lordy talk aboot here. Welcome to America." He extended a hand, which the boy timidly accepted. "What is yer name, lad?"

"George Peeper, sir."

"Father." Virginia tugged at the sleeve of his blue serge coat. "Can we afford any more?"

Jamie Munro's eyes widened and he blinked at his daughter. "More? Just an hour ago, ye upbraided me aboot the evils of purchasing people, and now ye want more? 'Tis no' like buying ribbons for yer bonny red hair."

"I know, but this is important." She leaned toward him. "Do you see the tall man in lavender silk?"

Jamie's nose wrinkled. "Aye. Who could miss him?"

"Well, he wanted to purchase me—"

"*What?*"

She pressed the palms of her hands against her father's broad chest as he moved to confront the dandy. "'Twas a misunderstanding. Please."

His blue eyes glittering with anger, Jamie clenched his fists. "Let me punch him for you, lass."

"No, listen to me. I fear he means to buy one of those ladies for . . . immoral purposes."

Jamie frowned at her. "And what would ye be knowing of a man's immoral purposes?"

"Father, I grew up on a farm. I can make certain deductions, and I know from the way he looked at me, the man is not looking for someone to scrub his pots."

"What can I do aboot it?"

"If he decides he wants one, you could outbid him."

"He would just buy another, Ginny. I canna be buying the whole ship. I can scarcely afford this one here."

She bit her lip, considering. "You could buy one more if Aunt Mary pays for George. She can afford it much more than we."

"Nay." Jamie shook his head. "I willna have my sister paying. This is the least I can do to help Mary before we leave.

Besides, I seriously doubt I could outbid the dandy even once. Look at the rich way he's dressed, though I havena stet clue why a man would spend good coin to look like that."

The ship rocked suddenly, and Virginia held fast to her father's arm. A breeze wafted past her, carrying the scent of unwashed bodies. She wrinkled her nose. She should have displayed the foresight to bring a scented handkerchief, though not as overpowering as the one sported by the lavender popinjay.

Having completed his leisurely perusal of the women, Mr. Stanton was now conversing quietly with a young boy.

"Look, Father, that boy is so young to be all alone. He cannot be more than ten."

"Aye," Jamie replied. "We can only hope a good family will be taking him in."

"How much for the boy?" Mr. Stanton demanded in a loud voice.

The captain answered, "You'll be thinking twice before taking that one. He's an expensive little wretch."

Mr. Stanton lowered his voice. "Why is that?"

"I'll be needing payment for his passage *and* his mother's. The silly tart died on the voyage, so the boy owes you fourteen years of labor."

The boy swung around and shook a fist at the captain. "Me mum was not a tart, ye bloody old bugger!"

The captain yelled back, "And he has a foul mouth, as you can see. You'll be taking the strap to him before the day is out."

Virginia squeezed her father's arm. "The boy is responsible for his mother's debt?"

"Aye." Jamie nodded. "'Tis how it works."

Mr. Stanton adjusted the lace on his sleeves. "I have a fancy to be extravagant today. Name your price."

"At least the poor boy will have a roof over his head and food to eat." Virginia grimaced. "I only hope the dandy will not dress him in lavender silk."

Jamie Munro frowned. "Oh, dear."

"What is it, Father?"

"Ye say the man was interested in you, Ginny?"

"Aye, he seemed to like me in his own horrid way."

"Hmm. Perhaps the lad will be all right. At any rate, 'tis too late now. Let me pay for George, and we'll be on our way."

An Excerpt from

TURN TO DARKNESS
by Jaime Rush

Enter the world of the Offspring with this latest novella in Jaime Rush's fabulous paranormal series.

CHAPTER ONE

When Shea Baker pulled into her driveway, the sight of Darius's black coupe in front of her little rented house annoyed her. That it wasn't Greer's Jeep, and that she was disappointed it wasn't, annoyed the hell out of her.

Darius pulled out his partially dismantled wheelchair from inside the car and put it together within a few seconds. His slide from the driver's seat into his wheelchair was so practiced it was almost fluid. He waved, oblivious to her frown, and wheeled over to her truck. "As pale as you looked after hearing what Tucker, Del, and I went through, I thought you'd go right home." He wore his dark blond hair in a James Dean style, his waves gelled to stand up.

She *had* been freaked. Two men trying to kill them, men who would kill them all if they knew about their existence. She yanked her baseball cap lower on her head, a nervous habit. "I had a couple of jobs to check on. What brings you by?" She hoped it was something quick he could tell her right there and leave.

"Tucker kicked me out. I think he feels threatened by me,

because I had to take charge. I saved the day, and he won't even admit it."

None of the guys were comfortable with Darius. His mercurial mood shifts and oversized ego were irritating, but the shadows in his eyes hinted at an affinity for violence. In the two years he'd lived with them, though, he'd mostly kept to himself. She'd had no problem with him because he remained aloof, never revealing his emotions, even when he talked about the car accident that had taken his mobility. Unfortunately, when he thought she was reaching out to him, that aloofness had changed to romantic interest.

"Sounded like you went off the rails." She crossed her arms in front of her. "Look, if you're here to get me on your side, I won't—"

"I'd never ask you to do that." His upper lip lifted in a sneer. "I know you're loyal only to Tucker."

She narrowed her eyes, her body stiffening. "Tuck's like a big brother to me. He gave me a home when I was on the streets, told me why I have extraordinary powers." That she'd inherited DNA from another dimension was crazy-wild, but it made as much sense as, say, being able to move objects with her mind. "I'd take his side over anyone's."

"Wish someone would feel that kind of loyalty to me," Darius muttered under his breath, making her wonder if he was trying to elicit her sympathy. "I get that you're brotherly/sisterly." He let those words settle for a second. "But something happened with you and Greer, didn't it? What did he do, grope you?"

"Don't be ridiculous. Greer would never do something like that."

"Something happened, because all of a sudden the way you looked at each other changed. Like he was way interested in you, and you were way uncomfortable around him. Then you sat all close to me, and I know you felt the same electricity I did."

She shook her head, sending her curly ponytail swinging over her shoulder. "There was no electricity. Greer and I had a ... disagreement. I needed to put some space between us, but when you live in a house with four other people, there isn't a lot of room. When I sat next to you, I was just moving away from him."

Darius's shoulders, wide and muscular, stiffened. "You might think that, Shea. You might even believe it. But someday you're going to realize you want me. And when you do, I want you to know I can satisfy you. When I'm in Darkness, I'm a whole man." That dark glint in his eyes hinted at his arrogance. "I'm capable of anything."

Those words shivered through her, but not in the way he'd intended. In that moment, she knew somehow that he *was* capable of anything. Darius might be confined to a wheelchair, but only a fool would underestimate him, and she was no fool. Especially where Darkness was concerned. The guys possessed it, yet didn't know exactly what it was. All they knew was that they'd probably inherited it, along with the DNA that gave them extraordinary powers, from the men who'd gotten their mothers pregnant. It allowed them to Become something far from human.

"Please, Darius, don't talk to me about that kind of thing. I'm not interested in having sex with anyone."

The corner of his mouth twisted cruelly. "Don't you like

sex? Maybe you've never been with someone who could do it well."

For a long time the thought of sex had coated her in shame and disgust. Until that little incident with Greer, when she'd had a totally different—and surprising—reaction.

"Look, I'm sorry Tuck kicked you out, but I don't have a guest bedroom."

"I'll sleep on the couch. You won't even know I'm here." His face transformed from darkly sexual to a happy little boy's. "I don't have any other place to stay," he added, building his case. "You just said how grateful you are to Tuck for taking you in. I'm only asking for the same thing."

Damn, he had her. As much as she wanted to squash her feelings, some things did reach right under her shields. And some people . . . like Greer. Now, Darius's manipulation did. "All right," she spat out, feeling pinned.

Her phone rang from where she'd left it inside her truck.

"Thanks, Shea," Darius said, wheeling to his car and popping the trunk. "You're a doll."

She got into her truck, grabbing up the phone and eyeing the screen. Greer. She'd been trying to avoid him since moving out three months before. But with the weirdness going on lately, she needed to stay in the loop.

"Hey," she answered. "What's up?"

"Tuck and Darius had it out a while ago. Darius has this idea about being the alpha male, which is just stupid, and Tuck kicked him out. I wanted to let you know in case he shows up on your doorstep pulling his 'poor me' act."

"Too late," she said in a singsong voice. "Act pulled—very well, I might add. He's staying for a few days."

"Bad idea." Always the protective one. He made no apologies for it either.

She watched Darius lift his suitcase onto his lap and wheel toward the ramp he'd installed for wheelchair access to her front door. "Well, what was I supposed to do, turn him away? I don't like it either."

"I'm coming over."

"There's no need . . ." She looked at the screen, blinking to indicate he'd ended the call. ". . . to come over," she finished anyway.

She got out, feeling like her feet weighed fifty pounds each, and trudged to the door. All she wanted was to be alone, a quiet evening trimming her bonsai to clear her mind.

There would be no mind-clearing tonight. There'd be friction between Greer and Darius, just like there had been before she'd moved out. Tuck had eased her into the reality of Darkness, he and Greer morphing into black beasts only after she'd accepted the idea. Tuck told her it also made them fiercely, and insanely, territorial about their so-called mates. She hadn't thought twice about that until Darius and Greer both took a different kind of liking to her. She was afraid they'd tear each other's throats out, and she wasn't either of their mates.

"Two days," she said, unlocking her front door. "I like living on my own. Being alone." Most of the time. It was strange, but she'd sit at her table in the mornings having coffee (not as strong as Greer's killer brew) and be happy about being alone. Then she'd get hit with a wave of sadness about being alone.

See how messed up you are.

"You might like having me around," he said. "If that guy

who's been creeping around makes an appearance, I'll kick his ass."

"Well, he's too much of a coward to knock on the door." She didn't want to think about her stalker. He hadn't left any of his icky letters or "gifts" in a few days.

She figured out where Darius could stash his suitcases and was hunting down extra sheets and a blanket when the doorbell rang. Before she could even set the extra pillow down to answer, she heard Darius's voice: "Well, look who's here. What a nice surprise."

Not by the tone in his voice. Damn, this was so not cool having them both here. They'd been like snarling dogs the day everyone had helped her move in here. She hadn't had them over since.

She walked out holding the pillow to her chest like a shield. Greer's eyes went right to her, giving her a clear *Is everything all right?* look.

She wasn't in danger. That's as far as she'd commit.

Greer closed the door and sauntered in, as though he always stopped by. "Thought I'd check in on you. After what happened, figured you might be on edge." There he went again, sinking her into the depths of his eyes. They were rimmed in gray, brown in the middle, the most unusual eyes she'd ever seen. And they were assessing her.

"She's fine," Darius answered as she opened her mouth. "I'm staying here for a couple of days, which will work out nicely . . . in case she's on edge." His unspoken *So you can go now* was clear.

Greer moved closer to her, putting himself physically between her and Darius. He was a damned wall of a man, too, way tall, wide shoulders, and just big. He purposely blocked Darius's view of her.

She'd done this, sparked them into hostile territory. Which was laughable, considering what she looked like: baggy pants and shirt, cap over her head, no makeup. She'd done everything she could for the last six years to squash every bit of her femininity. Her sexuality. Then Greer had blown that to bits.

He hadn't knocked, just barged into the bathroom, a towel loosely held in front of his naked body. She was drying her hair and suddenly he was standing there gaping at her.

"Jesus, Shea, you're beautiful," he'd said, obviously in shock.

She couldn't move, spellbound herself, which was ridiculous because she wasn't interested in anyone sexually. But there stood six feet four of olive-skinned Apache with muscled thighs and a scant bit of towel covering him. And the way he'd said those words, with his typical passion, and his looking at her like she *was* beautiful and he wanted her, woke up something inside her.

Breaking out of the spell and wrapping her towel around her, she'd yelled at him for barging in, stepping up close to him and jabbing her finger at his chest.

And what had he done? Lifted her damp hair from her shoulders, hair she never left loose, his fingers brushing her bare shoulders. "Why do you hide yourself from us?" he'd asked.

"Don't say anything about this to anyone." Would he tell them how oversized her breasts were? Would they wonder why she hid her curves, talking behind her back, speculating? "Leave. Now."

He'd shrugged, his dark brown eyebrows furrowing. "No

need to get mad or freaked out. It was an accident. We're friends."

He left, finally, and she looked in the steamy reflection. She didn't see beautiful. But she did see hunger, and even worse, felt it.

"How's your big job coming?" Greer asked now, pulling her out of the memory. He was leaning against the back of the couch, which inadvertently flexed the muscles in his arms.

He remembered, which touched her even if she didn't want to be touched. Still, she found herself smiling. "Great. We're putting the finishing touches now that the hard-scaping and most of the planting is finished. This is my biggest job yet. My business has kept me sane through all this. Gotta keep working on the customer's jobs." She glanced to the window. If the sun weren't going to be setting soon, she'd come up with some job she had to zip off to right then.

Dammit, she missed Greer. Hated having to shut him out. Now, things were odd between them. He looked at her differently, heat in his eyes, and hurt, too, because he didn't understand why she'd pushed him away. Like he'd said, it was an accident that he'd walked in on her.

"Do you want to stay for dinner?" she asked, not sure whether having them both there would be better than being alone with Darius.

Greer glanced at his watch. "Wish I could. My shift starts in an hour."

Darius wheeled up. "Yeah, the big bad firefighter, off to save lives." He made a superhero arm motion, pumping one fist in the air.

Greer's mouth twisted in a snarl. "I'd rather do that than tinker with computer parts all day."

"Boys," she said, sounding like a teacher.

Another knock on the door. Hopefully it was Tucker. He was good at stepping in. But it wasn't Tucker. Two men stood there, their badges at the ready. "Cheyenne Baker?" one of them asked.

She nodded, feeling Greer step up behind her.

"Detective Dan Marshall, and Detective Paul Marron. May we come in?"

"What's this about?" Greer asked before she could say anything.

"We have some questions about a recent incident." The man, in his forties, waited patiently for someone to invite them inside.

Greer inspected the badge, nodded to her. It was legit.

Shea checked it, too, then stepped back, bumping into Greer. "These are friends of mine," she said, waving to Greer and Darius.

Marshall closed the door behind them, taking in both men as though noting their appearance. He focused on her. "You've heard about the man who was mauled two nights ago?"

Her mouth went dry. How had they connected that to her? Bad enough that it triggered two men from the other dimension to hunt down their offspring. "Yes, it sounded horrible." She shuddered, and didn't have to fake it. "Wild animals attacking people in their own home."

"We don't think it was a wild animal. Do you know Fred Callahan, the victim?"

"No, I—" Her words jammed in her throat when she saw the picture he held up, a driver's license photo probably. All the blood drained from her face. "I knew him as Frankie C." She cleared the fuzz from her voice. "I haven't seen him for six years." She wanted the cops to go, or for Greer and Darius to leave. "I'm sorry, I can't help you."

Marshall's eyes flicked to Greer and Darius before returning to her. "We found pictures and notes about you on his computer. There was a letter in his desk drawer addressed to you, indicating he'd written to you before. It wasn't a very nice letter."

Her knees went weak. Greer somehow sensed it and clamped his hands on her shoulders. "What are you insinuating?" His hands started warming her, one of his psychic abilities.

Darius wheeled closer. "You can't possibly think this slip of a girl could tear a man apart."

"I've been getting letters, creepy gifts," she said. "But I didn't know who they were from." Frankie. She had wondered, yes, but how had he found her? And why after all these years?

"May I see them?" Marshall asked.

She'd wanted to throw them away, but thought they might be evidence if things escalated. She went to the file cabinet in her office and returned with the letters, and the box.

Marshall frowned when he opened it and saw the dildo, the flavored lube creams. "Can I take these?"

"Please." *And go. Say no more.*

He looked at Greer and Darius. "Did either of you know who was harassing her?"

Darius snorted. "No, but I'm glad the sick fu—the guy is dead. It's wrong to harass a woman like that."

Greer shook his head, but his gaze was on her.

Marshall turned to her again. "Callahan worked at the phone company. That's probably how he found you. You haven't heard from him at all in the six years since you filed charges against him and the other two men?"

"No, nothing," she said quickly. "I'd rather not—"

"I'm sure the detective you spoke to talked you out of going forward with the charges. I read the file and agree that it was a long shot to prosecute the case successfully. Still, I wish we had. One of those other men raped a teenaged girl a couple of years back. He's in prison now. The other's been jailed a few times on battery charges."

She felt Greer's questioning stare on her. "I'm sorry to hear that." Her words sounded shaky. *Leave, dammit.*

Marshall glanced in the box, then her. "But Callahan hasn't had another brush with the law. We did find some rather disturbing items in his home, including sex toys I presume he intended to send to you. One was a pair of handcuffs, and they weren't the fuzzy kind. It's the sort of thing that makes me uncomfortable about where he was going with this. So if you"—he looked at her friends—"or anyone had something to do with his death, it may have saved your life. But still, we have to investigate. It's a crime to tear a man apart, no matter how much of a scumbag he is."

"Son of a bitch," Greer said. His hands tightened on her as she slumped against the couch, and then he pulled her against his body, his arms like a shield over her collarbone.

Oh, God. Had Frankie been planning to rape her again? That overshadowed anything else in her mind at the moment.

Marshall seemed to be giving them time to fess up.

"We didn't know who the guy sending that stuff was," Shea said. "You can see from the letters that he never signed them." They'd been crude letters, detailing what he wanted to do to her body, and she'd forced herself to read them because she needed to know how much he knew about her. Or if they contained an explicit threat.

"Was it because of your earlier experience that you didn't report the stalking?" Marshall asked.

She shrugged, though it felt as though she wore an armored suit that smelled of a citrus cologne. "I didn't see it as threatening. Only gross and annoying."

Wrapped in Greer's embrace, she felt safe in a sea of chaos.

Marshall gave her his business card. "If there's anything else you know or remember, please give me a call." He took a step toward the door but turned back to her. "Ms. Baker, if anyone ever hurts you like that again, call me."

As soon as he left, Darius wheeled in front of her. "The guy's dead, Shea. You don't have to worry about him anymore. Isn't that great?"

Thank God Darius hadn't asked for more information. If only Greer would let it go.

He turned her to face him. "What happened? What was he talking about, if you're hurt 'again'?" His concern turned her to mush, and then his expression changed. He cradled her face, and as much as she wanted to push away, she couldn't. "Oh, Shea."

She heard it all in his voice—that he'd figured it out from

the detective's words. Raped "another" woman. She felt her expression crumple even though she tried to hold strong.

He pulled her against him, stroking her back. Her cap's brim bumped against him and it fell to the floor.

No, she had to push away. She would fall apart right here, and he would continue to hold her and soothe her, and it felt so good because no one had done that afterward. Not even her mother, who had the same opinion the cops did: that she deserved it.

She managed to move out of his embrace by reaching for her cap. She shoved it onto her head, pulling down the brim. "I'm fine. It was a long time ago."

"What are you two talking about?" Darius asked. At least he hadn't gotten it.

That was the difference between them, one of many. She wondered if Darius just had no emotions, nothing to squash or tuck away.

"You'd better go," she said to Greer, her voice thick. "You don't want to be late for your shift."

He was looking at her, probably giving her the same look he'd been giving her since the bathroom incident. The *Why are you shutting me out?* one. She couldn't tell, thankfully, because the brim of her cap blocked his eyes from view. At least he'd also pushed back after the bathroom incident and gone on, continued dating. He'd been cool to her afterward. That's what she wanted. Even if it stuck a knife in her chest.

"I do have to go. Walk me out." He took her hand, giving her no choice but to be dragged along with him.

The air was even more chilling now that the sun was setting. He paused by his Jeep, turning her to face him. "Shea, that's why you hide yourself, isn't it? Why you freaked when I accidentally saw you naked." He pulled off her cap. "Three of them?" His agony at the thought wracked his face.

"I don't want to discuss this. I freaked because I don't want people to see me naked."

"Because you've got curves—"

She pressed her hand over his mouth, feeling the full softness of it. "I am not interested in discussing my curves or my past."

"You're hurting, Shea. It's why you shut down on me. I lost a friend once, because he was hurting, too. Holding in a painful secret. I left for a while, doing construction out of town, and when I came back, he'd taken his life. He couldn't take the pain anymore."

"I'm not going to take my life. I've survived, gotten over it—"

"You haven't gotten over it." He tugged at her oversized shirt. "You hide your body. All those years you lived with us, you hid yourself. Did you think we'd hurt you? Attack you?"

He had no idea. "Of course not."

"That's why you were so pissed about me seeing you. Your secret was out."

That he had right. "That's ridiculous." She took the opportunity to look down at her attire, to escape those assessing eyes. "This is just how I like to dress."

He took his finger and lifted her chin. "I suddenly saw you as a woman and not just the girl who's lived with us for the past few years. Seeing you as a woman changed everything."

She smacked his arm, which probably hurt her more than him. "Then change it back. I don't want you like that."

He slowly blinked at her statement. "Is it because of what happened to you? We can work through that."

"Is he bothering you?" Darius called from the front step.

Greer muttered something very impolite under his breath, and then said, louder, "Go back in the house. We're talking."

Darius started to wheel down the ramp. "Whatever concerns Shea concerns me, too."

"I'm going in now," she said, dashing off before Darius could get close. As she suspected, he turned around and followed her back to the front step. Greer stayed by his vehicle, giving Darius a pissed look. She was glad Darius had stopped that conversation. Way too close for comfort on many levels.

"I'm fine, Greer," she called to him. "Thanks for caring. Get to work."

"Did I interrupt a tense moment?" Darius asked once he'd caught up to her, watching Greer's yellow Jeep back out. "Looked like he was harassing you. It had to do with whatever he did to you, didn't it? Tell me, and I'll make sure—"

"It's none of your business." She stalked into the house to find something for dinner, anything to get her mind off what just transpired.

It was hard to think about spaghetti or leftover steak when one question dominated her mind: how could it be a coincidence that the man who had been mauled was her rapist?